Threaten To Undo Us

by Rose Seiler Scott

PROMONTORY
P R E S S

Threaten To Undo Us
Copyright 2015 by Rose Seiler Scott

All rights reserved. No part of this book may be used or reproduced
in any matter without prior written permission.

Promontory Press
www.promontorypress.com

ISBN: 978-1-927559-68-0

Cover design by Marla Thompson of Edge of Water Designs
Typeset by One Owl Creative in 12 pt Arno Pro

Printed in Canada

Enjoyed very much...made me feel like I'm transported to the cosiness of German home life long ago with the terror of the political atmosphere raging outside...couldn't put it down!

— Lynn Teefel, School teacher

Rose Seiler Scott weaves a compelling story of a German family in Poland during and after World War II. The effects of the war continue unabated to victims of the resentful soldiers and citizens....What an amazing story!

— Carola Meerkerk, Singer- Songwriter

Historical fiction based on true incidents...I haven't seen anything written before about the dilemma of German families living in Poland fairly peacefully for generations, then... finding themselves in the middle of a major war started by Germany. It's an incredible story, and I couldn't help just reading it straight through the night. Really a great writing job, I loved it!!

— Sharon Bernard, daughter of German expellee.

As an avid reader of historical fiction, I found myself captivated by the story of Liesel and her conviction to keep her family together. Her steadfast nature and determination are apparent as she struggles to survive. I could not put this book down. I highly recommend reading it.

— Bonnie Old, Registered Nurse

In memory of Eugenie

Dwell on the past and you will lose an eye.
Forget the past and you will lose both eyes

— Russian Proverb

INTRODUCTION
YALTA, FEBRUARY 1945

STALIN TRACED HIS FINGER ALONG THE CURZON LINE WHICH encompassed the cities of Brest and Lwów. Regarding the other world leaders with a steely gaze, he squared his shoulders so that his epaulets formed a straight and rigid line. "I will settle for the Eastern territories and nothing less."

All of those present knew that the co-operation of the Soviet forces, allied with the Western powers, had been critical in turning the tide against Nazi Germany.

Churchill tightened his jowls around his cigar. He was not comfortable conceding anything to Stalin and even viewed Roosevelt with some distrust.

Roosevelt flicked the ashes from his cigarette into the ashtray and coughed; a sound that rattled from deep within his chest. He pulled the matchbox towards himself and looked up, his pale face thoughtful. Shaking out a number of matches, he arranged them on the map along the crooked lines of the Oder and Neisse rivers. "If we do what you propose, perhaps it would be prudent to give the territories of Pomerania and Prussia to Poland."

Churchill removed the cigar from his mouth. "But what of the people living in that region? These are German territories and many Germans live within the General Government area as well. Surely we will experience more bloodshed if we make this part of the new Poland." His ample jaw hung slack. "These nationalities need to be separated. We cannot have Poles and Germans together and expect them to live in peace after the atrocities of this war."

Stalin stroked his moustache and waited for his turn to speak. Though a cunning and ruthless man, patience was one of his better virtues. When at last he had opportunity to answer, it was a gross exaggeration, but one that would likely accomplish his own aims of domination. "Most have fled the region," he shrugged.

"Well," said Roosevelt. "Why should we not simply evacuate the remainder of the German population—in an orderly and humane manner, of course, and assist Poland in the set-up of its new and independent government."

The discussion continued at the conference of Potsdam and when the proceedings were complete the map of Poland was once again redrawn. As a result, millions of ethnic Germans from east of the Oder-Neisse line were driven out of their homes, stripped of their human rights, and enslaved by the new Communist regime.

What follows is a fictionalized account of one family's story. While inspired by actual events, the scenes are embellished by imagination. The characters are fictitious with the exception of Oskar, loosely based on the late Eugen Oskar Kossmann, an author, historian and statesman.

The history is true.

Let goods and kindred go, this mortal life also.

— Martin Luther, *A Mighy Fortress is Our God*, trans. Frederick H. Hedge

CHAPTER 1

1945

ERNST'S FACE WAS CAST IN DARKNESS; HIS TALL FRAME A shadow in the open doorway.

"I'm in the army now," he said, his solemn voice fading as he backed away into the night. "I can no longer give you my protection."

Submerged in the blackness of loss, paralyzed to reach out, Liesel pleaded to her husband, "Come back!" Her voice echoed off the wall. Simultaneously she heard the rumbling of a truck motor and a tinny voice on a bullhorn. "All German citizens of the Third Reich are to evacuate as soon as possible. You are no longer under the protection of the German army."

Liesel's eyes fluttered open and her conscious mind recalled that Ernst had left their home in Poland months ago and was missing in action, somewhere in Russia.

The blackout curtains were securely in place. A single gas lamp, dimly lit, cast a soft glow on the green tiles of the *Kachelofen*. On the hearth ledge of the large ceramic stove, a few sticks of kindling poked out of the wood box. Above the mantel the cuckoo clock ticked softly, its pendulum swinging gently back and forth in counterpoint to Liesel's racing heart.

In the gloom, silent companions watched from the walls; Ernst in his *Wehrmacht* uniform and his brother attired in the black garb of the "*Schutz-Staffel*", sepia sillouettes of Liesel's parents and grandparents and a portrait of her children, taken near the beginning of the war.

Kurt and Olaf stood on either side of Liesel like miniature sentinels in the matching dark suits she had made for them. Edeltraud was only a baby sitting on Liesel's lap, wearing a perfectly tailored coat and a ruffled hat. Rudy stood next to the chair, his face turned slightly as if his attention was elsewhere.

The announcement reverberated down the street. "Allied forces are advancing. You are no longer under the protection of the German army. All German citizens of the Third Reich, General Government, are to evacuate to the west."

Startled, now fully awake, her heart pounded and icy fingers of terror crept over her. Reich citizens of the General Government of Poland. That meant her. Evacuate her home? With four young children? Thoughts swirling anxiously, she wondered how she would manage everything in her condition.

Pulling her sweater tight against the sudden chill of the room, she heaved herself out of the rocking chair she had fallen asleep in, knocking over a half empty glass of tea in the process. Amber liquid splashed on the braided throw rug and streamed out across the floor in several directions.

She felt the baby move within her. It would only be a few more weeks and she hoped for a girl, a sister for four-year-old Edeltraud. A girl wouldn't be drafted into the army.

Liesel forced herself to take a deep breath. Words she had learned long ago came to mind and she whispered them to herself. "The name of the Lord is a strong tower. The righteous run to it and are safe." She repeated this a few times until the panic receded enough for her to think.

A mental list began to take shape. She would need food, utensils, bedding, things for the baby. First she must tell the boys and enlist their help.

She put on her coat and headed out to the barn. The warm smell of hay and manure enveloped her with heavy sweetness. Kaspar brushed up against her leg, meowing softly. Kurt was mucking out one of the stalls, while Olaf sat on the stool milking Wande.

"*Mutti? Was ist los?*" Eleven-year-old Kurt replied, his voice mirroring the tone of his mother's.

"*Jungens*, we will have to leave quickly." She swallowed, choking on the enormity of her task

"Where are we going?" asked Kurt.

Olaf, less than two years younger than his brother, patted the cow. "What about Wande and Kaspar?" His voice was brittle and his eyes glistened.

Liesel lowered her voice. They must not sense her alarm. "We are — taking a trip. We'll take some chickens along if we can, but the rest will have to be left behind. Too many animals will slow us down," she explained, thinking things through even as she spoke. "Olaf, make sure there is hay and grain for the animals while we are gone.. Leave their pens open."

In case we don't come back.

"But mother, I don't want to go," Olaf said. Standing up, he gripped the top of the cow's pen. "Who will look after Wande and the goats if I am gone?"

Feeding, milking, and grooming were his jobs and Liesel had observed how seriously he took these tasks. At butchering time he was scarcely to be found, unlike his older brother, who had always been fascinated by the process at an early age and was not at all bothered to wring a chicken's neck or help pour the blood from a pig's head.

Liesel squared her shoulders. There was no time for obstinate children right now. Looking him in the eye, she grasped his ears firmly, an action that was reserved for only the gravest offences. "You must do as you as you are told."

Olaf's eyes filled with tears and he looked down. "Yes, Mother."

With the absence of their father and grandfather and the scarceness of hired help, the boys had borne much of the workload on the farm. Necessity had dictated responsibility at a young age.

Liesel felt a twinge of guilt for making Olaf cry, but the virtue of patience was worth little right now. There was no time to lament the sacrifice of their childhoods to this relentless war.

Turning back to her older son, the one most often to try her, she steeled herself against whatever he might say. "Kurt, you get the wagon and horses ready," she commanded, "and bring along some tools. We will need the shovel in case we get stuck, a hammer, nails, a saw, and some grease for wagon repairs."

Kurt's eyes flitted to Olaf. He shrugged his shoulders and walked over to the harnesses hanging from the wall.

Liesel left the boys to their tasks. *I can do this,* she thought to herself. With a surge of nervous energy, she began preparations, based on the little she knew—winter weather, a baby on the way, and limited room in the wagon. How long they would be gone she had no idea, only that they must head west.

In the pantry she took stock; crocks of sauerkraut, pickles, and a box of rye, which had been destined for the flour mill. A short link of sausages, rationed from the last butchering hung from a nail. Thankfully she had baked two loaves of bread earlier that day. Linen bags held dried plums and apples, but much of the food they had raised had gone to the war effort, and it was mid-winter.

In her bedroom she lifted the small stack of handmade sweaters, booties, blankets and diapers. She stroked her hand over the fine wool, comforted by its softness. What would the future hold for this child?

Not much if I don't move quickly. From the drawer she took out pillowcases and stuffed one full of things for the baby and the other with her own clothing.

When everything was ready, she sent Kurt to load the wagon.

Only the most difficult thing left to do.

She crept to the door of her mother's suite on the other side of the house and softly turned the doorknob.

Adelheid was sleeping, her breathing laboured and uneven.

Liesel lit the lamp next to the bed. Her legs shook as she lowered herself to the edge of the bed and took her mother's hand. *"Mutter."* Adelheid opened her eyes. The light of the flickering lamp cast grotesque shadows on the wall and accentuated her sunken cheeks. *"Ja, Liebchen,"* she whispered.

"We have to leave," said Liesel. "The Russians are coming." She felt the baby move suddenly inside her, causing a sharp spasm in her back. She squirmed in discomfort not wanting to believe her own words.

"Are you all right my dear?" Adelheid rasped. With a thin arm she reached up and brushed Liesel's cheek. "Your duty is to your children. You must be strong and take care of them." She coughed weakly, her voice barely discernible above the pounding of Liesel's heart. "I cannot make such a journey. I have lived a long life and I am ready to meet our Father in heaven. And your father too," she added. "Besides, what can the Russians do to me?" At this her lips twitched, a faint smile.

"Aber Mutti ..." Liesel knew her mother was right. She barely felt able herself to make this trip and had no choice but to leave her mother behind. She bent down and laid her head on her mother's chest. Tears slid off Liesel's cheeks, dampening Adelheid's nightgown.

"The Lord is my shepherd ... he makes me lie down in green pastures ..." Liesel whispered.

Outside the horses brayed and she heard the boys' voices as they loaded the wagon.

She clutched her mother's hand tightly. "Though I walk through the valley of the shadow of death, I will fear no evil ..." She lifted her head.

Adelheid's eyes were closed, her lips moving as she followed along in the final words of the Psalm. "And I will dwell in the house of the Lord forever."

In the distance a whistling sound was followed by an explosion.

Liesel jolted at the noise. If she were to save her children, they needed to leave now. She choked back her sobs and staggered to the door.

Outside, Max and Minka stood ready, stamping their burlap-wrapped feet in the cold. Their eyes were shrouded by blinkers; their breath white plumes of steam hitting the cold air. Behind the horses, the wagon overflowed with their belongings.

Liesel wondered if even the two strong Belgian horses could pull the load.

Edeltraud waited on the porch, bundled in her coat, hat, and mittens, and wrapped in a colourful quilt. Rudy, age seven, stood next to her, holding his arm out so she wouldn't lose her balance with all that extra weight. "Ha ha, she looks like a coloured cabbage" he laughed, as he led her over to the wagon. "Mutti, where are we going?"

If only I knew the answer to that, Liesel thought, walking around to check the harnesses. "We have to go away for a while. Go kiss Oma goodbye."

A few moments later the family clambered into the wagon, amidst a jumble of household possessions and a crate of squawking chickens. She had intended to slaughter and cook them, but ran out of time. Before the first rays of gray dawn broke through the shutters of the little house, they were headed west. Many of the inhabitants of their village were leaving in similar haste—abandoning homes and livestock in a race for their lives.

Not since her childhood, had Liesel felt such fear.

Poland agrees to embody in a Treaty with the Principal Allied and Associated Powers such provisions to protect the interests of inhabitants of Poland who differ from the majority of the population in race, language, or religion.

— Excerpt from Article 93 Treaty of Versailles, June 28, 1919

CHAPTER 2
1919

SIX-YEAR-OLD LIESEL HELD TIGHT TO HER FATHER'S HAND AS they entered the meeting house. It was just a villager's house, used on Sundays for the Lutheran church service, but the kitchen table had been pushed into the corner of the room and benches and chairs set up for the parishioners.

Behind the congregation, a young man accompanied the singing on a tabletop organ, but its reedy vibrato was drowned out by Liesel's father's deep bass joining with the other voices in the room. Like a blanket, the sonorous harmony surrounded her, filling all the spaces of the room, the air, and the empty places inside her. Liesel had heard the song so many times she already knew most of the first verse:

Ein feste Burg ist unser Gott,
Ein gute Wehr und Waffen;
Er hilft uns frei aus aller Not,
Die uns jetzt hat betroffen

A mighty fortress is our God,
a bulwark never failing,
Our helper he amid the flood
of mortal ills prevailing.

Even though she didn't understand all the words, she liked the idea of God being strong like a fortress.

At supper she asked, "Father, what is mortal ills?"

"Well," said her father, slicing a piece of cheese, "mortal ills are all the bad things that can happen in a war."

"But the war is over now, Fritz," said Liesel's mother. "So we don't need to talk about it anymore, especially in front of the children."

Liesel's father raised his eyebrows. "The Great War may be over, but the danger has not fully passed. There is still the border dispute and the Bolsheviks."

"Fritz," said Liesel's mother firmly.

Fritz stabbed a pickle with his fork and pointed it at each of his children in turn. "Do you hear that, children? Your mother has spoken. No mortal ills for you, but perhaps you would like another piece of bread."

Liesel had just bitten into her sandwich when the dogs began to bark furiously. Fritz got up and looked out the window. "*Bolsheviks!* Everyone to the cellar," he boomed.

This was not the first time their farmhouse had been invaded and Liesel's parents had devised a plan for safety during these raids.

"Liesel, you must hide behind the bed," ordered Fritz.

Her parents and siblings would hide in the cellar beneath the house, but it was crowded and often one of the first places bandits would look, so they had found her a little niche behind her trundle bed. Anyone looking would only see the trundle bed and in the dark it would appear to be against the wall.

Liesel trembled. *Was this one of the mortal ills?*

Her braids swung as she shook her head. "*Vati*, I don't want to go in there." She watched her older sister Josephine and their younger brother Emil descend the stairs into the darkness of the cellar. Mother held little Frieda with one hand and the trap door with the other.

"You will not argue, you will get behind the bed." Liesel's father said. He was not smiling, and his voice was louder and firmer than she had ever heard before.

Liesel thought of the dust and spiders that lurked behind the bed. "Please, *Vati*."

With his arm on her back he pushed her forcefully towards her bedroom. "You must do as you are told. *Aber Schnell!*"

Realizing she had no choice in the matter, Liesel scurried behind the bed. Through the walls of the bedroom she heard the trap door bang shut and a moment later, the front door open. The sound of cupboard doors opening and closing was followed by a scraping noise as the intruders dragged something heavy across the floor.

She hoped they wouldn't find her. With her eyes closed she imagined her bed a strong fortress held in place by invisible hands. Squeezing herself tight against the wall, she waited for the bandits to go away.

They clattered about the kitchen speaking a language Liesel was just starting to learn at school. She knew they were helping themselves to the supper they had just started.

Thinking of the food made her hungry. She worried about the *Pflaumenkuchen* her mother had made for dessert. How dare those robbers eat the plum cake? She clenched her fists in anger, wishing she had a weapon to hurt them.

Finally, the bandits left, slamming the kitchen door behind them. She waited in the silence, expecting her father to come get her. When no-one came, hunger and an urgent need to use the outhouse drove her from her cramped hiding spot.

The kitchen was in disarray. Muddy footprints covered the floor and half-eaten bread and sausage littered the table. But her family was nowhere to be seen. A large trunk had been moved over the trap door.

"*Mutti, Vati!*" Liesel cried out in alarm.

"Liesel, let us out!" Muffled voices called out beneath the floor. Little Frieda was crying.

Liesel tugged at the handle of the trunk, then pushed with all the strength she could muster, but it couldn't be budged. "I can't, it's too heavy," she sobbed helplessly.

"Run to the Zawadski's," her father called out.

It was nearly dark. From the window she could just make out the light at the neighbor's house. It seemed such a long way.

"Hurry, Liesel!"

"But I am afraid."

"Pray to God."

"*Ja*, I'll go," she whimpered muttering a desperate prayer under her breath. She ran out the door, imagining again she was within the walls of a great castle, where nothing could get her. Pumping her short legs across the yard and out the gate, she arrived next door panting for breath with one braid undone and warm wetness soaked through her stockings.

Embarrassed and terrified, she banged on the door with both fists.

Pani Zawadski came to the door, wiping her hands on her apron.

"*Hilfe*," Liesel gasped.

No translation was needed for their Polish neighbors. *Pani* wiped Liesel's tears with the edge of her apron and called her husband over. *Pan* Zawadski put on his boots and headed out the door.

Upon entering the house, Liesel pointed to the trunk over the trap door. Beneath the floor her father called out, "*Pomoc!*"

That means "help" in Polish, thought Liesel, mentally adding the word to her vocabulary.

Pan Zawadski easily pushed the trunk out of the way and Liesel helped him open the trap door. The family emerged into the kitchen.

Liesel ran to her father, wrapping her arms around him.

"Such a mess," said her mother. "But look, they didn't touch the plum-cake." It was sitting on the windowsill, right where she had left it to cool.

Fritz disengaged himself from Liesel's grip and shook the neighbour's hand. "*Dziękuję*. We are grateful for your help."

Adelheid handed Mr. Zawadski a generous plateful of plumcake to take home.

"Liesel," said her father, after they had cleaned up and had some supper. "I know it was hard for you to obey and that you were afraid, but you saved us."

Liesel smiled at her father's recognition and took a bite of cake, her fears receding as the tangy sweet flavor filled her mouth. "I hope those bad men don't come back," she said.

"I don't know," said Liesel's father, his eyes twinkling at the corners. "It all depends on who is in charge this week. Will it be the Russians or the Germans? The Hapsburgs or General Pilsudski?"

"I hope it's not the Bolsheviks," said Josephine, shuddering. She was almost eleven, four years older than Liesel, and had been attending school a few years already.

"Can't you be the Emperor, *Vati*?" said Liesel.

"Only if I have loyal subjects like you," he said, patting her head.

"Did you know," he continued, "that I have a cousin in Danzig?" Liesel and her siblings had never met this cousin, but he was often the subject of various stories and jokes.

"He has three sons."

"Really, *Vati*?" said Josephine. "Last time you said he had two daughters."

Fritz shrugged. "Well, he has daughters and sons. Now do you want to hear more or not?"

"Please tell us," chorused the girls.

"One son was born in Lithuania," said Fritz. "Another is a Prussian citizen and one was born in Poland." He paused to stroke his moustache and take a bite of cake. "Your mother makes such good *Pflaumenkuchen*, don't you think so, Emil?" he said, looking at his young son.

"*Ja*," said Emil, his mouth full of cake. He was only five, too young to understand the story.

"Tell us the rest," said Josephine.

"Oh yes, the story. All of my cousin's sons are from the city of Danzig. It is perfectly true."

"That's not a real story," said Liesel.

"Oh," said Josephine. "I know! They never moved, but the government keeps changing."

"Oh my girls," said Fritz, putting his arms around them both. "You are so smart!"

"And now it is time for bed," said their mother.

CHAPTER 3
1928

IN THE YEARS SINCE SHE WAS A YOUNG CHILD, LIESEL HAD not lost her love of her home and family and an overwhelming desire for security. She was fifteen now, but life was best in her opinion when she was with her loved ones, secure and close to home, gardening or working in the kitchen with her mother.

When Liesel and Josephine spent a morning weeding the garden, Adelheid said, "You girls have worked hard today. Why don't the two of you go for a walk?"

"I guess we ought to," said Josephine. "Since I won't be living here much longer."

"We'll work on your dress when you get back," said Adelheid, when the girls were almost out the door.

Liesel and Josephine ambled along the road. Tufts of daisies, blue chicory, and cornflowers surrounded the fields of rye. The flowers nodded gently in invitation.

Liesel accepted the gesture and picked a daisy. "I will miss you when you are married, Jo."

"I will miss you too."

Josephine plucked a cornflower and handed it to her. "Do you know the story about the Queen of Prussia?"

Liesel thought about their grandmother, who had been a noblewoman and once lived in a castle in Silesia, but she could barely remember her. "Is that a story *Oma* used to tell us?" Her grandparents had lost their land holdings in some long ago conflict and died before she really knew them.

"I am surprised you remember at all. You were so young when she died," said Josephine, plucking flowers and weaving them into a crown. "The Queen of Prussia was fleeing Napoleon and hid her children in a field of cornflowers. Weaving the flowers kept the children quiet so the soldiers couldn't find them." She set the crown on Liesel's head.

Liesel smiled and held her head high. "Now I am the Queen of Prussia." It was fun to play at being royalty and she was lost in her little daydream when Josephine spoke again. "There is something I want to tell you." She glanced around quickly, as if someone might be hiding in the fields.

Liesel leaned closer to Josephine. "What is it?" She felt honoured when her older sister shared confidences.

"Andreas and I plan to go to Canada after we are married."

The cornflower and daisy crown suddenly became very heavy. "Canada?" Liesel's eyes widened and her jaw went slack. "But it is so far away." She thought of the maps in her geography books. A country so vast, only Russia was bigger. She could hardly imagine it. "And isn't it cold and snowy there?"

"Well, yes, but they have summer too. The soil is richer and they grow wheat there. And so much land is available; we can have our own farm if we homestead."

The bouquet Liesel had collected with such delight hung limply at her side. A tear splashed on the ragged petals of a cornflower as she thought of her beloved older sister living in a country so far away it took a month to travel there by ship. Liesel's feet were rooted here in Schönewald and she had no desire to travel farther than the market in Łódź.

"When we will see you again?"

"I don't know, dear one, but I know we will meet again someday," said Josephine, putting her arm around Liesel. "We still have a few months before we are planning to leave."

Liesel frowned and shook her head. "I don't want you to go." She shuffled her feet along the road.

At the sound of thundering hoofs both girls turned. Out of a cloud of dust a runaway horse galloped, reins flapping along behind him.

"Watch out," said Josephine, pushing her sister towards the ditch, dislodging the floral coronet off her head. The horse bolted by, narrowly missing the two girls.

"We'll go home and tell father," said Josephine.

Liesel glanced behind her. Blue and white blooms lay scattered all over the road, their stems broken pathetically, pretty petals trampled in the dirt.

CHAPTER 4

It was maddening to Liesel that she could not see her older sister's face in the dream.

Josephine, wearing her wedding dress, led a cow through a field of flowers. But she was facing the opposite direction and when Liesel woke, she remembered that Josephine had left for Canada over a month ago.

She turned to Frieda, whose braids splayed out in two directions across the pillow.

"Time to get up," Liesel said to her younger sister. "Market day."

"Mmm," mumbled Frieda.

"We need to get our chores done first." Liesel sat up and lifted her clothes off the chair next to the bed. She slipped off her nightdress, and pulled on stockings, a petticoat, and a woolen skirt. Over her linen chemise she put on a blouse and jacket. Taking two hairpins from a tray on the dresser she grasped her thick ash coloured plaits and pinned them at the back of her head.

She opened the shutter.

Rays of sunlight streamed through the forest beyond the yard, dappling the fields between with variegated light and shadow. Closer to the house, a mist rose from the ground.

The rooster crowed proudly from his perch on a fence post as the chickens clucked about the yard.

Liesel went out to collect the eggs. Schwartz, one of the dogs, squeezed his way under a hole in the fence, back into the yard. The other dog, Bach scurried around barking and scattering chickens and dried leaves everywhere.

Liesel didn't have to wonder long why the dogs had gotten loose.

On other side of the picket fence separating the vegetable garden, a trail of half eaten potatoes and trampled greens littered the ground. The apparent culprit was a snuffling, snorting creature who pawed the ground and butted his head against the fence. His bristly hair stood up on his back and his tiny eyes were set back behind a pointed snout.

Liesel thought the boar's stink was even less agreeable than his hideous face. Her heart was pounding as she set down the basket of eggs and backed up a few steps. She spun around for something to use as a weapon and spied the pitchfork leaning against the chicken house. She grabbed the tool, hoping the boar wouldn't crash through her side of the fence.

"Help!" she called out weakly towards the house and waited, waving the pitchfork every time the boar threatened to break through the fence.

The wooden fence had just about toppled, when Liesel's father came running with a cumbersome old shotgun in hand. Fumbling, he loaded the antique weapon with shot and powder, but before he could shoot, the boar crashed through another section of fence and escaped into the forest.

"Too bad, I guess we missed some fine roast boar," said Fritz, laughing as Liesel helped him prop up the fence. "Only a young one though. I don't think he would have hurt you."

Back in the house, Frieda and Emil were already seated at the table.

"A boar!" said Liesel's mother Adelheid, setting down a plate of sliced cucumbers and tomatoes.

"You scared away a boar?" asked Frieda, her eyes wide with awe.

"Ha, it was probably just a baby boar," said Emil, selecting several slices of sausage and arranging them atop a slice of bread.

"Fritz, what happened?" asked Adelheid.

"It was nothing," said Liesel. "*Vati* scared him away."

"Well I think that amount of screaming would have scared away a bear!" Fritz chuckled. "It was a huge thing." Fritz winked at his daughter. "Haven't seen one that big in years and those boars are really dangerous."

Liesel felt embarrassed now by her fearful reaction. She bowed her head and put out her hands, hoping her father would just say the blessing and then they could talk about something else.

"*Lasset uns beten.*" Fritz said, taking Liesel's and Adelheid's hands in each of his. "Father in heaven, we are thankful for our many blessings and that you kept Liesel from harm today. Bless this food and keep us safe on our journey. In the name of our Lord and Saviour, Amen."

"Amen," the family echoed in unison.

"Are you going to Łódź market with us this morning, *Mutti*?" Liesel enquired.

"No," replied their mother. "I have too much work to do here, but don't forget to stop at the post office. Perhaps there will be a letter from Josephine."

"I won't forget that!" said Liesel.

"And you'll remember the sugar and coffee?"

Liesel nodded and lifted the basket of eggs off the sideboard. "I'm so glad they didn't break this morning. I almost dropped the basket!" she said to Frieda who emerged from the pantry with the butter.

Outside, Liesel, Frieda, and Emil climbed into the back of the wagon, sandwiched between sacks of potatoes and baskets of cabbages.

"I do hope there is a letter," said Frieda as they bumped along, past stooks of hay dotting the fields.

A large tree stood at the first crossroad. A garland of fresh flowers and greenery twined around its lower branches and a shallow wooden box with a cut out opening was fastened to the trunk. Inside stood a small statue of the Virgin Mary in a painted blue gown, her hands folded in mute prayer. Her serene wooden face gazed out on to the road.

"Those are called *kapliczka*," Liesel stated, knowingly to her younger sister. She loved the sound of the Polish word on her tongue and having gone to school the past few years with the Polish children, she had learned to speak the language well.

"Why don't we have a shrine like that?" asked Frieda.

"We don't put them up because we're Lutheran and the Poles are Catholic. You'll learn when you do catechism class."

Silhouetted against the morning sky, the twin spires of a Catholic church rose in the distance. "And why do they have such a beautiful building and we just meet in that old house?" Frieda asked.

"Because." Liesel thought a moment, "Um, there are more Poles and fewer Germans here, I guess. And because our pastor only comes every three weeks." Those were the most obvious answers to Liesel. "Anyways, you ask too many questions, little sister."

Piotrkowska street hummed with activity. In front of its elegant edifices, merchants and farmers displayed a variety of wares from carts and wagons. Makeshift pens held chickens and fattened pigs, presided over by their owners, who haggled loudly over prices.

A roadster turned down a side street. "A motor car," said Emil, jumping down from the wagon before they had even stopped. He was about to run after it.

"Emil," called Fritz, "come back and help me with the horses."

"But ..."

"Those are just a passing fad," said Fritz, offering some oats to Max and Minka. "It is ridiculous the length people will go so as not to use their legs or these gentle beasts the good Lord has provided." He patted the horses.

"I want to go see it," said Emil, tying the horses to a post.

"Just the other day, I saw two men pushing one of those contraptions past the village for almost a kilometre," said Fritz. "There are so many potholes they couldn't even use the thing until they got to the main road."

Emil was not dissuaded. He ran down the street, calling back to his father and sisters, "One day I will own a motor car."

Fritz shook his head.

At the back of the wagon the girls set out their crock of cultured butter. People were already lining up as Liesel lifted the lid and pulled back the chilled linen they used to keep it cool.

"Your butter is the best," said one woman, a regular customer, handing over her money to Frieda in exchange for two squares.

"Because our cows make such good cream, of course," said Fritz, observing the transaction from beside the wagon.

In reality the butter was the result of many days of skimming the cream and allowing it to culture in the traditional way. They took turns churning, since Josephine had left home, but being older and stronger, Liesel did more of the strenuous work. They rinsed the butter repeatedly with cold water, drawn straight from the well, until they could see no sign of milkiness. "It won't go rancid so quickly," Adelheid had told them. The girls did the job with special pride, as once the family had enough butter, they could sell the extra for their own pocket money.

After the butter and vegetables had sold, Fritz and the girls went to a grocery to sell the rest of the eggs. Baskets of apples, pears, and potatoes adorned the front of the store and bulging sacks of flour and sugar crowded a corner. Behind the counter, arrays of tinned and boxed goods were neatly organized on a shelf. In front were jars of candy—licorice, lemon drops and peppermint sticks.

"All right," said Liesel. "But we shouldn't spend all our money."

At the other end of the counter, the proprietor checked over the eggs and offered a few *groszy*. "No, that is much too low," Fritz argued.

"That is the highest price I am paying for eggs right now. Production is up with the bigger farms. Prices for everything are down right now," said the proprietor.

"Very well then," said Fritz, as he accepted the coins for the eggs. Most of it went towards their purchases of sugar and coffee. "Perhaps next time I shall visit the establishment at the other end of the street." He nodded goodbye politely. *"Do widzenia."*

Liesel had been listening to the proceedings. "Let's not buy the candy here," she whispered to Frieda.

They walked over to the post office.

"Are there any letters for the Bauers in Schönewald?" asked Liesel.

The postmaster selected a stack from the "B" cubbyhole and flipped through the letters, handing them a thin envelope. "Yes, here you are."

When the girls returned, their father was loading his purchases into the wagon. "I don't know where your brother is, but I suspect his disappearance has something to do with that motor car," he said, his brows knit together. "I need to stay with the wagon now."

"We'll look for him," said Liesel. "We wanted to buy some candy anyway."

"Be careful."

A block away, parked in front of a bakery, they saw the car Emil had run after. He emerged from the bakery, a half-eaten apricot pastry in his hand.

"Vati is looking for you," said Liesel. "What are you doing here?"

"It's a model J, Duesenberg," said Emil, stuffing the rest of the treat in his mouth. "Look at this!" He pointed to the distinctive bow tie bumper shining against the black body of the car like a gentleman in a tuxedo.

"It is a handsome vehicle, but father is waiting," said Liesel.

A man dressed in a bowler hat and striped suit walked out of the tobacconist across the street and swaggered towards them. "So you like my roadster? Just debuted in New York."

He eyed Liesel up and down and doffed his hat with a flourish and a bow. "My name is Charlie." He spoke German but with an accent, perhaps American, noted Liesel. "I've been chatting with young Emil here and would like to take him for a ride."

"Aber jaaa!" said Emil, placing his hand on the door handle.

"Meine Fräulein," he indicated Liesel and Frieda. "Would you like to join us?"

"Can we?" said Frieda her eyes wide with awe.

Liesel took a breath. She had never been in a car before. She looked at the elegant car and the smartly dressed man.

"Well, I …"

The man was a stranger and a foreigner and their father was waiting for them. If they went with Charlie, *Vati* would surely be disappointed in her and she felt responsible for her brother and sister. "Thank you for your kind offer sir, but no."

"Good day then." Charlie tipped his hat again and got into the car.

Emil scowled at Liesel. "When am I going to get the chance to go in a car again? You never let me do anything!" He scuffed his feet all the way down the street.

When they returned to the wagon father had the horses all ready to go. "I was just about to come find you. Emil, what will your mother say if I come home without her only son?"

"He was going to go for a ride in a roadster," said Frieda.

How quickly she had forgotten, thought Liesel. It was a good thing she hadn't given in to her younger siblings.

"What? You wanted to go too," said Emil. "Liesel wouldn't let us."

Liesel said nothing. Sometimes it was best to let things work themselves out.

"A good thing your sister at least has some sense," said Fritz. "Frieda and Emil, I think the two of you can shovel the stable when we get home."

Emil stuck out his tongue at Liesel.

"I think you owe us candy. We didn't get a chance to buy any," she said, but she knew she would not be able to coerce anything from her younger brother.

"Come on, let's read the letter," said Frieda ripping it open.

> *Meine Liebe Familie*
>
> *How are you all? I miss you all so much and send my love. I hope you are well.*
>
> *I regret that I have not written recently. The opportunity that awaits us is so much greater than we could hope for in*

the old country!

The streets are not paved with gold or anything like that, but it is possible to be given free land! 160 acres for only $10.00. If we clear and cultivate, in a few years we'll have our names on the deed. So, it will be hard work, but worth it.

We have purchased two draft horses and plan to grow wheat on our quarter section, but many of the farmers are using tractors to do their work.

Our house is just sod, but Andreas plans to build us a new house in the spring. I saw one in the Eaton's catalogue. Everything you need for building the house comes on the train, complete with all the wood and instructions! We will probably have to build our own though since we can't afford that one. Our "soddy" should be warm and cozy during the winter but I am so tired of the dirt everywhere. In the summer bugs fall from the ceiling into the soup! I would so love to have a proper house, with real curtains and real floors.

I have been told that winter is terrible; it can get so cold that everything freezes instantly and you dare not step outside unless you are dressed in six layers of wool from head to toe and cover your face with a scarf!

The prairie is vast, and people live far apart here, not in little villages like at home. I go weeks without seeing a soul other than Andreas. Our nearest neighbor is a half hour wagon ride away. Most of the other homesteaders are English speaking and have been here long enough to be really settled. I think people were a little suspicious of us at first, since I can't communicate in English beyond "Hello" and "Thank you." They enjoyed my cabbage rolls and Kuchen at a barn raising a few weeks ago, but I haven't made any real friends yet. I hope some other Germans will come to the area.

The nearest church is almost an hour away. The services are in English, so it would be hard to understand, but Andreas said we could try going after harvest. For the time he reads

from the Bible each night and we sing some hymns on Sundays.
Perhaps some of you will join us here in Canada one day.
I am well, aside from feeling lonely for my dear family. We
send our love to you and Andreas's family too.

Deine Josephine

CHAPTER 5

HARVEST WAS ALMOST OVER AND THE SCHOOL YEAR BEGIN-
ning.

Liesel watched as Frieda and Emil left the house. This was the first
year that she would not be going with them. She had graduated out
of the village school and the *Gymnasium* in Łódź was too far away to
travel every day.

"But Father, can't I just work at home now? I can read and do math."

"Absolutely not," said Fritz, putting on his coat. "Even young women
should have a proper education. Intelligence and good conversation
should not be confined only to gentlemen, but ladies as well. Poverty
of the mind is a terrible thing."

Liesel wasn't sure she agreed. She would rather work with her hands,
both inside and outside, but she also wanted to please her father and
did not want to be thought of as ignorant.

"My cousin Oskar is very smart." Liesel's mother reminded her. "At
the top of his class. You should consider it a privilege to be tutored by

him."

Cousin Oskar's credentials did not impress Liesel. She had met him a few times before and all he did was talk about politics, history and geography, subjects which bored her.

Later in the morning, he arrived, his slight frame staggering under an armload of books and bags. "I have just come from the university," he said, placing the books on the parlour table with a thump.

They spent the first part of the morning going over mathematical equations and Liesel's head began to sag with the weight of all the facts. She was relieved when her mother brought in a tray with tea and cake, served on the china she had inherited from her once wealthy mother. But the fancy china gave Liesel a vague sense that her mother had something other than just tutoring in mind when it came to Oskar.

After the break, Oskar pushed his spectacles up further on his nose and pulled out the history books. "Now, do you know where we came from?" he asked.

Liesel blushed.

"No, not that," he waved his hand in the air. His fingers were long, the nails clean and trimmed neatly.

Liesel looked at the back of her own hands, which bore several scratches from the rosebush she had trimmed that morning. Her nails were chipped and cracked, with dirt embedded beneath them that even the scrub brush could not eliminate.

"I am talking about the history of Poland and of ourselves, the Germans, here in what is now Poland. It is important for all of us to understand these things. More than just dates and rulers, the events of history affect us all."

Liesel looked out the window at the autumn sunshine. A magpie had landed on the fence and was pecking at the sunflowers, sending showers of seeds from the drooping heads. She wished she were outside on such a lovely day eating sunflower seeds, or walking home from the local Polish school she had attended with her sister and brother.

Oskar set two books in front of her. "I want you to write about the three partitions of Poland and the effect this had on the German populations in the area. That is due on Friday."

He added another book to the growing pile. Liesel looked at the cover, trying to hide her boredom, but if Oskar noticed her inattentiveness, he didn't show it. "We are going to examine one of Goethe's poems. This one has been set to music several times."

He flipped through the book while Liesel glanced over at the Victrola in the corner. Sometimes, when the day's chores were over, her father waltzed, first taking her mother in his arms, then dancing with his daughters around the room.

"Kennst du das Land, wo die Zitronen blühn?" Oskar read from the book, jolting Liesel into the present.

"A land where lemon trees bloom?" She smiled. "It sounds interesting," she said sincerely. She imagined a tree dark green and leafy with large yellow flowers. Botany, now that was a subject that interested her.

> You know that land where lemon orchards bloom,
> Its golden oranges aglow in gloom,
> That land of soft wind blowing from blue sky,
> Where myrtle hushes and the laurel's high?
> You know that land?
> That way! That way
> I'd go with you, my love, and go today.
>
> You know that house, its roof on colonnades,
> The halls agleam, the rooms of gems and jades?
> The marble statues eying all I do:
> "Oh wretched child, what have they done to you?"
> You know that house?
> That way! That way
> I'd go with you, my guardian, today.

A wife of noble character who can find? She is worth far more than rubies.

— Proverbs 31:10 NIV

CHAPTER 6
ERNST 1930

THE PUSHCART WAS STACKED WITH A LOAD OF LUMBER FOR Ernst's next few projects and he was almost back at his house, when a commotion on the other side of the street caught his attention.

Dominik Wolseski shuffled awkwardly, as if he was dragging one half of his body behind him. He carried a small sack. Several local boys followed, throwing pebbles and tormenting him, "Weakling. Feeble-minded idiot." One of them ran up and pushed Dominik over, sending apples and pears rolling all over the road. The boys laughed and ran away.

Ernst secured his cart and walked over to Dominik.

"Are you hurt?" he asked, picking up some of the fruit and returning it to the bag. Dominik said something, but Ernst did not understand Polish very well and Dominik spoke as if his whole tongue filled his mouth. Ernst helped him up and went back to his cart.

Poor Dominik. No-one really knew why he was the way he was, but many thought it was because his parents had been first cousins and their parents before them. He would never manage a farm or a trade. Someone would always have to look after him.

Back in his workshop, sunbeams illuminated clouds of fine wood dust as Ernst bent over a beech table. The muscles of his forearm bulged below his rolled up shirtsleeves as he slid the sanding block back and forth along the grain of the tabletop.

Business had been slow lately, so this table was one he thought he might keep for the future, when he set up a household of his own. But who the other person in that household would be, was a question that remained to be solved.

The incident this morning had eliminated any thoughts of marrying his first cousin. He did not want the risk of having defective children. Besides, though she had a fine figure and a dimpled smile, her overbearing manners and refusal to help with any task that she deemed menial did not make her a suitable candidate. He thought she was spoiled and lazy and would not make a good wife.

It was hot and his shirt stuck to his skin. His ankles were hurting again as they often did when he stood too long in one place. He wiped the sweat from his forehead with the back of his hand and saw his mother standing in the doorway.

"Lunch is ready and I just received a note from your sister," she said, handing him a folded paper. "Helga and Hans would like you and your brother to help with the haying on Saturday."

Ernst ran his hand over the table top, feeling for rough spots. He supposed a break in the routine would be good. He cleaned off his tools and placed them back in the chest. "I'm almost finished, but I guess I could go for a day or two."

"I'll tell them yes," his mother replied. "Let's hope Günther will agree."

On Saturday, Ernst and Günther arrived at Helga and Hans' farm when it was still early, but the sun was already hot when they parked their bicycles in the barn.

In the field men swung scythes rhythmically back and forth in wide arcs, the blades flashing in the sun as the grass fell in narrow strips with each swish of the blades. A short distance away, Helga, wearing a long apron and her hair tied back with a scarf, raked the dried grass into piles. She waved when she saw her brothers. "I'm glad you came. I'll be going in to prepare lunch shortly."

Ernst and Günther joined the group of neighbors, relatives, and hired men and worked for several hours, but by noon, the heat had sapped their strength.

Hans took off his hat and wiped his brow with a handkerchief. "Time to go see what Helga has for lunch."

Ernst leaned against the scythe. "I am a bit hungry." Truthfully, he was just about starving. He turned to look at his brother, who had stacked up a pile of hay and was sitting against it. "How about you Günther?"

"*Ja.* Lunch sounds good to me."

Tables for the workers had been set up in the shade of a tree. A selection of sauerkraut, cheese, pickles, tomatoes, cucumbers, dumplings, and cold smoked ham so tender it fell off the bone, was accompanied by coarse rye bread, fresh churned butter and *Apfelkuchen.*

Günther piled up his plate. "This is why I don't mind helping," he said, plopping himself onto a chair.

"She does make it worthwhile," Ernst agreed.

After most of the meal had been devoured and the hired help went to rest over in the shade of the barn, Günther went with one of the neighbors.

Ernst sat at the table sipping elderberry juice and wondered if his brother would return.

"So have you found yourself a '*Frau*' yet?" Helga asked.

Ernst smiled to himself, but did not answer. He took a mouthful of *Apfelkuchen* and shrugged, hoping she would change the subject. He did not enjoy people prying into his personal affairs. Not even his sister.

Helga was not so easily dissuaded. "Do you remember Hans's cousin from the wedding?"

Ernst recalled the girl at the celebration of Han's and Helga's wedding in the spring, but they had only been briefly introduced and he had gone back to sit with his family.

"Yes, but I barely know her."

"Your sister is relentless, is she not?" Hans leaned back in his chair and laughed heartily. "But Liesel is a good girl, sturdy and hard-working. My aunt and uncle have done quite well with their farm and our family has good connections. My grandparents were nobles, even rode a four-horse carriage. You could do much worse!"

"We could arrange something for you." Helga's eyes glinted brightly.

It was quite simple; he could just take a different route home. They informed him where the Bauer farmhouse was located so he could stop for a drink. It was customary to offer hospitality to strangers, especially fellow Germans. Ernst's own family had done so many times, sometimes inviting weary travelers in for meals.

"You mean today?" asked Ernst, trying to think of an excuse. He was hot and tired and shy of meeting people besides.

"Of course," said Helga." It is only a short detour on your way home."

"Maybe I'll stop by her house later." He supposed it wouldn't hurt, but he wasn't about to make any commitment in front of them. Covering his face with his cap, he sat back in the chair to rest a while before doing some more haying.

Heat still radiated from the ground in the late afternoon when Ernst and the others quit for the day. Günther was nowhere to be found. He hadn't joined them since the noon meal.

Ernst was wiping off his scythe when Günther came into the toolshed. "Tell mother I am going with some friends and I'll be back later," he said.

Ernst had hoped Günther would come with him and make his planned detour a little less uncomfortable, but there were bigger worries. Since their father had died in the Great War, Ernst had felt very much his younger brother's keeper, especially lately. Just the week before, Günther had stumbled home late one night, reeking of liquor. Ernst had smuggled him in the back door and insisted he go straight to bed so that their mother wouldn't find out.

"I think it would be better if you came home," Ernst said, hanging his scythe on a hook.

"I'm old enough to look after myself, you know," said Günther. His face was dark in the shadows, the pitchforks, pruning saws, and scythes casting sinister shapes on the wall behind him.

Ernst had to acquiesce. At sixteen, Günther should be responsible enough to go out on his own, but Ernst hated being in this position. "Just be back before midnight and stay away from the Neudorf brothers."

"*Ja, ja,*" said Günther as he walked away.

Ernst brushed the bits of hay off his shirt and went over to the rain barrel at the side of the shed to wash, splashing cool water on his face and head.

It helped to relieve the tension he felt. Slicking back his thick brown hair, he placed his cap on his head and retrieved his bicycle from the barn.

Helga saw him and came running. "Where is Günther?"

Ernst exhaled. "Off with some friends, or so he said."

"I hope he stays out of trouble," she said. She handed Ernst a small parcel. "Some *Apfelkuchen* for you and mother." Ernst put it in his rucksack and hopped on his bicycle.

Shiny mirages marked the dirt road between the fields of rye and barley. The effort required to pedal was strenuous, especially after haying all day. Sweat dripped off Ernst's face and his thighs burned. Several times the chain slipped off and he had to stop and replace it, getting grease all over his hands.

How had he agreed to this idea? He was tired and dirty, not fit to meet anyone today. He thought about just continuing home, but by the time he came in view of Schönewald, his throat was so dry he could barely have kept going. No one would question his need for water anyway.

He parked his bike and walked up to the gate, pausing to wipe his sweaty face with a handkerchief and smooth down his trousers.

Roses, peonies, and sunflowers grew along the front fence in a profusion of colour. Red and white poppies lined a short walkway to the house. A dog, tethered to a tree pulled at his rope and barked ferociously, sending chickens scattering for cover.

The freshly whitewashed house contrasted with the bright flowers in front. It was a large house with two front doors, and Ernst was trying to decide which one to knock on, when a man strode into the front yard. He gave Ernst a quick looking over and greeted him. *"Guten Tag! Wie geht es Ihnen?"*

Mustering his courage, Ernst cleared his dusty throat, "I would like a drink of water."

"Just a moment." The man disappeared around the back of the house and a few moments later a young woman, whom he recognized from the wedding, came out with a bucket and dipper in hand. He guessed her to be about 17 years old.

"I was going to water the flowers anyway," she said with a shy smile.

She strode across the yard to the well, glancing to see if he would follow. He did, barely keeping up with her. Tying the bucket to a rope she lowered it down into the dark depths and then pulled it up.

Ernst drank several dipperfuls, taking care not to spill the water down his shirt. He watched his young hostess as she poured the remainder of the water into a watering can. He liked what he saw. She wasn't tall, but he saw strength and solidity in the way she held herself and handled the heavy bucket. As he followed her back to the gate her thick braids swung back and forth and her skirt swayed gently above her lower legs.

"I think we have met, at my sister's wedding, *ja*?" he stammered.

"Yes, I am Liesel." she stated simply.

"Ernst. Helga is my sister." Oh, she already knew that, he thought with chagrin. He didn't know what to say next. His eyes scanned the large farmyard and he noticed a bicycle leaning up against the barn. "Do you ride?" he asked.

"Yes." She poured water onto the rosebush. Droplets streamed off the leaves and petals.

Hmm, a woman of few words. Well, he wasn't one for mindless chatter anyway.

"That is my bicycle", said Liesel. "My brother and sister and I rode to the wedding."

She laughed as she relayed the story. As the crowd had begun to disperse that day the rain had come down in torrents. By the time they had reached the main road they were drenched. She turned her bike sluggishly on to the road and began to pedal furiously, spattering mud everywhere as they went through potholes that had been dry a few hours earlier. The road before them had disappeared into a raging river of water and they had to continue home on foot, pushing the bicycles through sodden fields and muddy paths. "My dress was ruined and we didn't get home until after dark!"

Ernst smiled. So she could talk after all. "Would you like to ride with me sometime?" he blurted out.

"You can ask my father." She pointed to where her father was mending a fence.

"You are Helga's brother, is that right?" Fritz stood up with hammer in hand. "I am Fritz Bauer."

Ernst was taller than this man, but the way Liesel's father raised the hammer slightly, was enough to make Ernst feel uncomfortable. He gulped and nodded, his palms sweating almost as much as the rest of him.

"Well, if you live up to your reputation as a hardworking, morally upright young man, you may see my daughter again." Fritz's raised his eyebrow and the corner of his mouth twitched slightly.

Ernst was relieved when Herr Bauer squatted back down to his work. As Ernst reached the gate, he heard Herr Bauer call after him. "And promise me you won't take her to Canada!"

"*Vati!*" Liesel said. It was hard to tell which was pinker: the roses or Liesel's face.

CHAPTER 7

1931

ERNST'S MIND WAS TAKEN UP WITH TWO THINGS LATELY. One was Liesel, whom he had begun to court. This made him very happy and he looked forward to a future with her.

The other thing was Günther and that situation made him unhappy. Ernst wished again that he was not in this position. For some reason, maybe the lack of a father, Günther was constantly drawn to trouble, from which Ernst had to regularly bail him out.

One day he found his mother crying in the kitchen. "The marshall has taken Günther in for questioning. He is being blamed for burning a barn on a Polish farm." She looked up at Ernst. "What will we do with him?"

Ernst heard the desperation in his mother's voice and an idea crossed his mind. "Why don't we send him to father's relatives in Berlin?" He didn't know why he hadn't thought of it before, but perhaps Günther could continue his education in the city or find an apprenticeship.

There wasn't much work in Łódź these days.

"Yes. Let's do that." Ernst's mother dried her eyes.

When they approached Günther, he wasn't so taken with the plan. "Berlin? Why should I go there?"

"You were fortunate to stay out of jail regarding the incident on that farm," said his mother. "It will be a fresh start for you."

"I don't need you to send me anywhere. I told you I wasn't there," Günther insisted.

No-one had been able to place him for certain at the scene of the crime, but Ernst didn't know whether to believe his brother's account or not. The police would be watching the family and the situation had ramped up tensions between the Poles and the Germans in the area. The next time Günther might not get off.

"We have made the arrangements with your Uncle and purchased the train tickets," said Ernst.

"Thanks for making the decision for me!" said Günther sullenly.

But by the time they dropped him at the train station, he had warmed slightly to the trip and bid them goodbye, tipping his hat and waving from the train window. Everything seemed to be taken care of.

For now Ernst could focus on his own future. He settled into building furniture, especially with Liesel in mind.

Within a few months Ernst and his mother received a short letter.

> I am well. Working a few odd jobs and I have joined the HitlerYouth, part of the Nazionale Socialist Party. This is the future of Germany and for Germans everywhere. I participate in military exercises. We fight against the Communist 'Rotfront.' I will see you soon! Günther.

"It sounds like he is busy and not getting into any trouble," said Ernst's mother hopefully.

Ernst wasn't sure if it was good or bad, but he had read about the National Socialists in the newspaper. It was said they were improving the broken German economy and keeping the ever present threat of the communists at bay. "I hope so," he said, setting down the letter. He did not share his unease about recent violent events in the beer halls and on the streets of Germany. He hoped Günther was not involved in any of that.

He got up from the table. "Going to work on a dining cabinet."

CHAPTER 8
1932

AMBER FIELDS OF RYE BLEW GENTLY IN THE BREEZE NEXT TO cerulean oceans of flax in bloom. Bright yellow rapeseed and strips of sandy light brown soil where the crop had been harvested, reminded Liesel of a striped quilt.

A herd of cows passed by in front of them and Fritz stopped the wagon to let them cross.

Liesel was impatient to get going again and it seemed to take forever to finally see the smoke which billowed from the factories of Łódź.

"Each time we come to town, I see more factories starting up again," said Liesel. Just a year before, many of the stores and factories had been closed and ragged people lined the streets.

"Perhaps the worst of the hard times are over," said her father.

"Well, we never went hungry," said Adelheid. "And I think we can afford a bit more fabric this time, maybe some satin or silk." Josephine's wedding dress had been styled simply with as little fabric as possible.

For the past few years, Liesel and her sister had done without new clothes, but now Liesel wore her new cloche hat and a fashionable pleated skirt she had sewn herself.

They got down off the wagon, leaving Emil to look after the horses.

The strains of a Chopin waltz drifted from a café onto Piotrokow Street, reminding Liesel of all that was right and beautiful in the world. She thought of Ernst, whom she would soon marry.

"Łódź wasn't always like this, you know," Fritz told them, as they walked down the street.

Liesel smiled. Like Cousin Oskar, her father liked to share little snippets of history. "Łódź is renowned for the textile industry," he said, "in part, because back in 1815, the Czar allowed Germans land and gave permission to build factories. It is now one of the largest cities in Poland."

Liesel stopped listening. She had heard enough history and was glad to be done her studies.

Her father continued. "But unfortunately the Bolshevik Revolution put an end to Russia as a trading partner for her fabrics."

They stopped at a window displaying cotton prints, shiny silks, and satins next to thick and sturdy broadcloths, muslins, and percales.

All the colours made Liesel think of her flower garden.

Fritz opened the door and motioned his wife and daughters inside. He stood at the back of the store, while the women looked around.

Behind the counter, the shopkeeper was stacking bolts of cloth onto shelves. He wore a black vest and a tape measure was draped around his neck. He adjusted his skullcap and nodded at them. "What can I help you with?"

"Some fabric for my wedding dress," said Liesel. "Silk or satin."

He pulled down a bolt and held it out for her to touch its sleek surface. "A beautiful satin, for the bride to be."

Liesel was hesitant, fearing her hands, rough from gardening, might catch on the luxurious fabric. She could easily imagine her dress made of this.

"How about the crepe de chine for you?" Liesel's mother asked

Frieda, lifting a swatch of pink cloth towards Frieda's face.

"It will look lovely," said Liesel.

"But I like this one," said Frieda, pointing at a patterned silk jacquard.

"*Nein*, too expensive," said Adelheid. "Perhaps, if you were marrying Oskar, it would have been possible for your dress Liesel."

Liesel had hoped her usually gracious mother would have let that idea go by now. It hadn't occurred to her before what it had been like for her mother, who even with her noble upbringing had chosen to marry a farmer. Maybe she had regretted losing a life of wealth and ease, but in the end it hadn't mattered. The old world had crumbled after the Great war and nobles were a rarity.

Frieda interrupted Liesel's musing. "Well, for *my* wedding, I want the jacquard."

"Well then, you better find a rich husband," said Fritz, taking out his pocketbook.

"Maybe you can marry Oskar," Liesel joked at her sister.

Frieda shook her head. "Too old and too bookish."

"Well," said Fritz. "Let's not keep the man waiting."

"I'll take four metres of the satin and three of the crepe de chine," said Liesel standing up straight.

"Certainly, I will wrap that up for you," said the proprietor. He took the bolts over to the counter where he measured, cut, and folded.

A stop at the post office yielded a letter from Josephine.

"Can I open it?" asked Frieda eagerly. Liesel was about to hand it over, but Emil chimed in, with just a slightly whining tone clearly meant to annoy his younger sister.

"No, I want to open it."

"Give it to me!" said Frieda.

"Stop it, you two!" Liesel said. She took the letter and opened it herself, standing so the others could read over her shoulder.

> *Liebe Familie*
>
> *I miss you all so very much and send my love to each one of you. I think of you and pray for you all often. Happy news!*

Our son Heinrich Andreas, was born six weeks ago. I regret not having written sooner, but it is so busy with a new baby and all the work. I had to be back helping with the chores in a few days. We cannot afford hired help and though our neighbors have helped out some, they are so far away and have troubles of their own.

All the farmers are suffering. The drought has only gotten worse. Dusty topsoil blows everywhere. I have to sweep all the time and the baby must be covered when we are outside.

A grass fire came as far as the henhouse and burned my poor chickens. It was so dry the wheat crop shriveled to al-most nothing and then the prices had gone so far down we couldn't make the mortgage payments. The bank foreclosed on the property. Andreas and I are heartbroken and for a while I just wanted to come home. But we have decided not to give up and found a quarter-section to rent and work for now. We were able to keep the horses but the tractor will have to wait.

At least I got my wish for a house, though it is more like a one room shack.

Men come off the trains and to the farms looking for work in exchange for a meal and a bed. I was so frightened the first time one of these ragged men came to the door, but Andreas usually sets them to work chopping wood and we share a little food with them.

I must take Heinrich and lend a hand to Andreas with the planting. I miss you all so much. All my love and prayers to you my dear family and especially to you Liesel. I wish you and Ernst much happiness together. May God bless you.

Deine Josephine

Liesel felt like the sun had gone behind a cloud. "It sounds like they are having a difficult time," she said, folding the letter and handing it to her mother. She wished she could be there with her sister and couldn't imagine such hardship without the support of her loving family.

"They will be all right," said Adelheid. "Perhaps we can put together a package to send them, but for now, just focus on your wedding."

"Times will be better soon," said Fritz. He ushered his family into the wagon.

CHAPTER 9

MORNING LIGHT DANCED ACROSS THE FEATHERBED.

Liesel woke and stretched, pushing the bedding aside. Frieda had slipped out of bed early to do the chores for both of them and allow Liesel to sleep in on this special occasion.

Outside, Emil was buffing the carriage to a gleaming black. The matching horse team had similarly been groomed until their glossy coats reflected the sun. Not many farmers owned carriages and theirs was only used on special occasions. It had been a wedding gift from Liesel's grandparents to her parents.

And now it would be used for Liesel's own wedding. She was excited and nervous.

After a morning of preparations, the family pulled up to the church and Liesel's father helped the women out of the carriage.

She wondered what it must have been like for Josephine on her wedding a few years ago, to know that she was leaving home and family forever. And then there was little Heinrich, Liesel's new nephew and her parent's first grandchild whom they never seen. Liesel wished Josephine could be here on this special day, but of course it was impossible.

"What are you thinking, dear sister?" said Frieda. "You almost forgot your bouquet." She lifted the enormous bouquet off the carriage seat and handed it to Liesel.

Adelheid adjusted the delicate veil around Liesel's face and stood to admire her daughter in the dress they had made together. Gleaming folds of satin shone softly and cascaded around the bride.

"*Sehr schöne,*" said Adelheid.

"Yes, you look so beautiful," said Frieda her eyes wide with awe. "*Mutti*, I hope you will help me make my dress too."

"I'm sure she will," Liesel smiled. "We just need to find you a suitable husband first."

"It's time to go in," said Adelheid.

Gathering her dress in one hand, Liesel lifted the bouquet to her face and breathed the calming scent of lily of the valley and roses. Her father opened the door and Ernst, in his best suit, took her arm.

Relatives, friends, and neighbors smiled warmly at them.

Liesel felt like she was floating as they started down the aisle.

Nosegays, tied with pink ribbon, festooned each wooden pew. Bouquets adorned the front of the newly built church and candles glowed at the altar, illuminating the the whitewashed walls and the cross.

Pastor Schuldt, in his long robes, stood before the congregation waiting to officiate.

Liesel clung tightly to Ernst's arm, as they knelt for the opening prayer. When the congregation had pronounced their "Amen," the pastor began the marriage service.

"Gathered friends, we come together to ask God's blessing on the marriage of Ernst and Liesel."

Liesel thought of the life they would make together.

Pastor Schuldt continued. "In God's great provision, he established the family, to provide for children and establish peace and stability."

Children, yes, she wanted lots. She imagined dimpled cheeks and laughter.

"…marriage is given for mutual help and comfort, in prosperity and adversity…"

Liesel thought of planting and harvests, the bleating of sheep and lowing of cows. And of course her flower garden with roses, bluebells and poppies.

The pastor joined their hands together and Ernst turned to look at Liesel.

She couldn't remember where they were in the ceremony. Had she missed something important? She was relieved when she realized it was Ernst's turn to speak first.

"I, Ernst, take you Liesel, to be my wife. I promise to be faithful…"

Liesel repeated the same words.

Pastor Schuldt concluded with, "Those whom God has joined together, let no-one separate."

The organ struck a chord and the congregation rose to sing.

Afterward, at the banquet hall, the photographer was waiting with his equipment all set up. The painted backdrop with its colonnades and foliage reminded Liesel of the poem about the lemon trees.

He seated the entire family group and before taking the picture reminded them, "Look natural, no smiling."

What an impossible task, thought Liesel. It was the happiest day of her life and she was surrounded by everyone she loved, especially Ernst. How could she not smile? Obediently she set her jaw and waited for the photographer to take the photo.

The blinding flash made her blink. "It's like a picture plate negative," she said to Ernst.

"Everything is inside out, the dark is light, the light is dark."

"You are so beautiful," whispered Ernst in her ear, ignoring her observation. Liesel giggled.

"And now, I want just the bride and groom," said the photographer.

The family members got up from their seats. With a rustling of skirts and a shuffling of chairs, one by one they disappeared behind the curtain until only Liesel and Ernst were left.

"Place your hand here, on her shoulder," the photographer directed Ernst.

With Ernst's arm around her she felt protected.

Arbeit, ihr Mädchen,
Arbeit bringt süssen Gewinn,
Da schnurren am Rädchen
Lustig die neblichten Tage dahin.

Work, you maidens,
Work brings sweet gain.
The foggy days hum by joyfully
At the spinning wheel.

— Johann Georg Jacobi, Translation by Sharon Krebs

CHAPTER 10

THE NEWLY MARRIED COUPLE ACCEPTED LIESEL'S PARENT'S invitation to move into the spacious suite on the other side of her parent's house.

Ernst set up his workshop at one end of the grain barn.

That way, thought Liesel, everyone she loved could be close.

For the first few months, they were happy just being together, but Liesel soon realized that Ernst was quite the opposite of her boisterous father with his clever sense of humour.

"I like to work by myself," said Ernst to Liesel as he set down a load of firewood in front of the *Kachelofen.* "I don't want to talk all the time, discussing politics and horse breeds when there is work to be done."

"I've noticed that," Liesel said.

"And sometimes I don't know when your father is joking and when he is serious."

"Yes, it must take some getting used to," she admitted. She had to be loyal to her husband, but she loved her father dearly. At least there was mutual respect in the way they treated each other. She hoped that would be enough.

Ernst went back outside and Liesel watched out the window as the wagon pulled up to the grain barn to unload the flax for the threshing. After the hired man had unloaded the bundles, Ernst hitched the horses up to a shaft and wheel in a covered area outside the barn; inside, a threshing attachment separated the straw from the linseeds.

After that the the men soaked the straw in the pond, then set it out to dry on the fields.

It was Liesel and Frieda's job to turn the stalks over so the other side could dry.

"So smelly," said Frieda, speaking through a handkerchief tied over her nose.

"I think it smells even more ripe than usual," said Liesel. She thought ahead to the scutching, combing, and spinning that would take up every spare minute.

In November, tables and chairs were pushed against the wall and an imposing loom took up almost all the space between the kitchen and the parlour.

This was Liesel's favourite part of the process. She loved to see the fabric grow before her eyes and transform what had grown from the ground into a sheet of cloth. Later, the work of her hands could be sewn into a bedsheet, a blouse or jacket.

She adjusted herself on the bench, picked up the shuttle, and pushed it through the threads in front of her. Pressing the pedal brought the next set of threads forward and every clacking rhythm added to the fabric growing before her eyes.

But today she felt sleepy. The smell of sauerkraut fermenting in the pantry assaulted her senses in a way she had never noticed before.

She pushed the shuttle through on the other side and took it back with her right hand. But as she repeated the familiar action, the threads across the loom wavered in front of her eyes. After a few minutes, her eyelids drooped, her hand relaxed and as sleep overtook her, the shuttle hit the floor with a thud.

With a start, she woke to find her mother laughing from the spinning wheel in the other corner of the room. "Liesel dear, how can you fall asleep weaving?"

"Ha ha. It's not even lunchtime." Frieda added, looking up from her hand spindle.

Liesel didn't think their response was particularly funny. She swallowed. There was some kind of metal taste in her mouth and she felt ill.

Adelheid stopped spinning and pushed her spectacles up. She leaned in to look at Liesel. "Is the smell of the sauerkraut getting to you?" she asked. They were so used to its aroma permeating the house in fall and winter, it was rarely ever mentioned.

"Oh, I'm tired and I don't feel so well," said Liesel, creasing her forehead in a little furrow. "I don't know what is wrong with me."

"Oh, you will probably know in about seven months," said Adelheid beaming. "I think the stork is going to bring us a grandchild that we can visit."

CHAPTER 11

1933

GÜNTHER HAD RETURNED FROM GERMANY AND WAS VISIT-
ing. The men sat at the table looking at the *Neue Łódźer Zeitung*.
Headlines in bold print read 'Reich Chancellor Hitler.'

"So the National Socialists have finally made it to power in Germany,"
said Günther. "This is the beginning of a new day for Germany and the
German people."

"Better than the communists, I suppose," said Ernst reluctantly. He
remembered the conflicts leading up to the formation of the Second
Polish Republic, with the Germans and other minorities caught in the
middle. Even now the Bolsheviks could be a menace to anyone who
had acquired property.

"The Reds are definitely a threat," said Emil. "If Hitler can stop them,
it might be just what the German people need."

"I think the man is a scoundrel," said Fritz. "I read that awful book,
Mein Kampf, and I tell you that godless man is up to no good. There

are too many fools who will follow him. I predict disaster for Germany and all of Europe."

Bothered by her father's vehement and contrary opinion, Liesel lost count of her stitches again on the sweater she was crocheting for the baby. The politics were of little interest to her, but she felt concerned by the uncertainty. She hoped that what happened in Germany did not affect their lives here, but she knew their fate was inextricably connected. Based on ethnicity, they were German citizens.

Regardless, she was having a baby and must prepare. She thrust the crochet hook through the next hole, collected the loop of wool and pulled it back.

CHAPTER 12

1934

THE BABY WAS DUE WITHIN A FEW WEEKS AND ERNST HAD
been busy too. He set the cradle down on the bedroom floor.

"It's beautiful!" said Liesel, caressing the smooth birch.

"You can paint a design on it if you like," he said.

"I'll keep it simple, just a little border," she said, smiling up at him and
thinking of the baby who would soon be nestled safely in bed.

She started work on it that very afternoon after choosing stencils of
a flower and leaf design.

Standing to survey her work, halfway through the first leaf, she
thought it good, but an uncomfortable tightness around her expand-
ing waist made her loathe to bend down again. Reluctantly she put the
paints and brushes away.

She would not pick up them up again for almost a year.

Liesel walked around the house several times before knocking on the
door of her parents' side of the house. Her mother answered.

"I think my time is coming," said Liesel, holding onto her belly. "It's a little early."

"Come inside and sit down. I'll tell Ernst to call for the midwife."

As it turned out, there was no hurry. It was almost two days later that the old woman whispered to Liesel, "You have a little man." With a toothless grin, she arranged the little bundle, wrapped in a blanket at Liesel's side.

Liesel look down at his tiny red face. "We will name him Johann," she said, "In honour of Ernst's father." She untied the front of her nightdress and tried to feed him, but he only sucked briefly before beginning to cry.

"Like this," the midwife instructed the new mother, repositioning the crying infant at his mother's breast. "He will learn to eat."

Johann sucked a little more and slept briefly, only to wake a few minutes later.

"I don't seem to be doing it right," said Liesel.

Adelheid came in and picked him up. "Come to *Oma*," she said and then looking at Liesel reassured her. "He'll be fine, you rest a while."

But over the next few days, nothing could soothe little Johann. His cries were piercing and his feedings never appeared successful. He would sleep a short while, then wake crying. He suckled frantically, but Liesel's milk and attempts to comfort him were in vain.

She began to think it was something wrong with her. Maybe her milk was sour or not enough? Perhaps she was holding him the wrong way or spoiling him by holding him too much.

Her mother warmed blankets on the *Kachelofen* to put on his tummy. The midwife brought an herbal poultice. She laid her wrinkled hands on Johann and chanted a prayer in a singsong voice.

"I have a call in the next village to attend to," she said to Liesel. "You will both be fine."

Ernst's mother arrived to see her new grandson. "He is very small. Perhaps you don't have enough milk," she said. "Breast-feeding is vulgar and old-fashioned anyway." She pulled a baby bottle from her bag and set milk to boil on the stove. "This is the modern way to feed a child."

Liesel had mixed feelings when that didn't work either. She couldn't wait until her mother-in-law left.

She rocked the cradle for hours, staring regretfully at the unfinished design. She picked Johann up and walked around the house until she was too tired to put one foot in front of another. The two grandmothers tried in vain to comfort the child.

Liesel's lying-in time came to an end and she attempted to resume her household duties, but it was impossible. She had looked forward to being a mother and now she dreaded every minute of the day her baby was awake.

She was holding a squalling infant and staring at a basin full of dirty dishes when Ernst came in for supper. She had nothing ready. "I'm sorry." She handed Johann to his father. "I just can't manage with him crying all the time. I didn't know it would be like this."

Ernst jostled the baby in his arms. "You are doing your best."

"What about his christening?" she said. "He is going to cry all the way through."

"We can wait a few weeks, perhaps he'll be fine by then."

Ernst took Johann outside, but Liesel could still hear his pitiful screams. Her milk let down, dampening the front of her blouse.

She felt like a complete failure at motherhood.

Her eyes filled with tears, but she wiped them on her apron. Picking up a knife she attacked a loaf of bread and block of cheese as if they were her sworn enemies. They needed to eat after all and she couldn't always expect her mother to feed them.

As she set the table, she looked out the front window on the neglected flower beds. Weeds had come up alongside the roses and peonies. In the vegetable garden, peas and beans were falling over and needed to be staked, but she had been so busy with Johann she had no time to get out and do it.

Ernst returned in a few moments with his screaming son in one hand and a jar of amber liquid in the other. Liesel took the jar.

"*Was ist das?*" She was fairly certain it wasn't liquor. Some of their neighbors made their own alcohol but her parents would have nothing to do with strong drink, except for special occasions.

"Don't worry," Ernst smiled. "Your mother made some chamomile tea for him."

"Oh." Liesel felt silly. Ever since she had Johann she couldn't seem to think straight.

She went to the drawer for a spoon and together they tried to get some of the fluid down the baby's throat without making him choke.

Finally they summoned Dr. Zalman from town.

Liesel answered the door with her noisy red-faced infant in her arms. Strands of hair fell over her face and her apron was dirty.

She hoped the doctor, in his long dark coat and wide hat didn't think her slovenly.

"*Oy vey,* he is a loud one," he laughed, setting down his bag on the table. "Come here young man."

Liesel willingly handed Johann over.

Doctor Zalman examined him from head to toe and listened to his chest with a stethoscope. Finally he shook his head.

"I can't say I know what is wrong with him, but some babies cry a lot." He handed Liesel a vial of medicine. "And it is not your fault little mother," he admonished her before he left.

Every few hours she administered two drops. She noted that Johann's crying was quieter, his sleep more frequent.

But a week later, he was up again, his cries now weak whimpers.

Liesel paced the house for hours, then sat down exhausted on the rocking chair, so tired she dozed off.

In the middle of the night a draft blew through the silent room.

Liesel woke up and touched Johann's back. It was cold. She put a finger in front of his nose. The warm breath, which she had known to be in every living creature, was absent.

Liesel lifted his limp body, and saw that blood had soaked through his diaper, staining her nightgown; a moment of anguish she would never be able to forget. "Ernst." Her voice shook as she called out, shattering the stillness.

He came running from their bedroom and took Johann from her

grasp. "He's gone," Ernst said, his face a pale mask.

The next morning, Liesel watched numbly from the parlor doorway as Johann's grandmothers and aunts laid him out in what was to have been his baptismal gown. They placed him in a basket on the table surrounded by lilacs, cornflowers and roses.

Johann's tiny face was peaceful at last, but the scent of the flowers, was repulsive to Liesel.

She stifled a sob and retired to her bed.

Visitors came by bearing food and flowers, but Liesel refused to see anyone. Ernst retreated to the workshop to build a casket.

On the day of the funeral Frieda entered the bedroom. "It's almost time to go." She sat on the bed next to Liesel and put an arm around her. "You'll have another baby. I know you will."

Liesel knew her sister was only trying to make her feel better, but it wasn't working. Fresh tears spilled onto her cheeks. "I don't want another baby. I just want Johann." She clutched the pillow on the bed as if it was an infant. "I wanted to make him better, to feed him and love him. I wanted to watch him grow plump and rosy."

"I know," said Frieda. "But now you need to say goodbye."

Well of course Frieda didn't know anything about having a baby, thought Liesel, but she swallowed the lump in her throat and splashed cold water on her face. She pinned up her hair and let Frieda help her into a black dress.

Outside the sun shone. Birds chirped and flowers bloomed amid the weeds as if nothing had happened.

Liesel's mother took her arm. Her father opened the door of the carriage and Liesel got inside.

They waited while Ernst placed the pine box he had made on the floor of the carriage. It wasn't much bigger than a wooden bread box. Ernst's hat covered his face, but Liesel could read his sadness by the stoop in his back and the slow methodical way he moved. Wordlessly, he climbed in and took Liesel's hand.

On the ride to the church, Liesel gazed stoically at the miniature casket engulfed by a wreath of white roses and carnations. *'Im Himmel, mit den Engeln'*, the ribbon on the wreath proclaimed.

Liesel could not imagine that distant place nor its celestial inhabitants.

Old Pastor Schuldt read the funeral service for their infant son, his words of comfort like a droning bee to her ears.

The casket was lowered into the ground and she was led to place dirt upon it.

Overcome again with sobs, she was unable to speak, so reserved quiet Ernst had to do the talking as people offered condolences.

A few days later, she wrote to Josephine.

> *Dearest sister,*
>
> *By now you have received the telegram of the birth and death of your nephew.*
>
> *I don't understand how the rooster can crow every day and the sun rise each morning when my baby is gone.*
>
> *I work to forget the pain, but nothing can change the fact that my baby died before I ever really got to know him. A year ago, I was happy just being married, I couldn't imagine a baby and now I don't know how I can ever go on.*
>
> *Liesel*

CHAPTER 13

ERNST AND LIESEL DID NOT ATTEND CHURCH SERVICES FOR A few weeks, preferring to grieve away from the eyes of others, but Liesel was soon drawn to find solace in the familiar hymns and rituals of her faith.

On Sunday morning, she was dressed for church and ready to go with her parents, but Ernst was still in his work clothes.

"I'm not going to church today," he said. "Max is unwell."

Liesel frowned and gathered her hat and purse. "You were just plowing with him yesterday." Their Belgian draft horses were the picture of health and strength.

"Horses can worsen very quickly. We can't afford to lose one during planting season."

Liesel went anyway with the rest of the family, but when they returned the stallion was in the pasture, munching grass.

At dinner Ernst explained. "Probably just ate some bad hay."

"You really have to watch that colic in horses," said Fritz. "The pain can get bad very quickly. You were right to keep an eye on him."

That just made Liesel think of the pain Johann must have experienced before he died. She pushed her plate away. "I'm going to go lie down."

Ernst spent the week working in his shop or helping Fritz with the farm. The following Sunday he noticed an urgent problem with the well.

"Please come with us," said Liesel.

Ernst frowned at her. "Don't tell me what to do."

His chastisement stung. She just wanted him to be with her.

"We express our grief with tears," said Adelheid to Liesel, when Ernst missed yet another Sunday. "Men follow another path. Give him time."

Time. There was plenty of that. It stretched out endlessly before her in the rhythms of that summer. Sowing, weeding, harvest, threshing.

Liesel threw herself into the work, but none of it had any meaning or brought any joy to her.

In the fall, her brother Emil went to Breslau to study. Frieda got a job in Łódź, only coming home to visit some weekends. Ernst worked long hours; the fields by day, the woodshop in the evening, sawing and sanding furniture.

Liesel felt more alone than ever, but she did not know how to fix the divide that had come between them. She felt abandoned by her husband.

One evening, hoping Ernst would come to bed before she was asleep, Liesel went out to the woodshop. Four freshly made chairs were stacked together. Ernst was fastening hinges to a cabinet door.

"I'm going to Breslau next week to deliver this dining set. Do you want to come with me and visit your brother?"

"Yes," she said, thinking a trip would do her good.

But when the day came she woke up with a bad head cold, unable to make the journey. She had so wanted to go.

"Give my greetings to Emil," she said, sniffling as Ernst climbed into the wagon.

"I should be back Thursday," he said, snapping the reins.

When he returned, Liesel was mending by lamplight.

"You're still up," he said. "I brought you something." He handed her a box.

Liesel put down her sewing and opened it. Inside was an intricately carved cuckoo clock.

"I bought it in Breslau, but they make them in the Black Forest," he said. "The other 'Schönewald.'"

He hung it above the mantle and they sat on the sofa together, quietly watching its workings in the flickering light, until the fire in the Kachelofen died out.

Before Christmas, Liesel felt tired and queasy again.

One minute she was excited to be having another baby; the next minute, she was terrified that the baby would die, as Johann had. To take her mind off her worries, she cleaned the house thoroughly and baked until she had used up almost all the flour and spices in the house.

"You should be resting," said Adelheid. "You've made enough cookies for the whole village and your side of the house is clean enough for the Duchess of Prussia."

"Yes mother," said Liesel.

But she was determined to do everything differently this time. She made a whole new set of clothes for the baby and ate more fruits and vegetables. She attended church and said her prayers faithfully in hopes that Providence would smile on her and grant her baby the gift of life. Finally, she finished painting the design on the cradle.

Nearly a year after they had lost Johann, Kurt was born. He was chubby with rosy cheeks and, though he cried loudly at times, he was comforted at her breast or rocking in his cradle.

Liesel loved being his mother. Everything was the way it was supposed to be this time.

Some, among the Volksdeutsche were hell-bent to become junior partners in the Aryan master race and did all they could to deliver their communities as a fifth column for the Nazis.

— Charles M. Barber in foreword to *A Terrible Revenge*

CHAPTER 14

1937

ERNST HELD HIS SON ON HIS KNEE AND JOSTLED HIM GENTLY, but it was nearly impossible to keep the boy quiet. Kurt constantly tried to wriggle away. Liesel was enthralled not only by the wedding, but by their youngest arrival, Olaf, who slept in her arms.

She smiled calmly, as she watched her sister Frieda, and her husband-to-be, Ludwig, repeat their wedding vows. She turned to Ernst and squeezed his hand. "I am so happy for Frieda and Ludwig."

He thought it was good to see Liesel happy again, but Günther's behavior was once again cause for concern.

At the wedding dinner, Günther sat amongst several pretty women. He plucked a flower from a centerpiece in front of him and placed it behind the ear of one girl. "And you are looking lovely today." She giggled, even as he filled the wineglass of a young woman on the other side of him.

Ernst wondered when Günther might get married. Of course first he would have to settle on one particular girl. Perhaps marriage would help him to lose his fanatical notions.

Since Günther had come back from Germany, the rift between them had grown. Günther had always been more outgoing, more daring and more prone to finding trouble. Ernst and his mother had hoped that Gunther's experience in Germany would have matured him and diverted his energy. Instead, he had come back idealistic and arrogant, in addition to being a card-carrying member of the Nazi political party.

The political situation was like a keg of gunpowder waiting to be lit, thought Ernst. Recently, skirmishes had erupted between the Poles and Germans in the area over the future of the city of Danzig. Prominent Bolshevik leaders had gone to trial in Russia and pro-communist forces were protesting that. In addition both Germans and Poles in the vicinity had grown increasingly intolerant of the Jewish presence in the area since the economic downturn at the beginning of the decade.

Oskar was also seated at Gunther's table , and already they were discussing politics.

"It doesn't matter how long the Jews have lived among us," said Günther with an oily smile, in response to something Oskar had said. "A Jew is a Jew and he cannot become anything else, any more than your grandfather could become a horse by living in the barn." Laughing at his own joke, he emptied the rest of the bottle of wine into his glass. "They really do not belong with us."

Oskar pushed his spectacles up on his nose and looked at Günther darkly. He appeared to be measuring his words with care. "Well, then I do not agree with the National Socialists."

At this Günther snickered and turned to his female companions. He pretended to push imaginary spectacles and mimicked the young professor.

Ernst turned his attention to Liesel and Kurt. He did not want her to witness how her cousin was being treated.

CHAPTER 15
1938

LIESEL COULD HARDLY BELIEVE HOW QUICKLY TIME HAD flown by.

"Boys, shhh!" Liesel had asked Kurt and Olaf several times, but they were too young to understand what was happening. She held two month old Rudy, the most recent addition to their family in her arms.

Her father and Ernst had turned their chairs to the radio set and were listening to a news broadcast. "Police and fire brigades stood back as synagogues and Jewish-owned businesses and homes were burned and vandalized."

Fritz shook his head. "Despots. Have we completely lost our human decency, that people would go and destroy the property and livelihood of others?"

"Hitler has apparently sanctioned the actions," said Ernst, turning the dial of the radio off.

"Well, Hitler is a criminal and a war-monger," Fritz said, mumbling under his breath. "There *will* be a war. I don't know when, but that man and his National Socialists will stop at nothing."

Liesel was shocked to hear her father speak so strongly, as if these politics were a personal affront. She did not remember when he had been that angry. Political affairs did not interest her much, but she thought back to her days of being tutored by cousin Oskar and her study of the instability of the Polish state throughout history. She hoped her father wasn't right about a war.

"Time to finish the chores," said Ernst. He was about to stand up when there was a sharp rap at the front door.

He answered it and Liesel was startled to see a man in uniform standing there with a hat shading his eyes. She thought he was a policeman until he thrust out his right arm, lifted his head and beamed at everyone, lips peeling back to reveal even rows of large teeth. "Heil Hitler!" He wiped his boots on the mat and hung up his hat on a hook. "My good brother, how are you?"

Günther greeted Ernst with a sound pat on the back. Smiling, he took Liesel's free hand into his grasp and gave a small bow. "Liesel, you are as lovely as ever." Turning his attention to baby Rudy, he said, "Your new son looks just like my brother!"

Liesel nodded. "I guess he does," she said politely, observing that Günther's smile did not cause his eyes to crinkle.

Olaf looked at his uncle, then toddled over and grabbed Liesel's leg.

"And here you are in the kitchen surrounded by your little future soldiers," said Günther. "The *Führer* would certainly approve."

She found his comment patronizing and she let her hand slip from his grasp. She cared for her family because it was her joy, not because Hitler or anyone else thought it was her duty.

Günther pulled out a chair and sat at the table. His voice was animated as he spoke, commanding their attention. "Der *Führer* is planning to Germanize Poland and make it part of the Reich, just like Austria and the Sudetenland. Danzig and the Corridor belong to the Fatherland. And there are so many Germans here, we need space to live. We are the ones who have settled and civilized this land. *Nicht wahr?*"

Liesel poured coffee.

"And what will that mean to us?" Ernst took a sip.

"Maybe an end to those thieving, lazy Poles. *Ja*, Ernst?" he chuckled. "It is we, the Aryan race, who have made this land a success. Our farms thrive."

No thanks to Günther, thought Liesel. Ernst had told her that many times his younger brother had shirked his chores to go out with friends and Ernst had had to do them. Even now Ernst was the one who regularly went to his mother's to help out. Günther was never around when her roof needed thatching or it was time to butcher.

"Poland will become a part of the Fatherland," Günther continued, his slate gray eyes glinting like shards of metal.

"Hmmph," said Fritz. He spoke gruffly. "War never brings anything good. I am old enough to remember the last war. You young people have no idea."

"How does Hitler know he won't lose this war like Germany lost the last one?" asked Ernst. He thought of his father who had died in the Great War.

Günther pulled out a gold case and withdrew a cigarette. "Adolf Hitler is a brilliant leader. The Hitler Youth organization has prepared us for military life."

"We have a decent life here. Why would we want to fight?"

"The German minorities here deserve a better life. Europe needs to rid itself of those filthy cheating Jews and the communist Bolsheviks, who steal us all blind." Günther leaned back in the chair and blew a puff of smoke across the table.

Liesel opened the window. She thought of the communist bandits who had caused such fear in her childhood. She shivered as she considered what could happen to her children. On the other hand she didn't trust Günther either.

"The Poles are no good," he continued, "making liquor with their potatoes instead of building up their farms. This land would be better off without them. The Slavs and the Jews are sub-human." He stubbed out his cigarette on the edge of his saucer.

Liesel picked it up and cleared the ashes into the dustbin.

Günther capped off his diatribe with a challenge. "The Aryan race is superior."

"We are all made in the image of God," said Fritz solemnly.

"Well, I don't care about any superior race," said Ernst. "And not every Jew is a cheat."

Liesel thought of kindly Doctor Zalman who had attended Johann before he died.

"We live next to these people," said Ernst. "I have no wish to fight them."

"You need to join the *Selbstschutz*. We are organizing communities of Germans— *Volksdeutsche* like ourselves—for self-protection of course."

"I am not interested in this cause," said Ernst.

"Just be careful what you say, brother. You do not want to be thought a traitor by your own people. Besides, the Poles are rising up against us."

Günther wasn't going to let go. He gestured towards the boys playing on the floor, "Don't you want to ensure the safety of your family? Things here will change, and you will have to change too." He stood up.

Liesel was waiting at the door with his hat and coat.

CHAPTER 16

Liebe Kusine Adelheid

I am working in Berlin now towards publication of my book about the history and geography of Łódź, particularly as it pertains to the German settlement of our ancestry. However, given the present political situation, I will be doing the majority of my work from here. I hope I can come to Schönewald at Christmas and I will visit if possible.

Dein, Oskar

Adelheid and Liesel were reading the letter when Ernst walked into the room. "Did you hear, Ernst?" said Liesel. "Cousin Oskar is in Berlin now and he is working on a book."

"Oh," said Ernst. He had met Oskar on a few occasions, but found his expansive discourse on this and that excruciating. Way too much book knowledge for one person.

"He will probably come to visit at Christmas," said Adelheid.

"I guess we will see him then," said Ernst. "Going to work in the shop now."

Oskar's promised visit that Christmas was welcomed, at least by some members of the household. According to Adelheid, her younger cousin could do no wrong and she appeared to hang on his every word.

Ernst was at a loss what to think. First of all, he didn't understand half of what the esteemed Professor said, with all his university learning and secondly, every time Oskar looked through his spectacles at Liesel, Ernst felt a vague sense of unease. Not that he could put his finger on anything.

Liesel brought out a tray of cakes and cookies.

"You have your mother's talents for baking," said Oskar, taking a slice of *Weinachtsstollen*. He turned to Adelheid.

"I remember all those goodies you made for us when I tutored Liesel."

"Yes, she has such fond memories of that year," said Adelheid. "You imparted such an appreciation of literature and poetry to her."

"I loved that poem we did," said Liesel, 'Where the Lemon trees Bloom.'"

Ernst had never been into poetry. He tried to assure himself that their exchange was nothing more than familial affection.

"Ah, yes, Mignon's song," said Oskar. "Such a poignant ode to one's longing for home."

"Of course I was completely hopeless at math and bored with history," laughed Liesel. "I was probably your worst student."

"Trust me, I had many worse when I taught at the high school the following year."

Fritz changed the subject and Ernst was glad he wouldn't have to listen to any more reminisces between teacher and pupil.

"What do you think of the *Anschluss* in Austria, Oskar?"

"Many of the Austrians seem to be in favour, but I think it is an indication of Hitler's intentions for the rest of Europe," Oskar answered. "First Austria, then he took the Sudetenland. Poland is only a matter of time."

Adelheid poured him another cup of tea and Oskar continued. "The other ethnicities in these regions need to be respected. Herr Hitler's insistence on racial superiority and purity does not extend fair and equal treatment of all people. The situation is becoming problematic."

"Tensions are running high," said Ernst. "The Poles here are restless."

"One could hardly blame them," said Oskar. "If I was Jewish I would be even more concerned about Hitler's policies. In Germany, they can't own businesses and they have expelled Jewish children from schools."

"As a minority here, we also may need to protect ourselves," said Ernst, thinking out loud about the *Selbstschutz*.

"Of course," said Oskar. "It seems reasonable, but I am just not sure what the future will bring if everyone takes up arms."

*German people, your country and mine are now at war. Your country has bombed
and invaded the free and independent State of Poland ... because your troops
were not withdrawn in response to a note of the British Government to the German
Government, war has followed.*

— Prime Minister Chamberlain on BBC Radio broadcast in the German language,
September 4th, 1939

CHAPTER 17
1939

GÜNTHER HAD BEEN RIGHT ABOUT THE CHANGES, BUT THEY
were not all good. Try as she might, the war and occupation of Poland
were impossible for Liesel to ignore.

In the past most people in the village of different nationalities had at
least tolerated each other and sometimes co-operated. But now Liesel
hated to go out. People kept to themselves and Germans and Poles were
not on speaking terms anymore. The Poles who had been neighbors
were now the enemy. Even the Lithuanians and the Ukrainians had to
take sides for the Nazis or against. Some, who had a German parent
or grandparent or spoke the language well, claimed German heritage
and signed the *Volksliste*.

Ernst entered the kitchen wearing his *Selbstschutz* uniform.

Liesel had to admit he looked handsome and she was proud of the
sacrifice he had made, but she still seethed with anger that Günther had
questioned her husband's loyalty to her and the children.

After more pressure from Günther , Ernst had reluctantly joined the local "Self-Protection" unit. He only wanted to be a carpenter and a farmer, but in the end, he had felt compelled to make sure no harm would come to the family.

"I'm out of sugar," said Liesel. Usually she would have just gone to the neighbor, old *Pani* Zawadski. "I was going next door to borrow some."

Ernst shook his head. "You can't," he said. "I am on patrol and I cannot be seen to be associating with the enemy in any way. And that means you cannot mix with any of the Poles either."

Ernst had said little about what he was doing. Some sort of police work Liesel assumed. She did not really want to know, but her life had definitely changed. She thought about all the ways that their lives had intersected with those around them. The neighbors, the hired help, and the shops in Łódź that she had frequented.

Shopping had become an annoyance. Many of the stores she used to patronize were off limits now, as Germans could not be seen at Jewish establishments without repercussions. Furthermore, since the occupation, they were calling Łódź "Litzmannstadt" after some important Nazi General. The Nazis had renamed so many streets, it was confusing to get around the city.

Ernst cut into her thoughts. "I had to fire young Jan. I caught him stealing potatoes, probably to bring to the partisans."

The other hired help had quit, mostly to join the Polish army. This meant that her father and Ernst had full responsibility for the farm.

She would just have to make do by boiling down some beets until she could get to town to buy some sugar.

In October Günther returned, this time to convince Ernst to join the German military officially.

"Join the *Wehrmacht*, Ernst. Or even better the *Schutzstaffel*," he said, fingering the SS emblem on his collar. "It is for the good of our people. To unite Germans everywhere. Many on the *Volksliste* have already joined. So far we've driven the Polish army out of Łódź, but there is much more to be done."

Bullies with uniforms, thought Ernst. The SS was out of the question for him, but he couldn't say so in front of Günther.

"I am already in the *Selbstschutz*. That should be enough. Besides, I have plenty to do around here," Ernst gestured toward the window.

The wagon, minus one wheel, was on its side in the yard. "The wagon to repair, an order for some chairs. The rye to plant. I can't expect Fritz to do it all."

Günther shook his head. "Whether you like it or not, whether they are your neighbors or not, the Poles are the enemies of the German people and the German army is cracking down on its enemies. You want your family to be protected."

Ernst looked across the room.

One-year-old Rudy sat on a braided rug in front of the *Kachelofen*. In each chubby hand he held a wooden block, his eyes nearly crossing as he brought them up close. Intently he examined them and then hit them together several times.

"Join the army!" insisted Günther. "Your family will get more rations. Food shortages are coming."

No wonder, thought Ernst, if people have to join the military instead of planting their crops. Already officials had come and taken what amounted to half the harvest. They had also counted the animals and had told Ernst that after butchering, the army was entitled to half the meat.

Rudy put a block in his mouth and attempted to chew on it. A few feet away Olaf was building a fence with the rest of the blocks, surrounding a little set of wooden animals that Ernst had made for the boys last Christmas. Ernst tried to commit this scene to memory, because he had a sense things were about to change.

"And," Günther's voice was smooth and well measured as if he was explaining something to a small child. "You will be protected from expulsions."

Liesel glanced over at Ernst. "Expulsions?" she asked. She put a hand on her thickening belly and Ernst knew she was thinking of the next baby that would join their family. She sighed. "Perhaps it will be best, Ernst," she said quietly as she made her way around the table collecting the dishes.

Ernst had heard enough. Now his wife was pressuring him, but he could hardly blame her, given her present condition. It was unthinkable that anyone would expel her from the home where she had lived all her life.

"I will have to think about it."

"Everyone will respect you!" Günther held his head high and thrust his chest out. The two embroidered lightning runes contrasted against the black collar of his SS uniform. Brass buttons lined up evenly down his tunic like a regiment. "You should see the young women when they see me in my uniform."

"Remember I'm a married man, so I don't need that kind of respect," stated his older brother. He picked up Rudy, who had toddled over. "I only want to protect what's mine."

Ernst postponed the decision, avoiding Günther whenever possible. But in November he discovered there really was no choice. Like all the other *Selbstschutz* members, his unit was being absorbed into the army. The price for being on the *Deutsche Volksliste* was being ordered to report for "service to the Reich" in the *Wehrmacht* army.

The day he was to register, Günther suddenly appeared in Ernst's workshop.

"So you've come to accompany me to Łódź?" said Ernst, hanging his saw from a nail.

"Aber natürlich," said Günther. "Of course, and it's Litzmannstadt now, remember."

Ernst was quite sure Günther's real motives were not brotherly companionship, but to make sure Ernst didn't try to leave the country as some people had done before the war had actually started. He thought of a few wealthier Jewish families in the area, suddenly disappearing after Kristallnacht, leaving homes and shops empty. He didn't know if they had found somewhere to go. The Anti-Jewish laws in Poland and Germany had become so strict now, it would be nearly impossible for them to even travel.

It would be almost as ludicrous, thought Ernst, for him to try to leave now or go into hiding. With three small children, a pregnant wife, Liesel's parents, and the farm, the thought had never seriously crossed his mind.

Arriving in Łódź, they parked the wagon near the registration office.

A number of shops stood empty, their windows boarded up. Across the wood someone had scrawled *"Alle Juden raus"* and other insults against the Jews. A few shoppers scurried furtively in and out of the remaining shops. Uniformed sentries stood at the end of the block.

Ernst swallowed and tried not to show his discomfort.

A man wearing a yellow armband on his shabby coat, swept up glass on the sidewalk. He shrank back against a storefront as Ernst and Günther approached.

Another SS soldier, his boots clicking ominously, strode toward the man. He stopped in front of him and spat. *"Schweinhund."* With his boot, he scattered the glass that had been swept right over the spittle. "You are not even supposed to be on the sidewalk, you filthy pig."

Turning to Günther and Ernst, he thrust his arm out high. "Heil Hitler."

"Heil Hitler." Günther responded and stood at attention with his heels together.

Ernst busied himself with the horses' harnesses.

"I said, 'Heil Hitler,'" the soldier demanded, looking straight at Ernst.

Ernst stood up and responded, lifting his arm slowly. "Heil Hitler."

"You are reporting for your duty to the Reich?"

"Jawohl," stated Ernst.

"Well you will need a little more enthusiasm than that for our *Führer*, Hitler. Perhaps a uniform will help."

Ernst left the SS officer chatting with Günther and went inside the registration office, which had once been a large shop. A desk with a typewriter had been set up in the centre of the room and an official sat behind it. "Name?" he demanded.

"Ernst Hoffmann."

"Viovodeship?"

"Łódź," repliedErnst. At every question he felt as if he were surrendering some part of himself.

"Litz-mann-stadt." The clerk enunciated each syllable as he typed it, making his point clearly.

Ernst was directed to a curtained area in the back where he undressed down to his undershorts. First a doctor checked his eyes then instructed him to look at the chart and read the letters.

"M, H, G, Q …."

"Your vision is excellent," said the doctor. He took a light from his pocket and briefly peered into each of Ernst's ears. "Now stand up." The doctor stepped back and looked Ernst over. "Not much flesh on these bones," he said, feeling Ernst's bicep, "but you are a strong one, a carpenter yes?" He took out his stethoscope and placed it on Ernst's chest. "Breathe." Ernst shuddered involuntarily at the cold implement and took a deep breath while the doctor listened.

"Gut."

"Now let me see your feet," said the doctor.

Ernst's ankles and knees leaned slightly inward and his bare feet rested completely flat against the floor. "Stand tall, shoulders back," the doctor instructed as he peered down at Ernst's instep. "Stand on your tiptoes. Have you always had this problem?"

Ernst had endured varying levels of pain in his feet for most of his life, mostly during times of heavy work or a lot of walking. "As long as I can remember. My father had flat feet as well."

Before the Great War, when Ernst was a little boy, he remembered his father taking off his boots after the day's work and massaging the soles of his feet. Sometimes Ernst's mother would bring a basin of warm water for him to soak in.

"Sit on the table," the doctor instructed.

Ernst climbed up, shivering as his bare thighs touched the cool leather. The doctor took Ernst's left foot in hand and examined it carefully. "Hmm. As I suspected you have absolutely no arch. You will be unable to march any distance, therefore I recommend you to some other duty." He picked up Ernst's chart and made a note. "It is too bad, you are such a fine Aryan specimen otherwise." He handed a paper to Ernst. "Give this to the commanding officer."

Ernst exhaled. At least he would not be in combat.

CHAPTER 18

"PUT THE JAM UP HERE," LIESEL INSTRUCTED OLAF, WHO lifted a jar of plum jam from a crate onto the pantry shelf. Sacks of dried beans, barrels of sauerkraut, salted pork, and pickles filled much of the remaining space.

Liesel felt satisfaction knowing her family would be well provided for, food shortages or not. Plus Christmas was just around the corner.

"Mutti," asked Olaf. "Can I have a pickle?"

"Maybe for supper," said Liesel. Her mouth watered at the thought of biting into the crunchy dills. In her mind she had perfected the flavor combination of garlic and the sour and salty tang of the brine that filled the crocks.

As she exited the pantry, her mother came into the kitchen. "Olaf, Kurt, you come with *Oma* so *Mutti* can rest, while Rudy naps."

"Thank you, mother."

Rest. That was a nice idea, thought Liesel, sitting down to her sewing pile, but right now "resting" usually included mending, sewing, and knitting for the baby. Three boys had nearly worn out everything and she had never been able to bring herself to pulling out the things Johann had worn in his short life. She set down the needlework and closed her eyes for a moment.

The door opened. "Here they are, just in time for supper," said Adelheid. "These young men are getting to be a bit too much for your father. He doesn't seem to have much patience anymore."

"I've noticed too," said Liesel.

The boys started to squabble. Kurt took a toy right out of his brother's hands and Olaf began to wail. Rudy woke crying from his nap.

"Kurt, give it back."

Liesel felt stressed and wished Ernst were home more, especially with the baby due any time. Always, at this stage in her pregnancy she would be reminded of Johann and wondered anxiously if everything would turn out.

The morning of Christmas Eve arrived but she didn't know if Ernst would be allowed much time at home. Mostly he had been policing in the area and she felt fortunate that he had not been sent far away.

She had just cleared away the lunch dishes, when she heard scuffling at the front door. "Sit," she ordered the boys.

"Who's there?" she called, with her hand hesitating on the latch. You couldn't be too careful these days.

"It's me," a muffled voice called back. "Let me in."

Liesel opened the door to a giant spruce tree filling the entire doorway, its fragrance wafting into the house. Ernst maneuvered it through the door and set it up in the corner of the parlor, where the top brushed the ceiling. He smiled, obviously pleased with himself. "Do you like it?" he asked.

"It's beautiful," said Liesel.

"We like it, Vati!" Olaf and Kurt said in unison.

"Kurt, you take Olaf and Rudy," said Liesel. "Go see how Oma and Opa are doing and tell them Christmas Eve dinner will be at six o'clock tonight."

She stoked the oven and put in the goose, that she had prepared the day before, to cook for the afternoon. She pulled out packages from the closet and placed them under the tree. Together, Liesel and Ernst fastened candles and folded paper stars to each branch. Liesel hung coloured glass ornaments and Ernst placed the angel on top. They lit the candles and stepped back to admire their work.

"*Sehr schön*," said Liesel.

Ernst squeezed her hand. Christmas would be celebrated as it always had.

The older boys burst through the door followed by their grandparents. "Wow! Look at the tree!" said Kurt, the light of the candles reflected in his eyes.

Adelheid followed Liesel into the kitchen. "I am sorry we didn't come sooner," she said quietly to Liesel, "but your father is getting quite stubborn. He was not willing to put down the newspaper until he was finished. He is so worked up about the war and politics."

"When did he return from his walk yesterday?" asked Liesel. She had seen him go by the window after lunch.

"It was almost dark, I was getting so worried," said Adelheid.

Fritz came in the room and surveyed the steaming stuffed goose, cabbage rolls, carrots, potato salad with bits of ham, and gravy. "Adelheid, you cook almost as well as my mother."

"Fritz!" said Adelheid. "Liesel has cooked for us today."

"*Ja!* Of course," said Fritz. "Thank you, Liesel." He patted his daughter's shoulder affectionately.

The family bowed their heads and prayed slowly enough for the children to join in. "*Jesus, danke für die Speise, Amen.*"

"Boys," said Liesel. "Pass me your plates." She had just begun to dish potato salad onto the children's plates, when her father took her hand in his. Liesel was puzzled.

"Let us give thanks," said Fritz.

"But," Liesel was about to explain that they had already said grace when she saw that her mother had already bowed her head. Ernst shrugged and said, "*Vater,* you ask the blessing."

After dinner they went into the parlour. Olaf sat quietly in his grandfather's lap, while Rudy squirmed to escape his grandmother's grasp.

Kurt was jumping up and down with excitement. *"Mutti!* When can we open the gifts?"

"After we read the Christmas story," said Liesel.

She lit the advent wreath. Ernst picked up his mandolin and they sang together:

Ihr Kinderlein kommet, O kommet doch all,
Zur Krippe, her kommet in Bethlehems Stall,
Und seht, was in dieser Hochheiligen Nacht,
Der Vater in Himmel, für Freude uns macht.

Oh come little children, oh come one and all.
To Bethlehem's stable, to Bethlehem's stall
And see with rejoicing, this glorious sight
Our Father in heaven, has sent us this night.

Ernst opened the big Bible and read, "Mary laid her firstborn in a manger, because there was no room for them at the inn."

"You mean a manger like the cows eat out of?" asked Kurt.

"Yes," said Ernst, "like the cows eat out of."

Rudy had escaped his Oma's arms and was toddling toward the tree, his hand outstretched towards a candle. Ernst stood up. *"Halt."* He scooped up his son and returned him to their circle.

"But why didn't baby Jesus live in a house?" asked Kurt.

"They were far from home," said Liesel. "There was nowhere to go." She thought of the Zawadskis, her elderly neighbors who had already been forced from their home a few weeks after she had wanted to borrow the sugar. Had they found a good place to live? Ernst had told her there was nothing he could do, the policies of the General Government had to be enforced. The Poles in their village were being relocated by the *Volksdeutsche Mittelstelle,* a Nazi organization for the resettlement of Germans. Poles were being moved out, Germans from areas outside the Reich were being moved in.

Olaf patted Liesel's tummy, taking her mind off those sobering thoughts. The boys had been told about the baby. "Will our baby sleep in a manger?"

"Of course not," said Adelheid. "The new baby will sleep in the cradle your *Vati* made, just like Rudy."

"And Rudy will move to the bed with you big boys," said Liesel, though she wondered how he would ever agree to stay in it.

CHAPTER 19
1940

THE NEW BABY, EDELTRAUD, WAS A FEW WEEKS OLD, WHEN A run of spring-like weather and a tenuous calm in the area coincided.

"I am going to plan a get-together, for people to visit the baby and do some quilting," said Adelheid. "It is too bad we can't have *Pani* Zawadski. I miss them."

Liesel doubted they would ever see Zawadskis again and didn't think they had wanted to move at their advanced age. At least Frieda had been able to come from Łódź. She gave Liesel a hug and kiss. "Ludwig thought I shouldn't come because it is too dangerous, there may still be partisans fighting in the area. I didn't know when else I would get the chance to see you and mother. Finally, when I insisted, he agreed to escort me here early this morning." She paused to thread a needle. "Parts of the city are completely empty. It has become almost ghostly since the Jews are being moved to the ghetto now."

"They bring so much disease and filth to the city. We should be happy to contain them in one place," said Frau Schwab, an older lady wearing an absurd looking hat.

Liesel looked up from her needlework. She did not add anything to the conversation, but observed the expressions of those around her. Ernst had said to be careful what she said, so nothing was probably best.

She stood up. "I need to go check on the children."

Out in the barn a large pile of feathers and down had been collected in one corner on an old sheet to await their use in filling the bedding they were making. "Stay away from the feathers," she reminded the children, who were playing up in the loft.

Upon Liesel's return to the house, her mother handed her Edeltraud. "I think our little Edel is hungry."

"Well," said Frau Schwab. "You clearly have your hands full. Why don't you have one of the young women from *der Bund Deutscher Mädel* come for her compulsory service year? I am sure you would qualify as someone needing assistance."

"I can manage," said Liesel, seating herself on the other side of the Kachelofen and covering herself with a blanket to feed Edeltraud. She had no interest in having a stranger, even one of the German Girls League, come and stay at her home.

"I am not impressed with the moral character of these girls," said Adelheid. "I heard a few of them have children on the way and no husband in sight."

"More soldiers for the Reich," said Ernst's mother, biting off a thread. "Some of the leaders are actually encouraging it."

It was impossible for Liesel to tell where her mother-in-law truly stood. But Günther was her son as well as Ernst.

Liesel set Edeltraud, who had fallen asleep, in a basket by the window, next to Kristiana, a schoolmate and friend of Frieda and Liesel. The sun glinted off Kristiana's flaxen hair, coiled in braids around her head. She whispered over to Liesel and Frieda, "I heard of one girl who didn't want a baby, so she had it terminated."

"It's true," said Frieda. "There are doctors in Łódź who will bend the laws on abortion. Some of the women in the factory have told me. A girl can just claim 'rape' and they will get rid of it."

Liesel was a little shocked by the frankness of this conversation. She looked down at Edeltraud. Her tiny fists clutched the edge of the blanket as she slept and a smile flashed briefly across her face. How could anyone consider that a baby would be something to be gotten rid of, as if it were an animal carcass or a piece of moldy cheese.

Just then Kurt came running into the house. "Come quick! A bird flew into the feathers. They are scattering everywhere."

"You sit," said Frieda to Liesel."I'll go."

It is the duty of every SS man, to identify himself body and soul with the cause. Every order must be sacred to him and he must carry out even the most difficult and the hardest of them without hesitation.

— Theodor Eicke, commander of the SS Death's Head regiments.

CHAPTER 20
ERNST 1941

FOR TWO YEARS ERNST'S MILITARY ASSIGNMENT HAD BEEN in the Łódź viovodeship, which meant he had been able to come home regularly, but he knew it was only a matter of time before he was deployed east, where Hitler's troops were fighting Stalin's Red Army.

He climbed up the ladder with an armload of fresh thatch. He wanted the family to stay warm and dry in the coming fall in case he wasn't there. Shouts and laughter of his sons playing in the back yard carried up and over the roof of the house.

Inside, Edeltraud, now almost two years old, was napping and Ernst had been firmly instructed not to wake her while working up there.

The loud putt putt of a motor at the gate was quickly followed by Edel's cries. Liesel will not be pleased, Ernst thought as he climbed down the ladder to see a motorcycle pull up and roar to a stop. The rider removed his helmet and placed it in the sidecar.

Günther rifled his fingers through his cropped blonde hair and brushed the dust and creases off his coat. "Heil Hitler." He thrust his arm out straight and grinned at his brother. "How is my big brother?"

Ernst saluted. In civilian dress he had to, and Günther's position in the SS made Ernst wary. "You certainly seem like the big brother now," Ernst observed, eyeing his taller uniformed counterpart up and down. Günther had always had a knack for looking out for himself and whatever would benefit him, and right now he seemed to be benefitting from his loyalty and position in the Third Reich.

"Come with me, Ernst, I want to show you something."

"On that?" Ernst asked, pointing at the motorcycle.

"It's fine, you can sit here." Günther patted the sidecar. "It is perfectly safe."

Perfectly safe. That's what Günther had said when they were boys, just before he climbed into the bullpen. Ernst had tried to talk him out of that one, but Günther had never been dissuaded from what he wanted to do. Günther had nearly gotten his arm ripped off and had worn the scar like a badge for bravery.

Ernst's heart raced. He had never ridden a motorcycle before, but he reasoned it surely wasn't as dangerous as a bull. His heart raced a little.

"Come," said Günther. "Just a short ride halfway to Pabianice. We'll be back before you know it."

"Let me just tell Liesel." *That way she'll know what happened if I don't return,* he thought ruefully. *Besides he didn't want to be blamed for waking Edeltraud.*

Ernst had to admit he enjoyed the thrill of the ride, the sudden accelerations and watching the houses, fields and trees of the village rush by in a blur.

They stopped in front of a gated estate home with an expansive lawn. Two columns framed an ornate front door. Vacant windows looked out onto a yard of heavily laden fruit trees. A profusion of rosebushes lined the front walkway, filling the summer air with their delicate perfume.

"What do you think?" said Günther.

"It's a beautiful estate. But it looks empty," said Ernst. He knew the owners had likely been relocated due to an agreement between Hitler and Stalin. The Poles were sent east, so more Germans could come and live in the area. Part of Ernst's job had been to help keep order during the population transfers, but he had not enjoyed these duties.

Günther plucked a rose and handed it to Ernst. "For your Frau."

Ernst accepted the gift as if it was a potato straight from the oven. He began to think about what "resettlement" really meant. After planting and before harvest? The pit of his stomach felt hollow as he contemplated the large groups of refugees, escorted by military vehicles. And of course there were the ghettos in Łódź. All those people had come from somewhere.

Günther continued with evangelistic fervor. "*Volkdeutsche* are coming into the Reich from the Baltic states, Romania, Russia, all over. I am giving up our parents' old house for them. Mother is settled over at Helga's and this little mansion is mine by order of the *Volksdeutsche Mittelstelle*." He picked up his helmet. "Of course for now the SS will be using it for an area headquarters."

Ernst was stunned into silence. He was furious, first of all that his brother had given up their family home, part of his inheritance, to strangers without consulting him. Neither had there been any discussion about the well-being of their mother.

"And why was I not part of this decision?"

"Well, I know that you do not like to make decisions, so I made this one on behalf of our family." Günther slapped Ernst lightly on the shoulder. "You will, of course, be part owner of this estate, when the war is over." His arm swept over the property in front of them. "*Lebensraum!*"

It was all Ernst could do to restrain from striking his brother. "I don't want it," he said, but Günther had already started the motor. Ernst couldn't wait to get back home.

CHAPTER 21

LIESEL TWISTED ANOTHER CUCUMBER OFF THE VINE AND placed it in the basket. She heard a rustling sound and straightened up, stretching out her aching back. The top of Ernst's head appeared just above the corn stalks.

"I'm going to slaughter a pig tomorrow."

"Tomorrow?" Liesel stood up and brushed the dirt off her hands. It was the busiest time of year, she was still harvesting vegetables, and had planned to make pickles the next day. "Aren't you going to wait a few weeks? When it's a bit colder?"

"Can't wait." Ernst looked off into the distance. "I don't know how much longer I'll be here. Russia is the Reich's next target and a lot of men are being called up. Besides, the army sent a man today. Remember they get half our food. The sooner we deliver the less likely they'll come back to 'remind' us of our contribution."

The next day Liesel put on her oldest clothes and tied her hair in a kerchief. The day was cool enough she supposed.

Outside, a large fire burned under a cauldron of hot water. Ernst and Fritz were setting up tables and troughs and when Kurt saw the preparations he turned to Liesel. "Can I help?"

"I think you are old enough now, but you will have to stay out of the way and do as *Vati* and *Opa* say." She tied an old apron around him.

Liesel handed Kurt a large bowl. "You hold this to catch the blood."

Fritz slit the neck of the pig with a knife and blood poured like a small stream from the pig's head into the bowl.

Kurt smiled proudly.

The men scalded the carcass in hot water and Liesel gave Kurt a blunt knife. Together they scraped the hair off the skin, revealing the pink flesh underneath. They hung the pig up on a pole and Fritz sliced open the belly. Ernst pulled out the entrails.

Kurt watched, obviously fascinated by every step.

"That is the part we use to make the sausage," Liesel said. "After it is washed of course."

Fritz placed his knife on the table and stood with his hands at his side watching Ernst with his brows knit together. He scratched his head.

"Need to wash him out now," Ernst reminded his father-in-law, motioning to the cauldron of hot water.

Liesel was distressed to see her father so confused about a task he had done countless times. How many more things would he forget?

As if to dispel her worries, when they had finished, Fritz handed Kurt the pig's bladder, blown up like a balloon. "You and your brothers can play with it," he said.

Kurt's grin spread across his whole face.

CHAPTER 22
1941

ON AN EARLY AUTUMN EVENING JUST AFTER CURFEW, ERNST and another *Feldgendarm* were patrolling the edge of the village for any signs of partisans, the underground fighters of the Polish army. Even though the penalty for sabotage was harsh, not to mention harming or detaining the German forces, the Polish resistance fought fiercely and there was suspicion of recent activity in the area.

The radio crackled to life. "Reports of gunfire in the area at 1900 hours." Ernst hit the return button. "Near the woods at the edge of the village. I will investigate."

A dense grove of trees rose up before them, their twisted and tangled branches reminiscent of gruesome fairytales. Following the beam of the flashlight, the two men stepped along the overgrown path into a clearing.

The remains of a fire and a crude shelter were all that remained of their adversaries, but here and there the ground had clearly been disturbed.

Ernst kicked at a mound of leaves and debris with his boot, uncovering something solid. A body garbed in gray fabric; the uniform of one of their own. Each mound revealed the body of another German soldier or civilian.

With one hand on his revolver, Ernst pressed the radio button again. "Five confirmed dead, we are investigating more. Partisans may still be in the area."

Under a tree, Ernst uncovered the body of an SS man; his tunic riddled with bullet holes from a small calibre weapon. Ernst fell to his knees on the soft ground next to the shallow grave and brushed away the leaves covering the man's face. Fair skin, neatly cropped blond hair…

Bile rose up Ernst's throat. He retched.

"You recognize someone?" said the younger officer.

"Günther Hoffmann, Squad Leader, *Allgemeine* SS," Ernst choked out the words, trying to maintain his decorum. "My brother."

The officer put a hand on his shoulder. "Sir, I am sorry, but there are some civilians here too." He pointed to the bodies he had uncovered. "Do you know any of these?"

A shock of white hair and a homespun linen waistcoat caught Ernst's eye. The man's cheeks and hands were bloodied and bruised, his arms folded across his face as if his last moments were spent trying to shield himself from the blows.

Liesel lifted Edeltraud into the cradle that she would soon outgrow. "*Schlaf gut,* my little girl," she whispered, kissing her baby's forehead and tucking in the crocheted blanket around her. She felt so blessed to have a girl. Everyone should have some of each, she thought.

She pulled in the shutters and adjusted the blackout curtains. Outside twilight had fallen and the night was cool. In the distance she heard rumblings and gunfire. With every noise a dog barked as if in response and she worried about Ernst.

He couldn't or wouldn't reveal much to her about where he'd be or what he'd be doing, so she never knew when to expect him. It made her worry.

Kurt and Olaf were playing battle with toy soldiers in the other room, complete with imitation machine gun noises and explosions. Günther had generously given them the set at Christmas and they played with it often, especially as they had to stay indoors more now.

Combat and killing, as child's play, made her uneasy. "It's time to put those toys away and get ready for bed."

"But we have just about killed all the enemies," said Kurt.

"You can finish tomorrow."

Olaf began to pick up the soldiers and miniature artillery and put them in the toy cupboard.

"But Mutti," said Kurt, "now the *Amis* will win." Liesel would have never said it out loud, but she wasn't sure it would be so bad if the Americans and their Allies won the war. At least it would be over and they could go back to the way things were before.

"Time for bed," she said.

She was washing dishes when her mother knocked quietly at the door.

"Papa has not come home." Adelheid's voice was brittle with fear. "His wandering about the village and his confusion are too much. It is dark now and I'm afraid he has lost his way."

"We can't go look for him, it's not safe," said Liesel. "Ernst isn't home yet either."

Kurt ambled into the kitchen in his pajamas with Olaf and Rudy in tow. "Where is *Opa*?" he asked, taking a sudden interest in the conversation.

"We don't know," said Liesel. "Go get into bed."

Kurt stood on his tiptoes and reached for the lantern on the mantle of the *Kachelofen*. "I'll go look for him."

"No! It is much too dangerous," Liesel said.

"Can I have a drink?" Rudy asked.

Liesel poured him a glass of water from a jug on the sideboard. Behind her the door clicked open softly.

She jumped, splashing water over her skirt and the floor. "Ernst! You startled me!"

His hat was in his hand, his face the colour of the ashes she had swept from the hearth that morning. She stared at him. "*Was?* What is wrong?"

"Kurt, take your brothers and go to bed," Ernst said, his voice low and serious.

"*Ja, Vater,*" said Kurt.

Ernst pulled up a chair and sat down. He covered his face with his hands and took a ragged breath. "They are both dead."

"Who?" said Liesel, her heart in her throat. "*Vati?*"

Ernst nodded.

Adelheid's face crumpled. "*Gott im Himmel,*" she said. "I knew this wandering was not good, but how …"

"Both?" said Liesel, collapsing onto a chair. "Who else?"

"Günther." At this, Ernst's voice cracked. He thought of the last time he had seen his brother alive and how angry he had been. When he had recomposed himself, he said, "Of course there will be recriminations by the SS." Or would it be vengeance, he thought. The previous week, a few villages over, ten Poles had been hanged for the death of a single German officer.

But revenge was cold comfort for their loss.

"When is *Opa* coming over?" asked Rudy for the third time in as many days.

"*Opa* is in heaven with the angels," answered Liesel. She struggled to make the boys understand their grandfather and their uncle were not coming back. Ever.

"Is that where Uncle Günther is too?" asked Kurt.

That was a harder question for Liesel to answer, but she could not wish her husband's brother elsewhere. "I hope so."

She sent her sisters and brother telegrams to inform them of their father's death and followed up with a letter to Josephine.

Dearest Josephine,

While I do not want to upset you further, it is only fair that you know the unfortunate circumstance of our father's death. As mother has probably written, he had not been in good spirits lately and had taken to wandering. He was found on the other side of the forest, beaten to death we believe by Polish resistance fighters, who had no compassion on a harmless and helpless old man. We are deeply grieved by his loss as we know you will be. Ernst's brother Günther was also found deceased in the same area.

We are doing as well as can be expected. Edeltraud is growing so quickly and has helped to lighten the mood by her smiles. Mercifully she is too young to know what has happened. Rudy plays together with her well and is quite protective, that is, when he isn't leading her into mischief. Kurt and Olaf are busy with their own pursuits and mostly ignore her. It grieves me greatly to think she will not know her beloved grandfather.

Lovingly, your sister Liesel on behalf of the family

CHAPTER 23

LIESEL WALKED KURT AND OLAF UP TO THE GATE TO SEE them off to school. Kurt had returned for his second year and Olaf had just started kindergarten. "Don't dawdle on the way home, stay together," she instructed.

An army truck rumbled by. "And watch out for the trucks." She waved as they headed down the road towards the village school.

She returned to the house with a sense of emptiness, worried about her children and feeling the loss of her father. It helped to have her mother there, as they worked side by side caring for the children, making sauerkraut and recalling fond memories as they mended in the evenings.

But Ernst disengaged as he had done when Johann died. He got up early and spent long hours working, repairing fences and animal pens, making sure the farm equipment was oiled and secured for winter. He even installed a pump over the well, something Liesel's father had intended to do.

It was past lunch time and he hadn't come in so she wrapped up a chunk of sausage and a piece of bread to bring out to him. She knew now that working by himself was the way he would deal with his loss. The other thing that was becoming obvious to her was that he was preparing for her future, so she would not have to manage chores undone or items in disrepair. She couldn't fault him for that.

With the bundle of food in her pocket and a bucket of slops in the other, she trudged out to the pigsty and emptied the slops into the trough. Led by the sow, six piglets trotted over to their food, snorting and grunting as they ate.

Army officials had come to take inventory shortly before the sow gave birth and it was only a matter of time before they came back again. Liesel was not enthusiastic about doing her "part" for a war that had already taken her father and brother-in-law.

Inside the barn, the sound of hammering echoed out into the yard.

She went inside. "Here," Liesel held out the food wrapped in a napkin. "I brought you some lunch."

Under the loft, against the outer wall of the barn Ernst was erecting another wall, double thick, creating a small enclosure. He looked up.

Liesel was curious. "*Was machst du*?" she asked.

Ernst set the lunch down. "I'm nearly done. Can you hand me some straw?"

Liesel brought over a few armloads of hay and Ernst stuffed it into the enclosure. "Are you making a place to hide?" Liesel asked. "Or somewhere to send the children when they are naughty?" She knew he might not answer until he was finished. She had learned that husbands were that way sometimes; you had to wait them out.

Ernst wiped off his hands and took a bite of sausage. "The boards here are loose," he explained, pointing to an area in the corner. "You can easily pry them off when you need to."

Still mystified, Liesel scratched her head.

The area was completely enclosed, all the way up to the ceiling which formed the floor of the loft. He had used old boards so it blended with other walls of the barn. She followed him back outside as he scooped up a squealing piglet.

"Just old enough to be separated from its mother," said Ernst. "Half of these belong to the army and they may not stop at that." He placed the piglet into the enclosure. "We are in trouble if anyone finds out, but if you and the children want pork this winter ….." His voice trailed off. "It will be butchered with the others, but we will keep the meat," he explained. "Don't tell the children either; if they don't know they can't tell anyone."

A few days later Ernst received his orders. He was being deployed east.

Liesel couldn't seem to cut the bread straight and when she tried to scrape a bit of rationed butter onto a slice of the rye, the bread broke. She added a piece of head cheese and wrapped the sandwich in some paper. She had to re-open it when she realized she had forgotten the tomato. The first apple she selected from the fruit bowl had a large worm hole so she picked another. She selected a pear, but it was too ripe, the second too hard.

The cuckoo clock interrupted her fumbling attempts to pack his meal.

"The train leaves soon," said Ernst, putting on his jacket. "If you are going to accompany me, we have to leave."

"Yes, of course," said Liesel. "I just …" She stifled the sob that rose up. "…wanted you to have a good lunch." *In case it is the last lunch I ever pack for you.*

She added a generous piece of *Kuchen* to the package.

Ernst put his arm around her. *"Danke.* I will be the best fed of anyone in my battalion."

"I don't know how I will manage," confessed Liesel. Later she realized it sounded selfish. He was the one going off to an uncertain future in a war neither of them had asked for. What if he didn't come back?

"You are strong," he said.

"Only God is strong," said Liesel.

"He will take care of you," Ernst said, but Liesel heard the lack of conviction in his voice.

They left Edeltraud with Liesel's mother and took the wagon to the train station so Liesel could get back home quickly with the boys.

At the station a group of uniformed men and their families milled around. Women in their Sunday best wore brave faces. Small children clutched the hands of their parents while older ones waved small flags emblazoned with swastikas.

"When will you come home again, *Vati*?" asked Olaf.

"I don't know, but you must be good strong boys for your mother," said Ernst. "Help her as much as you can and stay out of trouble." He kissed Liesel and stepped onto the train. "*Auf Wiedersehen*." He clasped his sons' hands briefly, letting go as the whistle blew and the train lumbered away, puffing smoke as it clacked down the line.

Kurt and Olaf waved until they could no longer see their father.

CHAPTER 24

ERNST'S ORDERS WERE FOR AN ASSEMBLY POINT OUTSIDE
Lublin as a member of a supply unit. He was relieved he would not
have to face the moral dilemma of combat or suffer the pain of marching long distances.

Dusk was settled over the ancient city, its walls crumbling in the
gloom. The massive shadow of Lublin castle rose up before him, its
façade draped with a giant black and red flag.

"Once a castle, now a prison for enemies of the Reich," said the soldier next to him. He pointed toward an archway opposite the castle.
"Inside you will find food and drink, but thankfully no Jews! The SS
has rid Lublin of them all."

Ernst followed the group of soldiers flocking toward the entrance.

Inside the old city, the walls bore testament to the previous inhabitants, with small squares and diamonds forming geometric patterns,
but nothing that could be considered a 'graven image.'

Lusty male singing accompanied by an accordion drifted from one establishment, but Ernst eschewed that in favour of a smaller, less raucous pub in a corner. A signboard outside the door proclaimed pork chops, mushrooms and beer.

A man seated by the window proffered the seat next to him.

"Thank you," said Ernst, sitting down.

In the light of the window, he recognized the man.

"Horst!"

"It is good to see you!" Horst glanced around. "Of course, perhaps it would be better if it were not here, in this …" he paused for a moment as if trying to read Ernst. "situation."

Horst was from his village and they had gone to school together; however, they had not seen each other since Ernst had married and moved away.

"I married a Polish girl you know."

That made it easier. Ernst nodded. "I can see how that would be difficult in these times."

"Of course I am on the *Volksdeutsche* list and so is she," said Horst. "And so, I am on this new adventure."

"Yes," said Ernst. "To fight the Reds."

Their conversation was cut short by a waitress who placed steaming plates of pork schnitzel with mushrooms and mugs of beer in front of them.

"*Guten Appetit*," she said, pulling an errant strand of hair back behind her ear.

Horst lifted his glass of beer and laughed. "To the army."

Ernst joined him in the toast. "The army."

He was glad to have a friend.

CHAPTER 25

LIESEL AND THE CHILDREN WALKED BACK THROUGH THE train station.

The walls were festooned with posters. One showed a soldier in uniform, 'Just as we fight, so *you* must work for victory!' A stern-faced Adolf Hitler was captioned 'Be loyal and true to our great leader.' Smiling children on a train waved to a blond haired woman. 'Mothers, the air terror continues! Safety for your children is in the country at a KLV'

Rudy pointed at the poster. "Why isn't the mommy on the train?"

"Oh, maybe the children are going to visit their uncle," Liesel said. "She will go see them later." She had heard of the *Kinderlandverschickung*, an evacuation program for children who lived in and near the major cities. So far though, she hadn't felt any great threat. The children would be safest at home where they belonged.

She was relieved to arrive back at the house.

Every day she was up before the sun to feed the animals, milk the cow, and start the bread. Then it was breakfast for the children, getting the older ones off to school, and then out to the fields to finish the harvest. When harvest was done she had to get everything properly preserved and stored for winter.

There would be plenty to do then, catch up on mending and housework, and write long overdue letters to her sisters and brother. She missed the rhythm of spinning and weaving. They hadn't grown flax the past few years because of the pressure of growing food for the war effort. The death of her father and the absence of her husband would have made that crop an impossible burden.

And then there were the children, requiring constant vigilance.

Three-year-old Rudy grasped one-year-old Edeltraud under the arms and dragged her away from the Kachelofen.

"Put Edel down, she's too heavy for you," said Liesel for the third time that morning. She set down the broom and lifted her squirming daughter away from the danger of the hot oven. She had just started sweeping again when Kurt and Olaf came tumbling in one after the other through the door, dropping schoolbags and jackets and slamming the door behind them.

"It's only 10:00. Why are you home so early?" Even as Liesel said the words, she was quite sure she knew the answer.

"We don't have to go to school." Kurt's smile revealed large new teeth. "The teacher has to become a soldier, because of the war. We can't have a woman teacher either, because they have to work in factories and on the farms."

Liesel knew about that reality. "Well, I guess there will be plenty for you to help with around here!" she said.

"But lots of the other children at school are going away for a holiday in the country," protested Kurt. "They showed us pictures of children hiking and swimming. Can we go for a holiday in the country too?"

"You do realize that you would be going for a holiday without me?" said Liesel.

Olaf shook his head. "I don't want to go then."

CHAPTER 26
ERNST

IT WAS LATE OCTOBER ON THE EASTERN FRONT WHEN ARMY Group Centre received their long awaited orders from General Von Bock to capture the Soviet capital.

"Come on then," Ernst said tugging at the reins of the horses. "Moscow awaits."

"Moscow will be waiting a long time, if we can't get this cart unstuck," said Horst. He pushed his shovel into the sodden mud which clung to the wheels of the cart.

The team of horses was exhausted, maybe even more than Ernst and Horst, just pulling an empty supply wagon. How they would manage to pull it back to their base full of supplies and ammunition, he could only imagine.

Ernst and Horst were relative latecomers, but the army commanders had led the men to believe the whole thing would be over by summer's end. *Blitzkrieg* was what Hitler had called it; a lightning war, and in the beginning the German forces had taken the Reds by surprise with superior training and newer weapons. But the realities of the Russian landscape had overwhelmed their forces; the bogs and mud swallowing trucks, tanks, and men alike.

Ernst lifted the wheel out of the mud and Horst threw the shovel back in the cart.

"I don't know if the Russkis will be beaten back so easily."

"Better the *Feldwebel* doesn't hear you talking like that," said Ernst, though he agreed with Horst's estimation.

The Russians hid out in forests and swamps, in bunkers disguised with brambles, branches, and tangled wires. Strategically placed mines inhibited anyone who dared to discover and destroy their hideouts, and by the time the necessary experts had been called in to de-fuse the explosives, precious time in the push to the capital was wasted.

"Now that we've dug this thing out," said Ernst, "we'd better get going."

The wagon slogged its way towards the train station, through mud that had gone from soupy puddles to the consistency of fresh horse manure as the temperature had dropped. Progress was painfully slow.

When they arrived, several other supply wagons were unloading boxes off the train. Ernst and Horst pulled up to one boxcar and a soldier handed them a box labeled *munitions,* identical to dozens of other boxes, except for numbers indicating which weapon they were for. Box after heavy box was loaded onto the wagon.

"That is enough," said Ernst when the wagon was only half full. "The horses can't carry any more weight and I need room for some fodder."

They turned to go, taking the wagon alongside the train. The next boxcar was also ammunition. Tracks, wheels, and other tank parts were stacked in the next. Drums of gasoline were followed by crates of rations.

Ernst clapped his hands together, trying to get some warmth in them. "Anything labeled 'winter uniforms'?" he asked when they had almost reached the end of the train.

"No sir," said Horst.

Ernst breathed deeply.

The autumn air reminded him of entering a newly built icehouse, that coolness on the verge of freezing. Snow was imminent. He felt it in his aching ankles and smelled it in the air. What they really needed were proper winter boots, gloves, fur hats, and white camouflage so the enemy could not see them in the snow.

They walked in silence for a while away from the train, at turns pulling the lead rope, coaxing the horses, foreleg deep in muck, to take another step. At the same time they had to force their own legs up and out of the ooze. Caught in a deep rut, they dug the wheels of the wagon out only to sink again a few metres later.

Halfway back to the base, the horses collapsed.

The sight of their frothy mouths and quivering ribs made Ernst feel ill. "Take off their harnesses," he ordered Horst.

Horst glanced at Ernst, his eyes dark with sorrow. He knelt down to unbuckle the leather straps, speaking softly to the animals.

Ernst took out his pistol. "Stand back."

Horst gathered up the harnesses and moved out of the way.

Ernst aimed and squeezed the trigger.

With a loud crack, and another, the bullets hit their mark, the horses' chestnut flanks twitching one final time.

Their death stung Ernst. It felt like an act of treachery, as if shooting one of their own. He put the pistol away, wishing he hadn't pushed them so hard.

"They should have supplied us with trucks," he muttered, his voice low and hard.

They hitched the wagon to a tank, one of the few that hadn't yet been swallowed by mud. But that moved only a little ways, before it too became crippled.

"It's dark. We have to get back," said Ernst. He took several boards from the back of the wagon and strapped them together with some rope. "We will make sleds to drag over the mud," he said.

"Yes sir," said Horst, arranging one of the harnesses over his shoulders.

"*Feldwebel* Wagner will not be happy about this," said Ernst, securing several boxes onto the boards.

"Nothing to be done for it, Sir."

Ernst dreaded the wrath of his superior officer when he told the same story the *Feldwebel* had no doubt already heard several times today.

Leaving the rest of the supplies for the time being, they continued on foot back to the base, dragging the makeshift sleds behind them.

A few weeks later the *Feldwebel* called his exhausted troops together. "In case anyone thought they would be going home for Christmas, forget it. We are short reinforcements and the orders are to continue the offensive to Moscow."

The frost came heavy and fast, but not so winter uniforms. Rumor had it Berlin had refused, on the assumption the whole thing would be over by winter. Now it was too late.

Anti-freeze for the vehicles had not been issued either and the German army's campaign stalled in sight of Moscow; the elegant spires of the Kremlin rising in the distance above the snow.

Equipment abandoned in the mud was frozen in place until spring thaw and the men hunkered down for the winter, raiding nearby villages for food to supplement their rations.

In their underground bunker, Ernst came across a large stack of pamphlets. The front cover depicted a Soviet flag, its hammer and sickle ripped in half by a large fist. "*Was ist das*?" he asked a young soldier who was systematically unfolding them and pushing them up under his coat.

"Propaganda leaflets, sir. We thought we could use them to pad our clothing." He hesitated a moment, as if worried about Ernst's reaction.

"It is a good idea," Ernst said. He did not tell the young soldier that a few pieces of paper were hardly protection against the severity of the Russian winter.

Around noon of Christmas Eve, Ernst left the bunker to look for firewood. The sun, just visible above the treetops, would follow the trajectory of a small arc and disappear again from the pale sky before they sat down to their evening meal.

He swung the hatchet against a fallen branch. The sound of splitting wood shattered the silence of the forest, startling Ernst as if it was enemy gunfire.

If only he could bring himself to wear the felt boots they had found on the dead Russian. He had taken a turn at the amputation of the corpse's frozen legs. Later they thawed the legs out in front of the stove in order to take the boots off.

Ernst shuddered with the memory.

After a few minutes outside he could not feel his toes and ears; when his lips and fingers succumbed to numbness, he placed the wood on a crude sled and pulled it back to the bunker, handing down the wood, before climbing back into the dimness of their winter fortification.

The smell of smoke, wet leather, and coffee greeted him on his return.

A table in the centre of their abode was covered with a red floral patterned scarf, no doubt the spoils from some peasant girl. On this makeshift table cloth stood two candle stubs and several folded paper stars. Apparently another use for propaganda leaflets.

Ernst disentangled the woman's sweater that he'd been wearing around his head for warmth, stacked the wood next to the stove and poured himself a cup of coffee.

"*Weinachtsabend!*" said Horst, pulling out a flask of liquor and pouring a little into Ernst's coffee cup. Soldiers around the room produced bottles of vodka and wine from packs and under cots. Ernst had no idea where they had stashed so many bottles.

"To the *Wehrmacht Heer!*" toasted one.

"*Die Wehrmacht,*" the others chorused.

"The Fatherland!"

"To this filthy bunker."

"Marlene Dietrich."

Laughter echoed hollowly off the walls as they toasted everything they could think of; their mothers, wives, and girlfriends.

When they had eaten their rations and the booze had run out, a man with a deep bass voice began singing '*Oh du fröliche.*' Others joined in, their voices now slurred.

The irony of the joyful carol was not lost on Ernst. The frozen and hopeless circumstance they found themselves in was anything but joyful and the country they sought to conquer did not acknowledge God or the celebration marking his Son's birth.

CHAPTER 27
LIESEL 1942

THE SNOW OF WINTER HAD MELTED AND TUFTS OF GREEN
dotted the pasture.

It was time to get the animals out and Liesel was headed out to the
barn, when two uniformed men appeared. *"Guten Morgan, Frau …
Hoffmann,"* the older one said, glancing at a clipboard.

"Good morning," said Liesel. At least it had been a good morning
until they showed up.

"We are here to collect food supplies for the army."

She invited them in the house. "I'll just get the children out of the
way."

"Rudy, Edeltraud, go see Oma," she ordered. Her first thought was
the nearly grown pig in the secret stall in the barn. Just the other day
Rudy and Olaf had come in from playing in the barn and asked what
the noise was.

"Probably just a rat," Liesel had told them. She had felt guilty for lying, but the price was too high if one of the children had let slip.

If only the pig would be quiet today and not alert these soldiers to his presence.

She stood behind them as the men opened the pantry door. Everything was arrayed on the counters and shelves in testament to her industriousness. One man loaded crates full of bread, butter, sausage and dried fruit.

She gritted her teeth and swallowed her anger. If only she had thought to hide some of that as well.

"Where is the cellar?" asked the officer.

She had hoped they wouldn't ask, but they had to do what they had to do. And she had to do what she had to do, she thought, thinking of the pig.

"You are a busy woman, *Frau* Hoffmann", said the Kommandant, making notes on the clipboard. "Everything seems to be in order from our last visit. The Reich thanks you for your generous contribution."

After several trips up and down the ladder passing up a crate of carrots and a sack of potatoes, the second man emerged from the cellar with a sack of onions and a large ham. "*Das is gut,*" said the Kommandant.

Liesel was anxious to show them the door, but he placed the ham and a crock of sauerkraut on the table.

"We'll eat here," he said "Would you be so kind as to prepare us some soup and bread?" His voice was as smooth as her homemade butter, but Liesel knew his words were an order and not a request. The sooner she fed them the sooner they would be out of her home.

The Kommandant tucked the clipboard under his arm. "We will go take inventory of your animals while you are getting that ready. I trust you will be butchering sometime soon?" He smiled, as if he was a neighbor or friend coming to call.

Liesel's heart sank. She hoped Ernst would be home to do the job, otherwise she would have to tackle it herself so they could keep the extra pig a secret.

As the Kommandant was leaving, Kurt came in. "*Mutti,* I'm hungry, when is lunch? And who are those men?"

"They are gathering supplies for the army for all the soldiers, and they will be eating lunch here."

She thought again about the pig hidden in the barn. What if they heard it?

"Where is Olaf?" she said to Kurt.

"Up in the loft, playing with Kaspar. I think he is going to come down soon."

"Go back there, right now, up to the loft. You and Olaf need to … Go chase the cat around or something. Make some noise up there, but not too much."

"Why?"

"Because I said, is why." Liesel lowered her voice and set her jaw. "And don't stop making noise until those men are returning back to the house. Wait a few minutes, then you can come in for lunch. We will leave Rudy and Edel at Oma's for now."

When the men finally left, Liesel breathed a sigh of relief.

Later in the week she heard the sound like whistling wind, followed by staccato gunfire hitting the ground, the strafing at first far away, then closer. The undulating howl of the air raid siren followed.

Edeltraud sat on the floor rocking a doll in her arms and covered her ears to the sound. "Quick, into the cellar." Liesel scooped her up. "Rudy come." He picked up the truck and tried to gather the blocks he had been playing with. "Just the truck," said Liesel. "Leave the blocks."

He would have to make his own way down the ladder, but even if it was crowded, she wasn't going to send him to hide somewhere else. The fear of being separated from her family was still with her. Besides he was a busy little boy and wouldn't have lasted behind a bed more than a few moments.

With Edeltraud squirming in one arm, she opened the door to the outside where her mother stumbled over from her side of the house.

Adelheid clutched a pot of tea and a blanket. Her skirt hung loosely about her hips and her blouse billowed out from her thin frame.

"*Mutti, schnell,*" said Liesel.

Kurt and Olaf came from the yard, running in behind their grandmother, holding the trap door for her as she climbed into the cellar.

"It's really close!" said Kurt. "I could see the airplanes!"

Liesel shook her head. "Boys, next time you see airplanes, come inside right away. Don't wait for the sirens." Couldn't her boys understand the danger they were all in?

The remaining foodstuffs only took up a few of the shelves now and had been pushed aside for blankets, candles, toys and books for the children. There was a bench for the adults to sit on and some sacks on the dirt floor with an old straw mattress which sufficed as bedding for the times they had to stay awhile. She had tried to make it clean and comfortable but it was still a cellar; dark, musty, and a favourite haunt of spiders and mice.

Adelheid coughed.

"Mutti, you are not well," said Liesel.

"Don't worry, dear, it's just the stale air down here."

Liesel stroked Edeltraud's hair and thought of her father. It was at times like this that he had been a tower of strength for the family, always taking command of a situation and then lightening the atmosphere with jokes and stories. She also missed Ernst's quiet calming presence.

Was he thinking of them, she wondered. Was he alive?

CHAPTER 28

IT WAS OVER A YEAR NOW, THAT ERNST HAD BEEN GONE returning home on only one short leave. Liesel was exhausted by the work that had once been shared among her husband, father, mother, and hired hands. Some things had to be neglected, but she had determined that the Advent season would still be celebrated for the children's sake. A little contemplation and singing in front of candles would be a good respite for her as well.

She arranged evergreen branches around a wire frame and set four red candles into the wreath. Finished off with pine cones and ribbon it looked every bit as festive as it had other years. Each Sunday they lit a candle and read a verse about the coming of the Christ child.

The children delighted in this special time, their eyes glistening with the reflected light of the candles, their voices rising as they sang a carol together.

For gifts, she had knit mittens and sweaters for the children who were constantly outgrowing and wearing out the ones they had. By drinking her coffee and tea without sugar, and skimping on the butter, she had saved enough ingredients to bake *Weinachtsstollen* and *Pfeffernüsse*, the traditional fruitcake and spice cookies.

Out the window large flakes of snow swirled in the near darkness. The gate was closed; the road empty of vehicles and travelers.

Ernst would not be coming home for Christmas as far as Liesel knew. Frieda had just had a baby and with the uncertainties of travel these days, they would not be visiting either. She missed her father.

She sighed and went around the house lighting the lamps and candles in an effort to dispel the gloom she felt.

Christmas Eve dinner was simple, more in keeping with the Polish and Silesian tradition, carp, cabbage, and potatoes.

After dinner, Liesel was surprised when Adelheid got up abruptly. "I'll be right back."

In a few moments she returned laden with packages.

"What are these?" asked Liesel.

"Ernst left them with me when he was last here," said Adelheid, smiling. "He didn't want to chance the children finding them." Wheezing, she placed them on a table in front of the hearth.

For Edeltraud there was a wooden block puzzle. Ernst had made the blocks and Adelheid had painted animals and colourful designs on each side. Rudy received a little figure which tumbled down a small ladder. Kurt and Olaf's gifts were perfectly scaled wooden *Messerschmitts* also painted by their grandmother.

"*Wunderschön,*" said Kurt when he received his gift. His brows knit together as he examined the tail of the miniature aircraft. "But *Oma*, there is no *swastika*."

Liesel recalled her father's attitude to the Nazi regime, but it would not do to speak against it in front of Kurt. Anyways, he should be more grateful to receive such a gift. "Kurt, you need to thank *Oma* for her work and recognize what a thoughtful thing your father did."

"*Ja, Mutti.*" he replied, looking down. He turned to his grandmother and said dutifully, "*Danke Oma.*"

Olaf was less concerned about the emblem on the tail and lifted his plane in the air, imitating the sound of an aircraft engine.

Adelheid cleared her throat. "I suppose if you or Olaf want to paint your planes some more you can come over and use my paints."

Hoppe hoppe Reiter
wenn er fällt, dann schreit er,
fällt er in den Graben,
fressen ihn die Raben.

... Fällt er in den Sumpf,
macht der Reiter plumps!

Hoppity, hoppity rider,
If he falls, then he cries
if he falls into the ditch,
the ravens will eat him

... if he falls into the swamp,
he makes a big splash!

— Nursery rhyme

CHAPTER 29

1943

CHRISTMAS WAS OVER. THE SNOW HAD MELTED AND AIR raid sirens had not gone off for a few weeks. In defiance of the war, buds and leaves appeared on the trees and spring rains softened the ground.

Spring always made Liesel feel hopeful as she looked forward to what the earth would yield and she went out to cultivate the garden. It was strange to think that this work of disturbing the dirt should have such power over her, as if she too were in collusion with the season.

She sent the older boys to gather mushrooms and greens. Not only did she want to supplement their food, but she reasoned it would give them something useful to do. "Stay on our side of the woods," she told Kurt and Olaf, now eight and nearly seven years old. "Keep together and if you see anyone you don't know, come straight home."

It was the first time the boys had been able to leave their house and yard in months. Under the trees the ground was soft. Mushrooms pushed their way up through the rotted leaves forming a large ring. "I found some," said Olaf.

"Only pick the white ones with a little pink underneath," said Kurt, putting some into his basket. Many times his mother and grandmother had gone mushroom picking and they had taught the boys how to avoid the poisonous ones.

They had only been gathering a short while, when Kurt spotted a glint of metal under a small mound of leaves. "Look what I found!" Trembling with excitement, he picked up the unexploded mortar shell and inspected the device turning it over in his hands.

He remembered a trick Uncle Günther had shown them with some ammunition. Once he had even let Kurt fire his gun, but Kurt was not allowed to tell his parents and he had kept the secret. Uncle Günther had been really important, because he was a special kind of policeman for the National Socialist Party and the Führer who would save all the German people. Kurt missed him and wished he could show him what he had found. Still, maybe he could do that trick himself.

"Wait here!" he yelled to Olaf, who was picking dandelion leaves. "I'll be right back."

Kurt ran back to their yard. His mother wasn't in the garden anymore. In the workshop, he spied a two-by-four with a large nail sticking out of one end. As promised, he returned to Olaf in a few minutes. "Where did you go?" asked Olaf. "Mom said we were supposed to stay together."

Kurt ignored his younger brother. "Come over here," he said, pointing to a fence post.

Pushing and twisting, he inserted the brass casing of the mortar shell halfway into a crack in the wood, so that the copper end was exposed.

Olaf stood a bit back from the fence watching.

"Hand me the board," Kurt asked. He didn't even look at Olaf. He was thinking about the upcoming explosion, like Uncle Günther had made.

Hesitantly, Olaf picked up the board. "I don't think we should be doing this," he said.

"Hand me the board. *Aber schnell,"* commanded Kurt, with all the authority of an officer. "Now stand back."

Olaf ran about five metres away.

"Not that much! What are you, a scared rabbit?"

Olaf took a few small steps closer to the fence and covered his ears.

Kurt lifted the board over his shoulder and with all the force he could muster, brought it down onto the unsuspecting shell.

The nail hit its mark. A loud clap followed a flash of light as the force wrenched the board from Kurt's hands and sent it hurtling into the air. He was blown from the fence onto his back. Splinters from the fencepost rained down on him.

The impact made him feel like he'd been punched in the stomach and his ears were ringing. For a moment he thought he was blinded too, but then he realized it was just the smoke.

As the debris and dust settled, Olaf ran towards him.

"Are you hurt?" he asked.

Kurt could sense the concern in his voice. "No, I'm fine!" He stood up quickly, brushing bits of wood off his pants. *"Wunderschön!* Wasn't that great?" He wasn't going to admit that his ears were still ringing and his face stung.

They started back to the house.

"It's a good thing *Vati* isn't around, you would get a licking for sure," remarked Olaf.

"Well he isn't here and I won't get in trouble, because you're not going to tell *Mutti.*" Kurt was quite confident his little brother wouldn't tell on him and besides, their mother ignored them a lot because she always had work to do and Edeltraud to bother about.

When they arrived back at the house Liesel was stirring soup.

Kurt's stomach growled. "Is that all there is to eat?" he complained, looking at the small bits of cabbage and potato floating around the broth. He was hungry a lot these days and thought his mother should give him more to eat.

"If you complain anymore you will be doing the dishes and sweeping after lunch," said Liesel.

Olaf set the basket on the sideboard. All it contained was a handful of dandelions leaves and a few mushrooms. The bottom of the basket was still visible.

"What took you so long?" she asked, cutting up the greens and adding them to the soup. She turned to look at the boys.

Kurt's hair stood on end and blood had dried around small cuts on his forehead. Both the boys' jackets were dirty and covered in ashes and splinters of wood. The faint smell of burnt gunpowder wafted from their direction.

Liesel crossed her arms. Obviously they had been up to something besides gathering.

"What was that noise outside a few minutes ago?" She had almost gone out to check, but the soup was boiling over and she didn't want to leave Rudy and Edeltraud.

Olaf looked down at the floor.

"We'll go wash up for lunch," said Kurt, turning quickly away.

Liesel shook her head and sighed, but she did not have the energy to deal with this right now. "We will talk about this later."

After she had dished out the soup, the boys came back, slightly less dirty, and sat down.

"Kurt, you may say the blessing," said Liesel looking at him sternly.

Kurt pouted, but took Edeltraud and Rudy's hands in his own and bowed his head. Quickly he prayed, emphasizing each syllable in a sing-song tone, "*Jesu, danke für die Speise.*"

After lunch, Liesel sent the younger children to play, before she addressed her older boys. "You could have been seriously injured or even killed!"

"But I wasn't hurt!" Kurt interjected.

"Even if the mortar shell didn't hurt you, the neighbors might come after you for scaring their animals," she explained, trying to keep her voice low and even. "Or worse, the police might think you are partisans blowing things up. We could all get in trouble. What are you thinking?"

"I'm sorry, Mutti." A large tear drop formed at the corner of Olaf's eye and trickled down his cheek. Liesel knew this could not have been his idea.

"Kurt, you are the oldest. It is your job to protect and keep your brother safe, not lead him into trouble. You can spend the rest of the afternoon in the barn cleaning out the stalls. I will call you for supper. *Ja?*"

"*Ja,*" said Kurt in a small voice.

"Olaf, you are to be responsible for Edeltraud until her nap."

Every day now, part of Liesel's daily routine was to check on her mother. Even through the door, she could hear violent coughing. Adelheid sat by the window darning socks. Her face was flushed and dark circles ringed her eyes.

Liesel brought her a glass of water. "*Mutter,* are you all right?"

Adelheid put down the sock she was working on and took a sip of water.

"Fine dear." She stifled another cough. "Maybe just spoonful of honey." Liesel looked in the cupboard. The honey jar was almost empty and it would be hard to buy more. No doctors either; the ones who weren't treating wounded soldiers had been deported to who knows where.

A few days later Liesel was out weeding. Edeltraud was napping and she had left Kurt in charge, instructing them to go to Oma's if they needed any help.

Olaf came running, straight through the newly planted cabbage field.

"Olaf," Liesel called out when she saw him, "Stay on the path!"

"Rudy fell!" Olaf panted.

"Fell how?"

"Out of the hay loft. He piled up some hay on the ground and we were landing on it."

"*Komm.* He can't breathe."

Liesel dropped the hoe and ran to the barn. Rudy was leaning back against the barn wall, his breath coming in short gasps.

Kurt came running from the house with Adelheid shuffling behind him.

Liesel got to her youngest son first and knelt down on the scattered hay. Anger and worry mingled together in her mind and she struggled to contain her temper.

"I think he has had the air knocked out of him," said Adelheid. "Lift your arms, *Liebling*."

Rudy's short gasps graduated to longer breaths within a few seconds. Adelheid put her arms around Liesel. "See, he will be fine, dear."

This time. But how many more times would her boys do foolish things? Of course, they were boys, and all the big boys were off more foolishly fighting a war that had dragged on for four years now, leaving the little boys to figure things out themselves.

She had thought she could manage the children, put food on the table, and take care of the farm. But the older boys hadn't been as helpful as she'd hoped.

She made a decision.

Adelheid sat at the far end of the table. That way she didn't expose the others as much to her coughing. She had gained some strength as the weather had improved and would come over sometimes, helping with the younger children and housework.

"*Oma*," said Rudy. "Can you butter my bread?"

She selected a clean knife and spread the butter thinly taking care not to touch his bread with her hands. As she handed it back a spasm of coughing overtook her and she turned away.

When the coughing had ceased and the children had left the table, Liesel set a cup of rosehip tea in front of her mother. "I've decided," she said, "As soon as planting is done, to send the older boys to Breslau. Things are apparently stable there and I'm going to write to Emil's wife. She might be willing to keep Olaf awhile and there are camps for children Kurt's age. I think it might be good, especially for Kurt."

"You must do what is best for the children," said Adelheid. "I will help as much as I can."

Liesel shook her head. "Mother, you need to rest."

When an opponent states, 'I will not cross over to your side...' I say to him, 'Your child belongs to me already.' You will pass on, but your descendants stand in the new camp. Soon they will only know this new community.

— Adolf Hitler 1933

CHAPTER 30
KURT

KURT HAD BEEN AT A *KINDERLANDVERSCHICKUNG* CAMP, JUST outside Breslau a few months now. He sat in front of the school with hundreds of other children waiting for the parade and ceremony to begin.

The music of the approaching parade was exciting. He wished Olaf could be here with him.

The front of the school was draped in folds of red and black bunting around a large flag boldly proclaiming the swastika. Other flags on stands defined an outdoor stage area where the newly inducted young people would stand.

Kurt felt the thump of the bass drum reverberating inside him and could barely contain his eagerness as he strained his neck to watch. Maybe one day he could carry that flag or play in the marching band, he thought as he hummed along.

Once he had seen his father march in a band with a tuba that wrapped around his whole upper body. The unrelenting beat had made Kurt want to tap his feet to the music. He wondered how his father was able to carry such a big instrument and stay in step.

At the front of the procession a tall blonde-haired boy held a black flag emblazoned with a single rune. Two boys on either side held smaller flags which fluttered in the breeze. Following them a group of students wearing white shirts marched and sang accompanied by a brass band.

Much as he would like to play the tuba or the bass drum, all he could do for now was sing, so he added his voice to the other children singing the anthem and saluted along with the crowd as the parade wound its way to the front of the school.

> *Deutschland, Deutschland über alles,*
> *Über alles in der Welt,*
> *Wenn es stets zu Schutz und Trutze*
> *Brüderlich zusammenhält*

> Germany, Germany above everything,
> Above everything in the world.
> When for protection and defence,
> It always takes a brotherly stand together.

He felt if he was part of something bigger than himself; the glory of the Fatherland!

The students lined up on the steps in perfect formation, stiff white shirts and blouses bright against the colourful flags as they stood at attention. The *Jungvolk* Leader came up to the podium and spoke into the microphone.

"*Liebe Deutschen Jungen and Mädchen!* Today is a happy day for all of you as you are welcomed into the Hitler Youth and you begin a wonderful time in your life. Today you swear allegiance to our great Führer and enter into the community of all German boys and girls with this vow and commitment to bear the German spirit and honour! You become the foundation of an eternal Reich of German citizens."

Kurt yawned. He had enjoyed the parade, but long speeches were boring. Still, he wished he could be up front with the big boys. He made himself stand straight and tall, as if he was standing with them.

The *Jungvolk* leader's voice echoed across the *Platz*. "As you march in step, you will be trained to be a National Socialist faithful to your duty and the great future before us! The *Führer* expects your service, loyalty and duty. Ten year old cubs and little maids, you are not too young to be a comrade in this glorious community."

Kurt perked up at this. Soon he could join the "*Jungvolk*," march in the parade, and practice the drills. He could hardly wait to wear the uniform and sing the patriotic songs.

The Jungvolk leader droned on. "Millions of other young Germans are swearing allegiance to our great *Führer*. Before this audience of parents, the Party, and your comrades, we receive you into our community."

Kurt was disappointed his parents weren't there. He thought about Rudy and Edeltraud. Rudy would be old enough for school now, but there was no school for him. When he had left home Edeltraud could only say 'urt' for his name. But what if she didn't remember him when he came back?

He tried not to think of the bombs and the air raids. Was their house still standing?

It was hot that night, and Kurt tossed and turned in his bed at the dormitory. It was at night in the darkness that he felt most alone. He wished Olaf could be here with him, but Olaf wasn't that tough and Kurt would have to defend him against the older boys.

Sometimes, when their *Jungvolk* leader wasn't around, the older boys tried to get him into a corner and do things he didn't want to do, like pull down his pants or steal food from the kitchen. Fortunately Kurt was quick and able to squirm away out of their grasp. Some of the younger boys were bullied all the time.

In the morning Kurt woke up and put on his gym strip. First they had to salute the flag, then do morning exercises. That wasn't so bad, but then after breakfast came classes.

"Heil Hitler," said Herr Klein, raising his arm in salute the same as he did every day. He didn't even look old enough to be a teacher with his smooth face and only the shadow of a moustache. Like his name he was thin and small.

When the boys had first heard it they had all snickered, but Herr Klein had retaliated with his ruler and no-one laughed any more.

The students stood up. "Heil Hitler," they chorused and sat down.

"Take out your math books and do problems one to five, no talking," said Herr Klein.

Kurt struggled a bit with the words. When the school in Schönewald had closed he hadn't yet become very good at reading, but once he got through the words, the math wasn't too hard.

"Werner is Aryan," he read, mouthing the words and following the text with his finger. "His skull measures 51 centimetres. Jakob is Semitic and his skull measures only 47 centimetres. How many centimeters larger is Werner's skull?"

"Four," Kurt wrote down. That one was easy, he thought with relief.

"The Hitler youth are doing marching drills. There are 6 boys in each row and 8 rows in total. How many boys are in the parade?" That reminded him of yesterday's parade, but he had to read the question through again, before figuring out the answer. "Six times eight, 48 boys." He deliberately formed each letter in the curving script he had been taught.

Outside the older boys were playing soccer, their laughter and shouts floating up through the open window as they darted back and forth with the ball. Almost all of them were slim and muscular.

Kurt wanted to be out there with them. He resolved to discipline himself at the morning exercises, so he could be strong like the older boys. Silently he grimaced and flexed his muscles, first one arm, then the other.

"Hoffmann?"

At the teacher's voice, Kurt jumped up from his desk, sending his slate pencil clattering onto the floor. "*Ja, wohl?*"

"What is the answer?" demanded Herr Klein.

Kurt looked down at his slate. Words and numbers swam in front of his eyes and he didn't know what question they were on. "Um, 48 boys sir."

Laughter broke out. Herr Klein tapped his stick on the desk. "*Ruhe!*" he said sternly. "The question I asked was 'How many targets were hit?' We are on question *four*, Hoffmann."

Kurt looked down again. He had only completed the first two questions.

Herr Klein's lips were a thin line under his dusky moustache. "Come here."

Kurt walked to the front of the class, his eyes trained on Hitler's portrait.

The *Führer* stood proudly, one hand on his hip with the red, white and black swastika armband displayed above his elbow.

Kurt determined that he would not cry or show any sign of weakness. The *Führer* had no use for those who were weak. Kurt put his hands out and Herr Klein whacked them once with the stick, raising a red line across Kurt's palms.

"Sit down and pay more attention next time," the teacher said.

Kurt pursed his lips tightly and blinked. His hands stung, but he walked straight and tall back to his desk.

Herr Klein turned to the rest of the class. "A good soldier is attentive at all times and obeys orders. Our *Führer* expects nothing less. *Ja*, Hoffmann?"

"Yes sir." Kurt replied stiffly.

"Now everyone line up. We are going outside for a hike to the creek! '*Kraft durch Freude*'."

The words, 'strength through joy', always made Kurt glad, because it usually meant some sort of outdoor activity or adventure.

"*Heil Hitler*," the class saluted in unison and rushed out.

Early in the new year, Kurt received a letter from his mother.

> *Heartfelt greetings from your mother.*
>
> *I miss you very much and hope you are well. I am sorry I*

have not written much, but I have been so busy. Wande had a calf a few weeks ago too, but she has gone to the "war effort." I am sorry you did not get a chance to see her but at least Wande has enough milk for all of us.

Edeltraud is always chattering about something or making up little songs.

Rudy keeps us all entertained. The other day, he climbed up onto a chair and tried to take the cuckoo from the clock when it struck the hour. He wanted to know how the bird got in there. He misses you so much and remembers you faithfully in his prayers. I hope you remember to say your prayers too.

Study hard and listen to your teachers. I will send for you as soon as I can.

Deine Mutti

Kurt felt a little ashamed at being reminded to say his prayers. Religious sentiment was not encouraged at the KLV camp. There were no church services or prayers, only ceremonies to mark important occasions like Hitler's birthday. One of the teachers had scoffed to the class 'Religion is for the weak.' Kurt didn't want to be thought of as weak, but he didn't want to go against his mother's wishes or the faith of his family either.

After lights out, he just said prayers quietly to himself, while he was already in bed. That way, no-one else would know.

> *"Germans are not human beings … If you have not killed at least one German a day … you have wasted a day … there is nothing more joyful than a heap of German corpses."*
>
> — Ilya Ehrenburg, Red Army propagandist

CHAPTER 31
ERNST 1944

THE WAR IN THE EAST DRAGGED ON. COLUMNS OF SOLDIERS, accompanied by tanks and artillery, had marched with frostbitten feet through snow, rain, and bone-shattering icy winds over vast steppes into the cold heart of Russia. They shot and pillaged and their efforts were returned by ambush and slaughter.

At times the men on the ground and in the trenches thought they were gaining the upper hand, building up beach heads and a stable frontline, but the Russians moved their factories further east, quickly re-establishing production of military machinery. The German army's equipment came piecemeal and inadequately engineered to the conditions and climate they faced.

The chilled tentacles of winter had not let go.

Several kilometers behind the newest bloody battlefield outside Kiev, a supply wagon, pulled by two horses bumped its way over the frozen ground. Horst and Ernst wandered behind in the chill morning, a thin layer of ice and frost crunching and cracking beneath their boots.

Remnants of houses and barns smouldered at the edge of the forest and the smell of charred wood lingered in the air.

Earlier in the day, they had watched from a distance as a village had been bombed and shelled, its peasant occupants and their animals running for cover with only the clothes on their backs.

Retaliation had been swift in coming to the German side.

Ernst and Horst stooped over and picked up the body of one of their fallen companions and hoisted it into the cart.

The cold was an advantage in a way, thought Ernst. In the winter there was no stench and no flies. Frozen bodies felt more like wood than flesh making it easier to forget that the young soldiers were once someone's son or husband.

He surveyed the battlefield. "Doesn't seem to be enough firearms here," he said.

"Maybe someone else has already picked it over," said Horst looking over at the dense woods beyond what remained of the village.

The rest of regiment had gone on ahead towards the battlefront, but they still had to exercise caution as Russian partisans were known for surprise attacks.

Ernst tugged at a rifle that was partly submerged in a frozen puddle when a brief flash of movement in the woods to their left caught his eye.

Finger on his lips, he signaled to Horst. They crouched down and ran over to the cart for cover. As they ducked behind, shots rang out.

The horses snorted and reared their heads. Horst grabbed the harness to prevent the animals from bolting. Ernst reached for his pistol. "Into the wagon!" he hissed. He aimed the pistol towards the trees and pulled the trigger.

The men dove into the partly filled cart, but before the lower half of his body had made it over the side, Ernst felt a shaft of pain in his leg.

The horses were already on the move when Horst handed Ernst the lead rope.

Ernst tried his best to rein in the horses while staying out of sight. His leg stung, but he couldn't take his focus off the team.

"We need bigger fire power," Horst said, rummaging through the supplies they had collected and selecting a machine gun. "Found a round of ammunition. Just have to load now," he grunted as the wagon jostled along over the uneven field, but by the time he had set up the gun, they were past the danger.

He put the gun down and turned to Ernst. "*Ach du lieber*! Man, you are bleeding like a stuck pig."

"I'm not stopping until we get back to base camp," said Ernst, but the dampness soaking through his pant leg was making him shiver with cold.

Horst ripped open a package and pulled out a long bandage. He grabbed on to Ernst's leg and wrapped it tightly.

They returned to camp as the sun slipped behind the trees.

Blood had seeped through the dressing and Ernst's pants. His leg was throbbing.

"You need to see the medic, sir." said Horst.

The medic cleaned and re-bandaged the wound. "Get some rest and see me tomorrow. If you are due for a leave, maybe we can send you home for a while," he said with a sardonic smile, "but if there is any sign of infection, you will go to the field hospital."

Ernst took the advice about rest gladly. He doubted he'd be getting a ticket home, but he dreaded the prospect of an overcrowded field hospital filled with the groans of amputees and the dying.

He hoisted his injured limb onto his cot and looked at the barrel stove in the corner that barely heated the room. He thought of his cosy house and the green tiles of the *Kachelofen*. Pulling the woolen blanket up to his chin, he thought of how he'd like to hold his wife again under the softness and warmth of the featherbed.

It seemed only a few moments later that he opened his eyes. It was already light and his leg was throbbing.

"*Leutnant* Hoffmann, You've got ten days leave," said *Feldwebel* Wagner. "Pack up and get out of here; just make sure you are back in time for the next campaign!"

CHAPTER 32

ERNST COULD BARELY BELIEVE HIS GOOD FORTUNE. IT would only be a short leave, but he was pleased to be headed home. He could hardly wait to spend a few nights with his wife, eat home-cooked meals and recover from his injury.

With delayed trains and sabotaged tracks, the trip to Łódź had taken three days, but at last the train lurched to a stop. Through the grimy windows, Ernst read a faded and torn poster: 'The British and Americans have failed. No-one can defeat the New Europe.'

Whoever wrote that never fought on the Russian front, thought Ernst.

Woolen overcoats and leather boots had been no match for the Russians with their heavy felt footwear and fur hats. Many of the modern weapons of war, like the men from a more temperate climate, had failed to function in the sub-zero temperatures of the Russian winter. Frostbite, exposure, and sickness had taken their toll on the lives and morale of the soldiers.

Ernst collected his pack, stepped off the train, and limped across the platform where he was confronted with another poster proclaiming Nazi glory. The tall blonde soldier on the poster resembled Günther.

If only he could see his younger brother once again, he would have spoken out against the ideals Günther had espoused. Not that it would have done any good. Nazism and the SS uniform had ruined Günther. At the same time it had given him purpose and discipline, its ideals had filled him with arrogance and hatred costing him his life.

Ernst hitched a ride to the village with a truck full of soldiers.

"*Russland*?" one of them said.

"I hope you brought your felt boots," said another.

"Maybe a body bag would be more useful."

At Schönewald they helped him off the truck with half-hearted "*Sieg Heil*'s."

Liesel was bent over, planting peas. She stood for a moment to stretch her back.

He marveled at her strength under the stress of all the work, the children, and her ill mother. Of course she had always been stubborn too, a trait needed to handle those boys on her own. Perhaps it was that trait that had kept her going.

When she saw Ernst a smile spread across her face. "Ernst!"

Rudy careened around the side of the house, pushing Edeltraud in the wheelbarrow, almost tipping it over as he came to a stop a metre from his father. He tilted his head and looked up. "Are you *Vati*?" he asked.

Edeltraud clutched the side of the wheelbarrow with one hand and sucked her thumb with the other, watching Ernst warily.

"Don't suck your thumb," said Rudy. "Thumb sucking is for babies."

Edel had been little more than a baby the last time Ernst had seen her, now she was four. He picked her up, but she stiffened and held out her arms to her mother.

Liesel shook her head. "It's *Vati*."

Ernst felt emptiness in the pit of his stomach. His own children did not know him. His family had changed and grown and they had managed without him. He was a stranger here, and he realized he had seen and done things he would never be able to explain to his wife and children. Mechanically, as if Rudy were someone else's child, he reached out and patted him on the head. "I hope you have been a good boy."

Rudy grinned, his smile revealing a missing front tooth. "Yes, *Vati!*"

"Well he has been good some of the time," Liesel said. Ernst drew her close, kissed her lightly on the cheek, then stepped back to look at her.

She wore an old pair of his trousers, altered to fit, but the belt used to hold them up sat loosely at her hips, revealing angles rather than curves. Her hair was pinned into a bun at the back of her head, but wisps of untamed waves had escaped their confinement, falling over her face and brow. She pulled a strand of hair back behind her ears.

Ernst didn't remember the creases across her forehead.

At suppertime, Edeltraud sat, with her big eyes just looking at him. Did his little daughter somehow know what he had seen? Did his experience cling to him, like a smell or dirt that could not be washed off?

"I can milk Wande all by myself," said Rudy, breaking the silence.

"*Ja, gut,*" said Ernst, chewing absently on a piece of bread.

Liesel handed Rudy a plate of food. "Run this over to Oma please."

After he had left she said to Ernst, "Mother is not getting any better."

Ernst did not say anything. What did she think he was, a doctor? Perhaps his wife was mistaking him for some kind of hero who could fix anything.

She stood up to pour the coffee. "It's made of chicory and roasted barley since we can hardly get real coffee anymore."

Ernst willed himself to be civil. She had written about her decision to send the older boys away. "How are Kurt and Olaf?" he asked.

"Kurt seems fine. He is really looking forward to being in the Hitler Youth," she said, stacking the plates. "But Olaf sounds terribly homesick. I think I will send for them soon." She sat down as if waiting for Ernst's reply.

Ernst took a sip of the ersatz coffee and looked out the window. "Maybe you should."

Suddenly thoughts that had been simmering in his mind crystallized and he spoke without thinking. "It is all a big lie, you know. The Hitler Youth. He is just trying to raise child soldiers who will blindly die for the Fatherland. I have seen them." He put down his coffee cup violently, the brown liquid sloshing onto the saucer. "Young boys barely old enough to shave, bloodied and dismembered, crying out for their mother before they died."

Liesel looked on with an expression of shock on her face.

"Germany has lost the war," he said quietly, sliding his hand over his brush-cut hair. "It is only a matter of time."

Now we will settle the score with the German fascists. Our hatred burns! We will not forget the pain and suffering done to the Russian people by Hitler's barbarians. We have not forgotten … the murdered and the martyred. We will exact a brutal revenge for all they have done.

— Soviet Marshal Georgi Zhukov

CHAPTER 33

ERNST WAS BACK AT THE RUSSIAN FRONT. THE MEN HAD JUST finished breakfast and were standing outside for roll call. After inspection *Feldwebel* Wagner called them to attention.

"*Achtung!* We have orders to move our forces southwest of here. After the unfortunate events at Kursk, we will maintain our position at Kiev, before the Soviets do. You will be happy to know that we can soon return to the Fatherland and to your families. Prepare to take down this camp and march westward."

He clicked his heels together smartly and left the way he came.

"So now we are in retreat," said Ernst to Horst. "Let's get this done." He glanced over his shoulder to make sure no-one else was listening. "Before they change their minds or the Russians finish us off."

"*Jawohl*," said Horst in agreement.

The camp was dismantled in record time. Their supply unit had been assigned trucks in Ernst's absence and after everything was packed up, they started on their way.

The soldiers all knew the war was nearly over. Germans' visions of glory had dissolved into the desire for mere survival. The Allies were occupying the West, and the Axis powers and their enemies had all sustained terrible losses on this Russian front.

Ernst's unit had been one of the last to be issued trucks, but he was glad of the shelter and the sense of control, however small, he had when behind the wheel. He squinted against the brightness of the sunshine on the snowy steppe, broken up only by a trail of white camouflage figures, barely visible as they trudged through the snow.

Other soldiers rode in the back of the truck with Horst amongst the supplies. Throughout the day, the foot soldiers would take turns riding.

It was April and the days were getting a bit longer. It might even thaw a bit later in the day. And, they were headed southwest.

The soldier next to Ernst spoke, his words slicing through the brittle air.

"I heard a unit over by Voronezh was taken prisoner." Some of the man's words were lost over the noise of the engine, but Ernst heard a word which made him shiver. "*Siberia.*"

The man closest to the window said, "And some have deserted."

"We know what the punishment for that is," stated Ernst. It was a desperate action taken by desperate men. The penalty was often execution, no questions asked. But who could blame them for trying, thought Ernst. Treason could not be supported publicly without repercussions. But no-one dared speak his true opinion on the matter, even now. The less said, the better their chances of getting home.

Late in the afternoon they came to a small town. A few men went to inspect the buildings while Horst and Ernst stayed in the town square, close by the truck.

Debris and shrapnel were everywhere. Roofless houses, some with the entire front blown off looked over the town square. What had been a fountain was now frozen and still. Green and black leaves lay suspended in their decaying state, trapped under a layer of ice.

Would someone ever clean out the leaves, Ernst wondered. Or would they just rot away in the spring?

"I left my pack in the truck," said Horst, getting up to walk the few metres away.

Ernst sat down on a stone bench and pulled a tin from his ration box.

It had taken a while, but he had learned most of the codes that would tell him what was inside. As he suspected this one was ham. Cold, but filling. In the early years of the war, if you didn't know the code, you could end up with canned peaches for supper. The *Knäckebrot* he put in his pocket for later. Maybe someone would light a fire and they could make tea or hot cocoa.

An old lady wearing a headscarf and a faded skirt wandered the square, glancing about furtively as she stooped to pick up pieces of wood.

She looked harmless enough.

Ernst was tired after driving for hours. He let his eyes close for just a moment.

But his nap was interrupted by loud shouts piercing the air. German and Russian voices, Ernst thought with alarm. Where had they come from and where was Horst?

Reaching for his gun, he realized it was too late. Across the town square he watched as their company accompanied by several Russians, was marched over to the edge of the town, hands behind their heads. Glancing back at the truck, Ernst saw Horst come around the side, followed by an Russian soldier, pointing his gun. A headscarf was draped around the soldier's fur cap and a woman's skirt had been tucked into his belt.

A clever disguise, thought Ernst, angry that they had been caught off guard.

"*Komm,*" said the Kommandant to Ernst. They were led over behind a building where the others had been taken captive. A truck stood waiting.

"Your weapons. Here," The Russian pointed them to a large pile of German army weaponry.

Next, he pointed his gun at one of the German captives and asked him questions..

"*Jak ma Pan na imie?*" The Russian asked his name, then branch of service and unit.

The young soldier's brow creased in bewilderment and he shook his head, replying in his native German. "*Ich verstehe nicht.*"

Clearly he didn't speak or understand Polish, thought Ernst. But why were the Russians addressing their German captives in Polish?

The Kommandant pointed towards the building and sent the man over to wait with others inside. Horst was next in line. Again the Russian addressed him in Polish. Horst's reply was fluid, without hesitation. Ernst remembered that Horst's wife was Polish.

"The names of your children?" demanded the Russian. Ernst was puzzled. Why would the Russian want to know?

"I have a daughter—" Horst paused ever so briefly, his eyes flickering to the right, "Katya, and a son Carol."

Ernst knew the children's names to be Katrina and Karl.

"Take out your papers for processing." Horst was directed to the waiting truck.

Ernst felt like there was a rock in his belly as it dawned on him. Poland was now allied with Russia, and the Soviets were giving amnesty to any Poles who had joined the German army.

"And you," the Russian addressed Ernst again in Polish. "What village you from?"

Ernst dared not attempt the Polish pronunciation of his village. How he wished he had properly learned the language of his hired help and neighbors. Even though he understood quite a bit his rudimentary pronunciation and grammar would be not be mistaken for his mother tongue.

He cleared his throat. "Near Łódź" he mumbled, pronouncing it "wudge" as the Poles did. At least he knew how to say that.

"The names of your wife and children." Too late Ernst realized what Horst had done, but he lacked the imagination and the fluency to lie so smoothly under the duress he was feeling.

"Lidia," he substituted for Liesel, hoping that would pass, but it wasn't enough.

"Your children," said the Russian.

"Kurt, Olaf, Rudy—." Could they pass as Polish names? He didn't know. Each name evoked a memory of tousled hair, and toothless smiles, but the faces were blurred and indistinct.

He wondered if he would ever see them again.

CHAPTER 34

LIESEL ROLLED OVER AND PUSHED BACK THE FEATHERBED. Even though she had slept late again, she felt sluggish and there was so much to do.

She had sent a letter asking her sister-in-law to make travel arrangements and the boys were due back soon.

But she had not heard from Ernst since he had been home on leave over two months previous. She thought about his fatalistic-sounding words about the war being lost and tried not to think of the possibilities that meant for him. She had heard far too much already from other women in the village who spoke in hushed and horrified tones about the young men returning disfigured, dismembered or worse, not at all.

Liesel's fears knit together in the pit of her stomach and made her feel like retching. She turned her head towards the wall and closed her eyes to pray for her husband and for peace and safety for her family.

When she sat up, another wave of nausea swept over her. She vomited into the washbasin.

She could no longer attribute the signs to anxiousness or the flu. How could it be? Ernst had only been home a few days. Anger rose up with the bile in her throat. How could he leave her in such a situation, barely able to manage the farm and look after the children, never knowing if or when he would return home. And now another child to bring into chaos and uncertainty!

She remembered the time at the beginning of the war that the neighbors had got together to quilt and talk.

Perhaps she could find a doctor in Łódź ... Surely there were other desperate women in this time making difficult choices.

She looked over at Edeltraud sleeping on the trundle bed in the corner, tendrils of golden hair across her flushed face. And then she thought of Johann, whom she would never hold again. How could she *choose* to go through the grief and loss of losing a child? It was impossible. Ending a pregnancy was wrong. Perhaps the war would be over soon. Ernst would come home, they could rebuild the farm and go back to a normal life. She could never keep such a secret from her husband; that she had chosen to end the life of a child they had conceived in love.

And what if Ernst were to die? Would she be able to forgive herself, knowing she had caused the death of the last child to bear his image?

No, this baby had to live. Children are a blessing; a gift from God, she reminded herself.

Even if she was hungry and overworked, she would carry this baby.

She left Edeltraud sleeping and went to wake six year old Rudy.

The large bed that he had shared with his brothers seemed much too big with just him in it and his spare frame was completely hidden under the eiderdown. Only a thatch of hair the color of coffee was visible. She shifted the bulky bedding over.

"Time to get up, *Liebchen*. Go feed the chickens and bring in the eggs." She handed him his shirt and trousers.

"*Ja, Mutti.*" He rubbed his eyes a bit, gave her a lopsided grin, and began to dress. He looked sleepy still, but Liesel knew it wouldn't take him long to wake up. She headed outside to begin what she knew would be a long day.

Wande, her udder heavy with milk, waited patiently, her brown eyes blinking and her jaw moving back and forth leisurely as she chewed her cud.

Liesel reached for the milking stool and placed it next to the black and white Holstein. She rested her forehead against Wande's warm flank and grasped a teat in each hand. Steaming streams of milk rang into the pail, like a calming song.

She carried the milk to the to the cool room off the porch and poured it into the cream separator.

Down in the cellar, a box of sand held the last few carrots. There were still quite a few potatoes piled in the grain barn, but the ones in the sack were sprouting eyes.

She would plant those in the garden for a late crop.

Just yesterday, army officials had come demanding more food from their dwindling larder. Liesel had tried to convince them that her family needed to eat too, but it was to no avail. They could take whatever they wanted. Everything was rationed so the soldiers and people in the cities would have food too.

A small succession of piglets had been stashed in the secret sty.

If she could keep that fact from the army, at least they would have some meat this winter. Or, if they were caught they might be treated as traitors. It was a risk. Have her children go hungry or be shot, she thought cynically. Which would be the better way to go? And now on top of that, there would be another mouth to feed.

She climbed out of the cellar, and looked out the window.

Rudy stood still in the middle of the chickens, dropping feed around him. He whirled around quickly. The chickens scattered. Again he stood still and dropped seed; then, when the chickens were busy eating it he would move suddenly, laughing as his thin limbs splayed out in every direction sending the chickens off clucking.

Such a little boy and she was relying on him so much. She opened the door. "The eggs, Rudy! Hurry up. We need to eat some breakfast and you shouldn't scare the chickens like that or they will stop laying."

"Yes mother," he said, not even looking up as he headed off in the direction of the henhouse to collect the eggs.

Liesel sliced bread and scraped butter thinly over each slice. When Rudy finally arrived with the eggs, she put three into a pot of water and set it to boil. When all were cooked and a weak tea from yesterday's leaves brewed, she dished out the plates with half an egg each and the bread. She placed one plate on a tray with a glass of tea.

"Take this tray to Oma and then wake up Edeltraud," she instructed Rudy.

He picked up the tray, but before he had crossed the kitchen floor, he tripped. Everything crashed to the floor.

"Rudy!"

"I'm sorry, *Mutti,*" he said, scrambling to his feet and picking up the pieces of egg and bread.

She saw that he was trying his best and that was all she could expect. She helped him collect the food off the floor. The glass was broken and the tea spilled, but everything else was carefully dusted off before going back on the plate.

"Never mind," she said. She put the salvaged plate at her place and made up the tray again for her mother.

After they had eaten, she told Rudy, "I'm going outside to work on the garden. When you are finished eating, clean up, then bring Edeltraud outside."

In the vegetable garden, the beans were in bloom and the peas and lemon sorrel were almost ready to eat.

She started clearing out the weeds around the seedlings, piling the young dandelion leaves into a basket for a salad. Pushing her spade into the soft ground, she made holes and filled each with a sprouted potato.

The dirt was soft and warm, yielding to her touch. She took joy in watching the earth yield good things. But she missed her flower garden, which had gone to near ruin since the war had begun. Occasionally she took a moment to trim a rose or scatter some poppy seeds, but there was so little time for such pursuits.

She heard the door of the house open. Rudy and Edeltraud burst out in a rush. Edeltraud ran, laughing into the yard in her stockinged feet with Rudy fast on her heels.

"Come get your shoes on!" he called.

Liesel shook her head in frustration. Leaving the hoe in the garden, she opened the garden gate, caught Edeltraud by the hand and scooped her up.

"Where are your shoes, little one?"

"I don't want to wear shoes," said Edeltraud, squirming to get free. "I want be barefoot like Rudy."

"I want some milk," said Rudy.

The nausea of the early morning had left and Liesel wanted a glass of milk too.

"All right," she said. "You put away the hoe for me. After you help me some, I'll pour you a glass of milk."

She stopped at the pump to wash her hands and rinse Edeltraud's stockings, then carried the child to the porch and put her down. "Edel, hang your socks here," she directed.

In the cool room at one end of the porch, she found the cream had been sitting long enough to separate. As she rotated the handle, a stream of cream poured down into the butter churn. She poured the milk into two cans; one to be collected for the army and a smaller amount for her family. At least the children were entitled to an extra ration and now she would be as well.

Rudy came in.

"Rudy, come start the butter churning, then I'll pour you the milk."

"It's so hard," he complained.

"You are a big strong boy," she said. "I'll come finish it in a few minutes." Rudy pouted just a little, but went over to the churn and began thrusting the wooden paddle up and down with both hands.

"Can I have my milk now?" Rudy called from the cool room. "And a piece of bread?"

She looked at the cuckoo clock. Only 10:30 and already they were all hungry.

"*Ja, Liebchen.*" She set down a glass for each of them, and went to finish the churning. The cream had barely started to thicken. She continued working the paddle until it resisted. She poured the buttermilk into a jar to use for baking. She added water to the churn and continued paddling to rinse it, repeating until the water poured out clear. Finally she scraped the glistening lump of butter onto a board for salting.

Liesel's mouth watered with its promise of pure fat, but that too was rationed.

Returning to the kitchen with the butter, she was surprised to see her mother sitting at the table.

Adelheid's face was flushed with fever and Liesel could hear her labored breathing. "Mother! You should be resting!"

"I know, but you are working so hard," Adelheid replied. "I thought if I came over it would save you trouble."

Liesel chopped potatoes and set them to fry in a small amount of lard on top of the stove. She added a few scraps of ham and the greens she had picked from the garden. When the potatoes had browned she dished everything out and sat down.

Steam rose from her meal and as if it were melting her resolve, her eyes filled with tears. Setting down her fork she tried to brush them away with the back of her hand.

Even though she wanted to be strong for her mother who was so sick, she could not face this pregnancy alone. "I am going to have another baby."

Adelheid looked at her and placed a nearly transparent hand on Liesel's. "Oh, my child. Remember that God is our help in time of trouble."

"I know mother, but I can barely manage things now."

"I wish I could help you more."

"You cannot help it that you are ill."

"Your boys will be back soon," Adelheid reassured her daughter. "They will be older, stronger."

Liesel hoped that was true.

CHAPTER 35

Leaving Edeltraud and Rudy with her mother, Liesel met the boys coming off the train. Kurt stepped off first, carrying his rucksack in one hand and his brother's in the other. He adjusted his cap and stood straight and tall, his head up past Liesel's chin. He was ten years old now.

His thick dark hair reminded Liesel of Ernst. "Oh, how you have grown," Liesel greeted him with a hug, but Kurt stiffened at her touch, as if he was too old for hugs and kisses.

"There was a parade," said Kurt. "You should have seen all the boys and girls joining the Hitler Youth. I am going to be a good soldier for Hitler," he stated proudly.

Liesel was taken aback. "I hope not, we don't need any more soldiers around here," she said. That kind of talk reminded her of allegiance to God. Hitler was just a man. A man with ideas that was making her world worse, not better as he had promised.

"But mother, you must not talk like that," Kurt said. "We are going to win the war. Hitler says Breslau will be a fortress and cannot be defeated. "

She didn't really want to know what else had he learned at camp.

She turned to Olaf, who returned her embrace. "How are you? I am so glad to have you boys home."

He leaned into her. "Did Kaspar have her kittens?"

Liesel tried to remember what she had written. "Yes."

He wouldn't know how many. The fact was she had only kept two and sent the rest to Kristiana's father to be drowned in the pond. You couldn't have cats overrunning what was left of the farm, but she knew Olaf would be upset if he found out.

"One is a grey tabby like Kaspar and the other is solid grey with white boots." She also chose not to mention that the old mare the children had enjoyed riding had been sent to the slaughterhouse. These days people were glad to have horse meat.

"I have one more thing to tell you. We are going to have another baby." She pasted on her best smile. "Probably sometime after Christmas." She had tried not to think about it, but there it was, as real as her sons standing before her.

"Oh," said Olaf. "When we get home can I play with the kittens?"

A few days later the children were in the barn with the new kittens when Liesel heard a sharp rapping at the front door.

She wiped her wet hands on her apron and speculated who it could be. Not many people were being neighborly these days and, with the "resettlements," she had not the time or opportunity to meet the new Germans in the area. A *Kaffeeklatsch* was a luxury she had not enjoyed in a long time.

Perhaps it was news from Ernst, but a knock at the door couldn't mean good news. She hoped it wasn't army officials wanting more food. She had given more than her share already. Just in case it was someone malicious she grabbed the poker from the hearth of the *Kachelofen* and opened the door a crack.

A young man stood there, his smooth rosy cheeks and hairless face betraying his youth. A shabby uniform hung on his small frame and loose threads on the sleeve hinted at some previous insignia of a higher ranking official. Nonetheless, he wore a serious demeanor under his courier's cap.

Barely older than my boys, she thought, still rankling at Kurt's idea of becoming a soldier.

"Heil Hitler," said the boy, standing at attention. He raised his arm so fast in the Nazi salute he almost hit Liesel in the face.

Her heart thumped wildly. She stepped back and nodded, one hand clutching her sweater around her thickening waist, the other loosening slightly its grip around the poker. Was she now a widow as many others had become?

The boy's voice cracked as he announced. "Registered letter for Frau Hoffmann." Liesel's hand shook as she reached for the blue envelope.

"Signature please." Liesel scrawled her name on the sheet. The courier saluted her smartly again, clicked his boots together and was up at the gate in a moment.

She ripped open the envelope.

> *"This letter is to inform you that Leutnant Ernst Hoffmann*
> *is missing in action and presumed to be taken prisoner..."*

Her heart plummeted like a rock. She dropped the poker and collapsed into a chair.

Presumed to be taken prisoner. That meant he was alive, but even she knew that to be taken prisoner of war by Stalin's Red Army was almost surely a death sentence. People in Eastern Poland had been taken at the beginning of the war, and never heard from again.

One of Liesel's worst fears had come true. But, she reasoned she was powerless to do anything but what she was already doing—look after her children, her mother and the farm. Prepare for her baby and pray to Almighty God that the child would not be left fatherless.

She tucked the letter into the drawer of the writing-desk and vigorously swept the floor, as if to sweep away her fear and worry.

Not knowing was terrible, but worrying was worse. She pushed her anxiety to a corner of her mind and determined to build a wall around it, otherwise she could not go on. The children did not need to be told just yet either.

When she was done sweeping she picked up the dustpan, opened the door and threw the dirt outside, shutting the door forcefully behind it.

She was hanging out the clothes a few weeks later, when a man in civilian clothing entered the yard, his hat in hand. Though he was much thinner than she had remembered, she recalled him as Horst, a friend of Ernst's from his village who had been deployed at the same time.

Horst glanced quickly in both directions and over his shoulder, as if he were afraid someone had followed him.

Liesel beckoned him inside."*Kommen Sie herein.*" She invited him in and tried to keep her voice controlled and calm, as she thought of what this visit could mean. Did he have news of Ernst? "*Kaffee?*" Liesel asked. "*Ja.* But I cannot stay long," he said. He looked at the children playing on the floor. "This must be Rudy and Edeltraud.

"And another is on the way," Liesel said, though she thought it must be obvious by now.

"I see your hands are full."

"Yes." Liesel couldn't bear any more pleasantries. With a note of desperation she looked at Horst.

"What do you know?"

"I came to tell you I saw Ernst alive in the early spring. The Russians took him captive." Horst took a sip of the substitute coffee, grimacing at its bitter flavour.

"But how did you get away?" Liesel asked.

"I was let go, because the Soviets have made an agreement to give amnesty to the Poles. We're allies now. I spoke well enough to satisfy the Russian, but Ernst …" He shook his head.

No explanation was required; Liesel knew her husband would not have been able to pass for Polish.

Horst lowered his voice. "Of course I will be training to serve with the Polish militia in co-operation with the Soviets now."

Nazism, Communist. It was all the same to Liesel. Taking sides and fighting meant soldiers killing and taking the property of others. Hard work and hunger for the women they left at home. "Ernst gave me this to give to you." Horst pulled a worn piece of paper from his pocket. "A lot of the soldiers agreed to write letters, just in case. There were only a handful left of us."

Liesel unfolded a short note, scribbled in pencil, on a field pad.

>*Dear Liesel,*
>
>*If you get this letter you will know that I am either dead or captured. I am so sorry to leave you and our children. Keep faith that someday we will be re-united. All my love to you and to our children,*
>
>*Your loving husband, Ernst.*

Liesel's eyes welled up with tears for the first time since she had heard of Ernst's fate. She clutched the letter to her chest.

"I am so sorry, Frau Hoffmann," said Horst. "I wish there was something I could have done." He patted her arm lightly.

Liesel picked up Edeltraud off the floor and placed the girl on what remained of her lap.

"This is not official." Horst twirled his hat around. "Perhaps I should not be telling you, but when it is over, you probably won't be safe here."

Evidently he had taken a great risk in coming to see her.

He placed his hat on his head and was about to turn the doorknob. "If I were you I would prepare to leave, the sooner the better."

CHAPTER 36
1945

LIESEL WISHED SHE HAD TAKEN HORST'S WORDS SERIOUSLY, but this was the only home she had ever known and she was in no condition to leave, pregnant and with four young children. His words of warning rang in her ears as she took one last look at her home and farm. She was leaving behind everything her family had worked for, without knowing if she would ever be able to return.

The wagon jostled passed the churchyard. She saw the steps she had come down as a young bride and the graveyard beside the church where little Johann and her father were buried. She hadn't even had time to place any flowers or say a final goodbye.

As if ringing from the steeple, the words of Luther's hymn came back to her.

Ein feste Burg ist unser Gott,
Ein gute Wehr und Waffen;
Er hilft uns frei aus aller Not,
Die uns jetzt hat betroffen.

A mighty fortress is our God,
A bulwark never failing;
Our helper He, amid the flood
Of mortal ills prevailing.

Und wenn die Welt voll Teufel wär'
Und wollt' uns gar verschlingen,
So fürchten wir uns nicht so sehr,
Es soll uns doch gelingen.

And though this world, with devils filled,
Should threaten to undo us,
We will not fear, for God hath willed
His truth to triumph through us.

Whether the song was about a spiritual battle that the forces of good would win or a physical battle did not matter to Liesel. She found strength and comfort in its ancient words and rhythmic cadence.

It was not quite dawn as they turned onto the road headed south west, towards Breslau, and the river Oder, which had frozen over this winter. An endless caravan of people were fleeing their homes in hopes of crossing into German-held territory, away from the advancing Red Army. Silhouetted against the bleak sky were covered wagons, carts, and wheelbarrows loaded up with bundles and furniture piled so high they looked like they might topple. Oxen and horses strained at their load. Animals led by rope and halter bleated, brayed, and squawked as they were pulled reluctantly along.

She had never seen anything like it.

The wheels of their own wagon creaked and groaned over the frozen ground and the utensils, pots, and pans clanked out a tuneless melody each time the wagon hit a pothole. As she maneuvered her rig onto the road she saw Kristiana with her elderly father. Kristiana's young son Erich rode between them on their covered wagon.

Kristiana wore a heavy scarf over her head as protection against the cold wind, but Liesel knew that underneath the folded fabric were those beautiful blonde braids coiled neatly around her head.

Liesel had always admired the younger woman's smooth hair while struggling to keep her own unruly ash-coloured tresses under control, but petty jealousies of the past were not important now. Nice hair was useless at a time like this.

A wagon in good repair, a set of strong co-operative horses and intangibles like determination and faith in Providence were the only things that counted now.

Kurt and Rudy sat up with Liesel on the front bench sharing a woolen blanket pulled almost up over their heads. Olaf held Edeltraud in the back, sandwiched between boxes and crates and covered with layers of featherbeds and blankets under a canvas tarp.

The children did not make a sound as the wagon jostled along the road.

Cold wind stung Liesel's cheeks and nose. Like shards of ice, it gusted up her sleeves. Inside her gloves, her fingers were getting numb.

She gripped the reigns tight with one hand and adjusted her scarf.

Progress was slow as overloaded wagons broke down, blocking the road. Horses and oxen had to stop for food and water. As morning wore on, fine snow fell, stinging Liesel's face and obscuring the wagons ahead of them. Following the long river of humanity, they plodded west.

Every jolt and pothole jarred her belly as she tried to navigate the icy road. By evening, her stomach was firm; the weight of the baby inside leaden.

Liesel halted the wagon at the edge of a village to rest. The horses needed to rest and so did she.

Next to an abandoned barn, Kristiana's father, Herr Schroeder, had pulled down the back of his wagon and lit a portable stove. A small kettle whistled; the merriest sound Liesel had heard for days.

"My wagon is covered, you can park inside the barn," said Mr. Schroeder, guiding her horses in and helping Liesel down from the seat.

"Come children," said Liesel, lifting down the basket of food she'd packed.

She lumbered over to Kristiana with ham, bread, and tin mugs for each of them.

"May we have some tea?"

"*Ja*, certainly. Are you feeling all right? Is your time soon?" Kristiana asked, filling the children's mugs halfway.

"It might be sooner than I had thought." Liesel did not share her fear that the baby would probably come early, perhaps in the next day or two. "I will manage somehow," she said with much more confidence than she felt, allowing the steaming cup of tea to warm her numb hands.

Faint sunlight marked the next day. As the snow melted, the road became a bed of muck. Max and Minka strained at the load, their stamina diminishing as they slowed and became less responsive to her direction.

She stopped them and climbed down clumsily from her perch. "Boys," she stopped to catch her breath and waddled to the back of the wagon. "We need to lighten this load."

Ignoring the warm dampness under her skirts she selected the heaviest items first—her grandmother's china set, a family heirloom that had been a wedding gift from the Crown Prince of Prussia.

It made her sad to have her boys hoist the crate to the side of the road. So many memories of family dinners eaten off those plates. She had loved looking at the delicate figurines depicted and many times had run her fingers over the gold filigree around the edge.

But it was not a difficult decision. She would not trade her life, or the lives of her children, for a set of china.

They threw off some chairs and books. Why had she brought books?

In the distance planes roared and artillery fired. The horses whinnied at the rat-tat-tat of machine gun fire and the flash of incendiaries.

Liesel comprehended the fear of the spooked horses as if she were one of them.

"Back in the wagon," she ordered the boys.

Fields on either side of the road were strewn with the horrors of battle. An abandoned wagon with a broken wheel lay on its side, surrounded by pieces of broken pottery and clothing.

A soldier, one their own, sat up against a tree. His helmet covered his face and his rifle lay at his side, but his legs were bent at an awkward angle and a dark stain covered the front of his tunic. A slaughtered horse lay in the ditch, its guts spilled over the icy water.

Liesel wished she could hide these grisly scenes from the children, but it was not possible.

They travelled into the night. She wanted to get to safety before this child was born.

Around midnight she let Kurt take a turn at the reigns, while she closed her eyes for a little while. A dull ache in her back woke her up and the weight of her unborn child seemed to be pressing against her spine. Her woolen skirt was damp through now, but even more alarming was a low rumbling sound nearby, a sound she had not heard before. The horses reared up as the ground seemed to vibrate under them.

The wagon lurched to a stop. "We are stuck," said Kurt. He gave the team a flick of the reigns and they strained and whinnied but one wheel of the wagon sank further into a deep pothole and the weight of everything in the wagon shifted.

"I'm caught under a box," Olaf cried out.

Liesel willed herself to breathe. "Everyone will have to get out now."

In the near darkness she could not see the Schroeders ahead and as far as she could tell there was no-one else behind her.

Cradling her stomach, she inched off the bench.

"Olaf," she said. "*Was ist los?*"

"I'm stuck. My leg hurts and it's underneath this box." He was in the corner of the wagon trapped by a box of grain.

Liesel reached over to see if she could shift the heavy box off of Olaf's leg, but the slightest movement caused her back to go into spasm. "Kurt, help me," she commanded. Kurt tried to lift the box and then the two of them together, but it was impossible at this angle.

"Let's get the lid off and scoop some of the grain out," said Liesel.

She recalled nailing it shut. Nice and secure she thought with chagrin. How had they ever gotten that heavy box in there? "Olaf, can you reach anything to pry the lid off?"

He rummaged around, but there was nothing he could reach. Before Liesel could stop him, Kurt climbed up into the back of the wagon to find some implement they could use to free Olaf. "No Kurt, it could tip," yelled Liesel frantically, "be careful."

The wagon creaked ominously. Two wheels were stuck now, two wheels up in the air.

"I found the shovel." Kurt called victoriously, but as he pulled it out, his weight moved the whole rig and the box shifted again.

The horses whinnied and snorted.

"Ow! It hurts,"said Olaf.

"Here push it in like this."

Liesel held onto the other side of the wagon and prayed that it would not tip any further. She heard a creak as the boys pried the lid off the box.

"Here," she said, handing Kurt a pot and a pillow case. "We can't afford to waste that, scoop it into here."

She watched anxiously as the boys worked, trying to hold the wagon still even while her stomach contracted.

Rudy, who had been sleeping, sat up. "Oh! Look!" he said, his eyes wide as the near horizon flashed orange, lighting the wagon with a brilliant glow.

Liesel did not share his enthusiasm about the exploding incendiaries.

Edeltraud woke up whimpering.

"Take Edel," Liesel commanded Rudy, pointing to a large oak nearby, "and stand by that tree. If there are any more explosions, crouch down and cover your heads."

Kurt had succeeded in extricating Olaf from the box and Olaf climbed out of the wagon. Now they had to push it out of the mud.

By the time the younger ones were safely tucked in the back of the wagon and they were ready to move again, she could see in the distance the tanks that she had heard rumbling a short while ago. Planes whined overhead and left behind little puffs of smoke as they fired at each other. Flashes of gunfire and exploding rockets lit up the sky below. The insistent clatter of artillery added to the clamor as dawn broke.

Liesel trembled with fear and intermittent pain that fully consumed her.

She snapped the horses reigns. "*Hüh.*" They had to hurry.

Daylight had broken when she heard voices and what sounded like machinegun fire up ahead. Around a bend in the road, between some trees the caravan had stopped once again. Herr Schroeder was slumped over the side of the wagon seat and Kristiana's little boy stood next to it wailing.

Kristiana stumbled out of the bushes pulling up her skirt. Her coat and scarf were gone, and her blonde hair cascaded wildly down her back. Behind her followed two Russian soldiers, one was doing up his belt and the other was laughing. They pointed their guns at the oxen that pulled Kristiana's wagon and fired.

"*Whoa.*" Liesel gasped, jerking on the horse's reigns with all her strength.

She felt another contraction. It was too late to turn around, there was nowhere to go.

Her heart beat furiously. "Hide!" she hissed to the children as the soldiers walked towards them.

"Aha, another *Hausfrau,*" said one of the Russians. "Who first Ivan? Me or you?"

The one called Ivan pointed his rifle butt at her stomach. "Oh ho, is with child." He made a crude remark and Liesel felt her belly tighten again.

"*Nyet.* She big like horse! I like small woman."

"Like last one," remarked his companion. "But screamed so loud," he said laughing.

It sickened Liesel that they had raped Kristiana, but she hoped they would pass her by for their brutalities.

"We will take the horses." The men unharnessed the team and Ivan led them over to a tree. Liesel opened her mouth to protest, but nothing came out. It didn't take long for them to find the children.

"Oh look! Little Nazis." Ivan felt Rudy's arm. "That one is too skinny to eat."

He pointed his rifle at Kurt. "You come join Red Army."

"No." Kurt replied in a small voice.

"You say no?" The other soldier cuffed him at the side of the head.

Liesel winced. Kurt did not say anything more.

Ivan snatched the featherbed off Edeltraud. Liesel prayed they would leave her precious daughter alone. "So soft and warm. I will keep! Is good for our winter in Leningrad."

Edeltraud looked at the two strange men who had disturbed her warm nest and let out a shrill scream.

Ivan leered up to her, making a face like a fearsome old witch. "Be quiet or *Baba Yaga* will eat you!"

She cried louder as they emptied out a sack of pots and pans. They opened the chicken crate and stuffed the chickens into the sack. Opening the box of grain, they emptied most of what was left on the ground and discovered Liesel's father's gold pocket watch which she had hidden at the bottom.

Her jaw clenched with resignation, Liesel clutched her stomach and rocked back and forth as a wave of pain passed over her.

At last the barbaric strangers loaded up the horses with their plunder and led them away.

Liesel took a ragged breath as she watched Max and Minka go.

She surveyed the chaos the men had left. Torn and broken belongings lay scattered in the mud and snow.

Anger rose up even as the next contraction gripped her. She had to figure out what to do. Right now, before the baby was born in a ditch.

Ahead, a row of poplars lined the driveway to a small cottage.

"Olaf, carry Edeltraud piggyback," she panted.

"Kurt, fill the featherbed with whatever you can salvage, especially food." She was gasping and doubled over.

"Rudy, you carry this." She lifted a bundle off the ground that she had packed with a few essentials for the baby. She grabbed a few jars that had rolled unheeded away from the gaze of the soldiers and put them in a suitcase among their clothes.

Schlaf, Kindlein, schlaf!
Der Vater hüt' die Schaf,
Die Mutter schüttelt 's Bäumelein,
Da fällt herab ein Träumelein.
Schlaf, Kindlein, schlaf!

CHAPTER 37

WIND BLEW THROUGH THE SMASHED WINDOWS OF THE house, rattling the shutters and ruffling the shredded curtains like a ghostly presence.

The door, hanging from one hinge, yielded with a creak as Liesel pushed on it.

She staggered across the almost empty room to a corner, and hastily arranged a sheet on the floor. She took off her coat and folded it into a pillow. Her sixth child; there wasn't much time.

The children had followed her into the house and stood staring at their mother.

"Kurt, Olaf," she gasped. "Go find some firewood, but stay close to the house." The boys left out the back door.

"Rudy, Edel ..." she began, but an overwhelming force tensed her body.

Edeltraud's eyes were round as tea saucers.

"Come on, Edeltraud," said Rudy. "Let's find something to eat." He led his sister over to a table by the fireplace.

Liesel focused her gaze on a small cupboard across the room. Two birds enclosed by a heart-shaped ribbon decorated the wooden cabinet and the pattern repeated all along the outer edge. But a split in the wood at the corner had rendered one bird without a mate, the heart broken in two.

The pains came faster and stronger as Liesel focused her eyes on the centre heart, following each curlique and brush stroke around the shape.

The front door scraped open.

Liesel shifted her gaze to the door.

"Hide," she commanded the younger children for the second time that day.

Over the mound of her stomach she saw Kristiana standing there, one hand clutching a suitcase and the other clinging to her small son. They were wrapped in blankets and their faces were masks of shock. A draft blew through the open door behind them.

Liesel relaxed back against her makeshift pillow. Now she would have some help.

Kristiana clumped over to the corner of the room and slid down against the wall next to the cupboard. Her head was in her hands and she was weeping loudly. *"Gott im Himmel,"* she wailed. "What will we do? Those Russian barbarians. They will kill us or take us all to Siberia."

Rudy and Edeltraud timidly made their way out from under the table. Kurt and Olaf came in the back door and set down a few sticks in front of the fireplace. They looked first at Kristiana, then at their mother moaning on the floor, her skirt riding up above her knees.

"I'm going to light the fire," said Kurt. Then, with confidence beyond his years, he turned to the other children. "Mutti will be all right, but I think we better not watch." The children gathered around the fireplace.

Liesel felt an overwhelming urge to bear down.

Kristiana continued her ranting. "My poor father. There was nothing I could do. Nothing." Fresh sobs overtook her. "Filthy animals."

Suddenly, she looked up across the room as if seeing Liesel for the first time. "Oh, you are having a baby," Kristiana said, her voice like a small child's. She stood up, walked across the room and arranged a blanket over Liesel. Squeezing Liesel's hand, she said, "You are almost there." Gently she smoothed back the laboring mother's hair.

Liesel groaned as waves of searing pressure overtook her.

An explosion rattled the walls. Outside the roar of rockets and the rumble of tanks shattered the night.

Inside the little house, a plaintive cry pierced the air.

Tentatively Kristiana picked up the baby, holding it away from herself, as if she did not want to be soiled. "It's a girl," she said.

"There is a washcloth in my suitcase," rasped Liesel. "And a baby blanket." She lay back on her pallet. Sweat poured off her brow and she shivered with cold. Kristiana laid the baby on Liesel's chest.

"I want to name her Heidi," said Liesel, wrapping her arms around her newborn. "After my mother." Sorrow threatened to overwhelm Liesel as she thought of her mother dying alone and never seeing her namesake. She looked at Heidi's tiny face and happiness and love filled her heart, edging the sadness away.

Rudy appeared at Liesel's side. "Mutti, are you well?" He came closer and saw the naked baby still covered in the messy fluids of birth in his mother's arms. His eyes widened.

"A baby!" he said loudly, looking around the room. "Where did it come from?" He walked over to the fireplace and peered up past the flames into the chimney. "Is there a stork around here?"

Liesel couldn't help but smile. Rudy had been too young to remember Edeltraud's birth and Liesel had been too pre-occupied to prepare him properly for this event.

Kristiana returned with the damp washcloth and handed it to Liesel, but she had forgotten the blanket. "Rudy," said Liesel, "can you bring the little blanket, so we can wrap up your new sister and make her nice and warm."

Kristiana watched dully as Liesel cleaned off the baby herself and helped Rudy wrap the newborn in the blanket. When they were done,

Kristiana picked up little Heidi and sang breathlessly, *Schlaf, Kindlein, schlaf...*

> Sleep, baby, sleep.
> Your father tends the sheep.
> Your mother shakes the dreamland tree,
> down fall all the dreams for thee.
> Sleep, baby, sleep.

The noises outside receded into the distance. Huddled by the fireplace, the children fell asleep. As Liesel drifted off, the walls of the little house seemed to rise up around her, cocooning its occupants.

She felt relief and joy even if it was only going to last a moment.

In the morning she woke to snow blowing in through the broken window. She tucked the blanket around Heidi who made little sucking noises in her sleep.

Kristiana tiptoed over to Liesel with a steaming beverage in a chipped cup. Her hair had been crudely cut around her ears like the straw for a thatched roof. "They are coming," she whispered, her voice thin; insubstantial. "I need to leave now." She transferred the cup of tea to Liesel, her gaze distant and unfocused.

Liesel clutched the younger woman's hand in her own. She hadn't heard anything yet this morning. "Who is coming? Why don't you wait a little while and we'll go together."

Kristiana's eyes darted around the room as if the offending Russians might be hiding in the little house. She patted the baby on the head. "No, I must go."

If Kristiana wanted to go, then she would go and Liesel did not have the strength to detain her. "Thank you for your help," she said. "I am so sorry about your father and ... everything."

Kristiana shook her head and raised her hands. Clearly the subject was closed. She kissed Liesel lightly on the cheek and spoke brightly again, "Come Erich."

She picked up the suitcase, and her sleepy son and went out the door into the swirling snow.

Liesel never saw her again.

CHAPTER 38

THERE WAS NO HOPE OF GETTING ACROSS THE ODER NOW. TO the west was a battle zone, to the east and in every other direction was Soviet occupied territory.

The road was lined with refugees, mostly headed east. But now there were no horses or wagons, only weary people on foot clutching small children and bundles of whatever they had been able to salvage from the Russians. Around them lay the smoldering ruins of the countryside, burnt barns and charred bodies.

"We're going home to Schönewald," said Liesel. As far as she knew there was nowhere else they could go.

The younger children stayed close to Liesel, keeping a slow pace with her, but Kurt walked much faster. "You can go ahead a little, but don't wander," she said. "There could be unexploded mines or more soldiers."

Heidi began to cry and Liesel's attention was diverted.

Kurt was ahead of the group in no time.

A disabled Russian tank lay at the side of the road. It was sloped in front, simpler in design than the German panzers. They were faster than the German tanks Kurt had seen rolling across the landscape.

If he wasn't so afraid of running into more soldiers or the mines his mother warned about, he would have gone closer to look at it, maybe even climbed inside. He imagined himself in it firing the gun. But of course, he would have been fighting for the Germans, not the Russians. He came to a fork in the road, but in the snow, he couldn't see anyone and wasn't sure which way he should go.

He chose the path to the left.

Icy wind blew over the plain and he pulled the featherbed he was carrying tighter around himself.

Past an abandoned truck and several dead horses, he saw a Junker that had crashed onto a snowy field.

The *Luftwaffe* had done training near Breslau and when he was there, he had watched them flying overhead. Along with many of the other boys, he had memorized each model and some of the individual insignia that marked each plane.

While waiting for his family and the other refugees to catch up, he went a little closer.

The wings were snapped close to the fuselage and the front propeller was partially imbedded in snow and dirt. The swastika on the tail was riddled with bullet holes.

Kurt recalled the wooden model he had received when he was young, back near the beginning of the war. Oma had helped him to paint the swastika, guiding his hand with small brush strokes. He wondered about her now, so sick. Would she die while they were gone?

He hurried to get back to the road, slipping and sliding on the snowy ground. He thought the rest of the group must have come by now and be further up the road, but the longer he walked the more he feared that they had gone the other way.

At the KLV he had learned some map and compass reading. He knew he was somewhere west of home and that Łódź was to the north. Perhaps if he kept walking, he would find something familiar. He was confident he was still going in the right direction and didn't think it would be wise to back track now.

He pulled his cap down over his ears. He was hungry and thirsty, since he had not even had a midday meal. Nothing, since the slice of bread his mother had given them for breakfast before they left the abandoned cottage. He was tired of walking and getting more worried with every step he took.

It had stopped snowing now. A river meandered peacefully through the bare trees, its banks bordered with ice. At the side of the road a large willow tree towered above a short path lined with bushes that led down to the riverbank.

He turned towards the river. The ice at the edge crackled as he broke it with his foot. Using a piece of curled bark from the ground, he bent over to scoop some water to his mouth.

Suddenly two young men jumped out of the bushes and pointed their rifles at him.

They were dressed in long tunics and Kurt recognized the square "hen" caps they wore as part of the Polish uniform.

"What have we here!" said the taller of the two men.

"I think it's a little German swine." The shorter one sneered. "What are you hiding in the blanket?" He reached out to grab the featherbed and it unfolded onto the ground as he felt it all the way through.

"Are you sure there's nothing in here? Maybe some money, precious jewels?" he said. "You Germans! Trying to take all the wealth out of Poland."

Kurt was thankful that his mother had taken care of the valuables.

"Well, just to be sure …" The soldier dragged the bedding over to the willow tree and slung it up over a branch. He aimed his rifle and shot. Goose down, like snowflakes, floated to the ground.

He pointed the gun at Kurt again. "How about we do some target practice on you?"

Kurt was rooted to the ground in in terror, but his eyes couldn't help following the swirling feathers. Something at the side of the tree caught his eye.

"What are you looking at, Kraut? Do you think your beloved Führer will help you now?" the shorter man said.

Kurt was too afraid to say anything, but pointed to the side of the tree, where just out of view of the *militja* men, a brickwork structure was affixed to the wide trunk. It reminded Kurt of a miniature castle turret. Under a gothic arch the figure of Jesus held his hands out, the red scars on his palms a silent plea.

The men stepped over to see what Kurt was looking at and the taller man's eyes widened slightly. He crossed himself and nudged the shorter man. "Hey Olek, maybe this little Nazi isn't worth using up our ammunition on." He lowered the gun.

"OK," said Olek to Kurt, "how about we count to ten and when we're done, you'll be gone!"

Kurt did not wait for them to reach ten. He snatched his featherbed from the tree and ran, as fast as he could, back up the path to the road, bits of fluffy goose down trailing behind him.

He was almost out of breath when a man pushing a cart full of branches pulled up beside him. "*Dzien Dobry.*"

Kurt backed away, poised to flee if necessary.

"Where are you going, son?" the old man said, a smile crinkling his face around gray whiskers and missing teeth.

Kurt's story tumbled out in a torrent of Polish with a few German words mixed in. "I can't find my family. I … We had to get away from the Russians. They took our horses. I don't know where my Mom or brothers or sister are. My Mom has a new baby too." His chest heaved and hot tears stung his cold cheeks. "I don't know which way they went and two militia men tried to shoot me," he sobbed.

The man pushed aside the kindling in the little cart. "Climb in, I'll bring you to our house," he said. "I think you could use a little hot soup!"

Kurt's legs shook under him as he climbed into the cart. He pulled up his knees and wrapped the featherbed around him. A bit further down the road, they came to a farmhouse and the man's wife poured him half a bowl of steaming potato soup.

He would have eaten more, but he was afraid to ask.

After dinner the farmer's wife took out a needle and thread and sewed up the holes in Kurt's featherbed. She handed it back to him and pointed him to the loft where he could sleep. Early in the morning, before it was light out, she wrapped up a piece of bread and a small wedge of cheese.

"Here, we will bundle it up like this," said the farmer. He stuffed the featherbed into a potato sack and tied it onto Kurt's shoulders with some rope. "Then you can carry it on your back. Where are you trying to go?"

"Schönewald. It's not far from Łódź."

The farmer had not heard of the place. "We are not far from the city. Perhaps you can find your way from there."

"My aunt lives there." Kurt said eagerly.

The farmer drew a map with a stick in the dirt and made sure Kurt understood. "I hope you find your way," he said.

"*Dziękuję.*"

The farmer's wife crossed herself, said some words Kurt didn't understand and patted him on the head. "*Do Widzenia.*"

Kurt walked for several hours, but did not see Łódź. He waited as long as possible before taking off the makeshift backpack and pulling out the bread and cheese. Then he tried to take tiny bites and make it last, but it was only lunchtime. Within a few hours the light began to dim and his energy was gone.

Ahead, he saw a barn.

No-one was around, so he lay down on a pile of hay and covered himself with the featherbed. Eventually he fell asleep, in spite of wind howling through the cracks and knotholes.

He woke up cold and hungry, with aching bones and feet. Shuffling to the door, he opened it to a blast of winter air.

It was tempting to go back in and lie down again,but he had to get back to his family.

Walking was tedious. He felt every pebble on the road through the worn soles of his shoes and the cold bit through his threadbare jacket.

It was getting too small and the sleeves were above his wrists.

He was glad now that his mother had made him carry the featherbed. He hadn't wanted to.

Clouds hung low in the sky and he did not see the city until he was almost there.

Up and down the deserted streets of Łódź he wandered, trying to remember which one his aunt and uncle lived on. He saw a girl's face peeking out a window, but when he came closer she disappeared. A soldier crossed the street in front of him and Kurt ducked into a doorway so he wouldn't be seen.

At last he saw something familiar; St. Joseph's, an old wooden church. Joseph the carpenter, thought Kurt, so of course it should be built from wood. He had seen this church before when visiting Aunt Frieda. They had gone for a walk and she had pointed it out to them. So her house was only a few blocks away.

He came up to the row of houses, but the windows were boarded up and the streets were littered with broken glass and pieces of plaster and brick. He found the house and knocked. What if no-one was there? Or worse, what if there were more soldiers? "Please God, let them be home," he pleaded, forgetting that he had not spoken to God in a long time.

The door opened a crack. Kurt could see his aunt's face. "*Tante Frieda!*"

"Kurt! Is that you!" The door opened wide enough for her to yank him inside.

"*Ach du lieber!* What are you doing here?" she said. "Don't you know how dangerous it is? You look like a fright."

She locked the door behind him and wedged a chair against the handle. Once again, Kurt told his story, while Frieda listened wide-eyed. "We will get you home tomorrow. Your poor mother." She set down a plate of potatoes and a glass of tea in front of him. "You must be so hungry. I'm sorry we don't have much else."

Kurt lit into the potatoes with gusto. "Oh, and we have a new sister. Her name is Heidi."

"A sister? When did this happen?" asked Frieda.

"Oh, in an old house at the side of the road." Kurt said, his mouth full of potato. "We had to stop and hide from the Russians. Then Mom had the baby. I had to keep the other kids quiet," he stated quite matter-of-factly, as if it were an everyday occurrence.

"Little Anna and I were sick, we couldn't get away in time," said Frieda. "We will try to leave when things calm down."

The Russian-dominated Polish government has been encouraged to make enormous and wrongful inroads upon Germany, and mass expulsions of millions of Germans on a scale grievous and undreamed of are now taking place.

— Winston Churchill "Iron Curtain Speech" March 1946

CHAPTER 39

LIESEL AND THE CHILDREN WALKED FOR A WEEK WITH other refugees. When darkness fell and they could walk no longer they took shelter wherever they could. Occasionally someone would take pity on the displaced and offer a piece of bread or a hayloft to sleep in, but mostly, the Poles wanted nothing to do with them.

The women were skittish. At the slightest sound of a truck or the sighting of people in the distance that might be soldiers, they would grab their children and run for the nearest grove of trees or a ditch. Liesel did not have the energy to follow each time. She just hoped the soldiers would have compassion on a new baby and its mother. She kept Heidi close to her body, tied in a blanket for warmth, untying her only for feeding.

They came up to a large farmhouse. The front gate swung open in the wind. "You have a new baby, surely you won't be turned away," said one of the other refugees, nominating Liesel to inquire about food and lodging. No-one answered her knock, so she opened the door.

The kitchen table was set with four places. A jug of milk and an almost empty jar of jam sat in the middle. On each plate was a spoonful of jam and slice of bread.

"Hello?" Liesel called out. "Is anyone home?" She picked up the milk jug and sniffed. No sour smell. It was obvious they too had left in haste, perhaps even that very morning.

Liesel beckoned the other women and children inside.

The children looked longingly at the bread and jam. "Go ahead," she said, though she could not have ever imagined doing such a thing as coming into a stranger's house uninvited and helping yourself to food. It wasn't the kind of thing she wanted to teach her children.

"Why don't you go upstairs and rest with the baby," said one of the other women. "I will watch your children."

"Thank you," said Liesel and went upstairs. She tiptoed from room to room, afraid she might come upon the rightful occupants and be sent away in disgrace.

The largest bedroom was the most inviting. The bed had been made immaculately with a fluffy eiderdown and large pillows.

Liesel took off her shoes and sat down, sinking into the comfortable softness. She arranged the pillow behind her and unbuttoned her blouse to feed Heidi.

Except for Johann, she had always had sufficient milk for each of the children, but not this time. Her breasts did not feel full at all and she had not had a chance to recover from the birth.

In the past, her mother had tenderly cared for her and the latest family member, so that she, the new mother, could rest. That was as it should be, thought Liesel. This terror, women and children running for their lives from soldiers and guns was madness. She questioned if Heidi would make it until they could get home or if she would die too, like tiny Johann.

Tears rolled down her cheeks onto Heidi's downy hair as Liesel thought of her mother. It had been almost two weeks since she had left her behind. And Kurt? Where had he gotten to? It was almost too much to bear.

Exhausted, she slept, only waking once in the night to feed the baby. The next morning a woman brought her a cup of tea and a bowl of porridge. "We plan to go shortly," she said. "Your children have eaten and are ready too." The woman was about to leave the room, when they heard the door downstairs burst open.

"*Frauen.*" That word, when spoken by a Russian soldier only meant one thing. There was a clattering sound, a woman's voice and multiple footsteps on the stairs.

"Into the closets," Liesel heard the female voice, as small footsteps echoed in the hallway.

But the soldiers clomped up the stairs right behind them. "*Frauen. Komm.*" The male voices were loud and insistent.

"Under the bed," said Liesel. She scrambled in beside her companion, clutching tight to Heidi, willing her not to make a sound.

CHAPTER 40

TIME SEEMED TO STRETCH OUT. FIRST THERE WAS THE DREAD
of waiting and knowing they could not escape. Drawers and closet
doors slamming were followed by muffled shrieks and the sound of
thumping and creaking bedframes.

Liesel heard footsteps down the hall and then the men bashed into
the room where she had taken refuge. First the other woman, then
Liesel, who left Heidi sleeping under the bed, was dragged across the
floor. Liesel felt a knife blade against her neck and the rough stubble of
a beard. The man smelled like rancid sweat and wet wool.

"Please," Liesel pleaded, her heart pounding. "I've just had a baby."
But he did not care.

Several men came and left, thumping back down the stairs, leaving
their victims bruised and sobbing.

Afterward, Liesel lay curled up on the floor like a child. The other
woman moaned loudly. Liesel did not even know her name. Below
them chairs scuffed across the floor and bottles clanked. Male laughter

drifted up the stairs.

She wondered how they could laugh at what they had done. It was as if a Russian tank had gone right through her, rolling effortlessly over every obstacle in its path, crushing her inside and robbing her soul with violence.

She retrieved Heidi from under the bed and held her tightly, drawing comfort from her innocence.

When the men had drunk themselves into a stupor, the women crept away, determined to get back home to safety or at least to somewhere else. Liesel trod on, one foot in front of the other, clinging to her newborn, the children trailing along behind.

All of them except for Kurt.

At first she had been angry that he had left the group and was annoyed with herself for not keeping a closer eye on him, but anxiety and dread had taken over as she pondered the fate of a young boy in a war zone in the middle of the winter, with no food and no-one to help him.

As they passed through a village that appeared devoid of people, the sound of lowing and cowbells dispelled the silence. A mismatched herd of dozens of cows, and a few goats, rambled along followed by two women and a lone Russian soldier with a whip.

"Please," said Liesel to one of the women. "Some milk for my children."

"Hurry," said one young woman. "We are supposed to get them to the train station. Then he'll let us go," she gestured towards the soldier. "Mostly the milk just gets dumped anyway."

"Such a shame," said Liesel. She hated waste.

The soldier glanced over at them and Liesel cringed.

But then he turned away, as if pretending not to see her.

Later in the day another group of women and children pushing baby carriages and clutching meagre bundles trudged towards the little party. Blankets shrouded their pale faces mirroring the despair Liesel felt.

"Have you seen my son?" she asked. It was so pathetic, asking these suffering strangers to help her. "He is ten years old. We lost him on the way back."

An old woman carrying a toddler shook her head. "We are the only ones left from our village. Everyone else…" the woman's voice trailed off and she looked away.

"*Es tut mir sehr leid*." Liesel forced herself to acknowledge their sorrow as her own hopelessness grew. "If you see him, his name is Kurt. We are almost home now."

CHAPTER 41

THE OTHER REFUGEES HAD TURNED OFF TO THEIR OWN DES-
tinations and Liesel and her children were alone now.

The beech and pine forest that marked the edge of the village was familiar, but little else was the same. The bodies of two dead dogs and several sheep lay haphazardly around a neighbor's yard. A headless chicken hung from a nail on the barn door, its bloody feathers flapping lifelessly in the wind. What had once been another outbuilding was a smoldering heap of ashes.

Liesel wondered if Kristiana had made it home. Kristiana had not been in any state of mind for survival and Liesel felt guilty for not insisting they stay together.

The road was littered with debris and the smell of smoke hung thickly over everything. She motioned the children to walk quietly. It was the supper hour but only a few chimneys were smoking. She saw no-one but didn't want to be taken by surprise again by any stray soldiers or anyone else who might harm them.

Dragging one heavy foot after another they came to the gate of their house. Olaf set down Edeltraud, whom he had been piggybacking and opened the gate for them to walk through. Though they had left in a hurry, the house had been in reasonable order.

But now, pieces of furniture, books, and clothing lay discarded carelessly in the snow along the side yard. Chopped up pieces of beechwood and curved runners lay in an unruly mound, near the remains of the woodpile. The cradle that Ernst had made—reduced to a heap of kindling.

What had been the family's radio was now a pile of wood, twisted wire and broken tubes. Next to that lay Ernst's mandolin, broken in half.

Liesel shifted Heidi over to her other arm and stooped to pick up an oval picture frame. Dusting off the snow, she peered through broken glass at the smooth young faces of her parents. Wistfully, she removed the picture and put it in her pocket.

She handed Heidi to Olaf. "Hold her," she choked out the words in a whisper. "Keep the others here with you."

Liesel pushed open the front door, but it gave way suddenly and a woman brandishing what had been Liesel's broom stood in front of her.

"What are you doing here?" the woman asked, spitting the words out in Polish. Liesel was taken aback at the vindictiveness of this person who was apparently living in her own house.

"This is … my house."

"Well it isn't your house anymore, get out," the woman sneered.

"But, I have nowhere to go. I have small children." Liesel gestured to the side of the house, appealing to what she hoped was the woman's better nature.

Heidi began to cry, mewing weakly like a newborn kitten.

"You stupid Krauts. Reproducing like rabbits. Why would you give birth to a baby during a war?" The woman spoke as if children were a personal affront to her. "It should have been suffocated or thrown in the river."

Liesel hung her head, afraid she would burst into tears if she had to look at the woman.

"Well, what are you waiting for?" She flicked her hand as if to dismiss them. "Go." She tried to slam the door, but Liesel hung on, her boot just over the door sill.

"But please, my mother …"

"That old lady? She was dead when we got here. The Russian soldiers cremated her with the rest of them Nazis at the edge of the village." She pointed off in the direction of the forest. Liesel detected a slight softening.

"Go sleep in the barn, but don't bother us." She shut the door to Liesel's faint *"dziękuję"*. They could sleep in their own barn! The whole world had turned upside down. They laid down their bundles and rested in the hay loft. The animals were gone, but at least the barn was almost as they had left it. Perhaps Wande had been in the herd they had seen earlier. Obviously the Russians hadn't wasted any time in reassigning their home and stealing all their animals, Liesel thought. She remembered how many Poles had been rousted from their homes at the beginning of the war and "resettled" east and how her own brother-in-law had taken one of their homes. She had never seen Ernst so angry as when he told her.

Vengeance should not be surprising, she supposed, but that still didn't make it right, especially since she had not been part of the any of the decisions.

The next morning as soon as she had nursed Heidi back to sleep, she opened the battered suitcase. It was so cold, they were wearing almost all their clothes. All there was left to eat, was the remains of the sack of rye she had salvaged. Only edible if cooked or soaked in water. She climbed down from the loft and spied the milk pail hanging from its nail, right where they had left it.

No-one was in the yard and it was barely light. At the side of the house she scrounged through a pile of refuse and found a few tin cans. She walked over to the pump and began to work it, hoping that the noise wouldn't wake her inhospitable hosts. She rinsed the tins and filled the bucket with water, then added the grain to soak. That would have to suffice as breakfast for now.

She thought about what other food was available. In the grain barn, she found the pile of potatoes layered with straw as she had left it. There were the oats they used to feed the horses and a large bin full of turnips for the cows.

Returning to the barn she noted that the stalls were smelly; the animals must have been there until recently. Olaf and Rudy had begun to stir.

"Boys, get up. You need to muck out the stalls."

"Can't we have something to eat?"

"When you've done the job."

"It's too cold, Mutti." Rudy, curled up closer to his sleeping sister. Liesel frowned at him.

"No complaining. *Schnell!*" she replied sternly. She was not going to tolerate any complaining or disobedience. Strict discipline had always been important, but now, it was essential. And she would have to be the most disciplined of all.

Olaf began the job without enthusiasm, but when he saw Liesel putting the grain to soak in the bucket, he picked up the pace, pitching the old hay into a pile out the door.

Rudy came down the ladder from the loft.

A young man strode into the barn. "Mother told me about you filthy Germans. I am surprised she let you stay."

Liesel brushed the hay off her skirt and hair and stood up straight. She had gained resolve in the night and would not be pushed around by these people who had taken over what rightfully belonged to her. "My boys and I will work for food. We know the farm."

"These boys? Hmmph. They are scrawny babies," he said, squeezing Olaf's arm.

Liesel couldn't argue the fact that they had been underfed the past weeks.

"They can work. Come planting time, you will appreciate our help," she said.

At that moment she noticed a movement through the barn door. A boy with a bulky bundle over his shoulders came down the front path. His jacket was too small and his bare arms stuck out. A dark cap was pulled down over his hair and ears.

Liesel's heart jumped. "Wait," she said, striding out the door across the yard to greet her oldest son. She wrapped his thin frame in her arms, "Kurt! We thought you were gone."

"I'm fine. I walked to Łódź."

"To Łódź? By yourself? You should have stayed with us." She was angry and relieved all at once.

"Can I have some breakfast?"

She led him to the barn where the others stood looking on. Ignoring the eager questions of Olaf and Rudy to their brother, she turned to the youth she had been speaking to.

With a hand on Kurt's shoulder she said, "This one can work very hard."

"There are too many. You stay and work, but they cannot stay here. They will just get into trouble."

For the next few days, they worked. Liesel set her boys to doing anything and everything she could possibly think of, hoping they could stay together but within a few days another Polish farmer came around.

"I'll take that one," he said, pointing to Kurt.

CHAPTER 42
ERNST

THE ORDEAL OF THE FORMER *WEHRMACHT* SOLDIERS BEGAN with a forced march from the ruined village where they had been taken, back to Kiev. Some dropped quickly from cold and hunger. Others were shot trying to escape. At night they sheltered in barns and empty factories on cold dirt or cement floors without beds or blankets.

When they reached Kiev, its citizens watched as thousands of prisoners marched in columns, behind trucks mounted with loudspeakers and Soviet flags. Guards on horseback guarded the flanks of the bizarre parade, but it did not stop men, faint from hunger and exhaustion, from collapsing in the street.

Every bone in Ernst's ankles pressed painfully onto the fallen arches of his foot. Each step was agony, but he knew that to stop marching, to fall over, was certain death.

He did not understand the Russian words coming through the loudspeaker, but all around them crowds of people decried the Germans, their shouts of anger and derision needing no translation.

After this humiliation, the captives were taken to an old jail that Ernst thought must have dated from the time of Ivan the Terrible. The only light came from a small window facing an adjoining building. Water dripped down the walls and pooled by their feet.

Several men slept in the cramped cell, with only a thin layer of straw on the floor. Nights were marked by clanging of doors and loud voices.

One night the cell door opened and two Russian guards took Ernst to a windowless room. "Take off your shirt and lift your left arm," said one of the guards.

The other shone a flashlight under Ernst's arm, up near the armpit. "I don't see it. Do you?" Ernst knew they were looking for the small blood group tattoo that Günther had shown him once. All members of the SS had them.

"So you are not elite SS?"

"No."

"But you fight against Soviet army, yes?"

"Yes, but I don't fight, I deliver supplies," said Ernst. "Just a supply runner."

Ernst didn't see the hit from the rifle butt until he felt it at the side of his head.

"You will only answer question I ask."

More questions followed. They wanted to know the name of his village and the year he was born in.

"Your wife. What is her name?"

"Liesel." Ernst wondered now if somehow they would go after her.

"Your children. How old are they?"

Ernst said nothing. He wouldn't turn his family in.

His silence was followed by a blow to his jaw. Hour after hour they interrogated and beat him. When the tormentors had finally finished, they led him stumbling back to his cell.

Most of the others were gone.

Ernst collapsed onto the straw, holding his bloodied and throbbing head. Eventually he slept, and woke only when he heard the cell door slam again. Two guards holding an unconscious youth between them, entered the cell, dropping him unceremoniously on the floor.

Ernst dozed off again.

The young soldier came to, his moans for his mother intersecting with Ernst's own dreams of home and family.

A few weeks later, they were marched out again in the night to waiting boxcars.

The train inched through the vastness of Russia. Every few days a bucket of water and crusts of bread or pieces of salted fish were passed up to the prisoners.

But it was not enough. The men licked the frost off the boxcars.

Only the cold held back the smell of death.

After a week, the train stopped. The doors opened. The guards used a metal rake to pull out the bodies the captives had pushed to the door. After they had completed this grisly task, they returned to the boxcar.

"*Udyi!*" they called and motioned the men to get out.

With stiff and trembling limbs, Ernst climbed down from the boxcar, squinting his eyes at the daylight. In the distance, a collection of log huts marked a remote village. Peasants, bearing baskets of bread and sausage, walked toward the train, regarding the men curiously.

Ernst approached a woman in a heavy skirt and embroidered coat. She held out a small loaf of bread and smiled, revealing crooked and missing teeth. He still had a little money in his pocket, so he gave her a few rubles and tucked the bread under his coat.

Before the hungry men had completed all their purchases, the guard was calling them and hitting them with the butt of his rifle, motioning them onto another train on a different set of tracks. "Hurry up, onto the train."

On board , Ernst pulled off a piece of the loaf and tasted it. It was soft and delicious, not like the army rations, or the bread that had been distributed to them. He watched through the slats as the peasants and their food receded into the distance.

As the train rolled slowly east, the spring rains fell and leaked into the boxcar. Dampness became the new enemy and diarrhea was rampant, raising the stench and the death toll.

The train, with its decimated, weary load of men came to the last of many stops.

Nestled in the foothills of a mountain range, several crude wooden huts were encircled by a wood and wire fence. The huts stood on level sandy land, but almost all around the camp was thick bog. Bare and stunted trees grew grotesquely out of stagnant pools.

"Is this Siberia?" a young soldier asked.

"It could be the far side of the moon for all I know," answered another.

The guard chose three men. "You dig holes." He pointed to an area at the perimeter of the property, between the huts and the fence.

"Where are the shovels?" said one of the prisoners.

The guard shrugged. "You want shovel? You make shovel." He pointed to a pile of wood scraps. The men each selected a piece of wood and began to dig.

Other men were assigned to a kitchen hut and directed to peel potatoes.

A guard led Ernst and another group of men into one of the huts. Narrow bare bunks devoid of any bedding or mattresses save one blanket each, were stacked three high against the log walls. A small stove in the corner did not look adequate to heat the room. Wind whistled through the cracks and chinks in the wall.

"You fix," said their guard, pointing to a disarray of tools on a bench. "You get clay from the river."

Ernst looked over the tools. A broken butter knife. A crudely carved stick and a rag with what looked like caked-on mud. He picked up a wooden bowl. "I guess we better get started if we want to stay warm tonight."

"What, now we have to work for the Reds?" one man complained.

"I guess the alternatives aren't that great. I'm not going back on that train," said another captive.

When they ran out of clay, they were let out of the fenced enclosure, under a guard's supervision, but the supposed river was more like a slough and the clay was just mud. Ernst scooped some into the bowl.

"Even if there were no guards, I don't think we could escape," said one of the prisoners, pulling his boot out of thick mud and looking at the mountains in the distance.

"Well I'm not going to try," said Ernst, nodding towards the guard with his gun slung over his shoulder.

Returning to the barracks, the men started work.

Ernst used a stick to paste mud between two of the logs which made up the walls of the hut. After a while, he concluded that once he had the mud on the walls, it was easiest to spread it with his own hands, especially since tools of any kind were in short supply.

"We are almost finished," said Ernst a few days later. Soon they had worked their way through the huts, fortified only by potato soup. He thought the huts would be quite comfortable now, at least in comparison to the cramped boxcars they had come on.

"Does this qualify us as apprentice masons?" said one of the men.

"There was a mason on the train."

"Yes," said another man, "but the Soviets don't seem to be interested in the skills people bring with them."

"Let me guess, they sent him to the kitchen."

"Latrine duty, actually," said a younger man, wiping off the tin butter knife he had been using to spread the clay.

The next day the camp Kommandant came in. "You are being moved."

"But we just fixed this up," the men protested. "Where are you moving us to?"

The guard shrugged. "I have my orders. You must follow."

They were taken again by train to a larger camp, where they joined other prisoners.

"Take off your clothes and put here," said a Russian guard. Ernst joined a long line of naked men, awaiting a brief medical examination. A white-coated doctor felt his buttocks with a firm pinch and assigned him to stand with a group of men in similar condition.

"They are determining our fitness for labour," said one of the other men.

"Quiet!" said the guard.

Judging from the larger, slightly less emaciated men he was grouped with, Ernst was sure he had been chosen for full labour, whatever that would be. Apparently his flat-footed infirmity wasn't going to get him easier duty as it had in the German army.

He wasn't sure what was worse, the scarcity of the food or the quality. Breakfast was thin gruel with pieces of barley, like treasured pearls on the bottom. He saved the dark, tasteless bread ration for the noon meal, at work, when he could stave off his hunger that long. If he didn't wait to eat it, the evening soup of water and potatoes was all he could think of all afternoon. Maybe there would be some fish bones in the soup if they were fortunate.

But the evening soup was often too salty.

Over the next months, many of the men's extremities swelled. First their ankles, then their thighs became grossly distorted. When the swelling reached the belly, they would often die. 'The water sickness', they called it.

Salty or not, that soup was what Ernst was thinking of as he swung a dull axe methodically against a tree. He had been assigned to logging trees for use as railway ties.

But the guard wasn't looking at the moment and Ernst stooped to pick some mushrooms growing at the edge of the marsh. Maybe he could slip them into his soup, adding both nutrition and flavour. He was startled by a thwack and a crack; the sound of splintering wood.

"*Confound es nochmal*," said Ulli, a man who bunked next to Ernst. "My axe handle is broken."

"And mine is dull," said Ernst. He took a piece of broken crockery out of his pocket and buffed the edge of the blade with it.

"Why don't they give us proper tools to work with?" Ulli asked. Many of the prisoners had asked this over and again. If the Russians wanted this work done, the proper tools surely would have helped, but such requests were always met with a shrug and a re-iteration of their quota of logs per day.

If the quota wasn't fulfilled, they didn't get paid the few rubles that might be enough to purchase some small item from the canteen, like a bar of soap or a handful of millet if it was available. In the summer, a tiny basket of wild berries or some onions could be had, but the prices were premium, enough rubles for 2 weeks wages. Or, if you could manage to sneak away from work detail long enough, you could pick them yourself as Ernst had done a few times when the guard was distracted.

On the rare occasions they exceeded the quota, they were given extra bread rations. But as time wore on and they became weaker, it was almost impossible to do more than required.

"Let me see your axe handle," said Ernst.

Ulli shrugged and handed the broken implement to him.

Ernst examined the axe. "Maybe I can fix it for you."

With his own axe he split off a piece of a wood roughly the size of an axe handle. From his pocket he took out a crude knife that he had fashioned from a piece of tin. He whittled the end of the piece of wood until it almost fit the axe head. He dipped it into a puddle to swell the wood and then jammed it into place with the blunt end of his own axe. "There you go," said Ernst as he handed it back to Ulli. "A German-engineered axe head."

"The tradesman is superior here," said Ulli, with admiration. "My university studies in economics did not prepare me for this life."

"No-one could be prepared for this life," said Ernst.

Ulli positioned himself to strike the next tree. "I do, however, understand the futility of the enforced communist and collective system, unlike our Russians comrades." With this remark he nodded almost imperceptibly towards the guard who was leaning against a tree, smoking a cigarette.

As if on cue, the guard looked their way. "Get back to work you lazy Krauts."

Ernst smacked at a mosquito that had been sucking the flesh of his hand and swung the axe again. The blazing heat of the summer was almost as miserable as the cold they had arrived in and the relentless bugs added to the misery of constant hunger. All of the men who worked outside had red swellings on every exposed bit of skin.

Back at the barracks he pulled the handful of mushrooms out of his pocket and placed them on a handkerchief. Since he was on the top bunk, he reasoned they could dry without someone taking them.

But the next day, when he returned from work, there were only rat droppings.

Between capitalist and communist society there lies the period of the revolutionary transformation of the one into the other.

— Karl Marx in "Kritique of the Gotha Programme"

CHAPTER 43
LIESEL

EVENING SHADOWS ENGULFED EDELTRAUD AND RUDY, curled up in the corner of the loft, with Kaspar purring between them. Olaf slept on two bales pushed together next to his brother and sister.

Liesel leaned against a wooden crate nursing Heidi. It was still a slow process, but Heidi felt a little heavier than when she was born. Maybe if Liesel was able to acquire a bottle, she could give the child a little cow's milk, if she could somehow get it.

As Liesel's head drooped over the sleeping infant, she heard voices outside. She set Heidi down and opened the hay door a crack.

"Over there," said the son of their new landlord whom she now knew as Alphonz. He pointed towards the grain barn. Earlier in the day, Liesel had noticed him carrying lumber through the large doors. The other man had what appeared to be a barrel on the wheelbarrow and Alphonz held a large sack that clinked as he walked.

Bottles and a still, thought Liesel pursing her lips in anger. Her family had avoided strong drink, but for the most special occasions, and now these intruders were going to be cooking it up on her farm. But she was in no position to do anything about it, so she closed the door and lay down next to Heidi.

The snow melted, the days lengthened, and around the yard green shoots poked up through the ground.

At the garden fence, Liesel selected a leaf and chewed it thoughtfully. Like a sour lemon, the *Sauerrampfer* refreshed her taste buds, and memories of soups and salads she had made awoke her hunger again. She spent the morning gathering a basket of greens. Some she would present to Jadwiga for soup, but Liesel would make sure her own children got their share to supplement the turnips, potatoes and horses oats they had been eating.

Alphonz was busy too, she observed. The man she had seen from the loft was back and she had noticed the pile of potatoes in the grain barn getting smaller. Alphonz handed him a large sack, which he placed in a wagon. "There's more," he said, directing the man to the grain barn, where he retrieved a few large jars.

A few weeks later two Russian officers marched into the yard and began yelling at Alfonz. She thought this would be directed to his illicit activities, but she heard one of the men yell, "Where are those Nazi partisans you are hiding?"

"I don't know what you're talking about," he said. "There are no partisans here."

If they were referring to her, Liesel was relieved that he was not going to turn them in so easily. To his advantage, she thought cynically. He knows he would have no time for bootlegging if he had to run the farm. She opened the hay door a crack and listened.

"You are lying," the man continued. "We have reports of Hitler youth collecting weapons and sabotaging Soviet forces."

Liesel was neither a Nazi nor a partisan, but her reluctant hosts could stand to get in trouble if the Russians thought they were harbouring partisans. She would probably have to leave soon, but she had no idea where to go. The war was not yet over and travel anywhere was a risk.

She pondered what had happened to Frieda. Had she made it into safer territory? Ernst's mother and sister had likely fled their village too and she didn't even know if Emil had made it back from the battlefront to Breslau.

As the soldiers strode toward the barn, Liesel was thankful she had sent Edeltraud and Olaf to pick mushrooms. It was only Heidi and Rudy, up in the loft, she had to worry about.

She ran to the ladder and hoisted herself quickly up its narrow rungs, "*Schnell*, Rudy, the hay pile." She grabbed their bedding and clothes and threw it all under a bale of hay. She picked up Heidi and they hid in the large pile of loose hay just as the soldiers entered the barn. She could hear as one of them began to climb the ladder.

A mightly fortress is our God ... The song of the Reformation rang through her mind. "Father save us," she prayed. The soldier's boots pounded loudly across the wooden floor, in rhythm to Liesel's pounding heart but she was unsure of another sound. Not a footstep, but a walking stick or ... the pitchfork! She wrapped one hand around Heidi's mouth and clamped the other firmly over Rudy's just before the pitchfork pierced the hay with a thump a few centimetres away. "*Gott im Himmel*," she pleaded silently.

"No-one here. Let's go," said one man to the other. The pitchfork clattered to the floor and Liesel heard their boots clumping down the ladder.

It was a long while before she felt safe enough to leave the haystack.

A few days later she was on her hands and knees scrubbing the kitchen floor as Jadwiga had requested.

Jadwiga sat at the table drinking tea. The door swung open abruptly and a man dressed in a uniform with a red armband stood in front of Jadwiga. "Aha, so you are harbouring partisans," he said. He pulled out a gun and pointed it in Liesel's direction. "You will come with us," he commanded.

"I haven't done anything," said Liesel. She shook her head. "I don't know any partisans." She was just trying to survive, feed her family, keep the roof over their heads. How could she make them understand? The man had her by the arm and was hauling her out to the yard where a truck waited. "But my children," she looked towards the barn. "There is no one to look after them."

"We will bring you back in a few hours," said the man, who she now discerned to be a Polish communist.

Olaf came around the side of the house with a load of firewood. "Mutti? Where are you going?" He dropped the wood and ran towards her, but the soldiers pushed Liesel onto the truck. "Look after Heidi," she called after Olaf. "Ask Jadwiga for milk and oat broth. Give it to her every few hours."

Several other people were already on the truck. "Do you know where they are taking us?"

"No," said another woman, "but I'm sure this will all be cleared up soon."

"They think I was some big shot, because I was in the Hitler Youth," said a boy, who looked to be about fifteen.

They were taken to the police station and led down into the cellar. Liesel was pushed into a cell, its lone occupant, a young woman. She wore loose trousers, with suspenders hanging around her waist. Her hair was stringy and one cheek bore a large purple bruise. She sat on a bench in one corner; in the other corner was a smelly bucket.

"Why are you here?" asked Liesel.

"They think I am a werewolf; a Nazi involved in sabotage," she said, wiping her eyes with her sleeve. "I was in the German Girl's league and they didn't teach us anything about sabotage, only how to be a good mother to more soldiers."

Late in the evening a guard came to the cell and took Liesel.

Good, she thought, I can explain and then they will take me home.

She was seated on a wooden chair in front of the Kommandant.

"Frau Hoffmann, I'm sure we can clear up this little matter." He smiled, his blue eyes crinkling in the corners. Liesel felt confident. She hadn't done anything, she just needed to explain.

"Have a seat."

"Lieutenant Grabowski, some more coffee," he said, handing his cup to the other man.

The Russians and the Poles are working together now, thought Liesel. It didn't leave her in a very good position.

"So where is your husband then?" he said to Liesel.

"He was taken prisoner during the war. I haven't seen or heard of him in almost a year."

"I see," said the Kommandant. "And what were the nature of his crimes?"

"Crimes?" she queried. "He was just a supply runner. Not a combat soldier." She thought it was important they understood that he hadn't killed anyone, but she didn't volunteer the fact that he'd been in Russia. She added, "He was drafted into the *Wehrmacht*. He didn't have a choice."

"And where is he now?" the Kommandant narrowed his eyes.

"I don't know exactly." She shrugged and looked down. "Somewhere in the east."

"We know all about you and your spying activities. Your husband has been feeding you information, hasn't he?" His voice had taken on an accusatory tone.

"No," insisted Liesel. "I haven't heard anything from him." What did they think she had done? Did they know where Ernst was?

The lieutenant brought in a tray with the Kommandant's coffee. The Kommandant closed his eyes and sniffed the steaming beverage. "Ahh."

The aroma wafted toward Liesel. She could not remember the last time she had tasted or smelled real coffee. But her stomach was in a tight knot. Even though she'd had nothing to eat or drink for hours, she could not have swallowed a thing.

Setting the cup down on the table he spoke smoothly, as if to a small child, "Frau Hoffmann, all you have to do is confess. Your husband is a Nazi pig, involved in partisan activity."

Liesel shook her head. In another circumstance, she would have laughed at this ludicrous statement. "No, that is not true at all."

He pounded his fist on the desk. The coffee cup rattled. "Your husband is a partisan, is he not?"

"My husband is not a partisan. All I know is he was taken prisoner last year."

The Kommandant stood up. He was a large and imposing man.

"I can see we are wasting our time here." He shouted down the hall. "Lieutenant." Instantly the other man appeared and escorted Liesel back to her cell. He opened the door. "I guess you'll have a chance to think some more in here."

Liesel could not sleep that night. She had not been provided with a blanket and the bench was cold and hard. The lights were left on all night.

All she could think of was her children that she had left behind. If they kept her here, Heidi would surely starve.

She spoke to her cellmate. "I explained, but they think I am guilty of something!"

"It doesn't matter if you're guilty or not," said the girl. "They will make your life miserable. Whatever you do, don't sign anything."

The next morning they were brought tin mugs of water and a piece of stale bread each. Shortly after, Lieutenant Grabowski came to unlock the cell. "You," he pointed to Liesel.

Maybe this time they would let her go. Once again she was brought for interrogation, but this time it was in a windowless room. They sat her down and tied her wrists together behind the chair.

"You are accused of harbouring partisans. Sign this confession and you can go." It seemed a tempting offer, but the girl had said not to sign it. Besides, her hands were tied behind her. He thrust the paper in front of her and she puzzled over the unfamiliar script.

"But I cannot read it," she said. "It is in Russian. Can you translate it for me?"

"Sign it," he said.

"But what does it say?"

"That you have been involved in illegal counter-revolutionary activities. We know what you have been up to. Your neighbors have confessed. You too can go home after you have signed this paper."

Liesel had no reason to trust what they were saying. "I don't know what you are talking about."

"Do you realize the penalty for false testimony?" His voice was louder, more edgy. "Perhaps now you will confess."

Liesel reeled in shock. She took a quiet deep breath to steady her voice and keep herself from crying. Maybe they thought the young men brewing vodka on the farm were partisans. Surely they couldn't be mistaking those boys for partisans. Anyone could have easily figured out what they were up to, but mentioning them might make her situation worse.

"I told you I don't know any partisans."

He stood up again and untied her wrists. Would he send her back to the cell?

He spoke softly again. "Frau Hoffmann, my patience is wearing thin. Sign this confession." He dipped the pen in the inkwell and handed it to her with the sheet of paper.

"I will not."

He leaned forward and struck her across the face. She could not stop the hot stinging tears, but sat silently before him.

"Why are you staying in that house?"

"That is ... was my home."

"Why do you not live with your husband?"

She could not keep the impatience out of her own voice. "I told you: he is a prisoner of war."

He slapped her again. "You will speak respectfully. I am the Kommandant."

For several hours this continued, until Liesel was exhausted.

When at last the guard led her back to the cell, her hand flew to her mouth in shock and horror. The bucket that had been used as a toilet had been moved and upended, its foul contents spilled over the cracked cement floor. The body of the young woman swayed from suspenders tied to the light fixture above.

"I see your comrade has taken the easy way out. Maybe she can give you some advice tonight."

He left her by herself with the corpse.

Liesel curled up on the bench as small as she could against the wall and cried silently. What had she done to deserve this and what could she do to get out? The truth didn't seem to have any meaning to these men. Should she just do what the girl had done?

Heidi would probably die anyway and there was no future that she could see for her children here. Ernst was just a distant memory and probably now in Siberia, which to her was the outer edges of the world. He could not save her.

Desperate thoughts and prayers swirled in her mind all night long. But her moral sensibilities eventually won out. Taking her own life was wrong; a cowardly way out.

In the morning, a guard came and removed the girl's body. Liesel was handed a threadbare mop and a bucket of cold water.

"Clean this stinking mess," he said.

Late in the day, the cell door clanged open and two more women were brought in.

The older woman's face was worn with lines and her back was stooped. Both women looked as bewildered as Liesel felt.

"Why have you been arrested?" whispered Liesel.

"My husband is accused of being a Nazi, except he has been dead for ten years," the older woman said. "And my son-in-law is accused of hiding weapons and ammunition."

The younger woman added, "He was wounded so badly in the war, he will never walk again. And those filthy Russian soldiers took over our house, smashed the furniture to bits, and stole almost everything."

"It is of no use to reason with them," Liesel said. "They seem determined to terrorize us." She didn't mention the previous cellmate. "I have a newborn baby; I had to leave the nine year old in charge of her."

"So terrible for you," said the younger woman. "Surely they will realize there is some mistake and release us." Liesel recognized that same false confidence she had felt a few days ago.

"Maybe they will," said Liesel. She rubbed her wrist where the skin was raw from being tied to the chair and turned to the wall hoping for sleep.

She hoped the women were right.

CHAPTER 44

IN THE MIDDLE OF THE NIGHT SHE WAS TAKEN FROM HER cell again and tried to explain herself. This time it was to the Polish Lieutenant Grabowski. She spoke clearly with measured words. "My husband is away. I don't know any partisans. I have small children, please let me go."

The light appeared to splinter in front of her as he struck her brow.

"Frau Hoffmann, sign the paper, then you can go." He said exactly what the Kommandant had said the day before.

But now Liesel was numb, worn down. It had been two nights away from her children and she needed to get back. She accepted the pen. "You will let me go?"

"Of course," he said smiling.

She scratched out her signature on the bottom of the page, praying God would forgive her for her false confession.

"There," she said meekly.

She was escorted back to her cell by a different guard. "But the lieutenant said I could go."

"Tomorrow," said the guard.

Late the next morning Grabowski came to the cell. "Frau Hoffmann, you are being discharged. See, we keep our word."

She was a free woman, but for how long she wondered.

When she arrived back home, Rudy came running out to the gate so fast he almost tripped. "Mutti! You are back! I've missed you so much." He threw his arms around her.

"I missed you too." She let go reluctantly and led him to the barn.

"Why is your face all purple?" he asked. "And your hair has a white patch in front."

She had not seen herself in a mirror and had no idea of her appearance. She had no desire to think of those terrifying nights, never mind tell her children what had happened to her. "I have a white patch in my hair? Ach!" she patted her head. "So I look like a striped badger then?"

"No, you don't look like a badger," he tipped his head up at her. "You still look like Mutti." He cocked his head and looked at her closely, "Except for your eye that is half-shut."

"Come then," she took his hand. "I want to see how Heidi is." She tried to keep her voice light and not betray her fear.

"Oh and we heard a noise this morning," said Rudy. "Guess what it was?"

Liesel was desperate to find out how Heidi was doing and didn't have patience for a guessing game. "What was it?"

"Lufti came back."

"Oh," said Liesel, but all she could think of was Heidi. The nanny goat's apparent escape from the Red army was of no consequence.

In the loft, Edeltraud had been keeping vigil with her tiny sister, a spoon and tin can discarded at her side. The blanket was tangled around the baby's feet and the faint smell of urine drifted up. They were perilously close to the hay door. "I carried her to the window, so she could look out," Edeltraud said,

"*Liebchen*, you should not carry Heidi by yourself." said Liesel. But all the rules had changed. Young children taking care of babies without their mother to help. Babies not getting nourishment from their mothers. People living in barns instead of houses.

It was no effort at all to pick up little Heidi. Her tiny limbs dangled as if she was a rag doll. Her eyes were closed and her head leaned listlessly to one side. Red cracked lips stood out from the pale sunken face. Unresponsive icy fingers met Liesel's grasp.

Liesel shuddered and knelt to the floor.

In the most difficult of circumstances she had carried this child, through food shortages and back-breaking work, followed by a traumatic birth in an abandoned house, surrounded by the noise of bombs and tanks roaring outside. She wondered if it was all for nothing.

Shaking, she untangled the blanket and placed her hand on the baby's chest. It rose and fell in short puffs.

Olaf scrambled up the ladder. "I'm sorry, Mutti." He was almost in tears. "We tried to feed her some porridge, but she kept choking on the spoon. Pani Jadwiga wouldn't help us. She kept complaining that we weren't working hard enough and there was not enough food to go around." He knelt down beside her. "Is she going to be all right?"

Liesel shook her head. "I don't know." She sat down on a hay bale and unbuttoned her blouse, making no attempt to shield herself from the children's eyes. She offered the infant a flaccid breast, but Heidi was so weak, she did not have the strength to suck. Liesel switched the child to the other side but the results were the same.

Suddenly she remembered the goat. "Olaf, try milking Lufti …"

He came back in a few minutes with a little milk in a tin can. "That's all I could get right now."

"*Gut.* Try again in a little while," she instructed him.

She handed the baby to Rudy. Rummaging around her suitcase, she found a clean handkerchief, twisted the end, and pinched it between her thumb and fingers. She dipped it into the tin and let the handkerchief absorb a little of the milk. She placed this at Heidi's parched lips.

Slowly the baby explored this substitute nipple, choking with her attempts to swallow.

Liesel cooked potatoes and added the water to stretch out the milk and give it some starchiness and for every hour that night, she woke and repeated the feeding procedure.

Early in the morning, she woke Olaf. "Feed her like this every hour. More milk or soup broth, even water if that's all you can get." Loathe to place this on his shoulders, she continued. "You are the oldest and this is the most important thing right now."

"But what about my chores? *Pani* will be angry."

Heat rose up into Liesel's face. "Jadwiga," Liesel did not include the polite preface afforded all Polish adults, "should—"

Summoning all her upbringing and better judgment, she stopped herself from saying words of condemnation about another human being, however intense her hatred was becoming.

"Tell Rudy he must do your chores while you take care of Heidi. I plan to be back by this afternoon."

"Where are you going?"

"Łódź." She didn't want to give the children any false hope for the sister who might die before their eyes. "Jadwiga does not know I came back so don't tell her I have returned," she cautioned.

CHAPTER 45

FROM HER SUITCASE, LIESEL CHOSE A DRAB SCARF AND tugged the gray patch of hair out in front in hopes she would look too old to be of interest to any lecherous soldiers. A skirt and blouse that was only slightly rumpled completed the ensemble. If she looked too much like a gypsy vagabond, they might arrest her again.

It made her think of the Gypsy Roma, who had sometimes camped by the forest before the war with their painted caravans; colourful houses on wheels. Enticing lively music, like the smoke from their fires had wafted up from their bivouac. Women with dark skin and billowing skirts gleaned the fields while their men sought odd jobs. Once, Ernst had let a Gypsy man pick fruit for them. Liesel could still see his wavy black locks and a bright smile crinkling his weathered face, when they handed him a basket of apples and pears for payment.

But then, a boy was caught stealing a chicken from a neighbor and the Gypsies were pelted with rocks and chased out of the village, with cries of 'Schmutzige Zigeuner', dirty Gypsy, echoing behind them.

Liesel had never really considered their plight before. A life of wandering, with nowhere to go; followed everywhere with distrust and hatred. She had assumed they deserved the treatment they got because of the way they lived.

But they were all gone now; she hadn't seen any gypsies for years. Like the Jews in Łódź and the surrounding villages, the Gyspies had disappeared from the countryside. Perhaps they were in hiding or swept up in Hitler's campaigns. Only their faded, broken wagons abandoned at the edges of the villages testified to their existence.

Liesel shut the gate behind her and walked out of the village before sunrise, keenly aware of danger. Whenever she saw anyone else, she hid in the ditch or behind some trees.

Now, she realized, she was just like a Gypsy. No longer a citizen of the ruling class, a prosperous and respected German wife reaping the benefits of generations of toil before her on their own land, she was now an outcast, her children forced to beg for bread and steal milk.

In Łódź, she searched up and down the streets for shops that were open and might carry a baby bottle.

She remembered her frustration at not being able to save Johann and her suppressed anger towards her mother-in-law for suggesting bottle-feeding. She reasoned now that the woman was only trying to help and she wished she had kept the bottle, instead of giving it to Frieda.

Łódź had not been destroyed like Warsaw, but it was eerie to see the once bustling city centre almost empty. A few people walked quickly to their destinations, disappearing into homes and offices. She turned onto Piotrkowska street. On the building edifices, cherubic carved angels gazed out of archways at gargoyles and dragons guarding darkened windows.

She paused at a door below a gold and green sign, heralding the post office.

It would not yield her a bottle, but she didn't know when she could next get her mail. Perhaps Ernst had written.

A typewritten placard on the door read; *All male Germans between the ages of 16 and 50 must report, within 48 hours to the Labor Conscription*

Office with two sets of winter clothing, cooking utensils and food.

At least that did not apply to her right now. Still her anonymity would be compromised and she would be late getting back. If there was any news of Ernst or anyone, she didn't want to miss it.

She could see there were no other customers. Adjusting the scarf around her chin, she thrust it slightly upward and went inside. In her best Polish she greeted the postmistress, *"Djien Dobre."* Not too friendly, just be polite, she thought.

Liesel's greeting was met with a stony glare.

She stared right back, unblinking. Then she remembered her black eye. Of course people would stare. "Hoffmann," she said, cutting off any chance of being asked questions. She hoped her German name wouldn't prevent her from receiving her mail.

The woman behind the counter narrowed her eyes slightly, then retreated to the back of the room, returning with a box big enough for two loaves of bread. Carelessly, she dropped it on the counter with a thump and pushed a card towards Liesel. "Sign here."

The box was considerably lighter than she had imagined a box that size should be. She slid the parcel further down the counter, away from the prying eyes of the postmistress.

The Canadian postage stamps on the box bore the benevolent portrait of King George the VI. She ran a finger over the embossed image of his regal face. Impassive, she read only a hint of resignation in the set of his jaw. Monarch of the British and Canadian Allies; a sworn enemy of the Third Reich. He had given up a quiet private life because of his errant brother. Circumstances beyond his own control had compelled the duty placed before him, but he had accepted his fate to reign as King.

Under Josephine's address, the box was ripped. Inside, Liesel found a package of sweet biscuits, a small bag of rice and two tins. One was marked "Spam" and had a picture of some meat. The other tin was marked 'Klim.' She didn't know what that was, but underneath was a white band with the words 'milk powder.' *Milch.* She hoped it would not be too late.

Tucked inside was a letter from Josephine.

> *Dearest sister,*
>
> *We are all well. The children are growing taller all the time and I am always having to make clothes and buy new shoes. I have enclosed a pair that Heinrich has recently outgrown in hopes they will fit one of your boys.*

That is what is missing. Liesel thought with disdain of the person who had stolen them out of a package addressed to her. Olaf could certainly have used new shoes. She read on,

> *we have experienced rationing and shortages here, but I am guessing things over there must be worse so I am sending some food in hopes it may ease the burden for you, especially with Ernst gone.*

There was no time to read the rest, but Liesel went back to the counter and purchased two postcards. On one she scribbled a note to Josephine.

> *Dear Josephine,*
>
> *I cannot thank you enough for your thoughtfulness. While I do not wish to burden you with our situation, I beg of you, if you are able, please send more, especially milk powder. I have a baby girl. Her name is Heidi, after our dearest mother, whom I regret to inform has departed this world for the next, after her long illness. I am anxiously awaiting Ernst's return.*
>
> *All my love to you. Liesel*

She addressed a second postcard to Ernst, in hopes that his regiment number and name might be enough for him to receive it.

With her parcel in hand, she hurried down the cobblestone streets. An apothecary around the corner yielded the bottle she was looking for and she rushed home.

By the time she reached the countryside, she was faint with hunger, so she allowed herself one biscuit. Just one. She nibbled at it as she walked, allowing the sweetness of this manna from heaven to dissolve in her mouth.

Before she arrived home she had eaten half the package.

CHAPTER 46

ON THE EIGHTH OF MAY, LIESEL WAS SWEEPING THE FLOOR in the house when she thought she heard a crackling voice, like on a radio.

She crept down the hall to what had been her bedroom. The door was ajar and Jadwiga sat on the bed with what appeared to be a miniature radio. As far as Liesel knew, the Soviets had confiscated and destroyed all the radios. "Yesterday, Wehrmacht representatives signed the act of unconditional surrender for Germany. The treaty will be ratified later today in Berlin and hostilities will officially cease one minute after midnight."

So she wouldn't be caught eavesdropping and to avoid any threats Jadwiga might make, Liesel knocked on the door. She heard a click and some shuffling.

"What do you want?" Jadwiga called out, her voice even more annoyed than usual.

Liesel tried to keep her voice even, masking her relief over what she had just heard. "Just letting you know, I'm done the floors, I'm going out to do the weeding now."

She picked up Heidi from the parlor floor and took her outside. For a four month old, she was still much too light, but at least she was alive. When she was clearly out of Jadwiga's earshot, she lifted her infant daughter into the air. "The war is over, Heidi; there is hope for all of us."

She kissed the child's fuzzy hair and went to find the boys.

"The war is over," she told them.

Rudy announced the news to his sister. "Edel, the war is over now!"

"What is war?" she asked.

"You know, all the fighting and everything."

"Does that mean we can live in the house again?" asked Edeltraud.

"Will father come back soon?" asked Olaf.

"So many questions," said Liesel. "I don't know when Vati will come home. I don't even know exactly where he is, but they should let him out soon."

What difference it would make to their situation she did not know. The world leaders may have decided the war was over, but the Soviets were entrenched in their occupation of Poland and intent on subjugating anyone remotely accused of any sort of resistance activity, real or imagined.

Liesel anticipated the upcoming harvest. Much of the land lay fallow; only a fraction was being used for agriculture during this chaotic time. Seed and fertilizer were in short supply and the laborers were mostly women and children. Even so, she reasoned they should soon be able to enjoy some of the fruits of their labour.

At the end of June, Liesel and Edeltraud sat on the front step shelling the peas that they had picked that morning. Heidi slept in a basket by the stairs.

The smell of each pod reminded Liesel of spring and the pleasantness of the routine task almost made her forget her circumstance at this moment. Except that the peas weren't for her.

She took off her frayed sweater and let the sunshine warm her bare arms.

"Mutti, look a worm!" said Edeltraud, holding open a pod. "Ewww."

"*Guten Appetit*. Just pop it in your mouth, but don't tell Jadwiga." Liesel winked conspiratorially. Jadwiga had been a little more generous of late, but Liesel thought it was because she didn't know what would happen now the war was over.

Edeltraud wrinkled her nose. She picked out the wormy pea, threw it in the grass and brought the rest of the pod up to her mouth, sliding the peas out with her teeth and chewing them.

"You can eat the pod too." Liesel grasped the stringy end and peeled it off. She wasn't going to waste one thing. "Maybe she'll let us have all the pods." Like the prodigal son in the Bible story who was so destitute he wanted to eat the pods that were for the animals, she thought.

"But I want more peas," Edeltraud pouted.

"You can have more when we are done shelling them."

A truck rumbled up to the front of the house and a stout woman wearing a uniform got out and came through the gate. Liesel stiffened and set down the bowl of peas.

Oh no. She had thought that maybe they would be safe for now, that she could sit out in the open and enjoy the sunshine and the growing things.

"*Mutti?*" said Edeltraud, looking over at Liesel.

The woman from the truck walked over to them. "I am from the Ministry of State Security," she said in Polish. "You will be needed for the collective rye harvest. Your children will be put into foster care."

Did that mean they would be fed? Liesel wondered. With a start she realized she would be willing to give up her children if she knew they would be fed properly. She was weary of trying to do the impossible.

As if in answer to her unspoken question, the woman said, "Your children will be schooled. They will receive hot breakfast, bread, and hearty soup each day. They will be taught the virtues of hard work." The words were like a recitation that had been repeated many times.

Liesel bit her tongue. She was tempted to tell the woman that her children already knew plenty about working, more than young children should know, but instead she said, "They are hard workers, they can work here with me." But her resolve was weak against the officialdom of this uninvited state officer. Liesel wanted her children with her, but more than anything she wanted them to be fed and grow like children should.

"Gather their things, say your goodbyes. You have five minutes," said the woman looking at her wristwatch.

"But when will I see them?" Liesel had come to realize she wasn't being given any choice in this matter.

"We will make arrangements for you to see them after harvest."

Only a month or two, thought Liesel. And they will be fed. She repeated this to herself, hoping it was true. But just in case, she turned away from the woman's view and put a handful of peas into the pocket of Edeltraud's sweater. Heidi began to cry.

"Mutti? Do I have to go with that lady?" Edeltraud whimpered, pointing to the offending stranger and clinging to Liesel's skirt.

"Don't point," said Liesel. "It's rude."

Liesel nodded to the woman. There was no sense in fighting this new system. "I will get their clothes."

Back in the barn, she stuffed an empty potato sack with clothing and diapers and filled the bottle with some milk powder and water.

"You will get food to eat. Lots of food," Liesel said to Edeltraud. She had convinced herself it was true. Surely they wouldn't starve innocent children. "It's just until after harvest, then I will come for you."

"I don't want to go. I want to stay here with you."

"I know." Liesel hugged her daughter tight, smoothing down Edeltraud's hair, tightening a braid. Edeltraud pressed against her chest, where Liesel's heart beat quickly. "But there will be other children to play with. Maybe they will have school and you will learn to read."

Even as she said it, she wondered what kind of education the communists might provide. Probably not in line with her views on family and religion she surmised.

She kissed her daughter on each cheek. The woman official lifted

Edeltraud onto the back of the truck, but she began to scream. "Nooo. I don't want to go." She slid down off the open tail gate jumped onto the ground. The woman picked her up more forcefully this time and set her down again on the truck. Taking Heidi from Liesel, she placed her on Edeltraud's lap. Both the girls were screaming now.

The woman slammed the truck gate closed.

Rudy and Olaf came running from the pasture. "Where are they going?" Olaf asked as the truck pulled away, with the cries of the girls echoing down the road.

Liesel turned away, as she couldn't bear to look anymore. She tried to breath, but air would not fill her lungs.

She turned to the boys and rasped out. "*Łódź Kindersheim*. We will see them again after harvest."

But she didn't really believe it.

A few weeks later she stood over the washboard on the back porch, her arms up to her elbows in tepid dirty water. What little soap there had been had long since dissolved in the filth of the work clothes she had washed.

She hung up Jadwiga and Alphonz's items first. It would not take long for them to dry in this heat. Only a few weeks ago, she had been washing diapers, nightshirts, and Edeltraud's one extra dress. Now there were only the boys' pants and shirts and her own clothes. Everything was going threadbare. Since the ground had been barely warm enough the boys had gone barefoot, because their shoes were almost completely worn through.

The window opened and Jadwiga called out, "Listen!" She didn't seem to care as much about hiding the radio from Liesel anymore.

Through the static a voice blared, "As a result of the conference at Potsdam, millions of Germans are to be repatriated to the German territories. The Polish government will be assisting in the transfer of Germans …"

Liesel wondered what it all meant. Repatriated? Didn't that mean you went back to where you were from? But she was born here and had never known another home. How would Ernst ever find her if they went to Germany? Could they ever come home again?

When the announcement was over, Jadwiga poked her head out the window again. Her voice was taunting. "So you dirty Germans will not be staying here for long then!" Liesel hung up her blouse on the line and stood behind it, where Jadwiga could not see her. She could not stand to hear that woman gloat about how the Poles were the victors and now she would have the house.

Of course Jadwiga would have a good dose of humility if Liesel were to leave. Where else would the woman get three labourers for the paltry price of a bowl of soup and a crust of bread.

CHAPTER 47
KURT

OPENING ONE EYE SLOWLY, KURT GLARED AT THE BATTERED clock next to his lumpy bed. In the dim light from the attic window, he could see that it was five o'clock in the morning. He hadn't been allowed to go to bed until late the night before.

Bits of straw poked through the ticking and one thin blanket wasn't enough for the drafty attic room he had been assigned.

Rubbing his eyes he pulled the blanket closer, wishing for his warm featherbed and his brothers who had shared it with him. He felt guilty about all the times he had teased them and how he had ignored Edeltraud. He wondered about Heidi. He could barely picture her, since he had only seen her a few days.

Reluctantly, he got up and climbed down the ladder into the house.

Pani Plozchinsky stood at the stove stirring a pot of thin porridge. She dished out a few spoonfuls for her aged mother-in-law and a similar amount for Kurt. Two substantially fuller bowls were for herself and her husband.

Kurt sat down at the table and looked in his bowl. It wasn't enough. At age 11 he was developing an appetite that could never be satiated on porridge and potatoes.

He thought back to before he had gone to the KLV camp. Even during the war his family had food to eat and he had a warm bed to sleep in. It seemed like so long ago.

While Pani Plozchinsky's back was turned the old *babke* at the table scooped a spoonful of porridge from her own bowl and transferred it to Kurt. She winked at him and Kurt flashed a quick smile in return.

She reminded him of his own grandma. He missed her. Most of all he missed his mother. She worked so hard for all of them, cooking the food, making their clothes and teaching them how to do chores around the farm.

But he had not been very co-operative. Thinking of the times he had not done what he was told, there was always some punishment, swift and sure. He remembered a cold night spent in the barn looking after Wande, when he hadn't milked her.

Another time, he had foolishly tripped Olaf, who was carrying a basket full of eggs. Olaf had fallen and the eggs had rolled out, breaking all over the ground. Kurt had gotten a spanking for that and he supposed he deserved it. What he wouldn't give to eat one of those eggs now!

Maybe he even deserved to be separated from them. If he hadn't gone the wrong way, they would still be living in their own house, instead of that Polish woman. Perhaps it was his fault that the rest of his family was living in a barn. He should have been looking after them, but instead he was working for someone else. He regretted not listening to his mother and determined that when he got back, he would try extra hard to be good and helpful. More like Olaf.

Pan Plozchinsky staggered into the room. His hair was uncombed and his shirt buttoned up crooked. A few days' growth of gray stubble cast a shadow on his face and the odor of alcohol and vomit wafted into the room as he sat down.

Kurt wrinkled his nose.

"What are you frowning at, boy?" Plozchinsky snarled. "Get out and get to work. That is all you Germans are good for."

Pani Plozchinsky added, "I need water. There is wood to chop. Hurry up or the stove will go out, and I need to make bread."

Shovelling the rest of the porridge into his mouth and gulping down a glass of water, Kurt hurried. He did not want to be on the wrong side of old man Plozchinsky.

He ran out the back door and off to the woods pulling a small wagon behind him.

As soon as he was out of view of the house, where Plozchinsky couldn't see him, Kurt slowed his pace slightly. He passed the pond and a grove of pine trees.

Only a few more fields, and another grove of trees, lay between him and his own home.

He tugged the wagon over the uneven ground and the long grass on the other side of the forest. In the fields several people, mostly women, swung scythes back and forth, cutting a swath through the amber field.

His parents had taught him that he should never disturb the grain or carelessly trample the fields, but he was hungry and the ripe field beckoned. The harvesters were still a ways off and Kurt reasoned that if he just took a few heads of the ripe rye, he could put them in his pocket to chew later.

He picked up a few sticks and put them in the wagon. He glanced again at the field. As far as he could tell no-one had seen him.

He reached out. The heads were sharp and rough against his hands. With one hand he held the stalk and with the other he pulled off the heads and stuck them in his pockets.

In the shade of a storage shed at the end of the field, he removed the husks from several kernels and put them in his mouth, despite the fact they were almost hard as rock.

He spied around the edge of the shed. The harvesters were working their way toward him. A colourful headscarf one woman wore caught his eye. A hefty woman wearing trousers came from the other direction down the path towards the harvesters.

Kurt took cover behind the shed, hoping the overseer woman wouldn't see him.

"This is not good enough," she yelled at the workers. "You are all a bunch of fat lazy *kulaks*. You must work faster."

Kurt peeked around the corner again. The woman grabbed a heavy scythe from a slightly-built girl who didn't look much older than Kurt.

He thought the woman overseer was a fat ... whatever she said. And the rest of the harvesters didn't look overweight to Kurt either; in fact, most of them were skinny, as if they were not getting enough to eat, like him.

"Like this," the overseer swung the scythe in demonstration. "*Schnell*—like Frau Hoffmann," she said, pointing towards the woman with the headscarf that Kurt had noticed earlier.

His heart skipped a beat. It was his mother and she was only a few metres away.

When the overseer finally left, Kurt stepped out from his hiding place, over to the path.

Liesel leaned against her scythe and adjusted her headscarf, revealing a gray patch of hair. Under the heavy work apron Kurt could see the dress she wore. It was one that she used to wear on Sundays, but now it was torn and frayed and hung on her like a sack. Before, she would have ripped it up to make a rag rug or a patchwork quilt.

He had always thought of his mother as strong, but now she seemed fragile, as if she needed someone to protect her.

"*Mutter*." He whispered, so as not to alert the other harvesters to his presence.

Liesel looked over at him and gasped. "Kurt, what are you doing here?"

"I was collecting some wood."

"Where are you staying? Are they kind to you?"

He pointed over past the trees. "The second house past the pond." He didn't know how to answer the other question. He thought of Plozchinsky, who was either drinking, shouting, or passed out on the floor. And of Pani Plozchinsky who was always telling Kurt what to do, but never giving him enough to eat.

"They are all right, I guess," he shrugged. "I have to work all day, but there is usually some cabbage soup when I am done." He looked down at his dirty bare feet. "When can I come back?"

"I don't know. Soon, I hope." With the back of her hand, Liesel touched his face.

Her hand felt warm and rough. He so wanted to be with her, to be comforted by her, but he couldn't tell her how he felt. He was too old for that stuff.

"When they let us go, I will come for you," she said.

"I have to get back," he said, heading for the wagon. It was worth it seeing his mother, but he was going to be late.

Suddenly he remembered Pani's orders that morning. Water! He'd forgotten to draw the water and by now they would know.

With the wagon clattering along behind him, he ran back all the way.

When he got there, Plozchinsky stumbled down the back steps. "You lazy Kraut! I had to get the water," he bellowed. He let forth a stream of Polish curse words, some of which Kurt did not understand, then pulled his belt loose.

Kurt stood shaking behind the wagon. "Come here, you little dog." Plozchinsky folded the belt in half and went towards the left of the wagon. Kurt ran nimbly to the right and galloped up the steps, into the house.

As he was hoping, old *babke* was sitting at the table drinking tea. He ran in and stood behind her just as the red-faced Plozchinsky came lumbering in. The air was thick with his curses.

"*Pani Kochany!* Listen, to me son," said the old grandma. "You harass this boy too much, you drunken devil. Leave him alone."

Authorized representatives of the People's Commissariat of Internal Affairs of the USSR ... are...ordered to arrest anyone hostile to advancing Red Army troops who have liberated territory from the enemy...spies, saboteurs and terrorists of the German secret services; members of any German organizations and enemy intelligence to carry out subversive work behind the Red Army;

— L. Berjia, Soviet State Security Administrator

CHAPTER 48
LIESEL

THE HARVESTERS MADE THEIR WAY DOWN EACH ROW, FELL-ing the rye, as grasshoppers and the odd field mouse escaped ahead of them. Chaff rose like dust in the heat, coating their skin and clothing.

"We are almost finished," said a woman working a row away from Liesel.

"Yes," said Liesel. "Maybe the rations will be increased."

"Don't we all wish!" said the woman, brushing the chaff from her apron.

But they both knew that not all the fields had been planted. The men had been off at war too long, the women working the factories and farms.

The other harvester voiced the dread in Liesel's mind. "I hope I'm wrong about this, but I think they will find a way to make sure us Germans don't eat."

"Stop talking and work," yelled the overseer, cracking her whip into the air.

Liesel fell back into the rhythm, scything up the row. Swing, step, swish. There was only the present rhythm of work, eating and sleeping, dreaming of eating and more work.

At home, she stepped into the barn, welcoming its shade. Sweat dripped from her brow and her shoulders ached from swinging the scythe. Her feet and hips were sore from standing all day.

She looked at her raw, blistered hands.

Maybe the work would be worth it. Even if none of the harvest went to her family, she could still glean afterward for whatever was left. She would work quickly and bring home some grain and roast it or boil it for the boys. If she had time she could grind it into flour for bread, but of course Jadwiga would claim more than half of it.

She filled a jar of water at the pump and sat down to drink it. She had been surprised to see Kurt, but glad that he was still close by. If only there were somewhere she could go to have them all together, but the local communist appointed "Mayor" was in charge now. She had to stay put and do as she was told or she might be interrogated again.

Rudy came into the barn. He had not been wearing a shirt and his shoulders were sunburned. His ribs looked like a washboard.

"Mutti," said Rudy. "There is a truck here and a Polish man who says you have to come."

"Come where?" Liesel muttered, gulping down the rest of her water. She did not want to see any more trucks with uniformed people stepping out of them telling her what to do and taking her away.

"Liesel Hoffmann, by order of the Ministry of State Security, you are being arrested for crimes against the state."

"What crimes? I haven't done anything but work."

"We have a signed confession."

"I was forced to sign that. I couldn't even read it!" she protested.

"You must come with me. We are taking you to a detention camp." He grabbed her by the arm.

"But my children!" She argued with the official for quite some time. "I must have them with me," insisted Liesel.

"My orders are for adults," said the official. "Your children will be placed into state care."

Rudy stood watching.

She had already lost Edeltraud, Heidi and Kurt. What was the use of staying alive through all this, if she was without her children. What if Ernst returned to find that all his offspring had perished or were lost.

She had not heard anything about her girls. She had written a quick letter to themat the *Kindersheim,*, but she had no idea whether they would get it. At any rate, Edeltraud couldn't read yet.

From the back of the truck she heard a voice in her defence. "Let her bring the children."

Olaf came running across the yard. "Where are you going?"

"Hurry," said Liesel, "Grab Rudy and climb in."

The official appeared to realize he had lost and went to the cab.

"Where are they taking us?" asked Olaf.

"I don't know, but we have to do what they say." Liesel shook her head. Dozens of people sat on suitcases, clutching bags and bundles. She scanned the group for Kurt, but he was not among them. At each stop along the bumpy road, she hoped to see him, but he did not get on.

At the train station on the outskirts of Łódź, they were let off to a cacophony of voices barking orders in Polish and German. Children were bawling, women wailing in hopelessness and confusion.

Craning her neck over the people in front of her, Liesel tried to find her oldest son, but she did not see him. A guard filled up one car with people, but the last woman on protested that her mother needed help getting on the train. For her cries, she was beaten with a stick and pushed onto the train while the older woman hobbled over to join the line getting on the next car.

Liesel held tight to Rudy and Olaf's hands as they were all shoved onto a cattle car. It was chaos. No benches or seats, only a plank floor and far too many bodies for so little space. They wouldn't be able to sit down anyway.

With its live cargo sprawled and propped against the slat walls, the train plodded through the night, its rhythmic motion eventually sending some of its uncomfortable passengers to sleep.

Liesel woke to the pressure of a full bladder and was forced to use the only toilet available: a crude hole cut in the corner of the car. When she returned to her spot by the door the boys were awake.

"I'm thirsty," said Rudy.

"I know," answered Liesel. She ruffled his hair under her hand, but she had nothing to give him.

As the second day wore on, the boxcar became stuffy and hot. The smell of sweat, urine and feces hung thick in the still air. Liesel's dress clung to her and sweat poured off the brows of the boys.

Rudy whimpered for a drink again. "Shh, don't cry," said Liesel, wiping his face with the back of her hand. "You'll lose more water through your tears." She didn't know, but it was the best motherly wisdom she could think of. Rudy frowned at this new idea and with a smudged finger wiped a tear from his cheek and licked it.

An old woman next to them fainted. Her husband patted her cheeks as he held her head on his lap. "Does anyone have any water?" he called out.

From the back wall a man called out in reply. "If we did, we would drink it, you fool!"

Others soon fell to the heat and lack of water, but no-one else asked for water from their fellow travellers.

The sun no longer shone through the wooden slats when the train came to a stop. The door opened just enough for a guard to hand a bucket of water and two loaves of bread to Liesel. He grabbed her arm.

"This is for everyone in your car," he said.

"But it is not enough!" Liesel protested, but he had already closed the door on the stifling compartment.

The train started up again. Water sloshed out of the bucket onto her dress.

She passed the bucket to the man whose wife had fainted. "Be careful, there isn't much."

He took the dipper and placed it against her lips, but the old woman did not respond.

With glistening eyes he looked up. "I think she's gone," he said softly, placing a handkerchief over her face. "God rest her soul."

"There was nothing you could do," said Liesel, placing a hand on the man's shoulder.

The bucket of water was passed around the car, but when it returned to Liesel, there was only a mouthful left for her and the boys. Rudy began to whine. Olaf's lower lip trembled.

Liesel clutched the two loaves of bread as if they were babies. This time she had to make sure her children got something. She tried to think as the passengers pushed against her and called out, their voices indignant and desperate. "You cannot keep that for yourself!"

"I want some," said a youth in the corner.

"I haven't eaten since yesterday."

"Let the poor woman feed her children first."

"Children? They are no good to us. We should just eat them." This comment was from the same man who had told the others he had no water.

"Hold on!" said Liesel. In her loudest most commanding voice she called out to her fellow travellers. "*Warten Sie bitte*! I will divide it up!" She felt a slight relief of the tension in the crowded space. "Everyone will get some." She hoped her words would reassure them and they would stop crowding around.

She tried to count the people and estimated more than 40 hungry people in a small space and only two loaves of bread. She handed one of the loaves to Rudy and began to break the other loaf. "We will do it by family groups," she announced decisively, with much more confidence than she felt.

From the farthest corner each called out how many were in their family. Most were groups of two or three women, a few children, less men. She broke off pieces of bread, estimating how much would be needed by each family.

As people bit into the bread, they quickly realized it was barely worth waiting for.

"It's moldy," said a well-dressed woman. "They gave us moldy bread."

"I think it's made of sawdust," said an old man.

At the pace of a wagon, being dragged by an old nag, the train rolled through the countryside. Occasionally it stopped and food or water would be distributed, but some days went by with nothing. Other passengers died and they had to carry the bodies to the front to be unloaded the next time the train stopped. More people got on.

Olaf peered through the wooden slats. "There are trees. We are going through the woods." The shade and breeze were a welcome relief to the summer heat.

"Where are they taking us?" said Rudy, lifting his head from Liesel's lap. "Are we going to the sea?" He had never been there, but once before Rudy was born, the family had travelled by train up to the Baltic sea.

"Of course not," said Olaf. Though he had been, he was too young to have remembered anything. "I don't think it will be anywhere nice."

Liesel decided to steer the conversation back to that vacation. She recalled with fondness the special trip they had taken with the two oldest boys before the war. That train trip had been nothing like this one.

Tow-headed Olaf with his chubby legs was just learning to walk and had tried to wriggle from Ernst's strong grasp as they boarded the train. They had just put down their luggage, when three-year-old Kurt escaped out the door of their compartment. Liesel remembered his mischievous grin and charming dimples as he laughed and ran down the corridor. He was almost to the next car when Liesel had caught up with him.

"Olaf, you are too young to remember, but you had so much fun," she said, recalling the days spent on the sandy beach. "Kurt had a pail he was filling with sand and you kept putting your little hand in and trying to eat the sand." She paused, a lump in her throat, wondering what had become of Kurt and the girls.

The train squealed to a stop.

"Where are we and when are they going to let us out?" said Olaf.

"I'm so thirsty," said Rudy.

For hours nothing happened and the occupants became anxious

when no-one opened the doors. Time lingered and the light coming through the slats dimmed.

"What are they waiting for?"

"This is worse than the war!"

"At least we had food and could go outside!"

Exhausted, the travellers fell asleep. It was then, in the dark of night that the doors finally opened and the captives were led out.

The guards separated them, marching the men off to one building, the women and children to another where they were told to form lines.

"*Frauen hier,*" directed a guard with his hands. "*Kinder hier.*"

One mother tried to keep hold of her small child, but the guard grabbed the little one roughly by the arm, ignoring the child's frantic cries as he insisted. "Children here."

The line was long, snaking outside the door, and Liesel was faint with hunger and thirst. She had no idea what they were waiting for, but it soon became clear when she entered the large receiving room. The women at the front of the line were leaving the room naked and bald.

She cringed, but when it was her turn, she obediently pulled out the clips that held her hair in place.

Thick wavy hair escaped and cascaded down her shoulders.

To prevent the spread of lice, she told herself, as the razor buzzed around her ears. She recalled Ernst running his fingers through her hair on their wedding night. He had made her feel so beautiful, but now she felt shame and sorrow as the heavy locks fell, like pieces of herself, to the floor.

After stripping down, she threw her clothes onto a large pile. Looking over to where the children had lined up, she watched Rudy and Olaf disappear through another door.

An overwhelming sense of loss came over her. Everything and everyone was gone. Her husband, home, her mother, her children and now her hair. She felt a deadness inside, as if there was nothing left at all of who she was.

CHAPTER 49

EACH WOMAN WAS ASSIGNED A NARROW BUNK. A *KAPO*, A leader from each barracks, was responsible for the women under her. Like most of the inmates she was a German, but in return for special privileges or for some warped sense of power, she made the lives of those under her miserable.

At roll call the women stood in the pouring rain. Today, for some reason the prisoners did not know, they were made to put their arms up over their heads. After about ten minutes, Liesel's arms and shoulders ached so much they were shaking. Many of the women could not do it, so the *Kapo* came around with a baton and hit anyone whose arms did not stay up.

That night, before they went to bed, one young woman came in late. The Kapo pointed with her stick. "Squat on the floor." The young woman squatted, but started to teeter over after a few minutes. "Croak, like a frog," said the Kapo hitting her with the baton.

Liesel could not stand to watch. "Leave her alone. I think she has learned her lesson."

The Kapo turned on Liesel. "Shut up and mind your own business. I am in charge here."

"You are a German captive, like us," Liesel replied, her voice rising. "Why are you doing this?"

Before Liesel saw it coming, the baton swung across striking Liesel in the arm. She heard a crack followed by a collective gasp from the other women in the room.

Liesel sank to the floor clutching her arm.

The Kapo left the barracks.

The young woman who had been on the floor stood up. "*Blöde Kuh*," she muttered after the Kapo. "Are you all right?" she asked Liesel.

"I think my arm is broken."

The other women crowded around.

"I am a nurse," said a heavy-set woman with a lined face. "Let me see."

Liesel winced as the nurse felt her arm.

"There is a bump," said the nurse. "Probably fractured. With the force she used, I am not surprised." She went over to the woodpile by the stove and found a few straight sticks. "I need something to tie a splint," she said to no-one in particular. Another woman untied a sash from around her waist and handed it to the nurse.

She lifted Liesel's arm and placed it atop the sticks. "I heard she was in a woman's prison before the war you know." she told Liesel quietly. "Just a common criminal."

It was true, there were a few Nazi sympathizers and the odd criminal in the camp, but there had been no hearings and no trials. Most of the prisoners were civilians, people that had gone about their business during the war as best as they could, working, trying to feed their families, complying with the government that was in charge.

Liesel grimaced as the nurse set the bone. "But why do we all have to be lumped together?" she said. The nurse shrugged. "Perhaps in some way we are all guilty." She wrapped the sash expertly around Liesel's arm and tied the ends around her neck in a makeshift sling. "At least they seem to think so."

Liesel wished she hadn't bothered addressing the Kapo. It wasn't worth having a broken arm. She hadn't helped anyone and now she would be dependent on others.

The remainder of the summer wore on in monotony. Except for a few who were assigned kitchen duties there was nothing to do.

At least her arm had a chance to heal, she mused as she stared at her breakfast one morning. Weak black coffee, thin barley porridge and a piece of bread made with mysterious ingredients. Trying to guess what it was made of was one of the prisoners' few forms of entertainment.

"What do you suppose they put in here?" asked one woman.

"I sure don't know, but I'll bet there is very little flour."

"I think it's clay," said another. "I saw the dough in the kitchen hut the other day. Look." She broke off a chunk of bread to show a small grayish lump. "It looks like clay."

"And it tastes like clay," broke in the first woman.

"Yesterday was definitely potato peelings."

"That is why it was the colour of dirt."

"The dirt disguises the bugs in the dough."

"I heard there was a factory where they made flour out of sawdust."

"Well whatever is in there, it gives me the runs."

Almost everyone attested to that. Diarrhea was a problem and there was no help for it. A few cases of typhus were rumored, spread by the close quarters, the lice, and filth.

It started with a headache and then a fever. Soon the victim would be moaning in her bed, delirious and nonsensical. As soon as anyone showed symptoms, the nurse would do her best to isolate the person, but she had no medicine or hope to give.

Only a few people returned from the infirmary alive. The dead were hoisted onto a wagon and taken away.

The concentration camps were not dismantled, but rather taken over by the new owners. Mostly they are run by Polish militia. ... prisoners who are not starved or whipped to death are made to stand, night after night, in cold water up to their necks, until they perish. In Breslau there are cellars from which, day and night, the screams of victims can be heard.

— R.W.F. Bashford Confidential report filed with the Foreign Office

CHAPTER 50

"OH!" LIESEL'S BUNKMATE POINTED AT A LARGE MOUSE RUNning across the floor. "Disgusting rodents."

"I wonder what he found to eat," said Liesel, picking up the broom, which was just a bundle of twigs and straw fastened together with some string. Fine sand and dust blew into the barracks constantly. Bugs and spiders found homes in every cranny of the barracks.

Liese swept vigorously, determined to rid the floor of any filth the mouse had found or created.

Another woman sat on her bunk in the far corner, quietly turning the pages of a small book. When Liesel came closer she could see it was a Bible.

The woman looked up and saw Liesel looking at her. "Would you like to read?" she asked.

"*Die Bibel*?" There were only two other books in the barracks, both in tatters. Liesel had not dared to ask to borrow them. Her own books had been abandoned in their winter flight and were no doubt ruined by now.

"Yes." The woman nodded and smiled.

Liesel replied enthusiastically, "*Ja*, later, when I am finished." The woman closed the Bible and wrapped it in a handkerchief, handing it to Liesel. "Please take care of it."

"Why do you want to read the Bible?" Liesel's bunkmate asked. "It is a book of fairy tales." She pulled a nit from her scalp and squished it between her fingers. "How can there be a God when we are living like this? Like animals."

Liesel put the Bible under her blanket. "Because," she said. "It is the only place to find any hope around here."

She took the doormat outside and shook it. She looked down the long row of barracks across to the far end where the children were housed. She glanced around to make sure the Kapo wasn't watching. She wanted to stay clear of that stick and the woman's irrational vendettas.

In their compound, the children had been let out to play in a fenced area. Some boys rolled an old bicycle wheel through the dirt, trying to see how far they could make it go before it fell over. After a few moments they tired of this activity and sat down against the barrack wall.

Liesel thought it was much too hot for them to be outside without one tree for shade.

Seeing Rudy and Olaf among them, she approached the fence and waved.

"Hello *Mutti*,"said Rudy.

"We saw Kurt," said Olaf.

"Where?" asked Liesel. She hadn't seen him since that day in the field.

"He walked by with some of the men on their way to working. They are in a different section of the camp." Olaf pointed over to a row of barracks far beyond theirs.

"Was he all right?" asked Liesel.

"We couldn't talk to him. He just waved at us," said Olaf.

"At least he is in the same place as we are and we'll be able to find him when this is over."

"When will that be?" asked Olaf.

"I don't know," said Liesel. Truthfully she wondered if it would ever be over.

"Can we come stay with you? said Rudy.

"It's not allowed," said Liesel, feeling the need to change the conversation to something positive.

"What did you have for breakfast?" she asked, hoping it was more than she'd gotten.

"Just barley porridge." said Rudy. "It wasn't very good."

"I guess they don't know how to cook here," said Liesel brightly. Or, they knew how to cook and purposely made the food bad, either not salty enough or too salty.

"Maybe you could teach them!" said Rudy. Liesel did not know how to respond to his optimism without crushing him. Any *Dummkopf* would know how much salt to put in the porridge.

"The soup has wormy peas in it," added Olaf. "I don't like it."

Liesel put her hand in her pocket and felt her bread ration. She broke off two crusty pieces and reaching through the fence placed it in their hands. "I wish there was more. I wish it was better. Sometime they will let us out and then we'll grow lots of food!"

"I want to grow pickles!" said Rudy. "Lots of pickles."

"Silly," said Olaf. "You can't grow pickles. Mutti makes them out of cucumbers."

"Cucumbers then, and some beans," said Rudy, his brown eyes lighting up.

"What else?" said Liesel, said continuing the little game.

"I want tomatoes. Those little ones that taste so sweet," said Rudy. "Maybe some yellow ones too."

"How about you Olaf," asked Liesel, trying to draw her quieter son into the game. "What do you want in our garden?"

"Potatoes. Piles and piles of potatoes with no black spots. And I want gobs of butter with them and sour cream too. As much as I want, big trucks full," he gestured with his arms. "But no peas. I don't ever want to eat peas ever again."

She thought of her fragrant sweet peas, the lilacs, and rosebushes that she had once tended with loving care, as if they too were children. Trimming, mulching, washing off the aphids. Sometimes she would cut a bouquet for the table, but mostly she left them outside where everyone could see the joy of her labour. People walking by would stop to remark on them. If Liesel was in the garden she would pluck a few blooms for neighbors passing by.

The dahlias would be blooming now. She had collected every variety she could find, yellow and red pom-poms and king-sized blossoms the colour of peaches. Even during the war, she had dug out the tubers so they would be safe from the frost, but it wasn't likely Jadwiga would bother with them.

The area in front of her that the children had to play in was barren of any greenery. Not a blade of grass or even a weed. And the rest of the camp was the same coarse sand. Nothing grew for long. If a prisoner spotted a weed that looked edible they would eat it. If a guard spotted a weed they would uproot it.

A woman wearing a pinafore came out of the door of the children's building. She pointed to the boys.

"*Jungens*! Inside," she called harshly.

Liesel tramped back across the sand to her own barrack.

If anyone had a notion to escape, the sand prevented them from running fast enough and footprints would bear witness to their trail. A woman had tried to escape the previous week, but she had got cut on the barbed wire, leaving a trail of blood. Within an hour they had her back and hanging on the gallows in the middle of the road that divided the barracks.

The next week the prisoners were taken out in trucks during the day to work the fields; hoeing, weeding carrots, and harvesting potatoes.

On her knees, Liesel dug out potatoes and put them in a crate, but she noticed the small ones would sometimes go through the slats and fall on the ground.

The Kapo was further down the row, examining the piles of weeds for any hidden food. Liesel bunched up a little of her skirt into the waistband and tucked a few of the tiniest potatoes between the skirt and her underwear.

She might be punished, but extra food was worth the risk.

The sun was hot and the work hard, but she preferred the work over staying at the camp with nothing to do but watch fights break out between women that were hungry and afraid.

Summer became fall, then one of the coldest winters Liesel could remember. Only the area around the stove was warm.

A heap of clothing was 'redistributed' to the barracks. The women gathered around trying to select items that were an appropriate size and suitable for winter, but there were not enough coats and hardly any hats or mittens. They had been brought to this prison camp at the end of summer and most of the people were taken from their homes or workplaces with little or no notice. Besides they had not expected to be here so long.

Liesel selected a bulky knit sweater with a wide collar and generous pockets. She wore it for a few days, but found her hands and head suffered the most from the cold.

She recalled the old bicycle wheel in the children's yard. The next time she visited the boys, she came away with two spokes, which she repurposed as knitting needles. Unravelling one of the pockets on the sweater she rolled the yarn into a ball and knit a pair of mittens. The collar was made into a wool cap to cover her ears.

Soon other women were taking interest in this craft and crowding around her bunk offering advice and requests for clothing. Many were looking through their belongings to see what they had that could be re-fashioned into something else. Knitting needles and crochet hooks were made from nails, wood from the kindling pile, anything they could find.

Women who didn't know how to knit or crochet offered Liesel all sorts of things they had either kept or somehow acquired under the scrutiny of the guards—hair clips, shoes, extra bread. Mostly, Liesel was happy to be kept busy and shrugged off their offers.

Gretchen, the young woman who had been humiliated by the Kapo, sat down and watched closely. "My mother died when I was a little girl," she said. "I never learned to sew or knit."

"I will show you," said Liesel and sat down next to her. "Don't hold the wool too tight." For several evenings she sat with Gretchen, holding a small ball of wool and helping her make stockings.

Gretchen learned quickly, but one evening roll call, Liesel noticed that her young friend was missing. After the room had descended into silence, she heard sounds from a building behind their barracks, crashing and screams.

Before dawn Gretchen stumbled into the barracks. She approached Liesel, shivering and wet. "It is because my father was in the SS," she whispered so as not to wake the others. "I had nothing to do with his activities, but they threw buckets of ice water at me."

Liesel's hand reached up to her shorn hair. The gray patch would probably always be there, reminding her of her own interrogation. Sometimes she had nightmares of the Kommandant's fists coming at her and his angry voice accusing her of things she did not do.

She wrapped Gretchen in a blanket, but there was nothing she could say or do without putting herself at risk.

In the morning she had a splitting headache and didn't get up for breakfast. Soon she noticed others moaning and groaning in the bunks next to her and a stench that permeated through her subconscious.

She wasn't sure how long she'd been lying there when someone said, "Too sick for work detail, we have to move you to the infirmary." That is where people go to die, thought Liesel as the nurse and another inmate carried her to the building that served as an isolation ward.

"Typhus," said the nurse. "I can't do anything without medicine." She held a cup of water to Liesel's parched lips.

Days went by. Someone from the barracks would slip in from time to time with a bowl of soup or piece of bread for those who were afflicted.

Gretchen brought Liesel soup. Liesel sat up and tried to eat it. Her vision blurred and she saw her sister Frieda holding a spoon to her mouth.

"Come on—a few more bites," said Gretchen.

But Liesel thought it was her mother with a spoonful of honey. She tried to swallow it, but couldn't stop coughing. "Forgive me *Mutti*," she cried. "I never wanted to leave you."

More sick people came into the infirmary. Several left, but mostly they were carried out to the death wagon.

Liesel's head pounded and red spots broke out all over her body.

Gretchen came in and placed a cold wet rag on Liesel's forehead, but Liesel tried to push it off. She sat up suddenly. "My girls. Where are they?"

"You are dreaming, Frau Hoffmann, your children are in the barracks." said Gretchen. "Just lie down."

"No, no," Liesel protested. "If I lie down she'll die."

"Who?" said Gretchen.

"My baby," said Liesel, slipping into unconsciousness.

CHAPTER 51
1946

"SHE SEEMS TO BE RESTING ALL RIGHT NOW," SAID THE nurse. "See how her breaths are deeper."

"I didn't think she was going to make it," said Gretchen.

At the sound of their voices, Liesel's eyes flickered open. *Who were they talking about?*

Her clothing was damp and she was hungry. Her mouth was so dry. "Water," she murmured.

Gretchen brought a mug of water.

"I think you will make it," said the nurse to Liesel

After Liesel's recovery she was sent out to work in a little shop some distance from the camp.

Michal, the man who ran the store, lived upstairs and didn't bother her in any way, unlike the guards at the camp who often acted on what appeared to be a personal crusade against the prisoners. Michal told her only what she needed to know, brief instructions to stock the shelves or what was available to make for their lunch.

Not that he really cared what he ate. The few times he had eaten in front of her, he indicated little or no interest in what was on the plate or in the bowl. He would thank her politely then go about his work or retire upstairs. Liesel responded by working quietly and efficiently. All the time, her mind was elsewhere; on her children, her husband, and when she would get out of prison labour and be together with her family.

One afternoon when there were no customers in the shop, Liesel sat down behind the counter to eat some soup. To her, it was a lovely soup. She had made it herself with ingredients Michal had provided. Lots of potatoes with cabbage, carrots and onions.

She heard Michal in the back room, talking on the telephone to one of the distributors.

"It is a small store. Well under the regulations … of course I am a loyal Party member, but I'm telling you the supply system is not working," he said.

Every day, he spent hours on the phone or at local farms, trying to get goods and produce to sell. Often the shop shelves were nearly empty and it was Liesel's job to assure people there would be something to buy another day. She did not enjoy all the irate people coming to the door on a regular basis, but she tried her best to be helpful. If they wanted bread and there was none, she would suggest potatoes or some flour to make their own bread, but ingredients for baking a loaf were scarce too.

Michal's voice rose slightly. "Of course, the workers must unite as we work towards collectivization, but in the meantime we must solve this problem. What we need is a steady supply of basic goods—flour, sugar, coffee … Yes, comrade, of course. I shall be happy to receive a delivery of tomatoes … this morning. *Dziękuję.*"

He slammed the phone back into the cradle with a loud click.

"A delivery of canned tomatoes is coming in today," he said to Liesel. "Place a sign on the door."

Liesel knew what would happen next. She envisioned a long line of people, mostly old women and children, jostling for position. They could be waiting for hours. If the promised item didn't make it or there wasn't enough, they had to turn people away. Liesel hated to see the hollow look in the eyes of the people, especially the children, when she had to tell them there was none left and that whatever ration cards and zlotys they offered could not change that.

Late in the afternoon, while people were still lined up at the front of the store, a truck pulled in to the back. Liesel took the clipboard from the driver. It read "ten cases of canned tomatoes, twelve per case." She signed for it.

Michal and the truck driver unloaded the crates onto a dolly. Liesel was about to follow Michal inside when she noticed what was stamped on the side of the crates.

"It's milk powder," she said to Michal. "I signed for tomatoes!"

"Oh," said Michal. "They are so incompetent." He put down the crate and went over to the truck driver. "Comrade!" said Michal. "It's milk powder, not tomatoes! Our customers are waiting for tomatoes."

The driver shrugged. "Do you want it or not?"

"I will take it," said Michal.

"Why they can't tell the difference between tomatoes and milk powder I don't know," said Michal to Liesel as the truck drove away. "The people will be angry."

"Maybe not," said Liesel. "Everyone is hungry and their children are hungry. Which is more filling? Tomatoes or milk?" She wished she could somehow get milk powder to her children. She opened the door for him to push the dolly through.

"True enough," said Michal, prying open the crates in readiness for the crowd that awaited.

Liesel opened the front door and held up her hand, gesturing for quiet. She hated speaking out loud, especially to a crowd of people who looked hungry enough to eat her if given the chance.

"There has been a change. We have milk powder, but no tomatoes."

Murmurs went up from the crowd.

"How can I make cabbage rolls with milk powder?" said one woman.

Liesel was curious as to where she had gotten the other ingredients to make cabbage rolls. Horsemeat? Or maybe rice or barley for a filling? Her mouth watered at the thought of the cabbage rolls she used to make. She had filled the large leaves with a mixture of ground ham and beef, flavoured with garlic and onions. Topped off with mashed ripe tomatoes, the casserole would simmer at the back of the stove in a big crock until everything was tender and delicious.

She was jolted back to the queue in front of her, which stretched down the sidewalk. "Milk powder is fine with me," said a woman holding on to a baby buggy.

No-one left the line.

Liesel examined and stamped ration cards and counted out change, while Michal handed over the tins. Eagerly she watched, hoping there would be a few tins left, but the powdered milk came to an end before the line of people.

Her heart sank. She supposed it wasn't realistic to hope for anything for her children, even if she could somehow get it to them. She sat down behind the counter and began to count the day's receipts. She dictated the amounts to Michal and he wrote them in a ledger.

"I have to keep track of everything. Otherwise Party officials will be after me," he said. "Some stores are being taken over and run by government officials. Don't tell anyone, but I think I will become a Zionist, instead of a Communist."

A Zionist? Liesel hadn't even known he was Jewish.

Just then she noticed a small numbered tattoo on his forearm, below his rolled up sleeves. Before she was able to avert her eyes, he turned towards her, crossing his arms over his thin chest.

"I was in Auschwitz," he stated. "Do you know what they did to us Jews there?"

Liesel shook her head. She had heard rumors of work camps and re-settlement of the Jews, but no-one had said what had happened to them.

Michal's eyes were dark in the shadow of his face and he directed his gaze outside the window. The street and sidewalk were empty. Grey clouds had descended and drizzling rain fell against the window, running down the pane like a multitude of tears.

His voice was flat, nearly without inflection. "We were all taken from our home and thrown into the ghetto. My parents were beaten to death by the SS. On the way to the camp, my wife became ill and died on the train."

He paused and wrote in the ledger.

"I am so sorry," said Liesel. She couldn't think of anything else to say. It wasn't that hard to imagine the horrors he had experienced, with what she had recently seen. She thought of her girls and of Ernst; what kind of suffering were they being subjected to.

Michal continued. "We were forced to do hard physical labor with barely enough to eat. '*Arbeit macht frei*' the sign at the entrance said. 'Work makes you free.' But the only freedom from that place was death."

His pencil lead broke leaving a dark smudge on the page. His voice thinned to a whisper.

"Just a few months before we were liberated, my two beautiful daughters perished in the gas chamber. It is considered fortunate that I survived but I am not so sure."

She thought about Günther, so proud in his SS uniform. Had he been involved in such atrocities? She knew Ernst had felt pressured into joining the army, but there were others who had signed up long ago, as soon as the Nazis began putting people on the *Volksliste*. Was this what the Germans, her people, had done to Michal's people, the Jews?

As if to acknowledge her thoughts, he sighed. "I don't believe there is anything to be done for it now, but there are some who are exacting revenge." He looked at her more pointedly this time and closed the ledger book. "Perhaps you know what I am talking about."

Liesel nodded. She had seen a measure of human cruelty and hatred. She thought of her own imprisonment and interrogations in a dirty cellar and her broken arm at the prison camp.

It was not hard to believe what Michal was telling her.

"An 'eye for an eye' as the Torah states. I worked for the Office of State Security as a guard at *Zgoda* for a few months."

Not just the imposition of the Soviet state, but revenge, thought Liesel. What Michal was telling her explained so much; why young women like Gretchen had been savagely beaten and others even drowned in barrels of water. Few people had any understanding of why they were in the camps. Most had been picked up on hearsay of what they had said or did or just because they were German.

"I understand the pain of the survivors too well since I am one, but I could not agree with what the guards were doing to women and children. Most of the real criminals who ran the Nazi death camps escaped before the Allies liberated the camp. Torturing people … it is too much like what happened to us and it doesn't change anything."

It was the most Liesel had ever heard him speak.

"It wasn't right and I could not participate anymore." He put the ledger book and the box of receipts below the shelf. "The Russians and even the other Allies are quite happy to comply with anything State Security wants to do in there. Just turn a blind eye, so they can get on with their politics."

"Like the world turned a blind eye to you," said Liesel. "I guess we cannot expect protection from our former enemies."

"I am 'entitled' to have you work here for free, and you know I can't afford to pay you," said Michal, "but really you are better off here."

"I appreciate it," said Liesel, as she gathered her things and left to wait outside for the truck that would take her back to the camp for the night.

Michal had trusted her with his story, a story that left her sick inside. A wave of shame came over her. The Jews, the Germans, the Poles, the Russians. Once the Germans had been the spiders and the Poles and Jews the flies.

And now I am a fly, she thought. But the conversation gave her hope that perhaps she could trust Michal with her request.

CHAPTER 52

MICHAL DID NOT HESITATE. "YOU MAY GO, BUT DO NOT TELL any official at the camp that I gave you permission." He gave her money for the street car that would take her part way across town.

She chose a seat near the back. Her ragged appearance wasn't that much out of place. People kept their business to themselves these days, away from the curious ears of the communists and those who had sold out to them.

To her dismay, a young man with a red armband on his tunic got on at the next stop and sat next to her. "*Towarzysz*," He nodded to her. She tipped her head slightly, but didn't reply. She wasn't his comrade, she wasn't anyone's comrade and she saw no point in engaging in unnecessary conversation.

"And where are you going today?" his mouth was turned up in a sardonic smile, but his eyes were steely. Now she had no choice but to answer, in her best Polish.

"To see my daughter."

"She doesn't live with you?"

The lie slipped out easily. "She's in the hospital."

"Oh, would you like me to escort you there?"

"No. *Dziękuję.* I will be fine."

"Are you sure?" He smirked ever so slightly. "A fine lady like you needs a handsome man at her side, does she not?"

Liesel looked down at her shoes, tied with knotted string, and the frayed sleeves of the old sweater and almost laughed at the absurdity of it.

"I am afraid that would be impossible. She is quite contagious and being held in isolation." Liesel placed a hand at the side of her mouth as if to take him in her confidence.

"Tuberculosis you know." A disease no one wanted to catch.

"In fact," she added, "I am feeling quite ill myself." She coughed convincingly.

"Good day then." The young officer abruptly stood up and moved further down the car.

Liesel got off at the next stop. A number of windows were boarded up on the gray building that loomed before her. It was three stories high and paint was peeling everywhere. It did not seem like a home at all, never mind a home for children.

She walked up to the cracked and crumbling front steps. A small sign on the door declared it a home for foundling children.

A stern-looking woman in a gray uniform answered Liesel's knock. "Why are you here?"

"To see my children," said Liesel, her heart pounding.

"The children in this home are abandoned and orphans. Why have you come?"

How could she explain the circumstances under which she was forced to relinquish her daughters? It was impossible to understand this new regime or its ever changing policies.

"I wish to see them." Surely the matron could understand that she had not given up her children willingly.

"Very well then. You may come in for a few moments."

The door was opened further, to the familiar odour of unwashed bodies with a top note of urine and vomit. Liesel could discern no food smells.

"The children are having their exercise in the back." The woman spoke this as if she were in charge of an exclusive private academy. Liesel became somewhat hopeful. That was good, the children were getting some fresh air.

Past a small office, down a dim hallway, the door opened to a paved courtyard where a group of children sat shivering on the cracked pavement. One little boy squatted on the ground, playing with a stick. Other children sat lethargically. There was no running or laughter.

On a creaking, rusted swing a girl swayed back and forth, her feet scuffing on the ground. Dull blonde hair was cropped short around her ears and the thin dress she wore rode up her gangly legs. She looked up slowly as Liesel approached.

Suddenly her face lit up. "*Mutti*! You came! They said you would never come, that I would have to stay here forever."

"I have missed you so much." Liesel wrapped her arms around her daughter, feeling the child's ribs beneath the tattered sweater. "Where is Heidi?"

"I tried to take care of her. I tried so hard." Teardrops pooled in Edeltraud's eyes. Liesel's heart dropped. She turned to speak to the matron, but the woman had left.

"She is upstairs with the other babies," Edeltraud said. Liesel's hand flew to her chest. "Are you allowed to go upstairs?"

"Sometimes." Edeltraud led her mother upstairs to a room lined from wall to wall with babies and toddlers in cribs.

Dozens of pairs of curious eyes watched the newcomers enter the room. The stench of dirty diapers washed over Liesel and the cries from the children in the cribs was pitiful.

A young woman dressed in a grey tunic and apron passed out bottles to each crib. She spoke nothing to the children, nor did she pick them up. The milk in the bottles was almost transparent.

Edeltraud stopped at a crib in the far corner of the room, separate from the others. A tiny child lay on a filthy mattress. A rash covered her emaciated body and patches of hair were missing from her scalp.

Without lifting her head, she gazed at the visitors with dull green eyes much too big for her face.

Liesel reached into the crib as if to confirm by touching her, that this child was her own daughter. "She probably won't live long you know," said the young aide. Her face was hard and and she did not seem to have any more bottles of the dubious liquid.

"Aren't you going to give her a bottle?" asked Liesel, trying to mask her anger.

The matron walked into the room. "If you insist on prolonging the child's suffering," the woman sniffed airily. The younger woman left the room, returning shortly with another bottle.

Liesel reached into her pocket. Though she had thought it was all gone, Michal had stashed a case of the milk powder in the storeroom and had given her a tin. He had marked it down as damaged goods. Liesel had put some into a paper bag. She added a small amount to the bottle and lifted Heidi out of the crib to feed her. The feverish child slowly sucked the bottle empty.

Liesel drew Edeltraud close to her. For a few moments she cradled her children close and tried to forget where they were.

Outside, the shadows lengthened. "I cannot take you with me now," said Liesel "but I will come to get you as soon as I can."

"Please," Edeltraud pleaded, her eyes filling with tears again. "I want to go with you."

"You must listen to me," said Liesel. She handed the sack of milk powder to Edeltraud. "Try to add this to Heidi's bottle every day if you can. Don't let that matron catch you with it."

From the other pocket she produced half a loaf of bread. "Half of this for you, the other half for Heidi, if she is strong enough to eat it. Try dipping it in the milk." What a burden for a seven year old child, Liesel thought.

"I will come for you as soon as I can. Do not lose hope."

But Liesel had nearly lost hers.

CHAPTER 53
ERNST

IN RUSSIA, THE SEASON CHANGED SO QUICKLY, IT SEEMED like one day the prisoners of war were dripping with sweat, the next they were soaked with torrential rain. After that the frost appeared, like a fuzzy beard covering the shrubs and moss, and then icy shards at the edges of the marsh. When the snow came, the days grew short, the mercy of darkness eclipsing the work day.

Ernst stayed in bed as long as possible preserving what little warmth and energy he had to face the day. At long last when almost everyone else in the room was up, he sat up and took his jacket off the bed, where it had been used as a pillow and put it on.

Ulli handed him his boots. "It has been nearly two years and we are still here, still alive."

"For how much longer I wonder," remarked Ernst, wrapping his feet with rags and pushing them into the wooden shoes they had been issued. His padded jacket and work pants hung on his six foot tall frame like a sack.

Ulli rushed out the door. "I'm on serving duty this morning."

Ernst's teeth had become loose. The doctor had told them all to drink tea made from pine needles to prevent scurvy, but it helped only a little.

He hustled to the latrine, grabbed his cup and bowl, and marched to the dining hut as the last group was rushing out for the workday. Jostling for position, he ended up near the end of line.

He had figured out the middle of the line was the best. You were guaranteed to get something in your bowl. The front wasn't very good, because if there were fish bones or potatoes, they sunk near the bottom. The end of the line was a risk. If there was anything left you might get a few good chunks, but if they ran out …

Ernst decided not to think about that.

Before dishing out his helping of gruel, Ulli eyed Ernst's gaunt frame over, then glanced around furtively. He had not forgotten that Ernst had helped him in the past.

"Almost everyone has eaten." He filled the ladle right to the top and dished it quickly into Ernst's bowl, then handed him his ration of bread. "Thank you," whispered Ernst. He put the bread in his pocket for later and went to a corner table, hoping that his fuller bowl would not be noticed. He ate quickly so he wouldn't miss the transport truck to the quarry where he had been transferred.

He would have preferred the kitchen. The quarry was harder than logging, but he was so weak now he was only assigned four hours of work. Soon, he thought he would not be working at all and then there was only reduced rations and death by slow starvation to wait for.

The work was monotonous and offered no shelter in the cold. Chip large rocks into smaller rocks. Shovel rocks into wheelbarrow. Empty wheelbarrow into pile. Do again.

Once at the quarry, the men stepped off the truck. Ernst took a pick and shovel and chose a spot to work behind a large pile of rocks, hoping that his slower pace would not be noticed and he could manage his quota.

At night he dreamt of steaming bowls of hearty borscht, with real meat and globules of fat floating on the surface. Thick slices of rye spread lavishly with butter and a selection of head cheese, kielbassa, tomatoes, carrots, and green cabbages. Visions of *Apfelkuchen* for dessert with fresh whipped cream filled his mind.

The next day, the temperature had moved down further, but not quite enough to keep the men away from work. Roll call was excruciating. Before breakfast gruel and morning coffee, they had to stand outside and wait for the guard Nikolai to finish determining that everyone was there. Not that anyone in their right mind could go anywhere—kilometres of frozen wasteland, empty forests and bogs, not to mention wolves and bears, prevented any serious escape attempts.

Nikolai paced in front of the prisoners. He wore a full woolen coat, a fur cap with ear-flaps and his feet were shod in warm felt boots. He lit a cigarette while the prisoners stood at attention and turned to the other guard who was counting heads. "Have any escaped?"

"There is one missing, comrade."

"Each man must number himself," said Nikolai.

"One," said the first prisoner in the front row.

"Two," said the second man, waiting just a moment to answer. Standing outside in the cold was bad; work detail was worse.

"*Patarapis!*" said Nikolai, impatiently grinding out his cigarette butt with his heel.

"18, 19." The men were quicker now, but they still came up one man short.

"Who is missing?" said Nikolai.

"I think it is old Finkelmeyer from the bottom bunk in the corner," said Ulli. "He was coughing a lot last night. Maybe he went to see the doctor this morning."

As if that would do him any good, thought Ernst. The doctor, one of their own men, did his best, but with no medicine to speak of and only a drafty infirmary for recovery, there wasn't much he could do.

"You go look." said Nikolai. "The rest will wait here."

Ulli ran into the barrack and returned a few moments later, making a gesture as if to doff his cap. "He is dead. God rest his soul."

"Pff. Your God is dead, just like your comrade."

Nikolai took out his whip. "You will kneel." He lashed Ulli. "Repeat after me. There is no God."

Ulli said nothing.

Ernst wondered what he himself would do, if given the same choice. He had learned his catechism as a child, memorized all the answers. But they had rung hollow as he had become an adult, especially after Johann had died.

"Say it," said Nikolai. "There is no God."

"I will not say that," said Ulli.

Ernst tried in his mind to reason with Ulli. *Just say it, even if you don't mean it. We all know you wouldn't mean it.*

The silence was heavy, as Nikolai pulled back the whip.

"I will prove it to you. Take off your jacket."

Ulli removed his padded jacket and knelt wearing only a thin shirt. He trembled with hands folded and head bowed.

The whip sliced through the air and across Ulli's back. And again, this time, cutting through Ulli's shirt leaving a gash on his back.

"You see?" said Nikolai. "God did not save you." He wrapped the whip and put it away.

Ernst felt sick. Later in the day he had to wonder if Nikolai was right and God was nowhere to be found in the work camps of Siberia.

The Romanian prisoners in the next barrack had gained a reputation for making slippers out of old tires and Ulli had struck a bargain with one of them. That evening he returned to the barracks in his new footwear.

"What do you think?" he said to Ernst. "My boots give me blisters. After work I can wear these."

"Very fine," said Ernst. He wished he would have thought of the idea himself.

They hadn't realized anyone else was in the barrack, but suddenly Schmidt emerged from the shadows behind them. He was a hulk of a man given to fits of temper and everyone did their best to avoid him.

He walked up to Ulli, towering over the slightly-built man. "What are you doing with my shoes?" His tone was aggressive and angry.

Ernst stepped away.

"I just had these shoes made," said Ulli.

"They are mine. Give them to me," said Schmidt.

Ernst saw something in the man's eyes and he backed further away towards his bunk. He did not have the strength to fight, not even for his friend.

"OK," said Ulli, raising his hands in a gesture of surrender.

"It's not OK." Schmidt grabbed him by the collar with one hand and made a sudden motion with the other. As he let go, Ulli staggered backwards, out the doorway and fell into the snow with a soft thud. Blood gushed from his chest.

Ernst rushed over and knelt down. His head was spinning with the memory of Günther dying in the forest.

Ulli looked up at Ernst. His lips were moving and he gasped, "Forgive ..."

Schmidt ran out of the barrack and a guard was on the scene shortly. "Stabbing," said Ernst, lifting Ulli's limp arms and crossing them over his chest. He didn't offer any further information.

That night Ernst lay in his bunk utterly spent. The shock of the day's events had brought him to a level of exhaustion he had not felt before. Straight from the evening's thin soup he had come to his bed and he had not moved since, not even to brush the lice and bedbugs off himself.

He could hear the other men talking quietly. "Too bad about Ulli."

"He was a good sort, at least as good as they come around here."

Enforced labour and starvation brought out the worst in most people, it was true. But Ulli had been something of an exception, offering small kindnesses when cruelty and selfishness was the norm.

One of the men had caught a rat. Ernst could smell its singed hair and the oily meat roasting.

Even if he was offered some of the meat, he didn't even have enough energy to get up. He did not feel the least bit sorry for the rat. It was probably the one that had eaten his attempt at dried mushrooms.

He closed his eyes and saw Ulli. His lips moving, but no sound, his body falling, the white snow splotched with his blood.

Ernst hoped for a peaceful end for himself. Perhaps he just would not wake up in the morning, like Finkelmeyer. When the ground thawed, they would take his body away to be buried behind the camp with others dead from malnutrition and illness. A Christian burial was out of the question. The barbarian Russians wouldn't send his body home. How would Liesel ever know what had happened to him?

He didn't know what had happened to them either. With his struggle to survive and every waking thought about food, he had hardly thought of his family. Were they still alive? He had gotten only one brief post-card just before the war ended.

How tall were his boys? Were they helping their mother keep the farm going? Some men prided themselves on wives that were reserved only for 'Kinder, Küche, Kirche,' but Liesel had not only taken care of the children, the meals and regular church-going, but had been his partner in life, labouring by his side in almost everything. He had always appreciated her stamina, strength, and faith but he regretted not telling her what she had meant to him.

Guilt gnawed at him about the times he had stayed home from church meetings, always the first to volunteer for some urgent chore or a sick animal that had to be tended. Something in him had hardened after Johann had died. He did not understand a God who would take his child. He had followed the motions of his Lutheran faith, had his children christened, but his mind had wandered away during the sermons. Personal prayers had been neglected and he had deferred most of the spiritual training of the children to Liesel, especially during the war.

The room was quiet now. Everyone had gone to bed and the only sounds were the sighs of sleep and the creak of a bunk as someone shifted position.

Was life in this wretched prison a punishment for his half-hearted faith; his anger at the Almighty? Or perhaps his inability to stand up against what was wrong.

It had been a long time since he had prayed. *"Vater Unser in dem Himmel*, Holy is your name."* Pronouncing sacredness in the midst of the filth and evil around him seemed profane; as shocking as the stabbing that had killed Ulli.

"Your kingdom come, Your will be done, on earth as it is in heaven." Ernst was surprised at how easily the old words came and he repeated them to himself, even as he considered what the will of God was and its place here, where the Soviets had vehemently expelled God from their midst. Had the communist insistence of life without God brought about the cruelty of Stalin's revolution?

But the Nazis had been no better, eschewing traditional religious belief in favour of pagan notions; the idolatry of Aryan race and German statehood. Look what his own people had done. He himself had helped to "keep order" when people were expelled from their homes and herded onto trains and into ghettos. He had done his job, fulfilled orders without questioning where they were taking the people or what was going to happen to them.

If these political systems were indication of life without God, then he would prefer the world with God in it, even a God he could not understand.

"Give us today our daily bread." Soggy rye bread was all that stood between the prisoners and the grave.

"Forgive us our trespasses." So many times, he had been selfish and silent when he should have spoken up. "As we forgive those who trespass against us." Ernst knew in his heart, that even as he lay dying in the snow, Ulli was a man who would forgive, and there was no shortage of people to forgive—both guards and fellow inmates that had schemed and cheated others for anything to help them survive—extra clothing, bread, cigarettes. Ulli's death reminded Ernst of how Jesus had died, taking the penalty for sins and offering forgiveness to those who had hurt him.

"Lead us not into temptation, but deliver us from evil."

A sense of peace, even anticipation came over Ernst. He was ready to be delivered into the eternity of God's love. "Forever. Amen."

As he closed his prayer, he opened his eyes for one last time.

It was a spectacular night on which to die. The shutters had fallen open and a full moon shone through the distorted glass, its bright glare dimmed by filth and soot. Swirling ribbons of colour, like the Polish girls wore in their hair, danced across the inky sky.

The silhouette of a man passed over the window. Someone was standing there, but his face was in shadow.

At first Ernst wondered if it was Schmidt, come to kill him too, but Ernst did not feel afraid. Perhaps this was death, come to take him. He had already decided he would not resist and waited expectantly. He would go to a better place, like Ulli.

He felt a hand on his shoulder and a voice both soothing and authoritative. "Not yet." Warmth enveloped Ernst's cold aching body.

"Take courage," the visitor said. "All will be well." The man disappeared into the darkness.

Ernst slept until dawn.

CHAPTER 54
LIESEL

ROLLING OVER WAS A CHALLENGE ON THE NARROW BUNK without disturbing your bedmate, but it was better in a way than having the bunk to yourself thought Liesel, because you could keep warm.

Gretchen's eyes flitted open.

"Almost time to get up," said Liesel.

"Just another minute," yawned Gretchen, pulling the blanket closer. "I keep hoping that when I next open my eyes, I won't be here anymore."

The door to the barrack opened and the Kapo strode in.

"Oh no, it's the old witch again," whispered a woman in the bunk across from Liesel and Gretchen. "I wonder what misery she has for us today."

Would it be some new work detail? Liesel hoped not. Working for Michal was the best possible situation under the circumstances. More likely there was some new oppressive rule or communist dictate.

"Achtung," the Kapo called them to attention. "I have a list of names. If you are on this list, you will collect your belongings and report to the front gate for transit at 900 hours."

"Here is a paper everyone must sign," said the Kapo. Liesel read it through quickly. "...must never disclose the events witnessed in the camp."

There was the near-starvation diet, the lack of medical care, and the cruelty of the Polish camp administrators and the Kapo. The screams of Gretchen and the sounds of torture still echoed in Liesel's mind. Would no-one ever know what had happened here?

To sign or not to sign? Would it make any difference? She signed the paper, assuming it was her only way out of this hole.

Everyone wanted to know what was happening. Most of the women had never been tried for their "crimes" and had hoped for a chance at freedom.

"Will we be going on the trains again?"

"Where are we going?"

"What about our children?" asked Liesel.

"Shut up," said the Kapo. "I will do the talking, or you will be staying here."

Gretchen's brow knit together in a slight frown. Dark circles under her eyes made her appear older than she was. "I don't know," she said to Liesel. "Do we want to be on this list?"

"All I know is, if I am on it, I hope my children are too," said Liesel.

The Kapo read the list of names. "Adler, Albert, Baum, Dettner, Feingold, Halle, Hoffmann ...

Liesel began to collect her things and put them into her bag.

The Kapo closed the notebook, put it in her pocket and left.

Gretchen's name had not been called. "You have been like a mother to me," she said, embracing Liesel.

Even as Liesel felt the dampness of Gretchen's tears on her cheeks she thought of her own daughters. *"Auf Wiedersehen.* Until we meet again," said Liesel.

At the gate, a guard called them to attention. The women stood in one group, children in another. Relief washed over her when she saw Kurt, Olaf, and Rudy among them.

"When your name is called you are to take custody of your children and travel together on the truck."

Two hours later, they found themselves at a village and were taken to a roped off area in front of the town hall. A crowd of people had gathered around.

One by one people came up and eyed the newcomers up and down, having them turn around and asking questions about how strong they were and what their work experience was.

Liesel felt like she was a horse or cow being looked over by a farmer before he made a purchase.

The largest, sturdiest looking women and those without small children were chosen first. One of the villagers, a tall angular woman came up to Kurt. She turned him around twice squinting at him. "*Ile masz lat?*"

"Twelve." Kurt answered, looking at his mother with pleading eyes.

"You'll do," said the tall woman.

"Please, we want to be together," said Liesel.

"*Nie,*" said the guard who had travelled with them. He held Liesel's arm back. "There are too many of you."

Slumped over with his hands in his pockets, Kurt trudged off with the woman. Liesel hurt for him.

An unshaven man with massive shoulders lumbered over to the remaining group. The smell of liquor wafted from him.

Liesel stepped back, one arm around Olaf, the other holding Rudy's hand.

The man grabbed Olaf's arm and squeezed.

"But he is just ten," said Liesel. "He needs to be with me."

"I'll take him," he said, grabbing Olaf roughly by the shoulder. Olaf looked stricken.

Liesel felt helpless and empty.

Besides Liesel and Rudy only a half-witted girl and an old woman were left. Liesel clutched at Rudy. She would not let them take him without her.

She lifted her head up and saw a small house across the road. One window was boarded up and the roof sagged. The front yard was overtaken with weeds. A rusty potato harvester and an old plow sat at the side of the house covered by a lean-to.

An old man with a cane stepped out, holding the door. His wife followed. Her hair was covered with a scarf tied at the back of her head in the traditional Polish fashion and beneath her coat a faded skirt billowed below her knees. With halting steps, the couple made their way across the street to where the former prisoners waited.

It was a only a glimpse, a flash in the eyes that Liesel instinctively thought might be kindness or simple humanity, but it was enough for her to grasp at.

She straightened up and made eye contact. "*Dzien dobry,*" she nodded, deferentially.

The old couple stopped. "*Dzien dobry.*"

"I hope we are not too late," said the woman. "Has someone spoken for you?"

"*Nie, Pani,* I will come with you if I can bring my son."

"*Tak.* Of course." With a gnarled hand, she patted Rudy on the head and he rewarded her with a grin. "My name is Maria. Is this your only child?"

"He is the only one with me now." Liesel did not mention the circumstances of the rest of her children.

CHAPTER 55

LIESEL PUT HER BAG DOWN ON A BENCH, AND LOOKED around the room. The wallpaper was stained and old-fashioned. Straw had escaped from the faded upholstery of a sofa, like a gaping war wound.

"Your house smells funny," said Rudy, wrinkling his nose.

"Shush," said Liesel. "Don't be rude."

"I haven't been able to do much the past few years and Piotr has not been well either," said Maria, gesturing at the room. Her fingers were curled and deformed, the knuckles like knobs.

She picked up a stack of newspapers off a chair. "We have not had many guests lately."

A fluffy cat brushed up against Liesel's legs.

Piotr sat down. "We should have eaten him," said Piotr gruffly, poking the cat with his cane.

Maria shuffled over to the stove and ladled out the noon meal. "I am sorry there is no meat," she said, handing Liesel two steaming bowls half full of beet chunks, shredded cabbage and potato.

Liesel's mouth watered with anticipation as she breathed in the aroma. "Look Rudy! Borscht."

Rudy's eyes shone with delight as he lifted the spoon to his mouth.

"First we give thanks, young man," said Piotr, taking Rudy's hand in his own.

Liesel blushed. "I am so sorry. I, we haven't …" How could Rudy have remembered to say a blessing in the prison camp without her to remind him?

"We understand." Maria nodded and smiled.

"Bless us O Lord and these your generous gifts which we consume. Through Christ our Lord." Piotr crossed himself. "Amen."

Rudy frowned. He had not seen Catholics pray before.

"It is all right," said Liesel. "We pray to the same God in heaven."

She took a spoonful of the soup savouring the sweetness of the beets and the cabbage melting in her mouth. She looked at Maria, "And I am truly thankful for this meal, *Pani*."

Before Maria was up the next morning, Liesel had milked the goat, brought the milk into the kitchen and made coffee.

"What are you doing?" asked Maria, hobbling into the room.

"We are expected to work, aren't we?"

"You don't have to work so hard for me. I am sure the officials will be assigning you tasks, but you are not my slave. Oh I know they have told us that you Germans are all supposed to work for us now, but in this house we will be like family, *tak*?"

"Yes." Liesel sat down to her coffee. "But I like to get up early."

"Your little boy, he reminds me of my son, when he was young." She pointed to a photograph on the wall of a young man in uniform. "He died in the Warsaw uprising."

Next to the photograph was a wedding picture. "And that was my daughter. She married a Jewish man. When the Nazis came they were put in the ghetto and taken away. I never saw her again."

Liesel placed her hand over Maria's and looked up at the wall.

The older woman continued, pointing at another photograph. "This is my other son Tomasz. I don't know where he is."

After a few moments, Liesel said, "I hope I can see my other children again too. My girls are in a children's home in Łódź. My other sons are somewhere in the village."

"You could try to find them. Just be careful. There are still some Russian officials and those State Security people are always coming around. Do not speak German!"

In the late afternoon, Liesel went down the street, in the direction she had seen Kurt go the day they had arrived. The day was sunny and some villagers were out, burning piles of debris and working gardens. She scanned their faces for Kurt and Olaf and the people they had left with.

A young girl hoeing a newly planted garden watched her.

"Please, have you noticed any boys about your age working around here?" asked Liesel.

"There is an older boy at that house," the girl pointed down the street.

Liesel knocked on the door. The woman that Liesel recognized from the day they arrived, opened the door. "I am looking for Kurt."

"Who are you and what do you want?"

"I am his mother. I would like to see him."

"He is out in the pasture with the cows and he must bring them back before dark. I don't want any trouble!"

Liesel saw Kurt before he saw her. His sleeves were halfway up his arms and the boots he wore were much too big. There was no way of knowing who might be listening, so she waited until he came closer. "Kurt."

"Mother!"

"I wanted to see if you were all right."

"I am fine."

"Do you know where Olaf is?"

"I haven't seen him, but one of the other herders told me that Jaroslaw is the meanest man around. I think that is the man Olaf went with."

The sun was low in the sky now and had slipped behind a cloud, casting a grayness over the rooftops of the village.

"Poor Olaf," said Liesel. She wished she had been able to find her younger son first.

"Work hard," she said to Kurt. "And then ask if you can come visit Sunday. You better go, it's getting dark."

It was too late to go any further so she went back to the house.

A few days later she was scrubbing the floor. No matter that Maria insisted she didn't have to do so much, Liesel would not take their kindness for granted or be indebted to anyone if she could help it. Besides, working hard kept her mind off constantly worrying about the other children and wondering what had happened to Ernst.

An insistent banging at the door interrupted her thoughts. She draped the rag on the side of the bucket. She wasn't sure if she should open the door or go hide.

Cautiously she lifted the curtain and peered out the window. A boy with a swollen and purple face was standing there. Above one black eye was a cut and blood had dried on his forehead and cheek.

Liesel opened the door a crack.

The boy was panting as if he had been running awhile. "*Mutti.*"

Liesel pulled him inside.

"Olaf!" This was her son who would never hurt any living thing. What could he have done to deserve such punishment? "*Mein lieber Gott*, who has done this to you?"

"The little girl," he chuffed breathlessly.

"A little girl did this to you?"

"No." He shook his head. "The little girl is sick. She fell asleep in the haystack this morning and Jaroslaw beat her up with chains." Olaf's eyes filled with tears.

"I tried to stop him, but he beat me too. We have to go help her." He tugged at his mother's sleeve.

She thought a moment. She could not let Olaf go back there. But a helpless little girl? She thought of her own girls and how she would feel if she knew someone was hurting them. She had stepped in and tried to help Gretchen in the prison and gotten a broken arm for her trouble. If she was hurt she would be no good to her own children. Further, she might be putting Maria and Piotr in danger.

She put her arm around Olaf. "I'm sorry, the man might denounce us to the authorities." She smoothed his matted hair. She felt terrible, but she could not go around trying to rescue other people's children when her own were in peril. "I will ask Maria, I think she will let you stay here."

"Of course he will stay here," said Maria. "We will all share what we have."

Kurt was allowed to visit. Olaf and Rudy were with her now, but Liesel could not stop thinking about Edeltraud and Heidi.

CHAPTER 56

SHE ESTIMATED IT WAS ALMOST AN HOUR AWAY BY TRUCK OR train to get to Łódź. That is if she had a travel permit and access to transportation. And then there were concerns about bringing more mouths to feed in a household barely getting by.

The boys' appetites were increasing every day. Liesel noted with shame that sometimes Maria would push aside a potato or piece of bread off her own plate for Olaf or Rudy. "I'm old, I don't need so much food," she shrugged, "let them have it."

Food was severely rationed and the communist authorities had taken much of what had been harvested to "redistribute." Where, she could only guess. Germans were not entitled to any official rations of meat, butter or bread, because they were being expelled out of all the eastern territories, including Poland.

It was a hot night and Liesel could not sleep. She was thinking about picking the rest of the beans and potatoes for Maria in the morning, before going out to the fields.

There was a noise outside, a scraping like the sound of a shovel. She heard it again and sat upright. She put on a shirt over the nightgown Maria had loaned her. At the front door, she put on boots and grabbed Piotr's cane.

Outside, a harvest moon gleamed orange, its beams illuminating the yard. A weathervane on the barn roof, shaped like a stork, spun slowly against the indigo sky.

A man knelt in the garden, pulling the potato plants out and putting them in a sack. Glancing in Liesel's direction, he stood up and ran across the yard throwing the sack to a companion waiting on the other side of the fence.

That was it; she would have to harvest all she could before thieves took any more. She surveyed the cellar now. She had done the best she could, but three sacks of potatoes, a sack of beets and a few cabbages, would barely last the winter with five of them to feed.

At Christmas Piotr slaughtered the cock.

Liesel plunged the old fowl into boiling water and took it to the back room to pluck. Its skin was tough and leathery, the feathers yielding only with great effort on Liesel's part to separate them from the stubborn bird.

Into the soup pot it went, with extra potatoes and onions for their Christmas soup.

After dinner, Maria handed Olaf and Rudy a small package. "A little present for each of you."

Rudy and Olaf looked at each other. Liesel had told them not to expect anything. They opened the plain brown paper. Inside was a pair of woolen mittens for each of them that Maria had knitted.

"*Dziekuja Pani* Maria" the boys chorused politely, not realizing that they would wear the mittens almost constantly for the next few months.

In January frost coated the window. Rudy and Olaf scratched pictures on the glass with their fingernails; outlines of wagons, horses, trucks.

"No sense in peeling potatoes," said Maria, as she gave them a quick scrub and handed them to Liesel to cut. "It is too much waste."

Liesel looked over at the boys etching the frosty windows again. They wore the mittens now and used the back of a tin spoon, so their hands wouldn't get cold. Olaf had drawn a chicken leg and Rudy had scratched a large carrot, its leafy top mimicking the pattern of the frost. Next to that, Olaf drew a plump loaf of bread with wavy lines of steam coming out of the top.

Within a few weeks, the window artwork stopped. The boys did not play or draw pictures anymore, but huddled around the stove or lay on the sofa under blankets and coats for most of the day, only getting up for a bowl of potato soup.

When the temperature remained far below freezing and the woodpile had dwindled to almost nothing, Liesel suggested to Olaf they go look for firewood.

"Maybe if we follow the railroad tracks we will find some coal," suggested Olaf.

They wandered a few kilometres towards to the train station at the next village bending over to look for telltale black lumps among the rocks of the railbed. Several other people seemed to be doing the same thing.

At the whistle of the train Liesel stood up, watching to see if any coal would fall from the top of the freight cars. As the rumbling behemoth slowed, a young man dressed in rags hoisted himself up onto the train and scaled up the side ladder into the box. Showers of coal rained down onto the ground as he scooped the top of the pile.

His bulging rucksack landed on the ground with a thud in a cloud of coal dust before the owner scrambled down after it. As he stooped to pick it up, a uniformed guard appeared suddenly, his gun drawn. "Stop, or I will shoot."

The youth did not even turn around, but grabbed his bag and sprinted away. Liesel heard the shot and watched as his lithe body seemed to leap into the air, then stumble and fall to the ground.

The guard re-cocked his gun and aimed it at Liesel.

"Drop it and get out of here." Liesel willed her stiff fingers to let go the piece of coal.

"Let's go," she said to Olaf, but he stood rooted to the ground in fear.

The guard turned his gun on Olaf. "Go, or I will shoot."

"Olaf, come," Liesel pleaded with him. As if he had just woken up, he stepped towards her and with heavy steps they walked away back to the cold little house.

The drinking water in the bucket froze and there was nothing left to burn. Liesel offered again to look for firewood.

"*Nie*," said Piotr. "It is too cold and you have to go so far. Take the bench and chop it up. Liesel went out to the lean-to and chopped the bench into pieces to fit into the stove so they could heat the soup.

The flour was almost out too. To stretch it they used alfalfa hay from the barn and some sawdust. It tasted terrible, but it made it look like more, gave them something to chew on.

Piotr became ill with a fever. He lay on the old sofa, which they had moved close to the fire. Maria placed a cold cloth on his forehead, but he pushed it off muttering. "I am already too cold."

One day he looked at Liesel with stony eyes and said, "We barely have enough to eat. Why are we keeping these Germans here?"

He had never spoken this way about them before. Liesel thought of her father, who had become so confused in his last days. She missed her parents, but thinking how much they would have suffered had they lived, she decided perhaps it was better that they were gone.

And perhaps it was better to go along with the person who was ill, as much as possible to maintain the peace.

She spoke to Maria when Piotr was asleep. "I think it is best that we leave for now."

"No," said Maria, taking Liesel's hand, "You don't have to go."

"We will come back when he is better; when there is some more food," she said, putting on her coat and looking for the boys' mittens.

"Get your coats on, boys."

"Where are we going?" asked Olaf.

"We can't stay here right now," said Liesel. She had absolutely no idea where they could go or how they could live, but she couldn't risk Piotr becoming angry with them.

"I'm cold and tired," complained Rudy. "Do I have to go?"

Mostly he had stayed in bed lately and Liesel had not discouraged him. There was nothing for a little boy to do and it was better to save his energy. Olaf had helped a little here and there but in the last few days, he too had spent much of his time in front of the stove, feeding it with twigs, books, and broken furniture.

Liesel wrapped blankets around her head and shoulders and the heads of the boys. Flakes of snow spun in the wind and bit through their worn clothes like icy pinpricks, stinging them on the face. Before they reached the end of the road their noses and hands were numb.

They came up to the door of the house where Kurt was living and knocked hesitantly.

The door opened a crack. "You cannot stay here," the woman said.

"I can work very hard," said Liesel, hoping she would see how desperate they were.

"I could get into trouble," said the woman. "We are not supposed to feed Germans, only the labour assigned to us. I could get arrested."

Liesel couldn't disagree with that, but she couldn't see any other options. Kurt came bearing a load of sticks. "Please," he asked the woman he had been laboring for.

She narrowed her eyes. "You can come in and warm up. That is all, then you must go back to where you came from."

She served them some weak tea and a potato each. All the potatoes had black spots, but they ate them anyway.

Before it was dark Liesel, Olaf, and Rudy left. The only thing Liesel could think of now was getting warm, so they went back to Maria and Piotr's, where she guided the boys to the barn.

"Mutti, can't we please go inside the house," Olaf asked.

"No, we cannot risk Piotr denouncing us."

"What is denouncing?" asked Rudy, flopping onto a pile of hay.

"Denouncing is …," Liesel began. It was so hard to explain to a child, especially when hunger clouded her thinking. "Do you remember when we were all in the camp?"

"Yes," said Rudy.

"That's what will happen if we get denounced."

"It's like some people don't like us very much," said Olaf.

"Exactly like that," said Liesel. "Now try to go to sleep and I'll figure out what to do in the morning."

"I can't go to sleep, I'm too hungry," said Rudy.

Liesel took the bucket from the corner and climbed into the goat's stall. Grasping the flaccid teats, she squeezed desperately, but there was nothing. Not a drop for a hungry child. She slid down against the back of the stall and sobbed quietly.

In the morning, she looked out the barn to see if she should bother venturing outside. What little food she would be able to find required so much effort, maybe they should just stay in the barn and try to stay warm.

The snow had stopped and she had to use the outhouse. As she passed the henhouse on her way back to the barn, she heard the chickens clucking softly. Surely Maria would understand if she took a chicken, plucked it and brought it to the house. She was beyond fearing what Piotr might do.

She had succeeded in chasing a feathery pullet into a corner and was about to scoop up the hapless bird when something caught her eye. Nestled in the straw a white orb glowed in the dimness and next to it another. Liesel dropped the hen and stooped to pick up the eggs, cradling them like a treasure.

Quietly she knocked on the back door, holding the eggs triumphantly.

Maria opened the door, her face haggard and her eyes red. "Piotr is gone. He died last night."

For a long moment Liesel held the old woman close, the eggs clutched in one hand, the other stroking the old woman's hair. "There was nothing you could do."

"You must stay now," Maria pleaded. "I don't have anyone else."

"Of course." Liesel was sorry for Maria, she felt bad that Piotr was gone, but she couldn't help thinking it was one less mouth to feed and now she could come back into the house.

CHAPTER 57
ERNST 1947

ERNST WATCHED DULLY OUT THE WINDOW OF THE TRAIN, AS the snowy forests of Siberia became the wide Russian steppe. Occasionally the landscape was marked with a village or peasants working the collective fields.

On his lap he held a cloth bag, beyond which his knee caps bulged like small melons under his trousers. Knobby wrist bones protuded from his large hands, the blue veins transparent through a sheen of skin, dry and cracked as old leather.

With spidery fingers he pulled his final ration of bread from the bag and nibbled slowly at the crust. Looking at the similarly spent men around him he marveled that they had gotten out of the camp.

Yesterday they had called him to the Kommandant's office. "You are no longer of any use to us," the Kommandant had told him.

Ernst had been silent. Were they going to execute him after starving him?

"Sign this," the Kommandant had said. Ernst couldn't read the paper; it was in Russian, but he shrugged and signed it. He was willing to accept his fate now, whatever it would be.

The Kommandant stamped the paper and gave it to Ernst. "We are releasing you. Red Cross prisoner exchange. See, we are not such barbarians after all. We keep to our agreements."

Ernst's mouth hung open. He was stunned.

"Smile, Comrade," said the Kommandant. "Today your lucky day!" He handed him train tickets, his bread ration and a few rubles for food.

Luck or something else. So many had died, been worked into the ground, starved, or frozen to death. He did not even know why he was still alive.

At a tiny settlement, the train stopped and he bought some sausage and bread from a peasant woman. It was the most food he had seen in two years, but after devouring it, he promptly brought it back up, his deprived stomach rejecting the rich food soundly.

At Frankfurt an der Oder the former prisoners stepped off and a contingent of guards checked their arms for the SS tattoo. Many had tried to remove the telltale sign, by burning it off with a cigarette or cutting it out, but the scar was a giveaway.

Ernst was glad he hadn't given in to his brother's pressure to join the SS.

Continuing their journey on another train, Ernst developed a fever and napped almost constantly, dreams intermingled with nightmares of giant rats and putrifying bodies. His mind was in a fog and he was too tired and ill to feel any elation about going home, even though it was that very hope that had held him alive the past few years. Liesel, the children, his previous life were but a dim dream.

Weeks after the prisoners-of-war had left the Soviet Union, they arrived at their destination in the Western occupation zone, in much the same shape as when they had left the camp.

Ernst's every muscle and joint protested as he slowly stood up, hanging on to the rows of seats for balance. He stumbled off the train, into the arms of a young nurse in a white pinafore, with a large red cross emblazoned on the front.

Her shining dark hair was pinned neatly under her kerchief and her full lips parted slightly as she stared at him a moment, as if he were a ghost. Then she smiled, took his hand and led him to a stretcher. "We will take care of you," she said tenderly.

He thought her the most beautiful woman he had seen in a long time and he let her hold his hand all through the ride to the hospital. Mostly he slept, only opening his eyes for a moment to see if she was still there.

Upon his arrival at the hospital they took down his information, removed the prison garb he had worn for weeks, bathed him and put him in a hospital gown. The nurse took him over to a scale. She slid the weights back and forth and then again.

"*Unmöglich!*" she exclaimed and scurried around the corner.

Ernst swayed, clutching at the scale for balance. The gown was thin and he shivered uncontrollably.

The nurse returned with a doctor. Looking at Ernst and then the scale, he shook his head. "It is impossible! I do not know why you are still alive. 190 centimetres tall and you do not even weigh 40 kilos." More nurses and doctors appeared, some taking notes on clipboards, others whispering as if he were not there.

Around him the room and the people began to spin as the white walls of the hospital darkened around the edges and closed in on him.

"Can I sit down now?" said Ernst breathlessly.

"*Ja*, but of course," said the doctor. "Get this man under some warm blankets and start intravenous fluids," he told the nurse.

The blankets seemed so heavy Ernst could not move. Days or weeks he lived in a haze, not knowing how long he slept. Doctors and nurses came and went, measuring his heart rate, taking his temperature, and feeding him vile spoonfuls of vitamins and sips of delicious fruit juice. Daylight was followed by darkness. Darkness was followed by porridge and coffee, a morning wash, then being weighed again. At noon they brought him soup and canned fruit.

Obediently Ernst sipped at the soup. Beads of fat shone like gold on the surface. He identified bits of chicken, onions, carrots, potatoes and barley. He tried to get something different in every mouthful and chewed it carefully savouring each bite. It tasted good, but if he ate too much he couldn't keep it down.

After lunch was nap time. He drifted in and out of sleep for the whole afternoon, until dinner, then the daily cycle started again. He was only vaguely aware of the passage of time.

"How are you today, Herr Hoffmann?" asked the nurse.

"Getting better." He nodded, telling them what they needed to hear, but not volunteering anything else. All his energy was expended on strengthening his depleted body from the scourge of near starvation. Besides, he had no wish to speak of his experiences. No-one would understand what he had been through and he thought what was past should be left in the past.

One day he sat outside in a small courtyard among the remains of a garden, absorbing the radiance of a sunny day. Dried perennial stalks poked up through tangled weeds anddandelions had worked their way through cracks in the cement between last year's rotting leaves littering the ground. Discarded paper and cigarette butts littered the ground.

Ernst's gaze settled on a rosebush in the corner, its riotous pink blooms exploding all over. Petals littered the ground with pink confetti as if in defiance of the surroundings.

The rosebush made him think of Liesel and her beautiful garden. Pain, from deep within his chest rose up through his throat and burned a path out his eyes and down his cheeks.

Where was she? Did she even know where he was? Why, he asked himself, had he not made inquiries or written to her since he had come here.

He had seen some of the devastation of Poland as the train had rolled through. As a former German soldier though, he had not been allowed to get off the train but had to continue to the Western occupation zone. Could he even find her? Things were different now and he had changed over these three years. He wondered if she would know him; if she'd even want him.

Perhaps she had found someone else. She was still a handsome woman and it had been more than three years. Maybe he should just begin a new life here; start over.

But then he thought of his experience in the prison. That mysterious visitor who, whether a dream or a heavenly messenger, had brought him hope when he had given up. Besides, it would not be right to just leave her. She deserved to know what had happened to him. He would give her the choice, whatever she wanted.

As soon as he was well, he determined to find her.

The day came when he was strong enough, at least in body to go to the International Tracing Service. A long line of people were waiting in front of him.

"It is very difficult to trace people in the East," said the official. "All the Germans from Poland and Prussia, anywhere east of the Oder-Neisse line have been officially expelled from those zones and are being repatriated to the Soviet zone in Germany. We will make inquiries. Refugees are streaming in all over the place and some are crossing the border. She would have to come to you," he explained.

"I need to go find them," said Ernst. The man shook his head. "Go to Poland? I wouldn't advise it. They will consider you an enemy of the state and throw you in another prison. You of all people know what the Soviets do to their enemies."

"But I need to find my wife and children!" said Ernst. Now that he was finally well enough to travel, he knew his conscience and heart would not rest until he made every effort to re-unite his family. He smoothed back his hair, recently grown in, almost as thick as it once was. There was some meat on his bones now. He could walk a few blocks without becoming winded. Physically he had gained some strength, but he felt powerless to fulfill his obligation as protector and provider to his family.

He could only imagine the complications Liesel might face travelling with five children in hostile territory, not to mention hassling with papers, travel permits, red tape, and border guards.

"Can we apply to have her come here?"

"Certainly; however, dozens of refugees, even civilians, have told us that they have been accused of crimes, imprisoned, and forced into labour. It is even worse chaos than here and the Western zones have not been prepared for millions of destitute people."

"Destitute?" For the first time Ernst began to realize the magnitude of what had transpired since the war ended. Germany had been nearly demolished and he felt himself personally ruined by his experiences both in the war and the prison camp. Now he was estranged from his family and could never return home.

He leaned forward in his chair. "What can I do?"

"Try placing notices at churches, on street corners. Anywhere people congregate. Someone who knows her may contact you. Give it some time. If you can't find her, start a new life. There are plenty of lonely women who would be happy to have you."

He pushed Ernst his papers. "*Guten Tag.* Next!"

Ernst stood up and nodded at a shabby looking woman, clutching a sheaf of papers, waiting to take his place.

He spent the next few days copying out notices onto little cards and posting them around town; *Seeking my wife Liesel Hoffmann and children; Kurt, Olaf, Rudy, Edeltraud and baby. From the vicinity of Łódź, Poland.*

Anxiously he waited to hear something.

He pulled out the picture Liesel had given him the last time he was home. It was dog-eared and creased. Kurt and Olaf stood on either side of Liesel as if guarding her, their expressions impassive. Edeltraud was about two. Rudy looked like he was about to run off.

Ernst tried to imagine how they would look now. He pulled out the postcard he had gotten a few months before he left the camp. Liesel had only supplied him with the barest of details of the birth of the baby, Heidi. She would be older now than Edeltraud in the picture, a child, not a baby anymore.

Each week he returned to the Tracing Office for news and to check his bulletin boards.

At last he had a reply. A man who had permission to travel to Łódź on business had been a neighbor of Liesel's sister and would deliver the note.

"There is no guarantee that your wife's sister is still there," said the man. "Things in Poland are not as you remember them."

"I appreciate your efforts," said Ernst.

At home he looked in the mirror. His knees were now merely defined, not the knobs they had been and his ribs were almost invisible. The mirror revealed something of the old Ernst, but gave no hint to the man inside.

That man would not be the man Liesel had known.

CHAPTER 58

WITHIN A WEEK OF LIESEL'S RETURN TO MARIA'S, ONE OF the chickens was sacrificed to the cause of the soup pot. Every bone was picked clean and boiled for days to make a stock that was watered down to last as long as possible.

They were down to potatoes and cabbages again, when Kurt came to the door.

Liesel ushered him inside.

He put his rucksack on the floor and opened it. "Look what I brought," he said triumphantly, pulling out a sack of rice, beans, and a tin of milk powder."

"Kurt! Where did you get this?" Liesel was as incredulous as if he had come with a bagful of precious gems.

"Off a truck." He smiled, obviously proud of himself. "I hid underneath and when they weren't looking, I went shopping."

Liesel heard her past self speaking to her errant son. *It's wrong to steal. You must take the food back.* He would have been spanked and sent to his room.

But now, none of that mattered. How could she scold him when deception and theft was required in order to eat and live.

"*Danke.*" She hugged and kissed him. "But please don't do it again."

"I have to get back now." He shouldered his pack and went out the door.

Liesel did not wait for the rice to run out nor the ground to fully thaw before she sowed peas, radishes and onions.

Maybe now she could travel to Łódź to get her girls. She approached Maria. "I want to get my daughters."

"Well then you must," answered Maria, picking up her rosary. "I will say a prayer for you."

Liesel made her way to the village mayor's office.

"You want to travel to Lodz?" he asked her. "Why?"

"My daughters are there. I wish to take custody of them before we go to Germany."

"It is not our policy to give travel permits to Germans, Frau Hoffmann. You have been assigned housing here. I must follow the orders of my superiors. Come back next week and I may be able to help you."

The next week, Liesel returned, but it was a different official, who told her he would have to check with State Security first.

She could see they were not going to give her a travel permit, so before dawn the next morning, she left, meandering across fallow fields, side roads and forests. Checkpoints were everywhere, but these she avoided, along with anyone who wore a uniform.

She arrived at the children's home in the afternoon, tired and aching with hunger.

A woman in a gray uniform and kerchief met her at the door. She was not the same woman Liesel had seen on her first visit to the children's home.

"I would like to see my girls," stated Liesel. "Edeltraud and Heidi Hoffmann."

"Edeltraud is in school and the younger ones are having their nap."

"But I haven't seen them in a year."

"You will have to wait until later."

"I will wait then."

For over an hour Liesel sat in the office, watching the clock on the wall tick slowly and wishing she'd had more than a crust of bread that morning. Finally around three o'clock the matron returned with Edeltraud.

She was taller than the last time Liesel had seen her, and her hair had grown out enough for two tight braids.

Edeltraud looked at Liesel with hooded eyes. "You said you would come."

Liesel reached out to her. "I wanted to come, but I couldn't. I want us to be together now."

Edeltraud backed up against the wall. "Why didn't you come?"

Liesel felt the accusation of her tone as if she had been declared guilty in a court of law. Her knees shook and she felt like her head was floating. She wanted to make Edeltraud understand, but it was so hard to think and the matron was standing there, so she weighed her words carefully.

Gently she asked Edeltraud, "Are you allowed to leave here?"

Edeltraud looked puzzled. "No."

"Well, I couldn't leave for a long time either." She didn't explain about the conditions at the camp or Kurt stealing food. "And, there wasn't much to eat for a while."

"Oh," said Edeltraud softening slightly. "What about my brothers?"

"They are fine. We are all in the same village."

Liesel turned to the matron. "I would like to see Heidi now."

Her heart pounding with memories of the last trip up the stairs, Liesel followed Edeltraud and the matron up the stairs. This time they were led into a room with a large window, furnished with a rug on the floor and a few toys and books. Several small children dressed in identical jumpers played on the floor, with a young woman watching them.

Liesel noted the size of their arms and legs. Underfed perhaps, but not starving. She allowed herself to breathe a sigh of relief. Things had changed since the last time she had come.

A tiny girl with a halo of short hair sat on the floor looking at a book. She raised her head. Round green eyes, Adelheid's eyes, looked up at her, but there was no recognition on the child's face.

She was only a baby, why would she even remember me at all?

Cautiously Liesel approached the toddler and lowered herself to the floor. "Would you like me to read to you?" She picked up the dog-eared book and reached out for the young child, but Heidi stiffened and stayed rooted to her spot on the floor staring at Liesel.

Edeltraud watched from the doorway while Liesel read the book out loud. Heidi clutched her hair, and sucked her thumb a few feet away, staring intently. About halfway through the story, she inched a little closer.

Liesel stopped reading. "Would you like to sit in my lap?"

Heidi nodded solemnly. Liesel placed one arm around her and continued reading. The story was finished, but Heidi continued to sit in her lap, so she began again at the beginning. "Once upon a time ..."

Edeltraud sat down beside her mother and sister.

"there was a little girl dressed in a red cloak with a hood ...."

It all seemed so ordinary. Sitting with her daughters, reading to them, as she had once done with Edeltraud and the boys. Except for the gnawing in her belly, her heart felt full and hopeful.

Afterward she went back to talk to the matron. "I wish to take my daughters with me now. They will be sending us to the Soviet zone of Germany soon."

The matron interrupted. "But you surrendered your children to the state!"

"No... I." Liesel faltered. "None of what happened was my choice."

"Well, you cannot take them today!" The matron was incredulous. "It is impossible. You will need identification papers and exit visas. Come back with the appropriate papers."

Liesel looked at the clock. It was already half-past four. Too late in the day to find the repatriation office and speak with the appropriate officials.

Wearily she trudged down the streets of Łódź. She hadn't heard anything of Frieda since Kurt had been there. If they hadn't taken her away there was a chance she was still in her house.

A small girl answered the door, opening it all the way to reveal several other children and a few adults. A woman came to the door scolding the girl, "Who is there? You shouldn't let people in like that!"

"I'm looking for Frieda." said Liesel.

"She's not here; I think she was arrested a few weeks ago," the woman said. "Fortunately for us, we were out or they might have taken us too."

"Oh," said Liesel. It was dark now and she couldn't manage another hour of walking without food and rest.

"Well, don't stand out here. I don't know who is going to come around." She pulled Liesel in and closed the door. "I'm Ilse."

Liesel looked around the once familiar room. There were holes in the plaster walls and a number of floorboards had been pulled up. Besides the kitchen table and chairs, all that remained of Frieda's furniture was a heavy cabinet in the corner that Ernst had made for their wedding gift. The cupboard doors had been pulled off and instead of Frieda's china and crystal, the shelves held clothing and an assortment of mismatched chipped dishes.

"The Russians destroyed most of the place," said Ilse. Liesel's heart sank at the thought of her younger sister encountering Red Army soldiers. "Then we had to burn a lot of the furniture," said Ilse. "It was that or freeze to death."

She ladled cabbage soup into a small bowl and put it in front of Liesel. "We don't have much, but you look hungry."

It was all Liesel could do to stop herself from inhaling the soup in one gulp.

"Are you her sister?" asked Ilse.

"Yes, I just needed a place to stay for the night. I didn't know if she would still be here."

"Before she was taken, she said that if you ever came, to tell you that your husband is alive and in the American zone."

Alive. Ernst was alive and out of Russia.

"I don't think you'll be able to go there though," the woman continued as if reading Liesel's thoughts. "It is not so easy to get a visa." She continued, "They don't want us here, but they don't want us to leave either."

"It's like some kind of purgatory," said another woman, "and every time we turn around someone is being rounded up and taken away." She took a sip of tea out of a chipped cup, one of Frieda's wedding china pieces. "We don't know how much longer we can evade them."

Liesel's relief at knowing Ernst was alive was short-lived. How could she get to the distant western zone, when she hadn't even been able to keep her children together? Even if she could get the girls from the children's home, she had no idea how she would provide for them.

Early the next morning, she went to the Bureau for Repatriation. When she was about a block away, she saw the line up of people, mostly women and children. "Please. Is this the line-up for emigration?"

"Yes, maybe if you line up now you can emigrate in 1950," said a man in the line.

"1950?" said Liesel, not realizing the man was half joking. That was almost 3 years away.

"This is our third time," he said. "Each time, the rules change. They want different papers, they want everything stamped by various officials, then by the time I get everything, my travel papers have expired."

"Shh, you must be careful what you say," said a woman that Liesel presumed to be his wife, "you don't know who might be listening."

The line moved forward, a slow river of people. A few hours after she'd arrived, Liesel stood before the official. "These are all the papers I have. The rest were taken from me." Just in case, she didn't mention the camp where she had been falsely accused and detained, but they probably had records of that anyway.

"You say you have two daughters."

"Yes. The second one was born at the end of the war."

"You have no records of her? No baptism certificate?"

Thinking of the horror and chaos of those weeks, it seemed a ridiculous question in Liesel's mind. Explaining would be useless. "Nothing."

"Where is she?"

"Łódź children's home."

"They would have to sign a release form and you have to bring the children here."

"But ..."

Back at the children's home, Liesel pleaded with a children's worker.

"They said you need to sign a release form."

"You cannot prove the younger child is yours, Frau Hoffmann, she does not even know you!"

"Of course she is mine. I cannot help my circumstances."

"Leave her here," she shrugged, "we will raise her to be a good Polish worker in the new state."

Liesel shook her head. That was not what she wanted for her children. "Ask Edeltraud. She remembers coming here!" Liesel's legs wobbled and she clutched the desk. She had not slept much in the night and had nothing to eat since the cabbage soup the night before. "She is mine," she said, her voice trailing off as a dark curtain fell over her eyes and she crumpled onto the floor.

The noise brought the matron into the room.

Liesel felt cold water being splashed in her face. The two women helped her into a chair and left the room. Liesel could hear them outside outside the door.

"Comrade, sign this woman's papers," said the matron to the younger worker.

"I was only following the policies."

"Obviously the child is hers. What would a half-starved woman want with an extra child anyway?"

The door opened a few minutes later and the matron returned with a piece of bread and a glass of water. "We are not supposed to feed

Germans, you know, but I will make an exception." Liesel hoped that edict did not apply to her children.

"I want to get my girls back with me so we can get to Germany soon."

"Get your other papers in order and come back again in a week or two."

CHAPTER 59

LIESEL RETURNED TO MARIA'S. SHE PICKED UP RUDY'S jacket to mend, one that had been handed down from Kurt and then Olaf. The elbows were worn through and the sleeves frayed and much too short. As she picked up the scissors she heard banging at the door.

Two men in uniform barged in before she got there.

Liesel's throat was dry, her knees weak.

"You are ordered to await transport to a transit camp and from there you will be taken to the Soviet occupation zone. You are to be at the train station in 20 minutes."

"But I don't have my daughters." She feared she would never see them again, if she didn't persist. "Please, may I speak to your superior?"

"We will escort you to the police station."

"I give you my word," she told the commanding officer. "I will take a transport from Łódź, as soon as I have my daughters with me."

"You have one week, that is all," said the Kommandant at the mayor's office. He handed her a travel permit for Łódź. "If you do not show up, all your children will be placed in state care and you will be arrested."

She collected Kurt from his labour assignment and bid Maria goodbye. "Thank you for your kindness to us," said Liesel. "I pray that you will find your son someday." They left her waving from the window.

They made it to the door of the repatriation office in Łódź, with the boys and papers in hand shortly before it was due to close again.

The official went over her papers. "Full name of the youngest child?"

"Adelheid Hoffmann. We call her Heidi."

"Place of birth."

Liesel thought of the vicinity where she had taken refuge in the abandoned house that night, but she did not know the name of the village or even if it was within the Łódź Voivodeship. "I don't know the name of the place. It was nearly dark when we got there and we had to leave in a hurry."

"We have to fill this part in. What village are you from?" continued the official.

"Schönewald."

"You must give the Polish name."

"Sonina."

"You will need to take this certificate to the office of Vital Statistics."

"Where is that?"

"Inside the building."

That was closed for the day.

"Mother, I'm hungry," said Rudy.

She'd had no time to figure out what to feed them. The bread she'd brought with her had been consumed and she had no money, nothing left to barter. Begging from the wrong person could only get her in trouble.

"Come Rudy," she called out to him as he lagged behind.

"There is a park with a bench. Can we rest awhile?" he asked.

"Yes, you boys sit here a moment."

She got up and walked over to a spruce tree. No one was around. She pulled some needles off the branches and put them in her pocket.

Under an oak, she squatted down and felt around the wet grass for acorns and collected a pocketful.

She felt like a squirrel.

It began to rain and they rushed along the streets to Frieda's old house, where Ilse answered the door.

"May we stay a few days again," asked Liesel, "until I can get things sorted out?"

"A space on the floor is yours, but you will have to come up with your own food."

Liesel started a pot of water to boil and put the pine needles into the tea kettle.

She poured each of the boys a cup of the "tea."

"But what will we eat?" asked Kurt, eyeing Ilse's daughter who was eating a potato.

Liesel emptied the acorns from her pocket. "See if you can find a way to crack these open," she said to Kurt. "Then they need to be soaked before we can cook them."

She looked outside at the rain pouring off the roof into the small yard. "Did Frieda have a vegetable garden this past year? Before she was ..." Liesel exhaled, trying not to think of her younger sister in one of the labour camps or being interrogated, "taken away?"

Frieda had never been very excited about gardening and had relished her life in the city, at least before the war, but even she might have grown some food this past year if she had managed to stay in her home that long.

"Yes," said Ilse, "but I don't think anything survived the winter or the people that have been here since."

Liesel went out to the tool shed and found a shovel. She stepped into the garden bed.

Mud oozed up to her ankles amongst the soggy brown weeds and last year's bean stalks.

She pushed the shovel into the ground and pulled her foot out of the muck to step on it. Methodically she worked, shovel in the ground, pull foot out of mud, place on shovel and push, but not too hard. If there was any resistance she must feel it.

Every few moments she stopped, exhausted, to rest against the shovel, then rake her bare hands through what she had dug, squeezing the soil through her fingers for any telltale lumps.

Within half an hour she was soaked through and shivering with cold.

She collected a few weed roots, some new greens, half a turnip hollowed from decay, and one potato, mostly rotten. She put away the shovel and trudged breathlessly back to the house.

"Soup will be ready soon," she told the boys.

The Three Governments, having considered the question in all its aspects, recognize that the transfer to Germany of German populations, … remaining in Poland, Czechoslovakia and Hungary, will have to be undertaken … any transfers that take place should be effected in an orderly and humane manner.

— From the Potsdam agreement.

CHAPTER 60

IN THE MORNING SHE MADE A PORRIDGE OF SORTS OUT OF the acorns. Ilse donated two potatoes to the children's meal.

"It doesn't taste good," said Olaf.

"I'll eat yours, then," said Kurt.

"No," said Liesel. "Eat your own portion. It might be all you get today."

The next few hours were spent in line again at the office for Vital Statistics.

"Were there any witnesses to this birth?"

"Kristiana Schroeder of Schönewald." Liesel had no idea if Kristiana was still alive, or, if given her state of mind, she could even recall the birth.

"You need three witnesses."

Liesel thought for a moment. "My children were there too." She wished they hadn't had to witness that trauma.

The official looked at her as if she were an imbecile. "Children cannot serve as witnesses."

"But I need this birth certificate. We are being taken to Germany."

The man shook his head. He pushed the unstamped document towards her.

At the Office for Repatriation, she was told the next transport was tomorrow and she was to be on it.

She didn't know what to do next. She had to get her girls somehow.

"Let's go see your sisters."

The boys stood quietly waiting at the office in the Children's Home. The matron came in with the girls.

Liesel crouched down to Heidi's level. "Heidi, these are your brothers."

"Hello," they chorused. Rudy patted her on the head. "You have such fuzzy hair," he said.

"I remember when you were a baby. We lived in the barn then." Heidi held up her arms for him to pick her up.

After a few moments, the matron turned to Edeltraud and then Heidi. "Will you go with this woman?"

Solemnly, they both nodded.

"Good," said the matron. "I will bring them to the train station tomorrow then."

The next morning Liesel and the boys waited at the station platform with dozens of others.

A notice on the wall read:

> The German population of Łódź will be resettled to an area west of the river Oder.
>
> Each German is allowed to take no more than 20kg of luggage.
>
> Inventory of all dwellings and farms in an undamaged state are the property of Poland.
>
> Apartment and house keys must be left outside. Dwellings to

remain open.

Those who are not in compliance with these orders will be executed.

So this was it. She would be leaving, maybe forever.

A large clock hung above them, its indifferent hands pointing ten minutes to the hour. Liesel fingered the incomplete birth certificate in her bag. The train would be leaving at 9:00 and there was no sign of the girls.

She had to be on that train or ...

"I thought Heidi and Edel were coming," said Kurt, speaking Liesel's fear out loud.

"I thought so too," she said glancing around at the throng of people. Some had nothing but the clothes on their backs while others carried various bundles and were dressed in several layers of clothing. Guards milled around, keeping a close watch and organizing people into lines.

"Look," said Olaf, "there they are."

The matron had both girls by the hand. Each carried a small bag.

"I packed them some milk and sandwiches," the matron said.

"Thank you so much," said Liesel, taking custody of her daughters.

The train, made up entirely of open cattle cars pulled up and blew its whistle.

"All aboard," yelled the guards repeatedly, pushing people on board.

It was standing room only and once the train left the station they were exposed to pouring rain. Liesel huddled in a corner with her children, insisting they take turns crouching at her feet for shelter.

Once again no provisions were made for food and water. Whatever rain they could catch in their hands and the empty milk bottles was all they had to drink. The train travelled at the speed of a sight-seeing excursion, as if there was absolutely no hurry to arrive at any destination.

And what the exact destination was they had not been told.

It was almost two days before they stopped and for some, close to starvation already and in ill health, it was too late. Several dead bodies were hurled from the train like refuse, before buckets of water and bread were distributed.

Somewhere in what Liesel thought must be close to the Soviet zone, the train slowed to a crawl. *Good,* they'll give us some more food and water, Liesel thought.

Instead armed bandits climbed on board. "Your boots," said one of them, pointing a gun at a woman.

"But I don't have any other shoes," she said.

"Take them off or I shoot," he insisted. The woman was left with only her stockings.

The men went around the box car looking for jewelry and watches. They divested people of coats, hats, clothing, and anything else they wanted.

For once, Liesel was glad that she had nothing left worth stealing.

"Mother," said Edeltraud. "Can we go back now?"

"Back where?" said Liesel.

"To the children's home."

"Did you like it there?" Liesel was incredulous. After all she had done to get her children out of there and back with her, Edeltraud wanted to go back?

"Not really," said Edeltraud.

"Why do you want to go back?"

"Because I'm hungry."

After several more days of slow starts and stops the train pulled up to another prison camp surrounded with barbed wire. A wrought iron sign at the gate stated *"Arbeit Macht Frei."*

Liesel was dismayed. This again? She thought of Michal. His family had not been made free by work; she had not been made free by work. Freedom was only at the whim of the authorities and the only thing that would make her free was patience. Maybe.

A transit camp they were calling it. Maybe that meant they wouldn't be there for long. Liesel's papers were checked and re-checked; she was questioned relentlessly. Somehow they ignored the birth certificate with its missing stamp.

Once again, she was shaved, sprayed for de-lousing and separated from her children.

She wondered if her daughters would have been better off at the children's home. What kind of mother could she be to them?

CHAPTER 61
ERNST

HOF WAS CALMING FOR ERNST AND A GOOD DISTRACTION.

At the edge of the river Saale, he watched the boats go by. Beyond the river lay the forest and the mountains bordering the Sudetenland, part of Czechoslovakia, that Hitler had insisted on absorbing into Germany before the war began.

Ernst had left the hospital and been assigned a temporary home, sharing accommodation in a pension with three other former soldiers. Unfortunately the apartment was about the size of a bedroom, so most nights his roommates would go out to the bar, seeking women and beer to dull their senses.

"*Komm,* Ernst," said one of them, putting on his coat. "You are far too serious. Didn't you notice, the war has been over for nearly 3 years? There is wine and there are women. Lots of them to choose from."

"Well, maybe the wine isn't that good," said another of the roommates. "But the women!" He raised his eyebrows.

Visions of the nurse with her full lips and youthful figure, who had first cared for Ernst came to mind. He tried to think of Liesel with her strong supple body and thick waves of hair cascading down her shoulders, but her face was blurry; the features undefined like a watery reflection.

The men were already at the door, when Ernst picked up his coat. He had waited for months and had no word from anyone. He didn't even know the whereabouts of his mother and sister.

Maybe he would never hear anything, should he go on without living?

He followed his friends across the street into a smoky cellar where he ordered a stein of beer and watched the people around him. One of his roommates was cheek to cheek with a red-haired girl, the other two chatted with a woman in a corner.

A girl came up to him, "Do you want to dance?" she asked. Her smile was wide and inviting; her accent American.

Ernst wasn't much of a dancer, but he didn't want to hurt her feelings, so reluctantly he took her hand and led her to the middle of the room.

She was pretty, she was available.

Desire, dampened by years of hunger and sorrow, surged through him, catching him by surprise.

Over her shoulder he glanced at the barred street level window. Propelled by the music, couples moved in front of it, outlined by the glow of the streetlight beyond. His dance partner whispered something in his ear and giggled softly as the strains of a familiar waltz filled the smoky room.

Ernst thought of another window in another lifetime and a figure in front of such a window. He had never come up with a logical explanation for that nocturnal visitor in the prison, nor his strange prophecy. All Ernst knew, was that by some miracle, he was alive. He had experienced an overwhelming sense of peace and forgiveness that night. A re-awakening of faith that defied his rational mind.

The singer at the front of the room clutched the microphone and crooned the sentimental ballad, with a husky voice, her hair glowing like a golden halo under the stage lights.

Du, du liegst mir im Herzen
du, du liegst mir im Sinn.

You, you are on my heart.
You, you are on my mind.

Ernst had danced with Liesel to this very song at Frieda's wedding.
She had held little Kurt in her arms as Ernst's arms encompassed them
both.

And, and when you are so far,
To me your picture appears,
Then, then I wish so dearly
We were united in love.

The accordion and the bass accented each syllable until the song
schmaltzed to a stop. The dancing couples applauded the band and
Ernst stepped back from his partner's embrace.

"I have to go now," he said.

"But, the night is young. Stay and dance!" She squeezed his hand,
her eyes glistening.

"I can't," said Ernst, releasing himself from her grip.

This was his one chance. He had to be patient and give it more time.

But would Liesel still love him? Would she defer to him for protection
and discipline of their children? Kurt had shown signs of willfulness
at a young age and Ernst wondered how he had fared. Would his children remember him at all? He considered how Liesel, left to carry on
everything, could have managed the boys. Maybe she was better off
without him. As far as he knew, her second cousin Oskar had survived
the war. He had never married and Ernst had always felt that it was
clever Oskar that Liesel's parents had wanted her to marry. For all he
knew they were together now.

But it was too late, he had already sent the letter to Łódź with the
delivery man. He had made a reasonable effort to find them. Now it

was in God's hands and he must wait until he knew for certain, however difficult it might be.

CHAPTER 62
LIESEL 1948

IT WAS HARD FOR LIESEL TO BELIEVE ANOTHER SUMMER WAS approaching. Once again, the prisoners were assigned field labour, leaving the camp when the sun came up and returning for their evening soup.

As Liesel spooned the soup into her mouth she thought of how it was the soup that said everything about good or plenty. Before the war, when she was at home, soup stock was rich with chunks of meat, vegetables, beans, rice or potatoes, but meat and fat had all but disappeared from the bowls she had eaten in the past three years.

All that could be hoped for here was occasional bits of fish bones, usually rotten. At least the bread didn't taste like clay, but hunger remained a constant companion announcing his presence at every moment from waking and chores to trying to sleep on an empty stomach. She thought of her children trying to survive on such skimpiness and was grateful when she found out they were rationed a little milk and extra potatoes each day.

Day after day, she waited, wondering if they would ever be able to leave or if she would ever see her husband again.

One day another transport of women showed up. All pairs of eyes in the room looked at the newcomers, wondering who would have to share their narrow bed.

No-one moved.

Liesel scanned the new faces slowly, her eyes resting on a slender woman clutching a small bundle to herself as she looked around the room. Liesel stepped closer. It was hard to tell, when you hadn't seen someone in such a long time.

Like other women who had just arrived, her hair was shorn and her face and arms were covered with scabs. The soft contours of her face had become angular and her eyes were encircled with the same gray weariness as all of the other women Liesel encountered each day.

"Frieda?"

"Liesel!" Frieda dropped the bundle she was holding and embraced her sister.

Liesel felt every bone through the thin overalls Frieda wore.

"Come, you will share my bunk." She took her sister by the hand.

Other women in the room were squabbling over fitting two and three to a bed; some were asking of news from the outside or what village they were from. Did they have any news of so and so?

Liesel and Frieda sat clutched together, glad to see each other, sad that it was in this dismal place.

"We tried to get away. First I was ill and then I was in hiding, waiting for Ludwig, but he never came home. I think he is dead." She ran a hand over her bald head, as if still expecting to find hair. Her gaze settled on a spider lowering itself down the wall on a silken strand.

"The authorities kept moving us from place to place. And the Russian soldiers," she whispered, picking at the blanket. "They raped me," she looked up, tears pooling in her eyes as she took a ragged breath. "Over and over for days."

Liesel held her sister's hands tightly as she continued. "They even took some of the younger girls. It was so awful. I was ill for days and so afraid I would be pregnant by those pigs or get some dreadful disease."

"It happened to me too." Liesel whispered looking away at bedbugs crawling through a crack. She didn't want to relive that day.

As if reading her thoughts, Frieda changed the subject. "Tell me, how are your children? I could not believe it when Kurt showed up at my house that day."

"They are here in another section of the camp. I just got the girls back from a children's home in Łódź, but now I am missing them again." Liesel's voice trailed off. "They don't let us near them much at all. Apparently we might spread disease. But maybe if they'd let us wash properly and provided another set of clothes we'd be cleaner."

"Could they possibly be worse off than us?" said Frieda. "I think the communists are determined to turn them into little models of themselves, *ja*? So maybe they are all right. Probably getting more to eat than we are." Her laugh was brittle.

"Oh, oh," she said, reaching into her bundle. "I nearly forgot. I have this for you."

Liesel nearly tore the note from her hands.

> *Liebe Liesel,*
>
> *I have returned, in many ways from the brink of the grave and have almost recovered from my illnesses. I would like to find you and re-unite our family. My prayer is that God has kept you from harm. If you wish, please write to me.*
>
> *Ernst*

If I wish? Liesel thought it strange. Did he wish to leave her? Perhaps he thought the baby was not his. Liesel contemplated this for the night. Surely he must know that she would have been faithful. Or maybe it was something else, he had lost a limb or an eye and was afraid that she wouldn't accept him. If that was it, then she must assure him that she was still waiting for him and she would accept whatever had happened.

She was allowed to send a short card.

> *"It is my desire to be with you, dear one. Life has been difficult, but we are all hoping to be re-united with you."*

It was only after she sent it, that she considered the other possibility. Perhaps he had found someone else and really wanted her to set him free.

A week later, the barracks were humming with the news.

"I saw them through the windows of the storage room. Stacks of boxes—with a red cross on them," said one woman excitedly to another.

"You are surely joking."

"Maybe she's been having hallucinations from the rotten potatoes," laughed another woman. "Or all the worms in the soup."

But it was true.

Liesel stepped slowly towards her bunk carrying a box marked 'Red Cross', as if she might stumble and the contents of the precious box disappear. Some authority must have determined that they were entitled to food. Her heart welled with thanksgiving at this gift of kindness and humanity.

Over at her bunk she sat down. First she pulled out a package of cigarettes.

She was disappointed. Well, she did not smoke so what good were those?

"For barter," said Frieda, sitting down next to her. "I got one too."

The next thing was a tin of cocoa. Real cocoa.

Liesel could hardly believe her eyes. It had been years since she had tasted cocoa.

She had taken the children sliding around the frozen pond near the beginning of the war and had brought a thermos of cocoa. She pictured the mittened hands of her children as they took the tin cups filled with the warm beverage. She remembered Olaf and Kurt's faces lit up with toothy grins as they skated wobbly towards her. Rudy's laughter, as he slipped and fell against the sled pushing baby Edeltraud across the ice. Their white breath as it hit the cold air. It was a good memory, she hoped one that her children would also recall.

Back in the present, Frieda lifted out the next item. "And English biscuits, to go with."

"Milk powder," said Liesel.

Other women were coming in with their parcels. Someone began to sing quietly, and other women joined in, breathy voices filling the barrack, but not so loud the guard would hear them.

> *Nun danket alle Gott*
> *Mit Herzen, Mund und Händen,*
> *Der große Dinge tut*
> *An uns und allen Enden*

> Now thank we all our God,
> with heart and hands and voices,
> Who wondrous things has done,
> in Whom this world rejoices.

CHAPTER 63
KURT

KURT SWATTED AT A FLY ON THE WALL. IT FLOATED TO THE floor and he picked it up by the wings and held it up.

"That's twenty-two, for me!" he said, adding the casualty to the growing pile in the corner.

"Aww, I only have fourteen," said Olaf.

"Thirty-five," called Albert, an older boy lounging on one of the bunks.

"So, what," said Kurt, shrugging. "Are we going to eat them?"

"Ha," said Albert. "You can eat them if you want. Or you could just sweep them up, because if you don't the Kapo will give us all the whip."

"Why should *I* clean them up?" asked Kurt.

Albert climbed off his bunk and stood up. He was almost a head taller than Kurt and had a heavy build, even after months of lousy camp food.

"Because I said." He leered down at Kurt and looked over at Olaf who had stepped over towards the wall. "Or maybe you want to help your big brother," he said with a sneer. "In fact, if you don't, I'll beat both of you up. Who wants to go first?"

Olaf pouted and reached for the broom behind the door.

Kurt longed for something interesting to do. Anything to break the monotony of the camp, punctuated by lousy meals and being bullied by the older boys and the Kapo. Even going to school would have been preferable, especially if he could get away from Albert.

The next morning, the Kapo came in with a clipboard. "Hoffmann. *Ja*, you the older one. You will be assigned to the woodshop. Report after breakfast." Kurt tried not to look too pleased.

Mostly they built coffins and sometimes tables or benches. The finished coffins were stacked in the corner, the yellow pine glowing in the light from the window.

So much around the camp smelled bad; the rotten food, the overflowing latrines and unwashed bodies, especially in his barrack of older boys. But the coffins, they smelled good.

Kurt breathed in the scent.

It was strange, he thought. People died in the camp every day, but it appeared these coffins were not used for them. Most days a cart would go by with bodies piled on top. Other days a truck would come and they would load up the coffins and furniture and take them away. He wondered, when he died, would he be taken away in a sweet smelling coffin or hauled away on an old cart. Pushing the broom slowly across the floor, he bent over and picked up a twisted nail. The Kapo was nowhere in sight, so he put it in his pocket. He was supposed to straighten out any nails that might be re-usable, but he thought they wouldn't miss a few. He wasn't sure what he was going to do with the nails he was collecting, but he figured he would think of some way to put them to use.

He finished his work for the day, leaned the broom up against the wall, and ran to the barrack. He stuffed the handful of nails into a little crack at the end of his bunk. Then he went to find Olaf, who had been assigned kitchen duties.

Olaf was in back of the kitchen hut peeling potatoes for the evening soup. "Quick," said Kurt. "Give me some peels."

Olaf looked around and then gave Kurt a small handful. "Is that all?" said Kurt. "Shh," said Olaf, "if I get caught I won't get any supper."

"Well," said Kurt, stuffing the peelings in his mouth. "At least you didn't get latrine duty like Alfred."

"Definitely better than that," said Olaf.

Rudy walked up to them. The outline of his shoulders could be seen through his thin shirt. His pants were several inches above his ankles and his legs looked like toothpicks.

"You look like an old man." Kurt rubbed his brother's shaved head.

"Look, I lost another tooth!" said Rudy, pulling it triumphantly out of his shirt pocket.

Kurt snorted. "Don't expect any tooth fee for that."

Rudy frowned. "Why do you have to be so mean?"

"I'm not mean. It's just that … this place. I just want to get out of here."

"Me too," said Rudy. "There are too many bedbugs." He lifted his shirt to reveal dozens of angry welts.

"*Ja*," said Kurt. "I hate those things."

At night, Kurt climbed into the bottom bunk and pulled the threadbare blanket over himself. Just the thought of the bugs made him itchy, never mind the straw poking through the coarse ticking.

He heard Olaf snoring above him, but Kurt tossed and turned restlessly trying to get comfortable. It was hopeless. His stomach ached with hunger pangs. He was going to be fourteen soon and bread with watery soup for supper hadn't satisfied, especially now that he was working all day.

The next morning Rudy came by the woodshop, a grin between his hollow cheeks and pinched face.

"Watch out, you might split your face," Kurt laughed. He hadn't seen anyone smile like that since he'd been in these stupid camps. "Did you lose another tooth?"

"No. But guess what? Mom got a package from the Red Cross." He reached inside his shirt and handed Kurt four biscuits and a tin of corned beef. "These are for you and Olaf to share. If you can meet her later, there's more."

CHAPTER 64
LIESEL

THINGS WERE CHANGING IN THE CAMP. LESS PEOPLE WERE arriving, more were leaving, apparently for the Soviet sector of Germany. One day Frieda came to Liesel with a letter. It was from Emil's wife, Elisabeth.

> I was pleased to have word of you and hope your families are well. Sadly Emil died in the last days of the war, defending Breslau. Wrocław they call it now.

So much for Hitler's fortress, thought Liesel, saddened by the military folly that had taken her brother's life. She continued reading the letter.

> We had to leave our houses with almost everything in them. In fact some of the area leaders were insisting we leave the beds made up for the new inhabitants. I am in Potsdam now and if either of you want to make your way here, I will

find room for you somehow.

Liesel pondered a moment. "There is nothing for me there," she said to Frieda. "I have to get to Ernst." But she had no idea when or how.

In a few days Frieda had release papers. "I'm going to accept Elisabeth's invitation," said Frieda. "I don't know where else Anna and I can go."

Liesel thought of all the things they had been through in the camps. She thought back to her own childhood, so unlike what her own children had experienced.

She kissed Frieda goodbye. *"Aufweidersehen, meine liebe schwester."* Her dear sister was the only thread left of her past life, now with her parents and brother gone and her other sister an ocean away. More than ever, she needed Ernst.

A longing for her *Heimat,* her home, land, family and community overwhelmed her as she thought of the past few years and an uncertain future.

A few days later she too was handed her release certificate. The words 'Soviet Zone', leapt off the page.

"But I applied to go to the Western occupation zone," she explained to the camp Kommandant, handing him her papers. "My husband is there."

"Impossible," he snorted. "Those borders are closed. We can offer you freedom here in Poland. You speak Polish and we hear you are a hard worker. Become a party member." He smiled. "Stay here, work for five more years and then you can go." He spoke as if to a little child.

"But I want to be with my husband and he is in the West."

"Perhaps he can come here then."

Liesel did not mention Ernst's service in the army nor his lack of Polish fluency. It would be impossible for him to live freely back here.

"Our orders are for all Germans from the area to be repatriated to the Soviet German occupation zone."

Liesel opened her mouth to say something more, but the official stamped her papers with a loud thud. "Pick up your children tomorrow and meet at the front gate for transport."

Another train. This time they crossed past a checkpoint. They got off the train and Liesel and her children were put on a truck and taken a few hours away.

When they arrived at their destination, the first thing Liesel saw was a wide tower with a dome-shaped top, rising above the town. A small gothic spire pointed to the sky. Below the tower windows a band encircling the tower proclaimed, "*Ein Feste Burg.*" A mighty fortress.

Wittenberg, thought Liesel. Luther's town, where he had nailed his protest to the door of the church and penned the Reformation hymn.

She was buoyed by hope.

But the place she was assigned to live was not much better than the camps. A dozen families were crammed into a large hall, with "rooms" sectioned off by blankets and sheets hanging from bunkbeds. A clothesline ran the length of the room. A stove at each end provided heat and cooking facilities, where everyone took turns and frequent arguments broke out.

She was allotted a small amount of money for food and household goods, but it wasn't enough, so the boys spent their days wandering and scrounging up extra food from fruit trees and garbage bins. Liesel spent her time tramping around to various officials making inquiries about getting to the West. But despite her determination the answers were the same. "Impossible." Her papers were not in order. There was a quota for immigration and it had been filled.

She got a letter from Ernst one day. The authorities of the Western zone were permitting her to come and had granted a visa.

Now she had collected everything she needed. Or so she thought, as she stood in front of another petty official who told her, "Your travel permits have expired."

"But ..."

He shrugged. "There is nothing I can do." He stamped the exit visa 'Denied,' and directed his attention to the next person in line.

Hope was so close, but now she felt like she had been punched in the stomach.

She left the office dejected, clutching her sheaf of papers. It was a few minutes before she realized a man in a long coat seemed to be following her.

Her nerves were set on edge and she walked faster hoping to get beyond his reach, but her short legs were no match for his long stride. Was she going to be arrested again on another trumped up charge?

He caught up and brushed against her, handing her a folded note.

> *I know someone who can help you. I will sit on a bench at the riverside and read a newspaper. Wait five minutes then come sit on the bench with me. Make very sure no-one follows you.*

Liesel did not know what to think. Was it a trap? The NKVD, the Soviet police, could throw her without trial into one of their "special camps," reputed to be even worse than the ones she had come out of. Would she end up separated from her children again?

She had to find out. Trying her best to look nonchalant, she traipsed over to the path which wound its way along the Elbe river. Cautiously she sat on the opposite end of the bench, near the edge so she could slip away quickly if she sensed the man had malicious intent.

"We have a network that can assist you in your travels," he said, from behind the newspaper.

"I have five children. What do I need to do?"

"Five?" The man scratched his head. "That will not be a simple matter."

A yellow leaf fluttered down from a linden tree and landed in the river, drifting away on the current like a small boat. In a few months the edges of the river would ice over and when it thawed again, it would be five years since Liesel had last seen her husband. She was determined to grasp every chance given. "I have to do this. Can you help me?"

"Of course, there is a cost involved," said the man. "Our people are taking a grave risk."

"I don't have much money."

"Some people pay with valuables, jewels, silverware."

"Everything I had was taken." She thought of the heirloom china, smashed at the side of the road, and the Russians soldiers with her father's pocket watch. Jadwiga wearing her string of pearls.

"Ration cards are worth a lot," the man continued. "That is one advantage you have with so many children. If you wish to proceed, I will tell you how to meet your contact. Remember to be discreet and do not tell anyone, even your children, you are leaving. Do not pack large amounts of luggage."

"That will not be a problem," said Liesel.

CHAPTER 65

SHE HURRIED DOWN THE SIDEWALK. IT WAS LATE IN THE DAY and she had left the children on their own again. In the distance, Luther's church tower loomed, a beacon against the sky.

Most of the shops she passed by were boarded up or devoid of any desirable merchandise.

The exception was a bakery; and the aroma that wafted onto the street made her salivate almost unbearably. She turned from the window with its tantalizing display of bread and cakes and focused on the sidewalk ahead of her.

In a few moments she came to the building where she had been told to meet her contact. Cement stairs led down to a basement café and she entered the smoke-filled room and allowed her eyes to adjust to the dimness.

A bearded young man in a tweed coat sat at a table in the far corner.

Liesel took a deep breath and walked over to him, her heart pounding.

Smiling, he greeted her, as if she was his dearest aunt. "*Tante!*" He embraced her convincingly and kissed her on each cheek. It is so good to see you." Quietly he whispered in her ear, "Call me Reinhold."

"I am happy to see you too, Reinhold." She tried to sound equally convincing, though she had never been involved in play-acting. He gestured for her to sit down. A waiter came by and poured them each a cup of coffee. He placed stained menu cards in front of them.

Reinhold's eyes scanned the room and he spoke in a lower more confidential tone. "How old are the children now?" he asked.

Liesel recited their ages.

"And you are planning to take them with you?" His eyebrows rose up.

"Of course. They are all I have. I have kept them alive and they have kept me alive."

He spoke evenly now, "You realize you are taking a grave risk?" He sipped his coffee. "You and your children could be shot or taken prisoner indefinitely. It would be much safer for them to stay here. Perhaps you could find them a nice home or you can send for them later."

"I have no choice," said Liesel. "I don't see any life for myself or my children here. My husband is in the west and I won't leave my children behind." She spoke quietly but her resolve was firm. She had not come this far to be separated from them again.

"Fine," He shrugged. "It is your choice. I just want you to be aware of the risk you are taking." He spoke louder now, for the benefit of anyone overhearing the conversation. "Did you bring the pictures of my cousins?"

Liesel was initially puzzled, but his meaning became clear. He held up the menu slightly to one side and she did likewise. She reached into her pocket. Palming the small amount of cash she had saved and the stack of ration cards she passed them to him in one swift motion shielded by the menus. He turned his card towards her and pointed to a hand drawn map concealed inside.

"The schnitzel is very good. Memorize the ingredients, then perhaps you could make it at home."

She looked at the map and tried to memorize each detail. They recommended crossing near the Czechoslovakian border.

Reinhold's eyes flitted around the room again and he leaned across the table. "Look for our cousin who will meet you and take you part of the way. Rainy weather is best. On those nights the guards would rather stay under shelter than hunt down missing relatives." After a moment he turned the menu around and slipped the paper back into his pocket.

He reached across the table again, and patted her hand in an affectionate manner. She could feel a little lump and took it in her own hand. "That is medicine for cousin Monika, how old is she now? Four? Give it to her with a sip of schnapps and she should sleep the whole night. I hope she is better soon."

Liesel's heart was pounding at what she was about to do. Was it right she wondered, to risk not only her own life, but the lives of her children for freedom they could not even fathom and for their father, whom only Kurt and Olaf would remember?

Reinhold continued. "If there is a really good thunder or rainstorm, the noise will help to mask your footsteps."

"I wish you God-speed." He added loudly, "Do send my love to the cousins!" He stood as she did, embracing her once again and kissing her on each cheek.

CHAPTER 66

SHE HAD TAKEN KURT INTO HER CONFIDENCE, BUT THE morning they were to leave she sat down with the other children.

"Today, we are taking a trip."

"Where are we going?" asked Rudy.

"For a ride on a train, then a hike in the country." She hated lying, but so many times, she had felt cornered into it. "It is very important for you to do everything Kurt or I tell you without question." She looked at Edeltraud who was playing with her hair. "That means you too."

"What about dolly?" said Heidi, "Can she come?"

The "resettlers" had been given a bin of used clothing and household items and Heidi had acquired a worn rag doll. Liesel had mended it and sewn on a new face. Heidi carried the doll everywhere. Other than whatever she had played with at the *Kindersheim* it was the only toy she had ever owned.

"Yes, of course your dolly can come," said Liesel.

She crushed up the pill 'Reinhold' had given her and put it in some milk. She handed it to Heidi. "Drink this."

Of course, she was oblivious to the doll now, a deadweight in the arms of the guide they had met. He had provided a few sips from his personal flask to enhance the effect of the medication.

Kurt strode confidently ahead of the others and Liesel counted heads for the third time.

Olaf shuffled along in his makeshift footwear. His shoes had given way weeks ago; Liesel had not had saved enough money to buy another pair and they had bound his feet with extra socks, cardboard, rags and string.

Rudy and Edeltraud wandered back and forth zigzagging along the path. To them it all seemed a game.

A light drizzle fell. They had been walking for a few hours when Rudy asked, "Can we go home now? I'm tired."

"It's not a nice evening for a picnic," said Olaf. "And it's getting dark."

"We'll go home later," said Liesel. "There's something I want to show you up ahead." Another lie, but she would tell them when they got closer to the border.

Darkness fell.

Ahead, a post marked the road to the border. The guide, who hadn't given them his name, stopped. "I cannot go any further," he said, transferring Heidi over to Liesel. "Rest a while. Then it is about another hour. Cross when they change shifts at 0300 hours."

"What if they hear us?" hissed Kurt.

"Who?" said Olaf looking quizzically at his mother. "Where are we going really?"

"To the Western side of the border, where your father is."

"But what if they shoot us?"

"Try to sound like a wild boar or a bird. Who knows? It might fool them," the guide said, with a soft chuckle.

Liesel did not see the humor in the situation.

"Cuckoo," said Rudy, imitating their old clock perfectly. The guide ruffled his hair.

"Not now," said Kurt.

"Yes. We must keep quiet," said Liesel.

The man continued his instruction. "Go for the area directly between the guard towers. The hardest part will be to get through the wire."

Barbed wire. She thought of the camps they had been in and the dreaded razor wire that prevented even the most intrepid escapees, either slicing its victims to leave a telltale trail of blood or catching them by their clothes long enough to be noticed.

"I have to go now. *Machs gut.*" Their guide wished them well and disappeared down the path the way they had come.

After the family had rested, they walked until they came to a clearing where a sign proclaimed "*Achtung. Demarkations Linie 100 m.*"

Only one hundred metres to go. Liesel swallowed. There was no turning back now.

Ahead was a boulder-strewn hill which led into a sandy gully. Up the next hill from that was barbed wire, its ominous length ahead of them. Trees, shrubs, and darkness partially obscured their view from the border guards, but Liesel could hear voices as one shift took over the next. Her heart thumped so loudly, she thought the guards would hear it.

Once more she rehearsed everything with the children. She began to think she was making a terrible mistake. What if they were caught or if she was shot? Her children would be without a mother. Or if one of them … she could never forgive herself if any harm came to her children.

"When we get to the barbed wire, Kurt you help Edel through, Olaf, you take Heidi and I'll help you both. Rudy, I think you can manage yourself. Come children, hurry." Heidi's eyes opened and she looked around. "Mutti?" she said.

"You are fine. We are just going for a little walk." Liesel spoke softly, with much more calmness than she felt. If Heidi were to start crying, it could be over for all of them.

"Oh," said Heidi. She yawned and the long lashes closed again over her eyes.

The hobnailed boots of the guard clicking along the boardwalk by the guardhouse alerted them to his whereabouts. Every now and again they could see his silhouette and that of the rifle he carried over his shoulder against the guardhouse light. He was patrolling in the other direction when Liesel commanded the children in a loud whisper. "Now!"

They rushed stealthily over the open area and scrambled up the boulders.

The strings and cardboard had worn off Olaf's feet.

Liesel felt sorry for him as he navigated the sharp rocks barefoot.

Past the boulders they encountered sand. Liesel struggled to run over it, especially carrying Heidi. She was lagging behind the children. She pushed Edeltraud ahead. "Run to Kurt and let him help you."

When they came up to the wire, Liesel handed Heidi to Olaf and she tried to move the coil in such a way to allow the two of them to slip through, but it was tricky. Heidi was limp and too big to hold with just one arm so Olaf could not help himself much at all. Rudy was managing on his own. His scrawny build was a definite advantage at this and he was getting a bit ahead of the others. He turned back and told them to hand him their packs, he was almost through.

Kurt was struggling with Edeltraud.

"Let go! I can do it myself," she said. At the age of eight, she was asserting more independence.

"Do you want to die?" Kurt snarled at her, his teeth clenched. He was old enough to understand the gravity of the situation. "Mutti said for me to help you."

She stuck out her lower lip and glowered at him. Her braid caught on a barb above her and she tried to wrestle herself free. Kurt was almost through behind her.

"Wait." He came up behind her and struggled unsuccessfully to untangle her hair. Frustrated, he clamped a hand over her mouth. "Hush!" In one quick motion he yanked the strand of snagged hairs from her head. "Sorry," he whispered in a gentler tone. He pulled at the next wire to allow her through. Tears filled Edeltraud's eyes, but she allowed him to guide her.

Rudy pushed the packs through and was trying to help with Heidi and Olaf. The wires bit into Liesel's coat as if to imprison her once again. Fighting back, she was rewarded with a deep slice across the back of her hand. She felt a wet gush of blood and glanced back to where the guard had been. She could not see him.

"*Halt.*" His voice was authoritative, threatening. "Border sentry. Stop or I shoot!"

Liesel froze for an instant in terror. What if they had come this far only to die at the hands of their captors? She was prepared to give herself up if she could only get them through.

The children were almost free. Rudy pulled Heidi from Olaf's outstretched arms and was on the other side. Edeltraud and Kurt had made it and were picking up the packs. Olaf was just out of Liesel's reach. The guard called out again. "*Halt! Wer ist das!*" His voice was louder, closer. Kurt picked up a rock and threw it far over the barbed wire to the other side of the guard. Liesel's shredded coat hampered her progress.

"Take it off," said Kurt. She slid out of its scant warmth, pushed the bundled coat towards Kurt and, heart thumping, attempted something like a dive through, cutting herself even more on the razor edge of the wire.

"Take the children down the hill," she ordered Olaf. As Kurt grabbed her hand and they began to run, the gunshot cracked through the night air.

Bullets whizzed past their heads as they ran for the west.

> *I lift up my eyes to the mountains—where does my help come from? My help comes from the Lord...*
>
> — Psalm 121:1-2

CHAPTER 67

OUT OF DANGER THEY SLOWED THEIR PACE, SLOSHING through the mud of a sodden field and onto a dirt road.

Exhausted, they deposited their belongings in a little heap in front of a stile. Out of one of the packs, Liesel pulled out a threadbare blanket and spread it on the ground, settling the younger children there with packs for their pillows. She covered them with the one featherbed they had left. It was dirty and a bit wet but the down still provided some insulation.

Liesel wrapped her bleeding hand in a handkerchief. The cuts on her leg stung, but she did not care. They had made it, and soon she could be with her husband. She leaned back against the stile and slept like she had not for so long, in spite of a wet and cold bed.

In the morning the first thing she saw was the sun coming up over the hills.

"I lift my eyes up to the hills..." she began to recite in thanksgiving. Suddenly a border guard was standing over them. *Oh no, they've caught us*, was her initial thought.

"*Grüss Gott*," said the guard, his colloquial greeting of God's blessing informing Liesel that they were in Bavaria.

She stood up, brushed her shredded coat and smoothed down her unkempt hair, as if it would somehow erase her bedraggled appearance. "*Grüss Gott*," she replied, confident that her help had come from God.

"You have come across the border?"

"Yes," said Liesel. She wondered what would happen how. Would they be detained?

"I have something for your little ones," he said, reaching into an inner pocket. He pulled out a tin of lemon drops and offered them to Edeltraud and Heidi. They looked up at him with wide eyes, examining the candies closely. "Yes, they are for you, *meine Kinder.*" Enthralled they took the candies and willingly followed him.

The border station was a short walk and they were brought into a room with a table and a bench. There was coffee for Liesel and warm milk with a slice of rye for the children.

"No shoes, I see." The guard looked at Olaf's feet.

Liesel looked down in shame.

"I have seen it all," said the policeman. "Every stripe of refugee, from young to old. Some barely alive. I have seen people coming off the trains in nothing but their undergarments."

He looked over her papers. "Do you have anyone here in the west?"

"My husband. Last time I heard from him, he was in Hof, but I haven't seen him for 4 years."

"Four years? He has abandoned you then?" He eyed her and the little troupe surrounding her with dismay.

"*Nein*, he was a Russian prisoner-of-war."

"He got out of a Soviet POW camp? I have not heard that story very often."

"I would not have risked my life and the lives of my children to come here otherwise. He had applied to have us immigrate. There is a visa. Can you help us?"

"All refugees are taken to the reception camp until you have been cleared. You can arrange to meet your husband there, after everything has been sorted out."

Another camp. Liesel felt deflated.

"Housing here is critically short," the guard explained further. "Once you leave the camp you will have to share a home with others, and some are reluctant to share with refugees. Still, perhaps an improvement from what you've been through."

"I only ask to be re-united with my husband and for my children to grow up free."

CHAPTER 68

"Everyone on the bus," said a policeman, guiding a group of thirty people. "We are taking you to a refugee reception area."

The family got on the bus. The girls shared Liesel's lap and the boys squished together in the seat behind her.

As they travelled a smooth and recently paved road, Liesel glanced around her. She didn't need to wonder where the others had come from. Short-haired women with worn-out shoes accompanied children with hollow eyes and shabby ill-fitting clothing.

"Where are we going now?" asked Olaf, gazing out the window at the trees. Red and yellow leaves fluttered in a gentle breeze.

The display was stunning. One would almost think they were going on vacation.

"They said they would take us to Friedland," said Liesel, trying the sound of the word on her lips, *Fried*, peace. She wanted to trust what they said, but for years now she had been told lies.

Life had been completely turned upside down. But looking out the window gave her hope. The road was not riddled with potholes like the roads in the eastern zone. Homes they passed were tidy, with flowers growing in planters and smoke coming out of chimneys. Only a few piles of rubble marked the war now three years past.

The bus pulled up to a gate and was waved through. When they got off the bus, Liesel's legs shook. Friedland looked just like all the other camps. Rows upon rows of barracks.

But this was different. Smiling women in Red Cross uniforms waited to greet them. People milled around freely and Liesel noted that they looked neatly-dressed and properly fed.

She was directed to line up in front of an office. Next to it was a massive bulletin board on which hung hundreds of scraps of paper and photographs.

Last seen Berlin 1944, Ewald Mueller, b. 1920. Contact Otto Mueller. No doubt a young soldier thought Liesel. Probably never to be seen again. There followed an address in West Berlin.

A photograph of a smiling blonde woman with two small girls accompanied by a faded typewritten notice read:*Missing from Danzig, beloved wife Alma and daughters. Last seen January 1945.*

Liesel shuddered as she thought of her own flight in January of 1945.

"Probably on that ship, the *Wilhelm Gustloff,* that was sunk in the Baltic sea," said a woman behind her. "Thousands of people died. Mostly civilian refugees from Danzig and Prussia."

A cold shiver went down Liesel's spine as she thought of someone just like herself, a mother trying to save her babies from the icy waters.

Liesel was still looking at the bulletin board hoping to see a familiar name or face when she was called for registration. "Don't worry," said the woman behind the desk, "You will have time to look at the board later and post a notice if you wish. First you must be registered and then we will be able to process your ration cards."

With registration complete, they entered the dining hall, where the tables were set with real china and vases of flowers.

Liesel was astonished. Luxury like this she had not seen for years.

She sat down with her children. Each place at the table had a small package containing a toothbrush and facecloth.

"I expect you children to brush your teeth tonight!" Liesel said. She welcomed a return to being a normal mother who reminded her children to do what they were supposed to do and who wouldn't have to steal food or run and hide from people who would hurt them.

Dinner was a nourishing soup with applesauce for dessert.

"Mmm, this is so good," said Edeltraud, licking her spoon. "We never had anything like this at the Children's Home."

"I'm going to get some more," said Kurt, getting up from his place to join the line for seconds.

At night Liesel sank onto a cot with real pillows and clean linens, the softest bed since she had fled her home.

The next few days were a blur. She looked through files of people she might have seen somewhere. She sent a letter to Ernst's last known address. She was given a medical check-up, where this time she would not be declared "fit for work," but fit for rest.

Various cultural activities were offered. They attended a music concert where a group of children sang along to an accordion, its lilting strains joined by men playing a tuba and a guitar.

"La, la, la la," she swayed along with Heidi who clapped her hands enthusiastically, delighted at this novelty, but as Liesel sat there, the plodding steady tone of the tuba reminded her of the strong presence of a husband she had once had. Her voice caught in her throat. All these years, gone. What if he never came? What if he rejected her because she had been raped?

She could not stop the gasping sobs as they welled up and she wept. Tears of sorrow for the past years of her life. For her children's lost childhood and the hunger, fear, and deprivation they had experienced. She wept for the long separation of her girls and not being able to care for her boys. For the beatings and cruelty they had experienced at the hands of others. She grieved her mother whom she had left behind to die, for her siblings and relatives she might never see again, and for kind Maria. She cried for all the times she had to be strong but felt so weak.

The musical ensemble bowed to its appreciative audience and people stood up to leave.

"What's the matter *Mutti*?" said Heidi. "Didn't you like the music?"

"Oh yes, dear. It just made me a little sad," Liesel said, wiping her eyes with a newly acquired clean handkerchief. She stood, and took the hands of her girls.

As she headed towards the door, it was a massive bouquet she noticed first, almost as big as the one she had carried at her wedding. The colours of all her favourite flowers; pink and yellow roses, peonies and dahlias blurred through her tears like a French impressionist painting.

"Liesel." The voice behind the bouquet was tentative, familiar. Ernst grasped her hand and looked into her eyes. The past fell away as his strong arms enclosed her.

She was home.

ACKNOWLEDGEMENTS:

I HAVE AN OCEAN OF PEOPLE TO THANK.

Without some very special real life people there would be no book, as it was your stories that provided the inspiration. Thank you for your willingness to tell. I know it wasn't always easy. You lived through tough times, but have chosen to live your lives with the grace that comes from knowing God.

Andy, it's been a long haul, but you have always believed, always hoped. And sometimes prodded. Thanks for your input at many moments when you would have rather been doing something else, like fishing for instance.

To Ben, Jordan, Kyle and Shandelle: I know I could always rely on an honest answer when asking your opinions. Sorry for all those times that dinner was late and I ignored you. Love you all so much!

To Mom and Dad, thanks for being in my corner, for your encouragement and everything else!

Loranne, I don't even want to think about the "before" product! Your suggestions and guidance have been crucial in developing the story. Thank you for reminding me about the "magic." Writing a book is indeed a fascinating process!

To the team at Promontory Press: Ben, Lisa, Amy, Vance, and Sean. When I met you, I just knew, and everything since has confirmed my decision to publish with you. Or was it your decision to publish me? May you forge new paths in the world of hybrid publishing! Thanks Richard for catching all those commas that I missed! And to Jordan for making it all look like a book!

To my beta readers: Carola, Sharon, Lynn, Bonnie, Paige and others. It was a quick timeline, thanks for stepping up!

Sharon, I couldn't believe how many times my eyes deceived me. Thanks for the initial proofread.

Ed, your family anecdote has been included as part of the story. Some of this stuff just can't be thought up!

Genie, the information about life on the prairies in those days has been most helpful.

To my amazing friends and family: Thanks for listening when I prattled on about war history, writing and research frustrations! Will I shut up already? I can't make any promises but I hope the book is worth it!

Research material was scarce in the early days of my writing journey. I am grateful to some people I've never met, but whose work enabled me to do mine. Alfred de Zayas and his histories on the expulsions, including "A Terrible Revenge" and "Nemesis at Potsdam," have been invaluable in setting the historical tone. Christian Von Krockow's narrative, "Hour of the Women" based on his sister's expulsion from Prussia, was a compelling read. John Sack's controversial "Eye for an Eye" is deserving of mention, for his documentation of the post-war camps. In the same vein, "Death Camps of the Soviets 1945-1950" by Adrian Preissinger provided more first-hand accounts. Dr. Gerda Wever-Rabehl's "Inside the Parrot Cage" is a rare exploration of one man's memory. "The Wehrmacht Experience in Russia" by Bob Carruthers took me into life on the Russian front, something I could never have otherwise imagined. Grateful mention also goes to Susan Campbell

Bartoletti for her book "Hitler Youth: Growing up in Hitler's shadow" and to Jost Herman's memoir "A Hitler Youth in Poland" and to the account of Roman Stöcklein's life as a POW.

Wikipedia, you are a true pal and I can't imagine life as a writer without you! For those of short attention span (me), there is nothing like the instant gratification of information when in the middle of a paragraph. Thanks to your many contributors.

There are too many other resources to mention, each providing a piece of the puzzle.

If there is anyone I missed, thanks to you as well.

Finally, I must thank the Author of all creative gifts, the Giver of every good thing.

NOTES ON HISTORICAL SOURCES
AND QUOTES

CHAPTER 1

p 2: "Let goods and kindred go …"
Luther, Martin (1531) "A Mighty Fortress" (*Ein Feste Burg*), Martin
Luther, trans. Frederick H. Hedge 1853

CHAPTER 2

p. 11 "Poland agrees…"
Treaty of Versailles (1919), Article 93
Official texts in English: [1919] UKTS 4 (Cmd. 153); [1920] ATS 1
http://en.wikisource.org/wiki/Treaty_of_Versailles/Part_
III#Article_93
Compiled from versions published by the Australasian
Legal Information Institute, the Avalon Project (Yale
University) and Brigham Young University Library.
p. 11,12 "Ein Feste Burg…"
Luther, Martin (1531), Frederick Hedge (1853) "A Mighty Fortress"

CHAPTER 3

p. 18 Queen of Prussia *legend
Reid, Marilyn (2007). *Mythical Flower Stories*. Lulu.com.
p. 40. ISBN 978-1-84753-521-4.
Retrieved from http://en.wikipedia.org/wiki/Centaurea_cyanus

CHAPTER 5

p. 31 "You know that Land ..."
Von Goethe, Johann Wolfgang (1795-96) *Wilhelm Meister's apprenticeship*, "Where the Lemon Trees Bloom" (Kennst Du Das Land)
English translation by A.Z. Foreman, used by permission.
http://poemsintranslation.blogspot.ca/

CHAPTER 6

p. 32 "A wife of noble character ..."
Bible, *New International Version 2011*, Proverbs 31: 10

CHAPTER 10

p. 50 "Arbeit, Ihre Mädchen ..."
Jacobi, Johann Georg (d.1814) "At the Spinning Wheel", English Translation by Sharon Krebs (2006), used by permission.
http://www.recmusic.org/lieder/get_text.html?TextId=27788

CHAPTER 14

p. 65 "Some among the Volksdeutsche ...", A Terrible Revenge, The Ethnic Cleansing of the East European Germans, 1944 - 1950
De Zayas, Alfred (1986), English translation by John Koehler (1994)
Used by permission.

Chapter 17

p. 74, "German people…
Prime Minister Chamberlain in a BBC Radio broadcast in the German language, September 4, 1939.
http://ibiblio.org/pha/bb/bb-249.html
No. 144
p. 84 "Ihre Kinderlein Kommet"
Von Schmidt, Christoph (1811) *Ihre Kinderlein kommet,*
English Translation "Oh Come Little Children", by Melanie Schulte (d.1922)

Chapter 20

p. 89 "It is the duty of every SS man…"
Eicke, Theodore (1939) in a speech to concentration camp commanders
Cited by Gilbert, Martin. *A History of the Twentieth Century Vol 2, p. 265*
Used by permission.

Chapter 25

p. 106
The propaganda *slogans are compiled from several posters found at www.bytwerk.com/gpa/poster2.htm
www.bild.bundesarchiv.de/
Thank you to Randall Bytwerks, Robert Brooks and the German archives.

Chapter 29

p. 120 *"Hoppe, Hoppe Reiter…
Traditional rhyme, retrieved from: http://german.about.com/library/blhopp.htm

CHAPTER 30

p. 127 * "When an opponent states… "
Adolf Hitler, Nov. 6, 1933 in a speech.
Cited in William L. Shirer, "Education in the Third Reich," ch. 8, *The Rise and Fall of the Third Reich* (1959)

p. 128 "Deutschland, Deutschland uber alles…"
Von Fallersleben, August Heinrich Hoffmann (1841) *Deutschland Lied*
Translation retrieved from: http://en.wikisource.org/wiki/Das_Deutschlandlied
Licensed under GNU Free Documentation License

CHAPTER 31

p. 125 "Germans are not human beings…If you have not killed at least one German a day… you have wasted a day…there is nothing more joyful than a heap of German corpses."
As cited by De Zayas, (1994) *A Terrible Revenge*
According to De Zayas, Ilya Ehrenburg's call was distributed as a flyer, the original of which is at the archives of the German Foreign Office among "Beutepapiere"—enemy documents compiled by German intelligence. He was the first historian to publish it with the appropriate source.
Used by permission

CHAPTER 32

p. 137
see chapter 25 re: posters

CHAPTER 33

p. 141 *"The time has come…
Zhukov, Georgi, Soviet Marshall, from a speech to his men

From the Bundesarchiv-Militärarchiv
Quote cited in De Zayas, (1994)

CHAPTER 36

p. 160 "Ein Feste Burg ..."
Luther, Martin (1531) "A Mighty Fortress"

CHAPTER 37

p. 169, 171 "Schlaf Kindlein Schlaf...
*"Sleep Baby Sleep" Traditional lullaby
German lyrics retrieved from http://www.mamalisa.
com/?t=es&p=451&c=38
Generally accepted English version has been used.

CHAPTER 39

p. 180 "The Russian-dominated Polish government..."
Winston Churchill in "Iron Curtain" speech March 5, 1946.
http://www.winstonchurchill.org/learn/speeches/speeches-of-
winston-churchill/120-the-sinews-of-peace

CHAPTER 43

p. 199 "Between capitalist... "
Karl Marx in *Critique of the Gotha Programme* (1875). http://www.
en.wikisource.org/wiki/Critique_of_the_Gotha_Programme/
Part_IV
Used under Creative Commons license V 3.0

CHAPTER 48

p. 229 *"Authorized representatives..."
L. Berjia, Commisioner General of State Security (1945)
Original memo is believed to be contained in the Archives of the

Soviet Communist Party and Soviet State Collection Fond 89, Opis
75, Reel 1.1012, File 1, No. 00315 (99)
Cited in Latotsky Alexander, (2011) *A Childhood Behind Barbed Wire*

CHAPTER 50

p. 240 "The concentration camps...
Bashford, R.W.F. in a confidential report,
Cited in De Zayas, (1994)

CHAPTER 60

p. 304 "The three governments...
"The Potsdam Agreement" Foreign Relations of the United States,
XII. Orderly Transfer Of German Populations www.en.wikisource.
org/wiki/Potsdam_Agreement
Used under Creative Commons license

CHAPTER 61

p. 311* "Du, Du liegst mir in Herzen ...
"Du Du Liegst Mir in Herzen" German Folk song (1820)

CHAPTER 62

p. 318 "Nun Danket Alle Gott...
Kruger, Johann (1647) "Nun Danket."
English translation, Winkworth, Catherine, "Now Thank we all our
God." (1856)

CHAPTER 67

p. 357 "I lift my eyes up..."
Psalm 121:1-2
Bible, *New International Version 2011*

* AUTHOR'S OWN PARAPHRASE OR TRANSLATION

ABOUT THE AUTHOR

ALONG THE ROAD TO BEING A WRITER, ROSE HAS BEEN A bookkeeper, piano teacher and mother of four. She makes her home in Surrey, BC with her husband and their two youngest children. She enjoys singing, reading and travel.